Cry
Against the Wind

by

Fleeta Cunningham

Santa Rita Series, Book Five

This is a work of fiction. Names, characters, places, and incidents are either the product of the author's imagination or are used fictitiously, and any resemblance to actual persons living or dead, business establishments, events, or locales, is entirely coincidental.

Cry Against the Wind

COPYRIGHT © 2013 by Fleeta Cunningham

Contact Information: info@thewildrosepress.com

Cover Art by *Kim Mendoza*

The Wild Rose Press, Inc.
PO Box 708
Adams Basin, NY 14410-0708
Visit us at www.thewildrosepress.com

Publishing History
First Vintage Rose Edition, 2013
Print ISBN 978-1-61217-778-6
Digital ISBN 978-1-61217-779-3

Santa Rita Series, Book Five
Published in the United States of America

"I...I don't..." Audrey began.

"Socialize with clients? But I was a friend before I was a client." The smile behind his beard flashed. "And I really need your advice. Besides, I'd like to know more about the town and what goes on here. It would be the best arrangement for me. Can't you manage dinner?"

Everything about the bronze giant with the russet beard urged her to accept. Audrey remembered their numerous confidential chats and the camaraderie of her college days. She'd looked forward to her tedious hours in the library because of his companionship. It made professional sense to renew their previous friendship. Hal Lindstrom would be a good client to add to her business, and without her his library could be in terrible shape before he realized it.

"I'd enjoy it," she answered at last.

"It's a date." He listened a minute as the lilt of a familiar tune filled the hall. "Give me this waltz.

Praise for Fleeta Cunningham
and the Santa Rita Series

ELOPEMENT FOR ONE

"Well-crafted story... exciting plot... interesting characters... The love between the two main characters is precious, from beginning to the final, exciting conclusion.... I am now determined to read the rest of the series."

~The Romance Studio (5 Stars)

~*~

BLACK RAIN RISING

"One of the most fantastic books I've read this year... grabbed my attention from the first sentence.... A memorable, entertaining, and well-written story.... An author of increasing distinction who will never disappoint her readers."

~Two Lips Reviews (5 Lips, Recommended)

~*~

DON'T CALL ME DARLIN'

"A warm, thought-provoking book... an enticing hero and a wounded yet proud heroine. A realistic picture of 1957... an image of small town America that both warms and terrifies.... The best thing is she balances the build-up with a really good ending."

~WRDF (rated Fantastic)

~*~

HALF PAST MOURNING

"Delightful to read. Fleeta Cunningham slips in mores, styles, and pastimes of the 1950s era.... Her subtle, understated writing style moves along smooth as silk...a sparkling, enjoyable vicarious experience."

~Camellia, Long and Short Reviews (4.5 Stars)

Dedication

To all the "brave, old Westerners"
Lubbock High School Class of 1963

We earned our spurs.

Prologue

George Anderson wished the child would brush her hair back out of her eyes. The way the sandy brown bush tumbled over her forehead gave her a cornered, furtive look.

"You copied virtually every word in your paper from an article in an old issue of the *Georgia Historical Quarterly*," he repeated. "Even if I didn't have a copy of that issue myself, the style of this paper would make me suspicious. No high school junior is likely to use words that way." George fanned the pages of the rumpled folder in front of her.

"I didn't copy, Mr. Anderson," Dondie Marshall insisted, her haunting grey eyes barely visible through the screen of hair. "Honest, I wouldn't do that. Okay, maybe I used a reference and forgot to write it down? Or quoted something and didn't put in the quote marks? I wouldn't copy, not on purpose."

George thumbed the pages, shaking his head, partly in dismay, partly in resignation. He'd heard that plaintive tone from a plagiarizing student too many times. Giving the girl a moment, he glanced out the office window, wishing he were on the tennis court instead of dealing with the troubled child opposite him. Events so far suggested the 1959-60 school year would be turbulent. Echoing his thoughts, thunder growled in the distance as dark clouds blotted out the autumn sun.

"I taught history a good many years before I became a counselor, Dondie. The Civil War still fascinates me. Your paper caught my eye because your subject, Jubal Early and the battle of Gettysburg, is an interest of mine. A year ago I found the same article you did, and I kept it." He put a sturdy journal in front of her, opened it, and tapped the columns of print on a dog-eared page. "Take a look at this, Dondie. The article matches yours nearly word for word." He waited as she looked down. "It's no coincidence, is it?"

Tears had threatened earlier; now they began to slide down the girl's thin cheeks. She sniffled as her head drooped lower, the tangled hair falling forward to cover her face. Her words, muffled and rambling, were barely audible. "It was *hard*, and I didn't understand, and Miss Cleburne kept nagging me. I couldn't tell her how dumb I felt, could I? I didn't know what to do, and then last week I was poking around the library, and I found that magazine. I mean, look how *old* it is. I didn't know anybody ever read such dull stuff. Who'd want to? Nobody would know who that Jubal person was. I copied it, only I changed some things around a little. It wasn't exactly cheating." She looked up, her pale eyes gleaming with tears through the tangle of curls. "You understand, Mr. Anderson? I couldn't do the paper, but I had to turn in something. I did the best I could."

Her dismay seemed real. George looked over the office copy of her recent grades. Mediocre to poor since she'd been at Santa Rita. Her earlier transcript had higher marks, some even outstanding. Pity, he thought, reviewing Dondie's sketchy history. She'd been found abandoned at a church at the edge of town, three years back, apparently suffering deep emotional trauma. She remembered her name and age but no particulars of how she got to Santa Rita. The county social worker located school records from the Texas Panhandle, six hundred miles from Santa Rita. The family had never been traced, and the girl had been placed as a foster child with an older couple.

"You've been with the Vanderhills for quite a while now, Dondie." George put the folder aside and sat casually on the corner of his desk. "Have you remembered any of your life before you came here?"

"No, nothing. It must have been pretty terrible, I guess, or I'd remember something."

"Your mother, perhaps?"

"No, nothin' about her. Just bein' hungry and alone and scared."

"I can understand, especially the scared and alone part." George paused. "But the social worker was able to locate your previous school. Surely someone at the school or some of the people in the town would know you. We could try to find out."

The girl shied like a frightened pony. "Oh, no, no, I don't wanna know, Mr. Anderson. I like it here. What if someone made me go back? Or what if somebody there hurt me? I don't want to go back. It makes me feel all green-queasy just to think about it."

George saw alarm and withdrawal in her eyes, as if doors were slamming shut behind those strangely light grey eyes. "You know, Dondie, I've found things that scared me usually weren't nearly as bad once I actually faced them. You might find the same thing. Perhaps your people love you and are frantic with worry for you."

3

She shook her head, sending tangled hair flying. "They wouldn't have dumped me if they cared."

"Well, think about the other possibilities. You might have been kidnapped or taken by mistake. I saw a story the other day about a boy who had fallen asleep in the back seat of the car. A thief took the car without knowing the boy was there, and he left him at a gas station. The parents were wild with relief. You might have had a similar experience. Before Christmas break we could contact your old school…" He saw her refusal mounting and drew back. "Don't decide right now, Dondie. Think about it for a while. Talk to the Vanderhills, if you like, but give it some serious thought. I'll be glad to make some calls."

Too many sad stories and too many lost children like this one. George sighed, grateful his own three daughters were safely grown up. Still, the immediate problem was Dondie's research paper, or lack of one, and her blatant plagiarism. He could call Fred Vanderhill, he supposed, and let him deal with Dondie's transgressions, but that humorless, rigid old man would first mete out harsh consequences to the child. Dondie would still not be able to produce a satisfactory paper, which was the point of the assignment. He handed Dondie's fraudulent work back to her.

"We can make this work out all right for you, Dondie." He smiled. "You just need to follow the correct steps to reach the right result. I'll help you, and you'll be surprised at how easy it is, taking one little piece at a time."

Chapter One

"Hey, Dad, you look worn out. Hard day at school? Or did the rain hit while you were playing tennis?" Audrey took her father's red-and-grey jacket to brush droplets from the collar.

George Anderson wiped sprinkles from his glasses and slicked back his thinning hair. "No match today. I was late getting away from school, and we had a downpour by then. I know why the kids think the three o'clock bell will never ring. Today was eleven hours long." He made an obvious effort to push his day aside to concentrate on hers. "You're home early. What's the occasion? A hot date?"

Audrey shrugged. "No, Jared Pierce didn't get all his updates in, so I ran out of work at his office. With the nasty weather, I gave myself the afternoon off."

"Glad you did." Her dad's hug enveloped Audrey.

"I picked up a pecan pie, and I've just made fresh coffee. Come on back and have some."

While George left his damp shoes by the door, trading them for a worn pair of moccasins, Audrey hurried along the hallway to the bar dividing the kitchen from the high-ceilinged family room.

"So what made this day eleven hours long, Dad?" She poured coffee into the familiar blue mug and pushed it across the bar. "An unruly assembly, or a visit from the school board?"

"Just an unusual number of interruptions and emergencies." The stiff way he sat down confirmed his weary tone. "Ruth Cleburne's mother had a stroke, so Ruth had to leave early this morning. When we couldn't get a substitute, I took her classes the rest of the day. I forgot how much energy it takes to teach all day, I guess. Have to admit I'm beat."

"I'm sorry for Ruth. I hope her mother makes a full recovery." Audrey had a quick sympathy for the teacher, having lost her own mother two years earlier. "Will she be back before Thanksgiving?"

"I don't think so." George stared out the window into the grey November rain thickening the air. "That wasn't what concerned me. It was a counseling matter. I caught a student passing off a published article as her own work. I handled it without Ruth's input, and I'm not sure I did things the way Ruth would have."

"Plagiarism goes on, Dad. You stop it where you can." Audrey wondered why one such incident weighed so heavily on her father.

"I know, but this girl has some special problems. She's in foster care, her grades are poor, and she seems lost. She didn't grasp the mechanics of writing the paper, so I gave her another chance. I'm tutoring her for an hour after school for the rest of the week to see if I can help her pull her work together. I don't see any way she can begin her senior year next fall if she can't grasp the essentials of writing a research paper."

Audrey cut a wedge of pie and put it in front of George. He held his fork absently, and she could see his mind was still in the classroom. "How did you know she'd copied the article?"

"I'm sure the finished product would have alerted any of her regular teachers, but she caught my attention because she wrote about Jubal Early. I'd read the same article."

"Oh, bad luck for her." Audrey grimaced. George Anderson had been writing a biography of the irascible Civil War general for years. "Are you going to talk to Ruth about it?"

"No, Ruth has enough to worry with right now, and the girl would face some severe consequences if we had to bring in the foster family. If she honestly didn't know how to do the work, contacting them would be counterproductive anyway. I suggested we keep the situation between us, make another attempt, and have a good paper to show Ruth when she gets back."

"A supportive and compassionate direction, Dad. Why are you still fretting?" Audrey took her own mug of coffee and perched on the barstool beside him.

"I don't know, exactly." Coffee sloshed as he pushed the mug aside. "The girl is a mass of contradictions. In her former school she made decent grades—outstanding grades in math and science, in fact. Now, she barely scrapes through. Something catastrophic happened to her. She doesn't know how she came to be here or what happened to her family. Whatever precipitated her presence in Santa Rita, it's buried in her memory. A promising student got lost. I offered to help her trace her family, but she's terrified of the idea."

Audrey kissed his cheek. "Every kid is special to you. You want them all to be Einstein or Strauss or Hemingway, or at least have a family life like ours." She hugged him. "I have news to brighten your dreary day. Claire's coming home for Thanksgiving."

"You spoke to your sister? Claire called home?"

"Yes, just for a second. She didn't tell me much, just said she'd be here next week, Tuesday evening at the latest, and stay for the holiday weekend."

George grinned, suddenly looking less like a man approaching the midpoint of his fifth decade and more like an expectant father. "Claire will be here for several days, then. Maybe the glamour of the big city and her fascinating job are beginning to lose their hold on her. Or maybe she just misses us."

Audrey turned away to gather cups and plates so her father couldn't see her face. She doubted Santa Rita's charm called to her older sister. Claire had long since abandoned her hometown for a career in the faster pace of Dallas. Her trips home had been rare, brief, and usually played against a background of upheaval and argument with their sister Judith. Through the window, as if called by the thought, Audrey saw Judith herself racing through the rain. The middle Anderson sister slid across the wet terrace and tumbled against the french doors of the family room.

Drenched and chasing slippery bundles, Judith flung open the doors and shook off rain like a damp puppy. Her dark pixie hair held a fringe of raindrops. Black jeans clung damply to her long legs, her ebony silk shirt highlighted by beads of rainwater. Polished Western boots sported bits of grass and a wet gloss where their cream-and-jet tops met the crease of her jeans. Only the dangling loops of her turquoise earrings and the silver of her concho belt broke the somber tones of Judith's costume.

"Hey, family," she greeted them. "Everybody's

home early today. And do I smell fresh coffee?" She released the last of her numerous brown paper bundles to let them slide onto the bar.

Audrey filled another cup and put it in front of her sister. *What's Judith going to say about Claire coming home? Better let Dad tell her. He's better at handling Judith.* Judith gave neither of them the opportunity to speak.

"I have some fun news," she announced as if unable to keep it to herself. "Drake let me put three of my paintings in the gallery last week, and today a friend of his came in. This fella bought one of them—the thing with the cat, the fireplace, and the newspaper— and wants to see more of my stuff. He may let me do a one-woman show in New Orleans. He said he's been looking for someone with my 'lyric clarity'—whatever that is—for the gallery. Drake knows him and says the interest is legit."

"Jude, how wonderful! You must be sky high." Audrey hugged her sister. Judith with a brush in her hand and a painting in her head was intolerable, but Judith with the sale of a painting and the promise of more became a whirlwind of enthusiasm.

"Even higher, Baby Sis, higher and still flying."

For once Audrey didn't complain about the aggravating nickname. Judith was too full of excitement and anticipation to have meant to annoy her. The slim apparition in black kicked off her boots and spun about the room. "I'm going to have a show! Somebody loves my paintings! Hooray for me!"

"We're full of interesting news today, aren't we?" George commented as Judith dropped onto the barstool next to him. "We have another surprise. Audrey tells me Claire called. She's coming for Thanksgiving. For the first time in, oh, I'm not sure how many years, we'll all be together for a family holiday."

Judith put her cup on the bar and turned slowly on her stool. Her bright spirits drained away as if drawn down an invisible tube. Seeing thoughts clamoring to become words as Judith's black eyes narrowed, Audrey braced herself for a scathing reaction. *Better to get it over with now and skip the scenes or icy silences when Claire's home.*

"*Claire* is coming home?" She sat still, wooden in her pose. "That's a bombshell, all right." The tone of her voice dulled. She fiddled absently with her cup. "So the lady executive will grace us with her presence. The sophisticated city girl comes to see her bumpkin sisters. Should be *delightful* having Claire home." Disdain colored her words. "Anybody told Drake? He'll be tickled to hear his ex-wife is in town." She pulled an innocent expression. "By the way, didn't we invite him to Thanksgiving dinner?"

Audrey felt her stomach drop. The pecan pie remained untouched on her plate as she saw the joy of the holiday vanishing. Whatever else Claire's visit might bring, it would make the holiday miserable for Drake Chandler.

****

The next day when Audrey ran into her ex-brother-in-law in Luke's Drug Store she found Judith had already enlightened Drake. In one of the red padded booths at the end of the store she saw him bent over his sandwich and a colorful catalog. As he glanced up she waved, and he motioned her to join him. His Byronic profile and wavy golden hair made more than one young lady in the shop cast Audrey an envious look.

"Judith says Claire is coming home for Thanksgiving," he began, as if anticipating her first words.

"Yes." Audrey tried to gauge how the news affected him. She couldn't read his dark eyes, but she knew he still had strong feelings for the girl who had married him only to run away from him less than a year later. "Do you want to see her while she's home?"

A flicker she couldn't identify passed across his poetic features. His hooded eyes closed a moment. "I don't suppose she'll want to see me."

"You know Dad will want you to come over anyway," she reminded him. "It wouldn't be Thanksgiving without your marathon chess tournament."

"I don't think I'll be up for chess, somehow. Judith asked me to come during the week to look over some canvases. Kearnes, in New Orleans, called. He'd like photos of her paintings. Judith wants my suggestions for which ones to send. I'll try to come before Claire arrives, or sometime when she's out. Maybe your dad won't mind skipping the chess game this year. I know he'd like to have the three of you to himself."

"But you said you'd like to see Claire."

"It doesn't matter about me." He pushed his unfinished lunch away. "I'm a painful memory for her, and that's about all. She'd probably like it if I left town while she's here."

Audrey held a special affection for Drake. She wasn't sure what had caused Claire to leave the man who had been high school crush, college flame, and briefly husband. Almost five years back, before her senior year of college, he and Claire married. They separated just before her graduation and divorced immediately afterward. Claire left town without explanation and, when prodded for a reason, only joked with a bitter laugh that the ink on her diploma and her divorce decree had dried about the same time.

Drake slipped his catalog into an envelope and sat back in the booth. "Claire is next week's problem. Tell me about you. How is the legal industry? Are they working you to death?"

"No, not working me enough. I need more lawyers in town buying law books." Audrey waved at the thin file she'd dropped on the table. "Fortunately we have enough private libraries to keep me working for a while."

Audrey ran her own small business for the benefit of Santa Rita's attorneys. Law books needed frequent updating, either by loose-leaf replacement pages or new material added as pocket parts to the back of bound volumes. She maintained the libraries for a number of local lawyers, working under a contract to file, update, or replace materials on a weekly basis. It was a skill she had acquired working in the law school library during her college years. It had served her well since returning home to be with her ailing mother.

"You should get farther out in the county," Drake counseled. "We have lawyers in even the smallest towns who would probably love to have your help. It's hard to get someone dependable out in Kelvey and Barlow, for instance. Have you contacted people out there?"

"I haven't, but I'll have the opportunity this weekend. Jared is taking me to the Bar Association dinner Saturday night. I'll have a chance to meet more of the out-of-town lawyers and do some campaigning." Audrey nibbled her chicken salad and stirred her coffee. Drake's appraising look made her wish she had worn something more professional than her sneakers, work jeans, and University sweatshirt.

"You know the dinner is formal."

"Well, ya-esss," she drawled. "I do own a dress, Dr. Chandler. I didn't plan to go in my jeans."

He chuckled at her indignation. "You and Jared have been seeing a good bit of each other lately, haven't you? Anything I should know?"

Audrey lost her indignation in an ironic laugh. "Not a thing. Jared is like you, another brother. We're pals, but there's no attraction. He's still way too hung up on Judith to ever see anybody else." Audrey grinned at the thought of snub-nosed, freckle-faced Jared and his hopeless romantic inclinations for her sister. He worked hard keeping his small office afloat while cherishing his romantic aspirations.

"So Judith will get her paintings into a real gallery?" Audrey followed her thoughts and Drake's field of expertise.

"Mine is a real gallery," he chided her. "Chandler's may not be in the center of Manhattan, but it does showcase some fine talent—like your sister."

"Sorry, I meant a bigger gallery."

"Apology accepted, and, yes, I think Kearnes will give her a show. He doesn't like experiments, fads, or general loopiness. He admires and knows talent. Judith is his kind of painter, emotional but not sentimental. He wouldn't look at pretty-pretty, but he feels genuine passion. The power in Judith's work reaches anybody with an ounce of sensitivity."

Audrey had often wondered how Judith could endlessly trample the feelings of people who cared about her and never realize she'd done it, yet create a painting that spoke of loneliness or sorrow or love more clearly than words. The work she'd sold, the one she called the cat, fireplace, and newspaper thing, had a haunting quality. Somehow the viewer understood the silence around the solitary cat beside the hearth and scattered newspaper. The missing person of the scene would never come back. At the time Judith painted it, just after their mother's death, she had shut herself up in her studio in the attic and screeched at anyone tapping at her door. Her family's concern for her, her lack of sleep, her irregular meals, had fueled her temper, but she painted with frenzied energy.

"I hope it works out for her. Judith will be a lot happier with some positive appreciation for her work."

"And easier to live with?" Drake queried.

"Definitely." Audrey finished her salad in silence. "So we'll see you during the holidays?" She didn't intend to let Claire's arrival make too many changes.

"I'll try, Audrey. I really will try to come over, but I won't let my presence make things hard for Claire. She needs some time with her family, especially your dad. I have to honor her wishes."

****

Things were suspiciously placid at home for the next few days. The week ended without further communication from Claire. Judith shut herself in her studio and evaluated paintings in various lights. She worked a few hours every day for Drake at the gallery, her thin, black-garbed form slipping in and out like a shadow on the walls. Audrey, recalling Drake's unspoken criticism, made a survey of her wardrobe and went shopping for a dress for the dinner dance. School kept George tied up, as Ruth Cleburne remained at her mother's bedside. He canceled his daily tennis game, coming home late from school, overwhelmed and weary, just as the amber light disappeared from the grey November sky.

On Saturday evening, as she dressed for the Bar Association dinner, Audrey wished someone were at home to see her off. Everyone was out, George having driven over to pick up another teacher for dinner with members of the school board, while Judith was working at the gallery. Audrey knew the tendrils and coronet of curls the girls over at the Curl-Up 'N' Dye had created would be wasted on Jared. At least Judith or George would have noticed the sophisticated departure from Audrey's usual ponytail. The elegant peacock blue dress rated something more than the preoccupied look Jared would give it. Still Audrey felt pleased with herself. She might not have the dramatic gypsy flair Judith managed in her endless eclectic black outfits, and she knew she couldn't manage Claire's cool, madonna perfection, but, all things considered, she looked well. Her baby-fine hair would never be anything but sandy brown, and her blue-green eyes couldn't match the magnetic lure of her sisters' dark ones, but just for tonight she felt very pretty indeed.

The weather had cleared, giving the citizens of Santa Rita two days of dry, crisp autumn. A hint of oak leaves and wood smoke floated in a crystal blue sky. After considering the unpredictable season, Audrey added a cashmere shawl to cover the low neck and bare shoulders of her dress, finishing just as Jared's attack on the doorbell announced his arrival. She fled down the stairs before he could begin banging at the frosted glass.

"We've got to move along," he said by way of greeting. "The mix-and-mingle before dinner will give you the best chance to rub elbows with the local attorneys." As she'd predicted, he took no notice of the stunning new dress or the intricate hairdo as he rushed her out the door.

"Looks like a good crowd," he remarked a few minutes later as he slid his Silverado into the parking lot at the country club. Audrey wished he'd gone for an actual car when he replaced his beat-up Ford, but he'd told her repeatedly how practical the pickup was. It was practical for looking at a disputed land boundary or for chasing a deer off in the woods, she agreed, but it did little for someone in evening sandals and a cocktail dress.

"I hope some of them need a filing service." She slid out of the seat while struggling to keep her skirt within the bounds of decency.

"We'll find out." Jared shrugged into his black jacket and fumbled with the unfamiliar tie while heading for the clubhouse entry.

The crowd filling the room clustered near the bar, making a constant hum like the vibrations around a beehive. Audrey accepted the glass of white wine Jared handed her and studied faces in the groups nearby. She saw many acquaintances and a few old friends in the gathering. *Surely a few of them need my services.* Across the room, one profile drew her attention. A quiet magnetism seemed to flow around the man in the charcoal dinner jacket. His mane of bronze hair and the cropped reddish-gold beard reminded her of someone, someone who touched the corner of her memory. *No, it's a trick of the light. It can't be...*

"Who is he?" she asked Jared. "The man talking to Judge Lindley."

Jared, towering above Audrey's five-foot four-inch height, scanned the group near them. "Oh, the Viking? He's a trial consultant. He came to help with the jury selection for Crawford's big trial. Name's Hal Lindstrom. No point in passing your name on to him. He's teaching at the law school next year."

"Halvard Lindstrom!" She drew a sharp breath. "The Viking? Is that what they call him now?"

"You know him?" Jared sounded doubtful.

"When I worked at the law school library, he was editor of the law review. I used to pull books for him and hunt up archived material. I worked nights when staff wasn't available, so we got to know each other. He went with a prestigious firm in Chicago the next year. Why is he back in Texas?"

Jared shook his head. "Some big trial he handled wound up with a witness getting killed. He'd built a good reputation, but I guess he didn't like what he got into. Now he's interested in teaching and consulting for other attorneys. I hear he can read a jury panel like it was a newspaper. If he finds weak points in a case, he goes for them like a Norse raider. 'The Viking' was what the press called him. Crawford's trial looked hopeless, but the client walked out a free man." Jared glanced at the group thinning near the visitor. "Want to go say hello?"

"Oh, he'd never remember a freshman library clerk

from six or seven years back." Audrey turned toward the opening doors to the dining room. *No, he wouldn't remember...but I do.*

During dinner, Audrey chatted with several of the attorneys employing her services and passed her business cards to a few new acquaintances. Many of the wives attending commented on her pretty dress, asked about Claire's impending visit, or sent regards to George. A small town didn't really need a newspaper, Audrey mused, as she brushed aside the probing questions about Claire's homecoming, Judith's possible show, and other private concerns.

"The combo is setting up for the dance in the other room," Jared reminded her as she edged away from a pair of women intent on gossip and a critique of their closest associates.

"Good timing. I was just about to hear the intimate details of June Pressler's third divorce. Thanks for tearing me away."

"Glad I could help. I'm not a fan of the sordid details either. I hear enough of them during office hours."

"I love living in a small town, but it does seem like we know way more than we should about our friends and neighbors." Audrey followed Jared into the festive ballroom and listened a moment to the small group of musicians warming up. They sounded as if they could actually play dance music instead of the blast of uncoordinated noise she'd expected.

"Like to take a turn on the floor and see if I remember any of those expensive dance lessons Aunt Min paid for?"

He actually could dance, Audrey remembered. He

had a decent lead, and his feet managed to miss her toes. The strains of "I Can't Give You Anything But Love" swirled around them, and she heard Jared murmur something about the music being "for the old-timers in the crowd." Jared was pleasant company, and he'd taken a strong interest in her business, recommending her to colleagues and mentioning her services to other attorneys. He even said he'd hire her full-time for his office if his budget would permit it. She'd been well trained in legal research, and her grasp of resources was often better than his own, he frankly admitted. Convinced part of his support stemmed from his interest in Judith, Audrey was flattered but made no commitment. She preferred having her own business.

As the music ended, they exited the dance floor at a narrow gap where another couple stood. Hal Lindstrom released his partner, the wife of Santa Rita's county attorney, and as he turned to leave the floor he inadvertently bumped into Jared.

"Pierce?" He offered his hand. "Jared Pierce, isn't it? Crawford introduced us in the hallway over at the courthouse a week or so back. Good to see you."

"Yes, I remember," Jared answered, taking the offered hand. "I had the chance to watch you in action. It was quite a lesson."

Audrey felt Hal Lindstrom's attention turn to her. Jared must have noticed also and realized his manners were slipping. Hastily he performed introductions.

"I know you."

"Oh, I worked in the library when you were in law school."

"Yes, of course," Lindstrom responded. "You always kept the coffeepot hot and knew where all the ancient tomes were hidden. You saved my neck more than once. You had plans for law school, didn't you? Are you practicing with Pierce here in Santa Rita?"

Audrey felt rather than saw Jared's start of surprise. She'd never mentioned her shelved dreams to him. "No, I didn't go on after undergraduate school. My family needed me here at home."

"Audrey runs a filing service for local attorneys," Jared put in. "She keeps us current and out of trouble. I think she knows more law than most of us who practice."

"Too bad you didn't go on. You looked like a promising student." Hal Lindstrom paused. "A filing service?" Audrey nodded. "We'll have to talk. I have books for a small library I haven't unpacked or even checked to see if they're current. Maybe you can help me out?"

"I thought you were leaving private practice to teach," Jared interjected.

White teeth flashed behind the gold-tinged beard. "I'm leaving the trial work to the rest of you, and I'll be teaching next fall, but I'm doing some consulting while working on a textbook. I've taken the Tucker place as a combination office and residence. Santa Rita's great, and folks have really encouraged me to stay around." He glanced back at Audrey. "Miss Anderson, could I have a few minutes to talk to you? It sounds like your help is just what I need."

"Excuse me, Jared?" Audrey turned away from Jared to follow Hal through the crowd. She moved in the wake left by the broad shoulders pushing toward the doorway. *Maybe business will profit from the dinner dance after all.*

20

The consulting attorney found a deserted corner of the wide foyer and drew two chairs together as Audrey joined him.

"What do you have, and how much maintenance will it need?" she began as she took the chair he offered.

"Not too many titles," he answered. "It's not a full law library, by any means, just the basics—Texas Cases, TexJur, the Digests, Vernon's Statutes—but I bought them secondhand and don't have any idea how current they are. And I'll have a few loose-leaf services that will need upkeep. Why don't you come by one afternoon next week and take a look? You'll know better from an examination yourself than from anything I can tell you."

"I have Tuesday afternoon free," she ventured.

"No, I have appointments all day Tuesday. How about dinner that evening? Meet me at my office about 5:30 and look over the stuff. Then you can tell me over dinner what I need to get everything current."

"I...I don't..." Audrey began.

"Socialize with clients? But I was a friend before I was a client." The smile behind his beard flashed. "And I really need your advice. Besides, I'd like to know more about the town and what goes on here. It would be the best arrangement for me. Can't you manage dinner?"

Everything about the bronze giant with the russet beard urged her to accept. Audrey remembered their numerous confidential chats and the camaraderie of her college days. She'd looked forward to her tedious hours in the library because of his companionship. It made professional sense to renew their previous friendship.

Hal Lindstrom would be a good client to add to her business, and without her his library could be in terrible shape before he realized it.

"I'd enjoy it," she answered at last.

"It's a date." He listened a minute as the lilt of a familiar tune filled the hall. "Give me this waltz, and I'll take you back to Pierce."

Just as the ancient clock in the clubhouse entry chimed ten, the affair began to break up. Audrey retrieved her shawl and joined Jared at the doors.

"It's about time we headed home."

"Yes, I have things to do tomorrow to get ready for the holidays. I'll be pushed for time, and I gave my only free evening to Hal Lindstrom," she answered.

"You signed him up, then?"

"I think I'm going to. After I look at his library Tuesday, I'll be able to tell."

Jared gave her a hoist into the high cab of the Silverado, then climbed into the driver's seat. "So you and Lindstrom are old friends?"

"Oh, just college acquaintances. He bought some books that need evaluating, and he wants to know more about Santa Rita. I'm having dinner with him."

"Nice going, kid," was all Jared answered.

Companionable silence filled the truck as each seemed preoccupied with the evening until Jared pulled up to the brick colonial on Stafford Street. Audrey was surprised to see lights still on in the back of the house. Her dad must be up, catching the news or reading. She guessed Judith was in her studio, since there were lights in the windows of the third floor attic, as well.

"Dad is up, so there will be fresh coffee. Come in and say hello to him and to Judith, won't you?" she invited.

"Sure. I'd like to see Judith about something anyway. Aunt Min has a birthday coming up, and I want some help looking for a present." Audrey read Jared's unspoken words. He would appreciate any excuse to be near Judith for a moment.

They came in through the front entry, past the darkened stairs, and followed the sound of the television to the family room at the back. Audrey stopped without speaking. Something on the screen had electrified the room. George leaned forward, rigid and silent, barely touching the cushion of his favorite blue wingback chair. Judith perched precariously on the chair arm, a mug of coffee threatening to splash over the edge and onto the upholstery. A strained undercurrent surrounded them. Both turned as Jared crossed the floor to reach out to Judith. Something was wrong. Foreboding filled the air like an approaching storm.

"It's good you're here," George began. "Late news had the story. Beckwith and Tate are filing for bankruptcy. They won't open the doors on Monday. They're being investigated for fraud and misappropriation. I've been trying to get an update on the local channel."

Jared's open face had a bewildered expression. He glanced from Judith to her father in confusion. Audrey saw the news didn't register with him. "Beckwith and Tate is the firm Claire works for."

"I guess we know the reason she's coming home so suddenly," Judith blurted. "She won't have a job anymore."

Audrey started to protest, but the sound of the front

door opening stopped her. Through the shadowed hall she saw a tall woman in winter white slacks and sweater moving toward her. The elegant chignon of dark hair framed an oval face of magnolia delicacy. Eyes of deepest brown surveyed the group. One hand held a wire cat carrier, the bristling Chinchilla Persian inside regarding them with haughty disdain.

"Well, family, I'm home. Here we are, all together again." Her glance took in the room. "I see you've heard the news." Audrey bit back the questions. They didn't matter right now. Claire was home. Everything else would wait.

Chapter Two

"Have you seen Richelieu?" As if reluctant to enter, Claire stood in the doorway of the cluttered studio.

Judith looked up from cleaning brushes to answer her sister. "His Eminence the Cat?" She gestured to the bookshelf below the dormer window. "He's checking out the accommodations."

The silver-tipped Persian glanced their way and closed his eyes, one blue, one copper, as if annoyed by their chatter. Claire crossed the room and gathered the furry bundle into her arms. The cat whiffled a sigh of resignation and draped himself over the shoulder of her white sweater. Judith put her brushes aside and wiped down the top of the old card table that held her paraphernalia. She watched as Claire glanced across the way toward the Chandler house.

"So, will you be seeing Drake while you're home?" She kept her tone casual.

"It's a small town. Inevitably we'll run into each other." Claire turned her back to the window. "I won't go searching for an opportunity, but I won't dodge him. We aren't important to each other anymore."

Judith tightened the top of a paint tube and dropped it into a tray of other tubes. "He usually comes for Thanksgiving dinner. He won't this year, of course."

Claire sauntered back into our lives as if her presence wouldn't make a bit of difference to our plans. How typical. She's as arrogant as her cat.

Claire's eyes narrowed and held a hint of malice. "I'd think any number of women would be anxious to have a single, attractive man at their holiday table. Has he run through all the available women in Santa Rita?" She stopped as an assessing expression flashed across her face. "Or has someone here caught his attention? You're working pretty closely with him. Is he making it more than a working relationship?"

Judith snorted. "No time in my life for men, thanks. I love Drake dearly, but he drives me batty about once a week. Two hours of his neat-freak spit-and-polish is enough to ruin a perfect day." She picked up a sketchpad and pencil, doodled quick pictures of "No Trespassing" and "Keep Out" signs across one page. "He doesn't have room in his heart for any other woman. You're still his one and only."

"So he'd have you think." The look on Claire's face declared the subject of her ex-husband closed. She sat in the old red rocking chair near the window, a pale spill of light touching her dark hair and glinting off the silver tips of the cat's fur.

Judith turned to a fresh page of her sketchpad and let her pencil drift over it. "What about the situation with your firm? The news said 'fraud and misappropriation.' Are you going to be caught up in it?"

"I might have to testify, I suppose." Claire hesitated. "I don't know anything, really. Office managers order furniture and supplies and hire support staff. Sometimes a client needs special attention, lunch or parking privileges, but I never was involved in any of the financial matters. All I know is that one of the partners told me last week the firm was in deep trouble and I'd be wise to take a few days off. The lid blew earlier than he expected, I guess." For a moment she couldn't seem to bring words forth. "I never suspected fraud or anything illegal. Not at our firm."

Judith saw the look of disillusionment flooding Claire's face. Her pencil raced to capture it. Scant lines caught the pained eyes. A quick tracery of worry shaded a partial profile. A painting formed in her imagination: *Employee ruined by corporate greed, shattered dreams the by-product.* "So you came here to wait for things to simmer down?"

"Oh, partly, I suppose. I needed to get away, to think about the future." Claire's dark eyes closed as she stroked the cat. "I'll probably move, find a new city. I'm not involved in the firm's affairs, but my name's associated with them. It could be hard to get an offer in Dallas after all the publicity. And with the holidays coming, it may take some time to get the right connection."

"How long do you think you'll stay?" Judith continued to sketch, catching the tilt of Claire's head and the bit of sun across her forehead. "And what about your apartment? You have a lease, don't you?"

Claire flicked the questions away with one hand, her eyes still closed. "The lease is up at the end of the year, and I can pay the rent till then. I'll need to give the building manager notice, I suppose." She sounded too weary to deal with details. She turned to stare out into the pale November morning. "I didn't come to make trouble, Jude. Really, I didn't. I know you and I aren't very close anymore, but I needed to find safe ground for a while. You and Dad and Audrey are my only haven."

"You could still include Drake in that list."

"No." Claire rejected the thought with a pained expression. "Believe me, there are things about Drake Chandler you don't need to know. Take it as gospel and don't ask questions you wouldn't want answered." She dropped the cat back onto the shelf and stood. "It's Sunday, isn't it? I think I'll change and go to church with Dad."

Judith closed the cover of her sketchbook as her sister started down the stairs. The "Shattered Dreams" painting took on substance in her mind as she studied the retreating silhouette. A blank canvas waited on the easel. Paint and brushes stood ready. The idea of the painting filled her mind. *Before I lose the moment...* She only meant to block in the shapes, but the image took over. Paint seemed to spurt from her brushes. Roughed-out spaces became lifelike. Judith heard nothing, saw nothing but the canvas in front of her as the intensity of her inspiration took over.

By late afternoon Judith, exhausted, her fingers cramped from clutching brushes, knew she couldn't paint any longer. The walls of the house were too confining to remain inside. The rest of the family had scattered. Claire had moved from room to room, endlessly rearranging bits and pieces till everyone was grateful when she wandered upstairs for a nap. George took off for his tennis game, and Audrey, saying she had filing to do for Jared and would be out for an hour or so, pulled on jeans and a faded shirt and left right behind him.

With no particular destination in mind, Judith zipped her black leather jacket and escaped the silent house, walking toward the footpath that ran beside the river. The quiet flow of water could always ease her turbulent mind.

"It's not fair of Claire to turn up like this," she muttered to herself, her pace picking up speed as she left Stafford Street behind. *She could have called home, explained the trouble, and at least asked if it was convenient for her to come. With Claire home, Drake will be alone for Thanksgiving. Dad's worn out with all the extra stuff he's been doing at school, so he doesn't need the additional burden of Claire's troubles. Audrey has her own worries keeping her business going. And Claire's managed to take the shine off my little triumph—again.*

Judith grimaced. For years, anything she did, every success she'd had, Claire had spoiled. Claire's sudden wedding had taken all the attention from Judith's art school success. Judith felt obligated to leave her school in New York temporarily when Mom became ill; her art studies had blown up forever when Claire announced she had filed for divorce. Claire took refuge in her job in the city, so the burden fell on Judith and what help Audrey could give. At least, when Audrey graduated, she'd come home to share the responsibilities. But now, once more, Claire's affairs had taken everyone's attention, leaving Judith no applause for her efforts and ambitions, her one-woman show. *Trumped again!*

"Hey, you planning to walk all the way across Texas?" Judith heard the words above the clamor of a horn and her own chattering thoughts. She looked back to see Jared Pierce in his black Silverado bearing down on her. "Want a ride?" he added, swinging the passenger door open.

She looked around. She'd walked past the downtown shopping district, left the footpath, and was heading toward the river bridge at the highway, much farther than she'd realized. She nodded and grasped the hand he offered to lift her into the cab.

"Thanks." She pulled the heavy door closed. "It didn't seem like I'd walked so far."

"It's getting chilly, now the sun's going down. You looked like your mind was about seventeen counties away. Something wrong?"

"Oh, just Claire. One more time she's got all of us dancing to her tune. Nobody in the house can ever have a crisis or a stroke of luck without Claire coming along to trump it. And I'm sick of stepping out of her way. Now she may have to go to court about the accounting firm's business, and she needs to find a new job, and maybe she'll have to leave Dallas, and one more time it's *Claire, Claire, Claire!* Claire's problem always gets solved first, no matter what." Judith slumped into the corner in dejection.

"Judy, put a sock in it, will you?" Jared pulled away from the curb with enough force to squeal the tires. "Claire's problem is real, and she didn't plan to dump her troubles on you. Her situation has nothing to do with you or your show. You're acting just like you did in second grade when Pete Jones won the award for best fire prevention poster. You felt threatened because he did a better poster. Anytime you start blustering, it's because you're afraid somebody will see you're feeling threatened."

"I am not..." she began.

"Are too."

Sulky silence filled the truck cab as the wheels skimmed along the pavement and across the Santa Rita River bridge. Judith chewed at a fingernail. "Where are we going?"

Jared waved a hand at the farm-to-market road branching off the highway. "My place. You haven't seen what I've done to the old homestead. Give you a change of scenery."

The rustic cabin emerged from the landscape as they turned. Its weathered grey walls caught the last of the afternoon light, washing the open porch with fading autumn sun. The scene appealed to the artist in Judith. She pushed the truck door open and dropped eagerly to the ground.

"Your Aunt Min would be proud. It's even better than she left it." Kicking up pebbles before her, Judith skipped along the gravel path to the porch and the rocker tipping in the breeze. She turned in a pivoting circle to study the whole scene. "I'd like to paint this place one day."

Jared unlocked the door and invited her inside. "Anytime. I'll be taking Aunt Min out for dinner Thursday, and I'll tell her. She'd love to know you want to paint the old cabin. She hated giving it up when she moved into the retirement home, but she just couldn't be out here by herself any longer."

"I'll bet she's glad you're here, anyway. You grew up here, so it means more to you than it would to strangers." Judith looked around at the quilt on the bed, the copper pans hanging from a rack over the long-legged stove. "Even the interior could make a striking picture."

Jared pulled out a ladderback chair and offered it to her. "Okay, what's going on at the Anderson house? Just Claire?"

"Oh, just more of the usual." Judith didn't want to get into a discussion with Jared again. "Claire's got problems, I hope to have a show to put together, and Dad's too worn out from the extra load at school to put up with either one of us. One more thing on his plate would break it, I think. He needs a peaceful holiday, but with Claire home, all our plans are washed out. Drake can't come, with Claire there. Claire's in turmoil, I'm bouncing off the walls waiting to hear about my show, and Audrey's just too busy to be around much. Thanksgiving won't be tranquil, and it won't be restful. Dad will probably be glad to get back to school for the peace and quiet."

Jared leaned back in his chair. "Judy, I've known you all my life, you and Claire and Audrey. Remember when I took you to the Harvest Festival dance? You spent the whole night bitching about Claire's wedding and that poison-green dress she made you wear. You've been down on your sister ever since you left New York when your mom got sick. I think in some way you blamed Claire—guess you had to blame somebody. I don't know what went on with her and Drake, but that's all in the past—your mother's death, Claire's divorce, all of it. Stop looking for ways to get hurt. You've got your show to work on. Don't let this thing with Claire get in the way."

Judith paced the room. *Jared's the only one who ever says 'Judy' now. He still won't give up his crush on me, no matter how I push him away.* She was sure it could never be more than a leftover thing from high school. Jared was all wrong for her, as wrong for her as she was for him. She wanted to paint and travel and be left alone to work when the need was strong. He was just a homely, unimaginative, small-town lawyer she'd known all her life. He wanted a wife and babies and someone to show off at the Bar Association dinners, not a chaotic artist who wore turpentine instead of perfume and usually had dabs of color spattered in her hair. What did he know about how things were for her? She turned around to tell him off, to tell him to go find another girl and back out of her affairs before it ruined their friendship. She would take him down a peg or two. She turned and found herself nose to nose with him. His fingertip stopped the words she meant to say. One brown hand traced the arch of her lips and cupped the curve of her head. His lips grazed hers, and whatever her intended words, they faded from her mind.

"Judy, it's going to be okay. It will all come right. You know I'm always on your side, and I'll be here if you need me."

****

Hal Lindstrom had made good use of the old Tucker place Audrey decided as she hurried to keep their Tuesday appointment. The native stone building was one of the few from historical Santa Rita. The rough-hewn structure had been a trading post, according to local legend. Looking at the sturdy rock walls and worn stone floors, she could believe it. A bright fire in the deep fireplace greeted her as she entered. Cedar posts, thick as a man, held up blackened beams. Shelves had been set into the walls, and doors and windows were framed in the same ancient wood.

Hal had put in basic office furniture, a rolltop desk and swivel chair, but three cane-bottomed rockers clustered around the crackling hearth.

"I put the boxes of books in the other room." He pointed at a closed door. "It's pretty cold in there still. You want to take a quick look now, or come back when I have the heat working better?"

Audrey hated putting things off. "Let me dig in now, so I can give you an idea of what you're dealing with." She dropped her coat over one of the rockers and pushed up the sleeves of her corduroy shirt as Hal swung back the door, revealing piles of boxes stacked in disorderly clumps. "This may take some pushing and pulling," she muttered, skirting the pile to pry open the first carton. An hour later, with dust across her nose and a smear of ink decorating her chin, she sat on the table corner to note her findings. Looking up from her scribbles on a yellow tablet, she found Hal regarding her from the doorway.

"How is it?"

"Not too bad. Your Vernons need pocket parts, you're missing about three volumes of Texas Cases, and you'll need recent supplements for TexJur and Texas Digest, but nothing to lead you into instant malpractice. I can get this cleared up in a week or so."

"Then let's leave this icebox and continue discussions over dinner. You promised to show me something of Santa Rita."

Audrey slipped down from her perch, holding out dirt-stained hands. "I'd better wash off a layer of grime first. They aren't called dusty law books without reason."

He pointed her to a narrow, oval-topped door at the

end of the shadowed hall. "Soap and maybe even towels in there. We can take my car when you're ready."

"Oh, we'll walk. Magnolia's Grill is just around the corner. We're closer here than we could possibly park."

Half an hour later Audrey chuckled a little to herself as she led Hal Lindstrom to the small café. She could barely wait to see his reaction to the colorful landmark. He didn't disappoint her. He immediately noticed the bright neon sign flashing "Sorry, We're Open" to all by-passers.

"Magnolia isn't your average chef," she answered to his unspoken question.

"So I see."

Audrey considered how it might appear to eyes unprepared for the eclectic scene. The walls, a deep mustard shade, were filled with one long mural of dancing flamingoes, all shades of pink, red, and orange. The turquoise rafters arched only inches above Hal's head. The pterodactyl in pink tennis shoes, perched on an open beam as though ready to swoop down on them, was a papier-mâché mobile, but it looked real enough. A gallery of abstract paintings in brilliant colors took the only undecorated corner, and black pots of tall ferns filled odd spaces. A row of stained-glass suncatchers— marbled magnolia blossoms as large as dinner plates— dangled from each of the small windows along the street-side wall. No two chairs were alike except for the hot pink-and-gold paint they sported.

"Hey, Audrey! Good to see you," a hoarse voice called, and Audrey found herself swept up and swung about in an enthusiastic hug.

"Put me down, wild man, and let me make introductions before you run off a new customer." Hal seemed ready to duck back out the door. "Hal, this is Magnolia. Magnolia, Hal's a new lawyer in town. Be nice to him. You never know when you'll need a friend in court."

Magnolia, a man of formidable size, with skin like a weathered coconut, offered his hand. Hal shook it gingerly. They were much the same height, but Audrey estimated the chef had at least fifty pounds on the lawyer.

"Good to have you here," he rumbled. "Need new folks moving in to keep things interesting. You're a friend of Audrey's, then you're a friend of mine." He shook back a mane of grey-streaked hair and pulled a chef's toque down. "Take any seat, and I'll send Suzette over for your order." He gestured to the red-and-orange lettering on the blackboard above the bar that divided the kitchen from the dining room. "Don't see what you want up there, order bacon and eggs. This is what I'm cooking tonight."

Audrey led Hal to a corner table. Its red cloth and spray of dried flowers glowed under the light of a small wall sconce.

"You said you wanted to see some of the local color." They settled into the mismatched chairs. She laughed at the look on Hal's face but hurried to reassure him. "Magnolia came here years and years ago. Now this place is almost an institution. You'll see why. The food is great, and you get used to the atmosphere. Just don't come in with a particular dish in mind. Magnolia cooks what he feels like, and what's on the blackboard is all there is. He won't be tied to a routine."

Hal sat back in his chair. "I can see Santa Rita is going to be a new experience." He studied the handwriting on the board above the bar. "What do you suggest for dinner?"

Audrey followed his gaze. "Well, in Texas you can't go wrong with a steak, but if you feel adventurous, you might try the shrimp enchiladas or the chicken quesadilla."

After deciding to try the chicken dish, Hal seemed ready for local information. Audrey answered his questions and told him about the town and its Spanish Colonial history. Before she realized it, she was also telling him about her family, her sisters and their shaky truce, and her life in general.

"So how did you wind up here, running your own business, instead of tackling law school as you planned?"

"My mother was really sick my last year in college. I didn't know how bad till I came home for Easter my senior year. I almost didn't go back then, but Dad insisted. After graduation, going on was out of the question. I'd taken the exams and been accepted, but I couldn't leave Dad and Judith with the way things were. Mom died two years ago. By then I had the filing service going and found I liked having my own business. Dad was pretty racked up over losing Mom. Having me here eased things a little for him and my sister, so I just stayed on. I enjoy the research and messing around in the library more than I would like practicing law itself. I didn't know that then, but I've come to see it."

"You're going to be a big help to me," Hal predicted. "Will you be able to give me enough time to get my office up to speed?"

Audrey pulled an appointment book from her bag and flipped pages. "I can work you into my schedule, but you'd better look at my rates before you decide. I come pretty high." She passed him a card listing her fees and saw him grit his teeth.

"Yes, your service is expensive, but do I have a choice? I need your talented little hands taking care of my library." He put out his hand. "You have a new client."

****

All in all, Audrey told herself as she buttoned her blue quilted robe, Thanksgiving Day could have been worse, though the day had passed in strained silence and stiff politeness. Judith had reined in her tongue and kept her thoughts to herself. Claire remained cool, politely distant. George read and, after the traditional dinner and mid-afternoon nap, took a slow walk in place of his tennis game. Audrey herself had kept out of sight, retreating to the office off the formal living room to work on monthly invoices. At least, Audrey mused, there had been no open quarrels or damaged feelings.

Everyone seemed to be sleeping late this Friday morning. Audrey wasn't sure if her sisters were actually resting or just avoiding each other by staying out of sight. She padded into the kitchen in fuzzy slippers and robe just as George pushed open the deck door, a gym bag in one hand and the morning paper in the other.

"Finally up?" He left the paper on the bar and carried the gym bag to the laundry room beyond. "It's a gorgeous day out there. Too nice to spend it inside."

"I know, Dad, but it was a treat to sleep in on a weekday. How was the tennis match?" Audrey scanned the kitchen for a sign someone had made coffee.

"No match, just hitting balls for practice. Couldn't find anyone to play with." His tone was muffled by the sound of the washer filling. "Have you seen my red striped shorts?" He peered around the door of the laundry room with a questioning expression. Audrey knew exactly which shorts he meant. Her mother had made them, as a joke, from a Valentine print fabric, some years back. Though they were hideous, George wore them with pride. They were the last of the fond, foolish jokes he and his wife had exchanged in their long and happy marriage.

"No, I haven't seen them, Dad. Did you leave them in the locker room, or get them mixed up with the other laundry?"

"Don't think so," he answered in a puzzled tone. "I was sure they were in my gym bag." The washer began to hum and slosh as he came back to the kitchen and pulled out his usual coffee mug. "They'll show up."

"Oh, the washer eats one of a pair of socks from time to time. Maybe it's demanding bigger tribute. You'll have to wait for coffee. We must be the first ones up, because the pot is cold and empty."

A second day had gone quite well, Audrey concluded that evening as darkness closed over the house. Maybe they weren't in for the crisis she'd imagined. Judith had retreated to her studio, but she'd seemed open and remarkably agreeable when she said goodnight. Claire was closeted in the office, looking at positions listed in various metropolitan newspapers she'd picked up at the news stand. Audrey had been given a quick review of the possibilities when she passed the room. *Apparently Claire has resigned herself to making a change and is getting on with it.*

Jared had come by for a moment as he returned from his visit with his Aunt Min. Audrey knew he was disappointed Judith didn't spend a part of the evening with him, but he didn't make a fuss about it, only watched her vanish up the stairs with a stoic look on his homely face.

Drake had phoned but stayed away. His conversation with George remained between them, though Audrey guessed it concerned Claire's future plans. Still, the day had been fairly free of stress and conflict. Audrey joined her father in the family room to watch the late news before going up to bed.

"Will Ruth be back at school next week?" she asked during the commercial break.

"She'll be back, but only until Christmas. Her mother's in a nursing home for a few weeks. At the end of the semester, Ruth will go back and stay with her mother."

A quick sympathy filled Audrey. She knew what hard times were ahead for the teacher. "What about that student you've been tutoring, Dad? Did she get her research paper in?"

George sighed with tired exasperation. "No, she didn't turn anything in. I don't know what to think. I'll have to have a long talk with Ruth on Monday. I hate to start off her week with this, but I have no choice."

Audrey watched the end of the news and the weather but decided to forego the sports reports. She told George goodnight and had just reached the bottom of the stairs when the doorbell rang. *Has Jared come back, or possibly Drake?* She flipped on the porch light and through the glass panes of the door saw the dark fabric and dull gleam of a uniform. *Oh, drat!* She bit back her annoyance. *Someone's made mischief at the school again, and Dad will have to go over and take a look, I suppose.* She opened the door.

"Sheriff Hayes?" She was surprised to see the county officer. Usually he sent one of the two deputies for errands like this.

The sheriff, whippet thin, his silver hair shining under the porch light, raised his Stetson. "Your dad home, Miss Audrey? I need to see him, please."

"Sure, he's in the den. Come in, and I'll call him." She held the door back and waited till the sheriff crossed into the entry. Audrey gathered her robe closer as a chilly draft filled the room. "Just a minute." She hurried down the darkened hall. "Dad," she called, "Sheriff Hayes is here. I guess something's happened at the school again."

George rose from his chair and shut off the TV. He glanced at his slippers and robe. "He'll have to wait while I change. Go on to bed, Audrey. Maybe this won't take long."

Audrey paused to shut off the lights in the den, then followed her father along the hall. She was still in the shadows when George joined Hayes.

"Hey, Al, what brings you out on this cold night? Somebody TP'ed the gym again?"

Hayes looked up, and Audrey saw the strained expression on his face. *This must be pretty serious. Maybe one of the kids is in trouble and wants Dad to break the news to the parents.*

"Could I have a word with you in private?" Hayes asked George.

George led the way to the office off the hallway.

"Sure, come in here, Al."

Audrey pulled the belt of her robe tight and crept into the living room. Dad wasn't going anywhere in a ratty robe and slippers. She intended to get the details from him before he took a step up the stairs. She had a long wait. The clock under the stairs chimed the hour and then the half hour before George emerged from the closed room. He didn't start for the stairs. He opened the coat closet and pulled on his long overcoat. Audrey hurried to the doorway.

"Dad, what's wrong? You can't go out dressed like that. You'll take cold."

He looked up at her. His face was drawn and white in the dim light. "Got to go, Audrey. One of the students at school…" He didn't go on.

"Mr. Anderson has been accused of assaulting one of the students." Hayes stopped to face Audrey. "Sexually assaulting a girl, the Marshall girl—Dondie, she says her name is. I have to take your dad down to headquarters. You girls need to call an attorney, Miss Audrey."

Chapter Three

The temperature dropped during the night. Audrey, her mind wandering in less turbulent paths, sought refuge in mundane affairs. She should light a fire, dry out the damp, chill room. The den was the family gathering place in times of celebration and in times of trial. On this pewter-toned morning, it felt unfamiliar to Audrey. She hadn't noticed the worn spot in the rug, and the faded places on the old chair looked different. Judith hunched over a sketchpad, escaping in her own fashion, while a distracted Claire brushed Richelieu's silvered fur. Audrey, not knowing what to do, had wakened them after calling Jared. Stunned by the charge against George, the girls remained convinced his arrest was a misunderstanding. As hours crept by, they alternately paced, bickered, examined views, and rejected each other's conclusions.

"It's a mistake, that's all," was Claire's unwavering position.

"Jared doesn't have a clue about anything like this. Dad will be furious about our interference," Judith argued.

"I work with legal matters. I read the cases and rulings. This is serious, and Dad needs legal advice. Jared can help." Audrey wouldn't back away from her actions.

The atmosphere still vibrated with apprehension. In the faint light of a new day, they simply waited in exhausted silence. As light filtered into the room, the doorbell cut through their individual isolation.

"It's Jared!" Audrey ran, her slippers thumping along the polished wood floor. Her heart fell when she saw Drake on the other side of the door.

"Audrey, I saw lights," he began. "I wanted to catch Judith before the rest of you were up. I developed her photographs."

He wouldn't know, of course, Audrey reminded herself. Even the town gossips couldn't have scandal on their lips this quickly. "We're all up, Drake, and we have trouble." Audrey pulled the door closed behind him. She looked up into his hooded, dark eyes, eyes that always seemed wearied by unspeakable burdens. "I'm glad you're here. We'll need your help."

Without hesitation Drake followed her. Judith barely paused, shrugged, and returned to her pencil sketch. Her black hooded robe emphasized her emotional distance from the group. A brief flare lit Claire's face before her carefully schooled features slipped into remote placidity.

"George? Is he ill?" Drake glanced from face to face. "You should have called me."

"Yes, it's Dad." Audrey found no easy words. "It isn't illness. But it's serious." Feeling as if the mind that formed the thoughts and the lips that spoke them belonged to another person, she told him what little they knew. The sheriff had come, spoken to George, asked him to come to his office, and said to call a lawyer. She shuddered as she told him the charge.

"Rape? George? One of the students?" Drake's

face drained of color. "No! No one would believe that." His mouth tightened. "Jared? You called him?"

Audrey nodded. "I called him before Dad was out the door. He said he'd meet Dad and the sheriff. I woke Claire and Judith." Audrey shivered, anxiety running chills along her spine. "We believed it was a mix-up, and he'd be home any minute, but it's been hours. We haven't heard anything." She stuck her hands in her robe pockets, pain and confusion bowing her shoulders. "Jared should at least call us."

"I'm sure Jared is doing all he can. Let's light the fire in here, and get breakfast going. You can't run on just coffee and nerves." Drake started toward the fireplace, but Claire's scowl stopped him.

"We can take care of each other, Drake. You have a business to run." Her voice sharpened. "You do have something to do, don't you?"

Drake stooped by the stone hearth. "I still care about the people in this family, though I'm not technically part of it. I'll do all I can to help, even if it's only light a fire."

Judith moved so he could reach the woodbin. "Thanks, Drake." She shot a cold glance at her sister, who walked away, leaving the chair to the cat. "Most of us appreciate your help."

"Speak for yourself, Judith. I'll dress. Add outsiders to the problem if you wish." As Claire left the room, Audrey and Drake exchanged a look, then wordlessly went on with their tasks.

Claire remained upstairs until the jangle of the doorbell again sent currents of apprehension through the household. Audrey started for the door but saw her sister coming down the stairs. Claire insisted, "I'll go.

It's Jared, but he's alone."

As he came in, Audrey tried to brace herself for whatever news Jared might bring. Unpretentious face and honest eyes revealing nothing, he handed Claire his coat. Weariness clothed him and, as much as his rumpled shirt and unshaven chin, indicated he hadn't been home yet.

"Well, what's happening?" Judith demanded. "Jared, we've been up all night, and we're worried sick. Where's Dad, and what's going on? Surely nobody believes this stupid accusation. It's a mistake, isn't it?"

Jared put an arm around her, a hound dog protecting a spitting kitten. "Judy, your dad has a hearing with Judge Lindley at ten. I'll go down and manage the bail and the court business. I came to get him some clothes. He needs something warmer than his robe and slippers. He'll come home soon, but he's shocked and tired and in no shape to deal with questions right now."

"But, Jared, they can't think Dad would…" Audrey's words died. She couldn't give the foul accusation reality by voicing it.

"Belief doesn't come into it, Audrey. The Vanderhills made the charge based on an account given by the girl. Some intimate stuff they say belongs to your dad was in her book bag. He denies the charges, but the evidence seems to support her statements."

"So what happens now?" Drake asked. "Do we talk to the girl or her family? Can George reason with her?"

Jared shook his head emphatically. "You, all of you, stay away from the Vanderhills and the kid. George absolutely doesn't talk to her. Let the sheriff's office do the investigation. We stay out."

"But what *can* we do?" Claire queried. "People will be talking, whispering and gossiping. And the school! Lord, they'll have a field day with this in the teacher's lounge and behind bathroom doors. Dad won't have a moment's peace."

Jared led the way to the den and waited till they were sitting and quiet. "George won't be going back to school on Monday. It's school policy in this kind of situation for a faculty member to be suspended until the case is resolved. The policy hasn't been invoked before, but the board passed it some time back. George won't have to face the gossip at school. It may fill the halls, but he won't be there to hear it. Right now we have to make decisions about how we handle the charges."

Judith, sitting with her legs folded tailor-fashion, pushed the cowl of her robe back and leaned against the stone of the fireplace. "What decisions? Al Hayes investigates, Dad is cleared and goes back to school in a couple of days, the girl gets expelled for telling lies. Right?"

Audrey bit her lip to keep from snapping at her sister. Judith lived in a world limited to what she could paint. She dealt with real life through brushes and canvas. As with Mom's death and Claire's divorce, Judith created her own perception of reality.

Claire showed no restraint. "For God's sake, Judith, use your head! You know what kind of damage this will do to Dad, even if the girl admits she lied. This is a little town. Everybody knows everything about everybody. Some people will believe the worst, no matter what. The school board will suspend Dad. The reason will be made public. And the stain will always be there. He'll be 'the old guy who raped a kid at school.' Even if she tells the truth, people will say the girl retracted her story just to keep from facing the scandal. Folks will start whispering and speculating. Dad will be ruined, and the town won't ever forget why."

Judith looked about her, her dark eyes troubled and angry. "Dad and Mom helped kids all over town. They wrote letters and found scholarships—even loaned some kids money now and then. Nobody could believe Dad would touch a student. Nobody with any sense."

Audrey turned to Jared. "Tell us what we're up against. We've got to know the worst."

Jared drew a long breath. "Claire's right, Judy. The town will go wild with rumor and speculation. The school board is justified—obligated, in fact—to impose the suspension." He fumbled in his pocket for a worn notepad and the stub of a pencil. "Here's what you need to know. First, George has been seeing this girl Dondie Marshall alone in his office after school. He says he was tutoring her, helping her re-write a paper, one she's never turned in. She says he demanded sexual favors in exchange for not flunking her. George did see her alone, but a paper is in the file with the girl's name on it. Two things for their side. The foster mother was taking things out of the girl's schoolbag—she searches it daily it seems—and found a pair of men's boxer shorts and a soiled towel. When she confronted Dondie, the girl claimed she'd taken them last week after a rendezvous with George. Said she planned to use the items to force him to leave her alone. George says the towel could be his—it's a pretty anonymous plain green bath towel—but the shorts are definitely his. A gaudy pair, red stripes and hearts, pretty distinctive." Audrey bit back a moan of recognition. No, her dad couldn't deny those shorts, and the towel was the same color as the ones in the master bath upstairs.

Jared paused. Audrey felt as if he were reaching out, asking for understanding and some support. "It's not pretty, girls. The evidence is debatable, of course. The towel could have come from anywhere, but the girl had his underwear in her possession. As evidence, it's pretty damning."

"So what are you saying, Jared?" Drake sank down on the edge of the sofa next to Claire. She drew away from him, her eyes focused on Jared.

"Yes, what is it you're saying? Dad's guilty? He raped a girl of fifteen or sixteen? You know better." Claire's madonna coolness gave an iced edge to her words.

"No, Claire, I'm not saying I believe George did it. I'm saying an awful lot of other people probably will believe it, or at least talk themselves into believing it. By the time we can get to trial, the entire town will make the matter public property. George is condemned just by word of mouth. I might get to this kid on the witness stand, take her apart and make her recant, but public sympathy would be with her. George would lose credibility."

"But she's lying!" Judith snapped her pencil with frustration. "The girl is making it up. I don't know where she got Dad's things. And I don't know how she rigged turning in the paper, but Dad's been talking about working with a kid who plagiarized a paper. He's been trying to get her back on track. Surely you can show she falsified her work. Can't you show them the first paper?"

"Unfortunately, George says he gave the plagiarized paper back to her. He has no proof, and she denies it." Jared frowned over his notebook and stuffed it back into his pocket. "Look, there's no easy way to deal with this. George is going to be branded with scandal any way we go. A trial will drag it out, bring up personal matters—talk about the state of his mind when your mother died. Speculate about perfectly innocent concerns that are no one's business. They'll be debated and discussed all over town." Jared sighed. "And there's me. I'm a hometown boy. I'm a pretty fair lawyer, but a lot of folks still see me as just the town drunk's kid getting by on Aunt Min's charity. I've never taken on this kind of case, and I can't guarantee the outcome." Jared reached out to put a hand on Judith's shoulder. "I might get the charges lowered if George pleads No Contest. We could probably get probation and no jail time. He couldn't go back to his job, of course, but the nightmare would be over. It would be a brief, ugly storm, until something else took public interest. It wouldn't drag on for months or have the notoriety of a trial."

****

Jared had considered the alternatives as he drove away from the sheriff's office in the first light of morning. George Anderson was a beaten man despite his twenty-five years with Santa Rita High School. Neither his compassion and his devotion to the students nor his conduct had ever been questioned, but it wouldn't matter. Jared knew George worked with every student crossing his path. That wouldn't count either. In a small town of four thousand, in a quiet, gravel-roads rural society, the back-fence telegraph was the standard news medium. George's reputation would be shredded by nightfall. His job and his position in the community were gone. Jared could see no easy way ahead for the family. The stains of mudslinging and innuendo would never fade. The best thing, the young lawyer concluded, was to contain the damage, get the furor behind them. So he had rehearsed his argument as he drove to the somber brick house. And he reminded himself of the soundness of his position as he put the facts before the girls. He expected Judith to fly up in outrage at the suggestion. He counted on Audrey to see the practicality of his solution. As for Claire, well, she would soon move on, return to her fast-moving world. She probably would be glad to see the last of Santa Rita no matter how the case worked out. Drake was an element he hadn't included. And as he looked around the room, saw the white, stricken faces, felt the waves of shock rising, he realized he'd miscalculated.

"You bastard! You rat!" Judith whirled on him, her slim hand a hard fist beating his chest. "You'd let him live with a lie? Dad, of all people! He never turned his back on you, not when your drunken father tried to make you quit school, not when those folks accused you of taking their car, not even when you got suspended for smoking. He stood up for you. Went to court and got Minnie Travis made your legal guardian. Proved you didn't take the car and made the Campbell kid confess he'd lied so you couldn't compete in the track meet. He faced down everyone for you! He did the same for any kid who asked for help. And you'd let people believe this filthy thing about Dad?" Judith's voice grew shrill as her anger flooded over the room. Jared trapped her flailing arms and held her to his chest.

Her fury rocked him. Restraining Judith's explosion, Jared looked helplessly toward Audrey.

"No, don't look to me for support, Jared Pierce. I won't have it. I won't see Dad's good name covered with scandal and his life ruined. It's wrong. I know what fighting the charges will be like, and I know how ugly things may get, but somehow we have to prove Dad is innocent. I don't know why this girl is lying, but I know she is." Audrey's eyes flashed with angry green light. "If you can't help us with something more than talk about legal expediency, you aren't the lawyer I think you are." Audrey jerked the cord of her robe tighter. "I'm going to get dressed, and when Dad gets home, I'll talk to him. He has to know we're with him even if his lawyer tries to duck the fight." She stormed toward the stairs, her hem whipping about her heels with the force of her anger. Judith struggled to free herself from his hold and dashed after her sister.

Jared turned to plead with Claire and Drake. Surely they'd see the impossibility of George Anderson's situation. Claire crossed the room with measured tread. Her dark chignon seemed too heavy for her slender neck, and the cameo delicacy of her face was marred by a frown of concentration.

"You're trying to spare us the deluge of scandal, Jared." Her voiced was low, her tone one of reason. "An admirable goal in most circumstances, but not here, not now. My father won't thank you for it. He doesn't believe in giving in to public pressure. We'll face down the outrage and criticism."

Drake caught her small, pale hand in his. "You have no idea what will happen, my dear. George will be tried by public opinion, judged by gossipmongers, and sentenced by mob mentality. Unrelenting hell for him and for your sisters. Public outrage will be far worse than you realize."

Jared added his views to Drake's. "You can't imagine, Claire, and you won't have to live with it day to day. Once you leave, none of this will be real to you. Your daily papers won't rehash every innuendo. Your neighbors will never know the intimate details of your most private life. And people looking for gossip and rumor won't pick your life to pieces. You can't begin to know what Judy and Audrey will go through in addition to George's anguish."

Claire drew away from Drake and Jared. Her wide brown eyes reflected the turmoil around her. Jared thought he'd never seen this quiet, contained girl come so near to open emotion.

"You're quite wrong, you know. I've been through some relentless scrutiny myself. Not the same, I suppose, but near enough. One doesn't divorce the town's most favored son without being the subject of considerable speculation. And my former employers have managed to stir up quite a firestorm of negative publicity as well." She smoothed the pale pink wool of her skirt and pulled down the sleeves of the matching cashmere sweater. "I won't leave Judith and Audrey to deal with Dad's crisis alone. I'll stay in Santa Rita. Everything that matters is right here."

Jared felt the same stunned reaction that froze Drake in place. Claire and her ex-husband living on the same block? The arrangement could only add substance to the stories soon to spill over every dinner table and shop counter.

"I'll have to make a short trip to store my things

and close my apartment," Claire was continuing, "but I have until the end of the year. I'll be on hand to help here in any way I can. Judith and Audrey have their work, but I'm free to work for Dad."

****

An hour of discussion kept Claire from escaping the shock waves engulfing the household. At last she found sanctuary in her father's office when she withdrew to write necessary notes to workplace friends. She felt the door of the study opening as it created a draft and fluttered the pages she'd stacked on the desk. Over her shoulder she saw Drake's dark gold head, backlit by the lights in the hall. *Damn, I don't want to talk to him now.* Would this sense of aching loss never end? Would she ever be free of Drake Chandler? After five years, she still kept her distance, even when it hurt so badly she could barely make it through one hour without screaming at the unfairness of it all. She knew him for what he was, knew the spineless, flawed man living behind the charming smile. Others might be swayed by his poetic profile and posturing speeches, but not Claire Anderson. Not any more, not ever again. If only the ache would go away. If she could look at him and not itch to touch the wave just above his eyebrow or long to run fingertips over the fine-boned planes of his face. Surely one day all the pain would wear itself out.

"Did you mean what you said earlier?" He closed the door behind him. "Do you really intend to stay?"

Claire pushed her chair away from the desk and stood. She felt less vulnerable with her eyes nearly level with his. "Yes, of course I meant it. I'll stay, even though inevitably we'll run into each other from time to time. Surely we can be civil. I couldn't face being here when Mom was sick and dying. The situation overwhelmed me. But I think we're both adult enough to put our past away so I can help out now."

Drake frowned, his beautifully chiseled mouth thinned, and he paused before he spoke. Claire wondered what words he held back. "You're free to come and go as you need to, Claire. I won't get in your way. If I need to see Judith about something, I'll leave her a note or catch her at the gallery. I won't make things harder for you."

"Thank you. I'm sure I won't be here too long. Jared should be able to find a way to prove this charge is groundless." She started to turn back to her letters.

"Why did you leave, Claire? What went wrong with us?" Drake's words were much closer to her and she spun to face him, her legs braced against the desktop. She bit her lip to hold back the cry welling up in her. *Why? Why bring it up again?* He'd certainly known her reasons.

"Drake, I don't think we want to go over old pain, do we?" She forced her voice to be cool and remote. She couldn't let the floodgates open. He'd lose what little respect he had for her. "We have to deal with enough drama. Let's leave the past alone."

If she'd still been a foolish, small-town girl, Claire reminded herself, she'd have believed he was suffering unrequited love for her. But she was a big girl now, with years of experience behind her in the ways of man and woman. She knew better. His act hadn't changed, but she had her eyes open now. She had learned his fallacies and had moved on with her life. So why did the sight of him in that bronze ski sweater still stir memories? Had he worn it because she gave it to him? Gave it to him back when she believed their dreams were forever? Was it just memory and the present uncertainty urging her to throw herself into his arms? She knew one move on her part and he'd wrap her close to his heart. She'd be where she most wanted to be. And her hard-won self-respect and the fragile threads of her dignity would vanish. So would whatever regard he had for her.

"We were so good." She wished he wouldn't remind her. "Like Christmas lights and Ferris wheels and the glow of a warm fire. How could it just vanish, Claire? What happened to send your love into a blue-white freeze? What drove you to a place where no one can reach you?"

He was too close, and it would be easy to be drawn in again. She had to have distance. "Surely you have work to do at the gallery, Drake. You should go. I have a thousand things to tend to before Dad gets home." Claire used words to put a wall between herself and the man she longed to touch. She was grateful he didn't persist. She wasn't sure how much longer her will would have held her.

"I'll try to keep my distance, Claire," he murmured from the doorway, "but I expect you to answer me one day. At least I deserve to know what wrecked the best thing that ever happened to me." The door closed behind him, and Claire shivered. The room felt at least ten degrees colder.

****

Audrey parked her car beside the stone wall. She didn't know if the office would be open on a holiday weekend. Most people would still be grazing on turkey sandwiches, and with the football games now on television, many would be home watching the game. Why should Hal be available?

Still, she had to try. Jared couldn't do this alone. He'd been clear about his doubts. And his solution—no, his lack of a solution—wasn't something she could accept. Claire and Judith had agreed. Only one thing to do: seek help in any hopeful quarter, find light in any corner. At least she would ask. Audrey didn't know the man well, not anymore, but he had expertise Jared didn't. *The Viking?* Yes, they needed a swift and daring warrior for their cause.

Audrey opened the car door and slid out into the dank cold of a Central Texas winter. The temperature wasn't terribly low, but the damp, clammy air held a seeping chill that sank into flesh and bone. She wrapped her raincoat tightly and buttoned the top button. A fresh wind rose off the river, cutting through the coat's weave. Her teeth chattered, though she suspected she might be experiencing nerves as much as chill.

The door felt rough to her touch. More than a century of wind and rain had pitted the heavy planks and grooved them to a weathered finish. She turned the knob. Locked, locked tight, and no light showed through the wavering panes of the narrow window. What would she do now? Go back to the car and wait, or just give up and take herself home? She leaned against the unyielding door, a black despair washing through her.

"Audrey?" The voice startled her. A figure emerged in the half light. "Audrey, were you waiting to see me? I just ran out for the paper." Hal Lindstrom drew her away from the door. "You're chilled. Come in here. I've built a fire, and I have coffee in the back." She looked up at the bronze giant towering above her. His russet beard held a few droplets, and his mane of hair blew in the rising wind. He looked so fearless, so ready to face a storm. She took the hand he offered and followed him into the office that smelled of an oak fire, fresh coffee, and law books. She slumped into the rocker beside the fireplace.

"It's about your dad, isn't it?" Hal pushed a heavy mug into her nerveless hands. "Pierce called me a little while ago and filled me in. He thinks he's in over his head and wondered if I might help." He took the cane-bottomed rocker beside her and drew it toward the fire. "I won't lie to you, Audrey. It's a bad situation. You might be better off taking Jared's first plan and getting this thing over with. But he says you won't consider the quick solution, and I understand your feelings. You think going that way would be saying you believe your dad did what the girl claims."

Audrey nodded. "I just can't let Dad take the blame for something so awful, so foreign to everything he is. Claire and Judith agree. I'm glad Jared asked you to help, because I was going to ask you the same thing. Is there something we can do, some action we can take? This will ruin Dad."

"I've told Pierce I will help all I can. I need background, facts, histories, and some time with the law books. Jared says your dad is about at the end of his endurance right now. I'll do some thinking on this situation and look into some cases. Monday let's meet at your house—your dad, Jared, and you and your sisters—and see what we can do. If your dad is as anxious to fight this thing as you are, we owe it to him to make his case as strong as facts will let us."

"I don't know how to thank you." Audrey looked into the hazel eyes, saw the tiny lines fanning out from them, and remembered the brilliant mind behind them. She drew resolve from what she read in their depths. "I know your time is valuable and your help will be expensive."

"Audrey, we've got the reputation of a good man to save and the well-being of your family in our hands. Money is the least of our problems. Your dad has to be our first concern. Concentrate on keeping his spirits up and his health intact. That's your job. Don't worry about the small stuff, like money. Got it?" He sat so he faced her, his big hands wrapped over hers as they clutched the mug of coffee. "Now tell me all about this case, everything you know."

Chapter Four

Audrey went to church the next morning hoping she just might get through the day without having to deal with gossip. All was well until she heard the remarks that would forever define this period of her life. She caught the words from the other side of the aisle a few rows back.

"Well, I feel sorry for the youngest girl, that's all. Heaven only knows what George Anderson has put her through since her mother died. The middle sister is strange enough, all those freaky black clothes. Paints pictures nobody understands. Not flowers or fruit or even pretty landscapes. I've seen some of them over at Chandler's. They're nothing I'd want to look at every day, I'll tell you. And the oldest girl, what can a body think? Married Drake Chandler, then out of the clear blue ran off to, oh, Dallas, Houston, one or the other. Now suddenly she's back. Old George, he's a sorta funny guy. Living in that big house after Patsy died, never taking even one woman out in all this time. My sister tried her best to get his attention, but he never noticed. Shows you right there something's not quite right about the man. Think he'd welcome a little female companionship by this time. Guess he's got his interests in another direction." A derisive snort punctuated the comments. "A young girl! A schoolgirl and a man his age. Ought to be locked up."

"Ought to be locked up." The phrase kept echoing in her head as Audrey hastily slipped out. If people were whispering vile suggestions within hours of the accusation, public condemnation couldn't be far behind. The situation was as bad as Jared had predicted.

****

The day was wretched from Claire's point of view, as well. Her dad had looked haggard, silent and withdrawn, since he returned the day before. She'd sat with him a while to lend support, but it had been too long since they'd experienced the silent closeness of her childhood. Audrey's hasty report of public attitude hadn't helped. Judith flounced off to bury her fury in a storm of painting, while Audrey vanished into the office to reschedule appointments, leaving Claire to roam restlessly about the house. Afternoon sun cast a pale glow over the dormant garden. A sunny spot beneath an ancient oak tree enticed her. That stone bench near the tree had been her mother's favorite place. Claire pulled on a fisherman sweater and slipped out the side doors, pausing to let the golden rays touch her. In Dallas she'd missed such solitary moments, since her work had kept her from long, quiet walks in the afternoon sun. The city streets discouraged meditative strolls, and her workload made the idea impractical.

Claire hesitated a moment beside the low wall of the deck. Across the faded green she could see Drake's house rising above loblolly pines. Memories washed over her. She'd thought to live there, in the tall white house behind the pine-green grove, with Drake. They'd planned how they'd live there, first in the apartment above the carriage house, then later raising a family in the house where Drake had grown up. Sweet, wonderful dreams. Dreams now broken. Claire slammed the door on memories.

Tearing her glance from the silvery rooftop and its reminder of shattered promises, Claire shifted her gaze to the other side of the grounds. The corner sloped down, and the Anderson house was the last on the road. Beyond it the land dropped slowly to the river's edge. From her perch she could see a winking brightness as the river splashed an occasional wave above the embankment. She loved it here, loved the tranquility of Sunday evening, sitting alone in silent reflection. If it hadn't been for Drake and their ill-starred marriage, she might still live here, close to her family. Perhaps there would have been no terrible rift with Judith to drive the sisters apart. Audrey might be a friend, not just the grown-up edition of a teenage sister. She could have shared those bittersweet months of her mother's illness with her family, not been alone and racked with the sorrow of her mother's death.

She wouldn't let Drake push her away again. *I know Dad's relieved I'm here.* She could answer the phone so he wouldn't hear things like Audrey had heard that morning. She could shop and clean and keep the house pleasant. She was proficient at all kinds of office work, so she could assist the lawyers with the non-legal chores. Despite Drake's presence, she'd stay. Dallas had nothing for her. If she had ties, they were here in Santa Rita with the only people she could call her own.

Stepping over the low deck wall, Claire scuffed her loafers along the stone path half hidden by unclipped tufts. Leaves from the old oak scattered behind her footsteps, and sprigs of still-green ivy twined over the stone bench at the end of the path. She pulled the vines away and brushed the seat with a couple of tissues. She could still feel her mother's presence. Patsy Anderson had first heard her daughter's wedding plans as they sat together on this bench, about this time of year, a late fall afternoon filled with golden light peculiar to autumn. So many memories tied into this minute square of grass, yaupon, and chrysanthemums. Claire leaned against the weathered oak tree backing the bench. She felt one warm tear slide down her cheek. With eyes closed, she gave herself up to the moment. She couldn't be strong and resolute and removed from the current any longer. She was weary of always being in control.

****

Drake turned from his desk and glanced down from the window of the office that had once been his mother's sanctuary. The grounds of the Anderson house were visible through the tips of pine boughs. He took moments to look at it during the day, like a traveler taking a refreshing sip of cool water. An hour earlier he had noticed Claire standing at the wall of the deck. He waited, watching to see if she might look his way. He'd seen her quick glance, but then she averted her eyes. In the waning light, he could see her sitting on her mother's old stone bench, her white sweater against the gnarled bark of the live oak. Aware he was guilty of rudeness, if not spying, Drake started to move away. Something in Claire's pose stopped him. She leaned forward, her face buried in her hands.

Claire crying? He had trouble believing it. Claire didn't cry, not ever. Not when she told him she was leaving, not when she signed the last document ending their ten-month marriage. Not even when standing beside her mother's open grave. She had only stood tall and remote behind icy dignity. Something must have truly racked her to shatter her aloof poise. Drake tore himself from the window, loped down the stairs two at a time, and sprinted across the open ground between the two houses.

****

In the dark shadows of the garden, Claire felt two gentle hands draw her close. The sturdy shoulder cradling her head offered all the comfort she could want. Blinded by unstoppable hot tears, she took the consolation offered and clung with silent gratitude. Familiar fingers loosened the pins in her heavy hair, releasing it from the tight knot, as they kneaded the rigid tendons in her neck. No words could have touched her so deeply, and she drew on the hushed comfort of her companion. Like a top-heavy dahlia she let her head rest, her eyes shut to the distractions of the day.

"Has there been a new crisis?" The words were spoken as softly as a whisper.

"No, nothing new. I felt as if I was carrying boulders, with no way to put them down. No place to rest. I'm so tired, but if I let it get to me, I can't think."

"Of course it's hard to stay calm with the storm around you. It's not easy, not for someone with blood in her veins." The deft fingers stroked the hair cascading down her back and eased the knots at the base of her head.

"But I have to do it. I must! We can't all be going off like skyrockets like Judith or wipe tears and make notes like Audrey. Somebody has to keep the façade intact. Keep the vultures out of the front room." Claire drew a long breath. "I guess it has to be me."

"You don't have to do it all, Claire. I'm here, always close, if you need me."

Claire looked up. "Drake! I thought you were Jared!"

"Liar. You knew it wasn't Jared."

His arms offered a sanctuary she couldn't accept. If the walls between them fell, she was lost. Claire wiped her face with soiled tissues and drew as far from him as the bench permitted. "Were you spying on me? Did you see me in a weak moment and take advantage of it?"

Drake leaned his tall frame against the tree. "No, I saw you from the window and thought you looked like you could use a friend. Things are pretty hard around your place. I wanted to help."

He can be so plausible. Claire wouldn't let herself be lured back into false security.

"Things are awkward, but Jared is sure he can find the truth and clear Dad of everything. He's got a consulting attorney coming tomorrow to help. Someone with years of experience, who can see more options. We'll make it through this."

She gathered her loosened hair into a casual knot and fastened it with the two or three hairpins strewn over the bench. The knot held, but stray tendrils pulled free and curled about her face. Absently she brushed at them.

"All this anxiety is draining you, Claire. Please let me help. George is still family, in my mind. In fact, he's all the family I have left since Mother died last winter. I'd put a banner across the front of the gallery proclaiming his innocence if you asked me to." Drake stepped closer to her, holding out a hand as if offering physical aid. Claire took two steps back.

"No, I don't think you would persuade anyone that way. But I'll tell Dad you said it. It might give him a smile. He can certainly use one." She forced herself to walk slowly, keeping her head high, running away to keep from accepting Drake's tempting comfort.

****

Drake watched her retreat to the shelter of the house. *Well, something can still reach my ice princess.* He shook his head and started for his own house across the way. *What happened to her? To us?* He'd asked himself the questions a dozen times a day for almost five years. She'd been so warm, so loving, so filled with a passionate joy for life. She had been his salvation from a home of cold perfection and distant parents. Her flawless beauty had filled an ache in his heart and all the empty places where his soul walked alone. Overnight it had stopped. She'd drawn away, her joy gone, her love chilled to guarded politeness. *What did I do to hurt her? What killed all her passion? All her love?* At first he'd called and heard her softly drop the phone to break the connection. He'd written long, loving letters, only to have them returned unopened. Her family assured him they were as much in the dark as Drake himself. Through George and his wife, Drake had been able to keep some tie to Claire, until Patsy became so ill he didn't dare add stress to her life. With her death, he lost his link to Claire. She didn't come home any more. She paid brief visits at Christmas, but she didn't linger. She never, ever, followed the path between the two houses or ventured near the gallery. Somewhere Drake had wounded her beyond forgiveness. Though he picked apart every moment of their time together, he didn't know how or when he'd committed the unforgivable. He thought the thorns in his heart might cease their torture if he just knew what he'd done, even if the damage between them could never be repaired, but Claire remained aloof and silent.

****

It looks like any family gathering for the holidays. Jared surveyed the group around the table, knowing it wasn't. Powerful undercurrents of worry and fear and more than a little hostility threatened to destroy the superficial calm. Hal had proposed the Monday afternoon meeting, saying he wanted to see the family in their normal setting. He could measure their strengths and look at ways they could be used. Jared wasn't convinced, but he could see George, at least, was better off in his own dining room than exposed to an impersonal office. Hal Lindstrom leaned his elbows on the polished wood of the round dining table and took charge of the group.

"George, this is a terrible thing for you and your family to go through. I want you to feel free to call a break anytime proceedings are too much for you." He glanced at the others around the table. "Breathe, people. We won't make progress if you're wound too tight to think." Hal opened a new yellow legal pad and fanned pencils across it, then stacked folders beside the tablet. "Anyone have questions before we start?" No one spoke. Jared thought Audrey looked okay, but he could feel Judith simmering on the verge of rebellion.

Hal passed a set of stapled papers around and addressed George. "Jared told me you'd had some kind of difficulties with the…" He scanned his pages for a name. "The Vanderhills before, George. What was that about?"

George shook his head. "It didn't amount to anything, Mr. Lindstrom. Just the usual school ups and downs. The Vanderhills' boys were in school back when I taught history. I guess their parents didn't agree with some of my ideas."

No help, George, Jared thought.

Hal must have agreed. "Need a bit more detail, George. We're going to see a lot of each other. Let's make it Hal and George, okay? Save formality for the court proceedings." Hal waited until he was sure George was focused. "Now, tell me more about you and the Vanderhills."

George leaned back in the chair at the head of the table. He looked somewhere beyond the walls and drew a breath. "Fred Vanderhill is a good man, a hard-working, God-fearing man. He has a little store near the end of Main Street. It's not upscale enough to be a resale shop, but it's not seedy enough to be a junk store, either. He tends the grounds at his church, and his wife sings in the choir and teaches Sunday school. He's not mean or vindictive, but for him there are no shades of grey. Things are black and white. He didn't permit his boys to have extra-curricular interests at school. He expected them to work at the store if they weren't in class. All there is to his world is work and church and eating and sleeping. Play is a waste of time and social activities are sinful. He and I could probably agree on what day of the week it is, but not much more."

Hal nodded slowly. "I've known a few like that myself. Where did you two clash? Over activities for his sons?"

"Well, the boys wanted to do things other kids

were doing. Just natural," George answered. "We didn't have an official counselor then. I was still teaching history. Did what I could to help kids, give them direction, but I didn't get the title for another year or two. The Vanderhill kids asked my advice from time to time. I told them to do as their parents said while they lived at home. They could make their own decisions when they left. Trouble was, Vanderhill expected them to work in the store and stay in Santa Rita forever. The older one flatly refused and went into the military. The younger boy took the automotive classes at school and could fix almost anything. He stuck it out at the shop for about six months after he graduated, but then he struck out on his own, too."

Hal waited for more explanation. "But how were you concerned?"

"As I said, the boys talked to me a lot when they had free time. When they really put me on the spot, I told them they were the only ones who could decide where their lives would go. They made their choices, but Fred still thinks I led the boys astray."

"But he never accused you of anything? No suggestion of inappropriate behavior?"

"Oh, no, not anything like that. Fred's a narrow-minded, stubborn old coot, but he tries to live what he believes. I don't believe he's using this girl to get back at me."

"You've explained the background between you." Hal put his stack of papers aside. "Now about these tutoring sessions with the girl... What's her name? Donnie?"

"Dondie. Dondie Marshall," George corrected. "The girl got lost trying to cope with a major assignment. I attempted to help her out."

"Why?" Hal made notes on his pad. "Do you usually take so much interest in a student's problems with an assignment? Did she ask for help?"

"The girl is an enigma, troubled, even melancholy." George gave the group a quick summary of the story of Dondie's misfortunes. "I thought I might be able to save her academic year. Her grades from her previous school were very good, but her recent ones are abominable. Trauma or injury, something took her off track. I thought I might find the spark to getting her mind working again. Given her earlier grades, it was worth trying."

"I see," Hal responded. "The girl plagiarized a paper, got caught, and you tried to get her straightened out. You didn't want to see a promising mind lost. Is that the idea?"

"I didn't spell it out quite that way, but yes, her slipping grades were the motivating factor. Dondie doesn't have much of a future as things stand, not unless her marks come up."

Hal was silent. Jared could feel the next questions coming, and he shifted so he could see the face of each of the Anderson daughters. *This is going to be hard for them, especially Judith. She's closest to George.*

"Now about these things found in the girl's backpack," Hal began. "Can you be sure they are in fact yours? Undershorts and a bath towel, weren't they?"

George ran weary fingers through his thinning hair. Jared noticed more greying strands than he'd seen a week or so earlier. "I think we have to concede they're mine," George answered at last. "We could debate the towel, I suppose, but I do have at least ten in my bathroom just like the one the police are holding as evidence. The shorts we can't disclaim. They're unique because my late wife made them as a Valentine's joke. Instead of the sentimental stuff everyone else exchanges in February, Patsy and I always tried to come up with something outrageous and silly. The last year she was alive, she made me three pairs of those hideous shorts. The other two pairs have long since become dust rags, but I still have the one pair. They couldn't belong to anyone else."

"Then how did they wind up in the girl's book bag?"

George stood and paced the narrow distance of the dining room. "No idea, Mr. Lindstrom—Hal—none at all. I can't see how she came to have them. I wore them one day last week. I play tennis at school three days a week, to stay in shape. Sometimes I don't have anyone to play with, just practice some backhand shots alone. I shower, change, and sometimes pick up my faculty mail. Usually I toss my gym bag into the back of the car and come home. One day last week when I went to drop my clothes into the washer, the shorts were gone. Somewhere between the school and the washer, they just vanished."

"Those two things, the shorts and the towel, are a big part of the case against you. The Marshall girl's statements gain credence because your things were in her possession. We'll have to find an explanation," Hal said.

The Anderson daughters were being unusually quiet, Jared noted. He looked across to Judith and saw the flinty sparks in her black eyes. She wasn't taking the situation quietly. She was reining in her words with every ounce of control she possessed. He could feel the dam beginning to break under the pressure.

"Judy, see if there is a towel missing in your dad's bathroom," he suggested. "It may be important to prove the towel the police have really is or is not one from this house."

She threw him a disgusted look as if she could read the distraction for what it was. "Later. Right now, I want to know what our brilliant attorneys have in mind to get Dad out of this ridiculous mess. Are you really doing anything? Do you even have a plan for doing something? Or are we just going to sit here and talk everything to death?"

"Judy, is it?" Hal asked.

"Judith," she snapped.

"Judith, we don't have a plan yet. We've got to see where all the evidence fits and how we can make the best use of what favors us. It's like putting together a jigsaw puzzle. First you find all the pieces in the same color and put them in piles. Then you look for the ones with outside edges. You start building the shell and then little by little fill in the rest of the pieces as they connect, so you can see the whole picture. Right now, we're just sorting out the pieces to see what goes with what."

"Lawyer-speak for we don't have a clue how to fix this red wagon, right?" Judith pushed away from the table. "I can't sit still for much more of this. Kearnes is giving me my own show in New Orleans. I'm going upstairs and photograph paintings. It may not help you, but it will give me something to do besides sit here and imagine Dad in prison stripes." Judith grabbed a black smock from the back of her chair and fled the room.

"My daughter is wound a little tight over this thing," George explained at Hal's exasperated expression. "She'll be here if we need her, but she doesn't tolerate extended family scenes too well."

"Not unless she's creating them," Claire sniped.

"Your sister doesn't have your ability to step back and evaluate," George chided gently. "Her perceptions and understanding don't work in the same way yours do. She feels deeply and loves intensely, but she lives in a world foreign to most of us."

"Judy fusses and blusters and runs to a quiet corner when she's feeling threatened," Jared added. "Right now, it looks as if her father is going to jail for something so heinous and impossible to believe that Judy has to get away just so she can deal with it. Things affect her in ways most of us can't imagine."

"I see," Hal commented. "But we have to move along. She's right in saying I have no idea how to make our case. We have to keep sorting the pieces."

"More coffee?" Audrey picked up the coffeepot from the buffet and filled cups. Jared knew her well enough to know she had something on her mind. Something had snagged her attention.

"Dad, how much time have you spent with Dondie? I don't mean the last few days, I mean during the years she's been in Santa Rita. Is she a discipline problem? Does she come to you for counseling routinely?"

George stroked his lower lip in thought. "No, I've not actually spent any real time with the girl until Ruth's absence made it necessary. I knew her by sight, of course." He glanced up at Hal and added, "In a school our size, the faculty knows every student to some degree." He turned back to Audrey. "Dondie's never been in to see me, and I've not had to contact the Vanderhills. Her grades are poor, but she doesn't make trouble or demand attention."

Audrey moved closer, her nose wrinkled in concentration. "And during the time you were tutoring her, she never gave you any trouble? You didn't call her down or reprimand her for anything?"

Pursing his lips, George was silent a moment. "No, Audrey, I don't believe I did. I showed her proof that she'd copied someone's published work and claimed it for her own. It was unpleasant for her, but she had a reasonable explanation. She didn't have the fundamentals to do the work. I didn't see any point in scolding or attempting to lay guilt. She admitted what she'd done. My purpose was to figure out a way to help her. During our work sessions after school, she was polite, pleasant, and seemed to be industrious in her efforts. Several times I tried to talk to her about finding something of her background, perhaps tracing her family, but she just shut down. She has rather expressive eyes, almost translucent, they are so light, and anytime I mentioned her family her eyes just went blank. I think the idea of trying to look into her history terrified her, but I can't recall any time we were at odds. She was scared, not rebellious."

"And you don't think the Vanderhills are using her as a means of getting back at you for the choices their sons made years ago?" Audrey waited while her father considered the idea.

"No, I'm certain. It's not Fred Vanderhill's way of doing things. He and his wife honestly feel a righteous fury at what they see as sinful perversion."

Audrey rolled her cup between her palms. "Then what's happening here, Dad? What's really going on? You're no threat to the girl. You certainly didn't do what she accuses you of doing. And you don't believe the Vanderhills are behind her accusations. So why in the world is the girl doing it? Why is she risking the Vanderhills' wrath and public humiliation by swearing to such a pack of lies? Why is Dondie Marshall doing this to you? Why is she doing this to herself?"

Chapter Five

Claire felt a start of surprise. Audrey's question hung like an invisible cloud above them, a cloud too thin to see but weighty enough to be disturbing. She hadn't—and apparently no one else had, either—thought beyond George's immediate peril. Why was the Marshall girl doing this? What did she have to gain from creating such a situation?

"Dad?" Claire turned to her father. "Why is she stirring up trouble for you?"

George shrugged. "I don't know. I can't begin to read the girl."

With a puzzled frown, Audrey looked at her sister. "What's the usual reason for putting blame on somebody else, Claire? To keep from getting in trouble yourself?"

Claire thought a minute. "Dad, you said the Vanderhills are pretty strict. Maybe she's been slipping out at night, and the Vanderhills were getting suspicious, so she made up this story to send them in another direction."

"Is she devious?" Jared asked. "Rebelling against restrictions? Pointing a finger away from herself?"

"Good questions." Hal glanced around the table. "You're beginning to think, not react like shell-shocked victims." He leaned toward George. "Are boys hanging around her? I haven't seen the girl. Does she lead the boys on? Is she pretty, or trying to look like the teen queens?" Hal's questions sat in the air.

"She's ordinary, not pretty, not ugly, sort of plain," George answered at last. "Brownish hair, long and shaggy. Needs a decent haircut, but the Vanderhills believe women should let their hair grow. She's short, barely five feet, and thin. She doesn't have much in the way of clothes. No make-up, but as I said, her eyes are striking—very pale, almost silvery, with darker eyebrows. You always notice her eyes." He shook his head. "I haven't seen her holding hands or walking to class with a boy. Doesn't mean there's not one."

The silence was broken by a faint knocking. Claire noticed it first. Her listening attitude alerted the others. "Someone's at the deck door." She stood. "I'll bet it's Drake. Give me a minute to get rid of him."

"No, don't," Jared insisted. "I told him to come over if he heard anything around town that might be useful."

Claire steeled herself for another confrontation, but Drake's tall form didn't make the shadows on the french doors. Too short, too wide, and too female. *Some neighbor hesitant to come during daylight hours?* Claire unlocked the door and opened it.

"Is George in?" The woman hurriedly slipped into the room. "I'd like to see him, if he feels up to it." She paused. "Oh, you're Claire. I've seen your picture in George's office a million times. I'm Ruth Cleburne. I teach at the high school."

Claire realized Audrey had crossed the room and was holding out her hands to the newcomer. "Ruth, I'm so glad you're back. How's your mother? You've heard about our problems, I suppose. Come in. We're in the dining room having a powwow. Maybe you can help."

Claire stifled a sigh of resignation. *Bring someone else into this discussion? Dad is too tired to be gracious, and we're all too edgy to make the effort, even if this woman means well.*

She watched Audrey welcome the new member to the group and take her to Judith's empty chair at the dining table. "Do you want some coffee, Ruth, to get the cold out of your bones?"

Claire took a second look at the teacher. Ruth Cleburne might be anywhere from thirty-five to fifty-five, she thought. Short and square, with no discernible curves, Ruth Cleburne's form would forever remain boxy and stolid. Her dumpling nose and chipmunk cheeks wouldn't wither with age. The kelly-green shirt under the blue denim jumper spoke of her inattention to wardrobe. What she wore was clean and practical, but Ruth didn't seem to concern herself with style. From her sturdy walking shoes to her damp, frizzed hair, Ruth Cleburne was the embodiment of the spinster schoolteacher.

"Ruth, it's good of you to come," George began, "but was it wise? You might become as much an object of rumor as we are."

"I came up the back path," the teacher answered, then added, "Not because I was afraid of what people might say, but I thought I might be more useful if no one suspected I was trying to help. From what I heard at school, you have a war to fight."

George clasped her hand with a look of relief, then made introductions. "We need help, but I don't want to put you in jeopardy. Is the school an armed camp?"

A shadow passed over the teacher's rosy face. "No one says much, but the teachers and administrative staff don't believe the girl's story. Louise Tannerly is calling for an open discussion."

"Louise would," George agreed. The senior history teacher expected her students to discuss any and all controversial topics, filling her world history classes with disciplined but lively debates.

"I'm not worried about myself," Ruth went on. "I'll only be here until the Christmas break. Mother will need someone with her once she leaves the hospital, so the school must get someone to take my classes. I hope to see your name cleared before I leave. I'll help as much as I can while I'm here."

Hal focused on the newcomer. "I've not learned much about the girl herself. She's acquired damning evidence against George with no discernable motive for lying. Maybe you can give us some insight. Is she trying to distract attention from herself or a boy she's forbidden to see?"

"I haven't seen her with anyone." Ruth turned back to George. "Tell me how this all started, and let me see if I can give you any help." George gave her a quick summary, but Claire realized he'd toned down the girl's original misconduct. Still, the teacher understood the implications in spite of his careful phrasing.

"Dondie plagiarized a published article, George?"

"I caught her, and she admitted it, Ruth. She seemed confused about how to do the assignment, so she took the easy way out."

"I think she may have done it before," Ruth said slowly. "I didn't have any proof, but a short paper she did at the beginning of school sounded too skillful to be her own work. I thought she'd had some coaching from another student. I can't prove it, of course." She took a sheet from George's tablet and one of Hal's pencils. "You said she acquired some personal belongings of yours? That suggests planning and forethought, some maturity I haven't seen in her before."

"We were trying to understand why the girl is doing this. What does she gain?" Jared asked.

Ruth pulled at a tuft of her crinkly, taffy-colored hair. "I don't know. George would never do what she says he did, so the evidence has been manufactured. I have no idea why." She looked at George in dismay. "I may not be able to help you after all."

"Don't say that yet, Ruth. You probably know more about the girl than you think you do." George's words were reassuring, but the tired lines in his face were deeper than before. Claire heard hesitancy in his voice.

Ruth settled herself like a small hen on her nest. "I know her background and the confusion about her past, though sometimes I think she's remembered something. Once in a while she has an odd look in her eyes—and you notice those eyes, they're unique. It's as if something's connected, but then her dazed, bewildered expression is back."

George put a hand out to touch Ruth's. His eyes brightened. "I know the look you mean, Ruth. When I first talked to her, that day she turned in her paper, I asked her if she had any memory of her mother. For a second I thought she had. It was just a flash. Then she got scared and a glassy stare came back. Still, I was sure I saw a glimpse of comprehension or memory there."

Hal leaned forward. "You thought she remembered something of her past?" His voice held an eager note.

"Just a flicker, and I could have been wrong," George answered, "but I thought so at the time."

Hal's excitement washed over the group. Claire felt a breath of hope touch her.

"Do you think you might have, for just a moment, reminded her of someone in her past?" Hal asked. "Maybe someone who threatened or hurt her? Could she be transferring a buried memory? She may believe what she's saying but have past and present confused. Could she subconsciously rig the evidence to protect herself? Maybe, like a wounded animal, she's hunting a safe hiding place. Her accusations could be a reflection of an earlier incident."

Light filled George's face. Claire saw the hope Hal's words raised and knew the conclusion made sense to her father. The girl wasn't maliciously trying to ruin him. She was simply confused and trying to save herself. It made a kind of sense, more sense than Dondie Marshall striking out at a man who had only given her a safe haven and the benefit of the doubt.

"We need to find out about her history," Jared concluded. "If Hal's idea has any merit, the reason for this fiasco lies in Dondie's past. To help George, we have to know what triggered her to lash out at George. Then we can explain her confusion to the court."

Claire hesitated to accept the suggestion, but Audrey scrambled out of her chair to hug Jared and her dad. "I can see Dondie getting things mixed up, especially if she went through enough trauma to erase her memory. We can make the court understand. Maybe even keep the whole thing out of court. We might do that, Hal?"

Hal stretched his back and rubbed his fingers. "You're getting ahead of yourself, Audrey. It can only work out if the theory is right, and if there is time enough to make an intense search. Has someone made a hunt for Dondie's missing life?"

George nodded. "Yes, the county welfare office did, but I don't think they had the means to do too much. They found the girl's early school records, but her family no longer lived in the district. No trace of them ever showed up."

"Then we start with her old school and the town where she lived." Jared turned first to George, then to Ruth. "What do we know for sure? Where did she live before?"

George shook his head and raised an eyebrow at Ruth. "Some small town in the Panhandle, but I don't I recall the name." He looked to Ruth as if asking for help.

"I don't remember," she admitted. "Some little place with a funny name up near the New Mexico border. Not one I was familiar with."

"We need the school records," Hal told them. "We need mother's name, father's name, addresses, schools she went to, how often they moved, and where. Sometimes people go back to old stomping grounds. Did she have sisters and brothers who might be in school somewhere? I could subpoena the records, but it would alert people to what we're thinking. Might add to the gossip going around, as well."

"I can get the records," Ruth answered. "She's my student. I'll pull the file for my own use and make notes of anything helpful. I might do you some good after all."

"Do it as soon as you can," Audrey urged. "Do it before someone gets there ahead of us."

Ruth agreed. "I'll get to them first thing in the morning, during my free period."

****

Claire turned off the vacuum cleaner and wound the cord. The amount of traffic in the dining room the night before had left the rug rumpled and crushed with footprints. The meeting had been useful, all things considered. Ruth Cleburne had put a small key in their hands, giving Claire a stirring of hope. The sound of the front door closing made her turn just as George Anderson came into the room. His hair stood in tufts over his head as he swiped a towel over his face.

"Out for your tennis match so early, Dad? There's still frost on the grass. You must be chilled clear through." She noticed the long envelope in his hand. "Is the mail out already?"

"Special delivery by messenger." He snorted. "I had to sign for it. The messenger was waiting at the steps as I came back." He tossed the ivory rectangle on the dining table. "The school board didn't waste any time getting to the formalities. Here's my official suspension notice."

"Oh, Dad," Claire commiserated.

"I expected it," George went on. "But seeing it, the black-and-white reality of it—I guess it brings everything into focus. This nightmare is actually happening."

"This makes your position harder." Claire mentally wished all the plagues of ancient Egypt on the school board.

George pulled his shirt free of his waistband and wiped his neck and arms. "Claire, no matter what rabbits Jared and Hal pull out of the hat, nothing will be the same at school. I have twenty-five years in, and I can retire. Providing the guys manage to win the court case. If not, I won't have to worry about what I'll be doing. Either way, I'm branded forever."

Claire sat down hard on the chair beside the table. "Dad, you don't mean that. Jared and Hal are going to whip this thing. I'm sure we're on the right track and with Ruth's help…" She stopped at the grey look of defeat on his face.

"It won't matter. No one will ever let me work with kids again. They might move me to administration—something innocuous, like ordering audio-visual supplies or lab materials, but I'll never be in an actual school again. If I'm free to be anywhere."

"No fair, Dad. You didn't do anything. After the trial, if we have to go that far, we can write letters, get in touch with former students, go to our congressman and senator. We'll stir up such a racket we'll make the board give you your place back."

George laughed ruefully. "No, we won't, Claire. I'll take my retirement, if I have the chance, and go to work in earnest on my Jubal Early biography. I got my nerve up and sent a proposal and a couple of chapters to the Institute for Civil War Studies in Richmond before this whole situation blew up. If they show any interest, maybe I'll get the thing published. If not, I'll go on and finish it anyway, as something to leave my grandchildren." He gave her a slanting glance. "If my girls ever give me grandkids."

Claire was not to be sidetracked by his comments.

"Dad, look, you don't have to do anything. I know you don't want to contact people, but Judith and Audrey and I can do it. Get people, people you've helped, to help you."

George patted her hand but pushed her words aside. "I'm a lucky man. I have three beautiful, smart daughters who love their old man enough to jump in on his side regardless of the odds. But, honey, you aren't being practical."

"I can do things—" she started.

"You sure can, Claire, you sure can. You can manage things, make priorities, organize like nobody's business. That's your talent—managing things. You're efficient, Judith's artistic, and Audrey's practical. It's my life we're discussing, and I don't want you trying to fix it for me. Don't martyr yourself or alienate your sisters over this. Leave it to the lawyers, Claire."

****

"Audrey, how you holding up?"

Audrey looked up from her untasted sandwich to see the burly form of Chef Magnolia looming above her. "Oh, we'll get through it one way or another. It's nice to see someone who's not looking for some new tidbit of gossip to pass around."

"I know. I've seen the heads together and heard the chatter like a passel of magpies having a sit-in." Magnolia sank into the chair opposite her, its small frame creaking with his weight. "That girl, what does she think she's doing, making up stuff about George Anderson? Girl's got no bringing up at all." Magnolia waved to the waitress at the other end of the room. The lunch trade had thinned, leaving only Audrey and an elderly couple in the café. "Suzette, I'm taking a few minutes."

Warmed by the aging chef's support, Audrey relaxed and made more inroads on her lunch. "I don't know what she's doing, but she's made a mess of things around our house."

"Didn't seem the kind of girl to stir up trouble. Guess you never know about kids, how they'll jump, one day to the next."

"You know Dondie Marshall?" Audrey was surprised. "I wouldn't think the Vanderhills ever ate anywhere but home." She waved at the beer-and-wine list on the board beside the bar. "Especially in a place that serves alcohol."

"No, never seen them in here, but the girl now, she came in last summer looking for a part-time job. Couldn't take her because she's too young. Can't hire underage help. We talked a little, though. Asked if I was related to the Magnolia with the bar in Arlington, the one near the new GM plant. Told her I'd been there once, but I had no connection. Then she seemed to go blank, like she didn't know what we were talking about. Said thanks for seeing her and trotted off."

"Asked about a place in Arlington? Near the car assembly plant?" Audrey asked impatiently.

"Yes, so she said. That mean something?"

"It might, it just might." She pushed her unfinished lunch aside. "I have to run. Thanks, Magnolia."

Audrey, intent on getting to Hal's office around the corner, dropped two bills on the cashier's desk and dashed away without waiting for her change. Turning the corner, she banged abruptly into a man waiting to cross the street.

"Oh, pardon me, I'm sorry," she gasped.

"You're the Anderson girl," the man said.

"I'm Audrey Anderson." The man's hawk nose, the down-turned mouth, the faint grey stubble on the seared thin cheeks rang a bell in her memory.

"I'm Fred Vanderhill." One callused, clawlike hand caught her arm. "I want you to know we're praying for you all."

Startled, Audrey could make no reply.

"We are. We're praying night and morning that your daddy will make things right. He's got to face up to it. He's done wrong, and he's gonna be punished for it, but it's best all around for him to come clean and admit his sins. You're suffering, our girl's suffering, and even if he don't know it, George Anderson's suffering from the burden of his misdeeds. You tell him we're praying for him to see the light."

"Mr. Vanderhill, my dad didn't do anything wrong. He never touched Dondie. He couldn't do a thing like that."

Vanderhill nodded, a hint of sadness in his face. "You got to say that, of course. You got to show support and act like you believe in him. We know you're honoring your father like the commandment says. When he comes clean with himself, with you, and with God, we're all gonna be real relieved."

Audrey tried to pull away from the man. "Mr. Vanderhill, Dondie's had a hard life. There are things she can't remember. She's troubled."

"Dondie maybe can't remember what went on before, but the girl remembers real good now. That child didn't make this up, neither." Vanderhill released her arm and stepped back. "I'm obliged to be a witness for my beliefs. I never thought George Anderson was the right kind of man to be leading young folks. He's got loose ideas about right and wrong. Now, see where he's fallen. Still, we're praying for him. It might make a difference. We'll be praying for you and your sisters, too."

"Really, Mr. Vanderhill, you don't know my father, the kind of man he is," Audrey protested.

Fred Vanderhill didn't seem to hear. "May do no good, praying for your sisters. One divorced and living some kind of loose life, and the other making pictures, graven images, against the commandment. Don't like Anderson and never did, but that won't be a factor. Won't keep us from asking the Lord to move him to do right. Don't do to underestimate the power of prayers coming from good, worthy hearts."

Chapter Six

"I don't know that it means too much, Audrey. Don't get wound up over one small incident," Jared cautioned.

Audrey glared at him in frustration. If Hal had been in his office, he might have seen more significance in that scrap of conversation with Magnolia. Hal had been out. Anxious to share what she'd learned, Audrey had come to Jared to talk about the incidents of the day. "But Jared, if Dondie remembers being in Arlington, and it has to be pretty recently, because the car plant is only four or five years old, maybe we're looking in the wrong direction. That school up in the Panhandle may not be close enough to her trauma to give us what we need."

"And the Arlington thing may not mean beans. She *may have* been there, she *might have had* contact with this bar, but it's a bar, and she's a kid. Not a reasonable place for people to know her. We're certain Dondie Marshall lived in that Panhandle school district, and they did know her. We aren't chasing phantom memories there."

"We should at least look for a Magnolia Bar in Arlington, one near the plant."

Jared sighed and picked up the phone. He made a call to the information service. "Arlington, a place called the Magnolia Bar or Bar and Grill, something like that." He listened. "Yes, I see. No, I don't have any more information than that. Thanks." He dropped the phone into its base. "Found seven places with the name Magnolia something in the general area of Arlington but no Magnolia Bar. May have been there, but it's gone now. Bars go out of business, get sold, change names overnight. As a clue, that one's a dead loss." He pushed his chair away from the desk and leaned over the desk. "I'm more concerned about this encounter you had with Fred Vanderhill."

"Oh, it was nothing, just sort of uncomfortable." Audrey tried to brush the unpleasant moment aside.

"No, not just uncomfortable. It was threatening, and a veiled attempt at intimidation. Not to mention a breach of the court directive."

"I didn't take it that way."

"Turn the incident around. Suppose you went to Dondie and said she wasn't suitable company for other young girls because she cheated, or that you were praying for her to see the error of her ways. Do you see how the court might take that as intimidation? Vanderhill suggested your sisters live immoral lives because they don't live according to his philosophy. He suggested George is unfit to serve as school counselor because George has a different view of life. It may sound like just his moral judgment, but he's violating court rules by hounding you with it. That's intimidation."

"What are you going to do about it? Speak to the sheriff?"

"I'm not sure, Audrey. I've got to talk to Hal and see if we can use Vanderhill's statements to our advantage."

Audrey flinched at the idea of turning the Vanderhills' strong beliefs against them, but she did see Jared's point. If she had approached Fred Vanderhill or even Dondie with similar words, the Vanderhills would have objected and complained to the courts.

"What about Ruth Cleburne? Have you heard anything from her?"

"No, she can't get in touch with us during the school day, and I don't think she'd chance coming over until she's sure she won't be seen." Audrey glanced at her watch. "School won't be out for almost an hour. She might be able to give us a call then."

"She's our best hope at this point." Jared sent a look at the stacks of law books on the table behind Audrey. "I've been going through the court reporter publications and digests for similar cases." He sighed. "I've got to tell you, Audrey, this dirt never washes clean. Even when the accused is able to show he's innocent, something of the charge sticks. A suspicion, a hint, a question is always left in the public mind."

"It's so unfair," Audrey complained. "No matter what the girl's motives are, even if we prove she lied—or was honestly confused—Dad is the victim of the situation. He can't win."

"I'll do all I can, and so will Hal. He's giving us a huge boost, since this is his field far more than mine. His criminal trial experience alone is invaluable."

Criminal trial. Audrey turned the ugly words over in her head as she made her way home. The word "criminal" applied to George Anderson would be laughable if it weren't for the facts staring at her. The charge was criminal, and, if convicted, George faced a severe prison sentence. The tarnish it spread over her father's blameless life had become a reality she couldn't ignore.

****

Judith wiped a paint-spattered rag across her face, leaving a pale green stain above her eyes. The sawdust and grit on her hands stiffened her fingers till she could scarcely lift the rough boards stacked against the deck. Three more trips should see them all safely upstairs. Then she could knock together the crates to protect her paintings during their journey to the Kearnes Gallery in New Orleans. She felt disloyal in going on with her show, but Drake, and even Jared, insisted she should carry out her plans. Audrey had been supportive, too, though Claire had dismissed the show with a shrug of disinterest. George only said he would be proud to see her work in a gallery and she shouldn't pass up the chance. She had particularly wanted to be home for New Year's, but she needed to be in New Orleans to hang her paintings and then welcome guests at the opening the following evening. The choice was a difficult one.

"Need a hand with that?"

Judith looked up from her labors to see Drake coming across the open ground between their two houses. She tilted the pine board against the wall and dusted her hands.

"I don't think a three-piece black suit is recommended for hauling dusty lumber up two flights of stairs." She hoisted a smaller board. "You could hold the door for me. That shouldn't muss you up too badly. Did you come to see Claire?"

A quick shadow passed over his handsome face.

Judith wished she could capture that moment on canvas. "No, I saw you over here and thought I'd offer a hand." He slipped out of his immaculate jacket and unbuttoned the vest. Folding both garments and placing them over the rail, he heaved the remaining boards to his shoulder. "Shall we get these up to the studio?"

"You might be useful, at that." Judith started up the steps. "Watch for the landing. The turn is pretty sharp at the top of the stairs."

Shortly the whir of an electric drill and the bang of a hammer on wood filled the house. As the glow of afternoon faded in Judith's studio, she and Drake crated paintings and prepared them for transport. While Judith finished closing the last few crates, he retrieved his coat and vest after carting shavings and bits of wood to the trash bin.

****

"I saw your note on my office door, Audrey. Sorry I missed you. Was it something important?" Hal entered the foyer of the brick house on Stafford Street, the crisp tang of fall coming in with him.

"I thought so, but Jared looked into it and said it was nothing. He was disturbed because Fred Vanderhill stopped me on the street and—oh, he'll tell you about it. Dad's here, and I'd rather not get into it in front of him." Audrey led the way to the family room. Across the breakfast bar, George and Claire were holding a low conversation. From an upper room came the batter of hammer and nails and the sound of something being pushed across a floor. Hal raised an eyebrow in query. Audrey realized Hal couldn't know such racket was normal in the Anderson family.

"My sister has a gallery show and is getting her

paintings ready," Audrey explained. "She should be finished soon."

"I had a call from Ruth Cleburne." Hal spaced his words between thuds and bangs. "She said she called here but no one answered. She has notes from the Marshall girl's school records. I asked her to come over. She can get here without causing discussion. If she came to my office, she'd surely be seen."

"Jared? You called him?"

"He's filing papers at the court house. I suggested he come here when he's finished." Two more members of the group came into the room. Judith's pixie hair was well dusted with sawdust. Her black jeans showed spatters of paint between smears of the same dust, and her smock sagged from the weight of tools in the pocket. As always, Drake looked dapper, even in shirtsleeves, his jacket over his arm.

Audrey remembered that Hal hadn't met Drake and made quick introductions. Drake rolled down his monogrammed sleeves, wiped his hands on the towel Judith passed him, and took Hal's outstretched grasp. She couldn't remember at that moment just how much of the family history concerning Drake she'd given Hal. It must have been enough to make things clear. She saw the measuring look Hal gave him as they shook hands.

"Forgive my informality." Drake slipped on his vest. "I was helping Judith get things ready for her show." He buttoned his vest and straightened his tie. "Want me to take the crates downstairs?" He glanced at Judith, who was stowing the hammer in a small tool chest on the bar.

"Not till I'm ready to put them in the van."

"We won't need your help tonight, anyway,

Drake," Claire interrupted. "I'm sure you have concerns of your own to see to."

Shooting a silencing look at his oldest daughter, George dropped his dishtowel over the edge of the sink and joined the group. "If you can stay, Drake, I'd be glad of your opinion on some things I came across on Jubal Early. One article has a fine reprint of his portrait. You might give me some background on the artist and his work."

"Glad to, George. I don't have any plans for the evening."

"But, Dad, Jared is coming, and we need to talk about those notes *his associate* is sending," Audrey reminded him.

"We'll only be a few minutes, dear. I'd like to make use of Drake's expertise while I have him here. I'll be with you in a while." George and Drake withdrew to his small study.

Audrey knew Judith was about to rebuke Claire for her rude dismissal of Drake's help and was relieved to see Ruth Cleburne's rotund figure crossing the yard through moonlit shadows. She forestalled a sisterly squabble by hurrying to the door to admit the teacher.

"Ruth, it's so good of you to do this for Dad. Come in." She held open the door and admitted their guest into the family room. "Jared will be here in a minute. Come in and get settled."

"I need to get back as soon as I can. I'm expecting a call about Mama this evening, and I don't want to miss it."

Audrey and her sisters gathered around the teacher, and Hal leaned over the back of the sofa so he could see the notes she pulled from her tote bag. A skein of red yarn and a ruffle of knitting fell out as she removed the folder of notes. She glanced at it and chuckled. "Camouflage," she explained, "in case someone wondered why I was hauling that big bag around. A pair of woolly slippers for Mama."

The doorbell sounded, and Audrey answered it, admitting Jared and bidding Drake goodnight. She was relieved to see her dad had rejoined the group when she returned to the dining room.

"What do you have for us, Ruth?" Jared asked, as he pulled his crumpled notepad out of his pocket.

"Not as much as I'd hoped to have. The girl was in the same school her entire life before she appeared here in Santa Rita. She lived in Siding, Texas, from the time she was four or five. Mother is Donna Marshall, a widow, with no other children. Father, Gordon Marshall, died some time before they came to Siding. I have the address where they lived and a work number for the mother—Miss Bobbie's Dress Shop. Employed as an alteration lady. I called the shop but didn't get an answer. No home number listed for the Marshall house. The girl herself seems to have made a good adjustment to school early on. Her grades are good and the teachers' comments are positive and encouraging. They mention how quickly Dondie learns, how willingly she does her work, and what a joy it is to teach her. Math and science are her best subjects, but she shows enthusiasm for her art classes, too. I know it's not much, but the files didn't have anything more."

"Not a lot, but it gives us some place to look," Hal assured her.

"One thing," Ruth added. "I've always wondered about the girl's name. It's so unusual. The file shows that her name is actually Donna Denise. Named for her mother, I surmise, and called Dondie as a shortening of the two names, to avoid having two Donnas in the family. I don't know if that suggests anything."

"Doesn't suggest anything to me." Jared brushed the information aside. "I'm more interested in this place she comes from. Siding, is that the name? I've never heard of it. What's it near?"

George laughed a little. "You're talking about my old stomping grounds. I grew up in that part of the world, remember? Up in the Panhandle nothing is near anything. Towns of any size are pretty far apart. Unless it's changed a lot since my youth, Siding is a wide place in the road, maybe six or eight hundred hardy souls, that grew up around the railway about nineteen hundred. It was a lay-by for the railroad to hold up cars reconnecting with other trains. Since the railroad redirected its line, the place has sort of dried up. It may have some light industry, but little more. Siding is the last town in Texas before you cross into New Mexico. Pretty bleak and barren area."

"It's interesting that the girl has such a history of good grades and excellent school work," Hal interjected. "Now she's plagiarizing work and skating through on minimal grades."

Ruth handed him her notes and tucked the knitting back into her bag. "It's probably a reaction to physical injury or great emotional trauma."

George added, "I thought tutoring might get her back into her studies. If she liked school before, enjoyed her classes, she might respond if she got more involved with a project and had some strong encouragement."

"If something happened to her in that little town, in Siding, we should be able to find out fairly easily," Jared suggested. "I'll write to the school to see what they can tell us about the family. Serious trouble or some kind of incident—a fire, a traffic fatality, something shattering for the girl—they'll know about it. Ruth, your notes will help me frame my questions. Thanks for bringing them."

****

Santa Rita glowed with the lights and spirit of Christmas, now only a week away. The holiday had been less festive in the Anderson house since death had diminished the family. This year Audrey could barely tolerate the thought. She trudged along the sidewalk, ignoring the sound of bells and carols rippling from the doors of shops bright with tinsel and greens. Hal's office, a sanctuary blessedly devoid of season's greetings, gave her respite from the clamor outside. She draped her coat over one of the rocking chairs and drew up the brown-wrapped box sitting near the fireplace. The end-of-year updates for Hal's loose-leaf service on tax, she saw, as she peeled back the wrapping. Across the room Hal murmured into his phone and waved while she sorted the invoice and shipping documents from the banded packets of thin paper.

He's going to be tied up all afternoon, she told herself. *And there's probably nothing new to discuss. He or Jared would have called if there'd been developments.* Audrey gathered her work up and took it to the small room Hal used as a combination conference room and library. The room was chilly but had work space. She pushed up her sweater sleeves and removed the awkward binders from the shelf. The massive updates would probably take most of her afternoon.

Hours later Audrey heard the door behind her open and looked around as Hal came in. He grinned companionably and reached for one of the digests behind her. "I forgot you were in here. Must be a big filing. How's it going?"

"I'm about to finish up for the day." She stretched cramped fingers. "I don't suppose there's anything new? We haven't heard from the school up at Siding or anything?"

"I would have called you immediately, or Jared would have." Hal sat on the corner of her worktable. "How are things at home? I haven't had a chance to talk to your dad in a few days."

"We put up the Christmas tree last night, always a big thing in our house. We heat cider and put carols on the record player. Judith makes a special set of ornaments every year, something to commemorate the year's events. This year she painted clear glass balls with cartoons of Claire's cat doing some un-catty things, opening packages, reading the newspaper, going shopping. They're really cute, and we got a laugh out of them, probably the best moment we've had. It got pretty teary from time to time, even with everybody trying."

"And your dad? I know this thing is wearing him down." Hal's hazel eyes were gold in the afternoon light. His close-cropped beard picked up the glint of sun cutting a shaft through the room from the wavy old glass windowpane.

Audrey slumped back in her chair and closed her eyes. "I think Dad may be handling this better than any of us. He's putting all his energy, and hours every day, into this biography he's writing. He's been at it for years, but he says now he has time to pull his research together into a manuscript. He may be absenting himself from the day-to-day worry, but he's really involved in his work."

"Your sisters?" Hal pressed.

"Judith is head over heels into her show. She has to go to New Orleans right after Christmas for a few days. The gallery owner wants her to open the show, and we feel she should, but Claire needs to go to Dallas, too. She has to close her apartment and store her things before the end of the month. So they'll both be gone for several days, leaving Dad and me alone. We'll have to keep each other's spirits up."

Hal reached over and tucked a strand of loose hair back behind her ear. "You look worn out, little one. You need to get away from the whole thing for a while."

His warm touch seemed to linger on her skin, almost like a caress. She smiled, but she hid pain behind the smile. "A fine thought, but you don't know what it's like every time I go anywhere. This morning I stopped by the printer's to pick up some invoice forms. Three other people were in the shop, but I felt like a thousand eyes watched me. The minute I was out the door, I saw all three of them—and the sales girl—putting their heads together for a good round of gossip. Judith says she gets the same thing when she's working in Drake's gallery. We can't get away from it."

"Have dinner with me," Hal suggested. "We could leave town for an evening, see some new faces, talk about something besides your dad's case. You'll feel better for a little distraction, Audrey."

Hal Lindstrom was asking her out? A college fantasy coming true? Audrey started to draw away, refuse. *Not smart to get involved with Hal.*

"I see the word 'no' in your eyes. Please don't say it. I would really like to see you relax and even laugh a little. I remember we laughed a lot in the dark stacks of the old law library."

They had laughed, talked, and made long hours pleasant in each other's company. Hal, even as a law student, had been able to dispel gloom and raise hopes. Maybe, yes, she would take the chance. She didn't have enough friends right now that she could close the door on this one.

"All right, dinner and no thoughts of Dad's dilemma or my sister's squabbles," she agreed. "When and where will we go?"

"Tonight. And where? Oh, somewhere out of town, so we don't run into anybody you don't want to see. How would you feel about a drive over to San Antonio? It's only a little more than an hour, and the chance of meeting acquaintances is pretty small. Would that do it for you?"

Audrey felt a tingle in the back of her spine. San Antonio had a number of excellent restaurants in the old city. "I think that sounds lovely." The afternoon seemed brighter and her troubles smaller, for the moment.

"Good." He pulled the binder out of her hands. "Now, put these grubby books away and go on home. I'll pick you up in an hour and a half."

Audrey looked down at her work clothes and smudged hands. An hour and a half would barely be time enough for her to put herself together. "I'll see if I can find a dress and get a comb through my hair in that time. It may be a shock to my sisters to see me in girl garb for a change."

****

Hal's powerful Mercedes purred along the highway. A holiday radio concert filled the car. Passing lights of oncoming cars caught Hal in their flickering beams as he drove with conservative attention. Audrey was glad the music gave her a chance to escape for a while. She let the moment fill her senses. The soft copper silk of her dress curled around her knees, sensuously pliant over her lap. Her hair brushed lightly over her bare shoulders. With no time to do formal things with it, she'd left it loose, held back with a velvet bow.

"By the way, if I didn't mention it, you turned into a very pretty butterfly tonight." Hal brushed a fold of her skirt. "I like that dress even better than the blue one you wore at the Bar Association dinner."

"You remember that blue dress?"

"Miss Anderson, not a man under eighty in the room failed to notice that blue dress, or at least the girl in it. You're quite beautiful, you know."

"You're sweet, Hal, but you don't have to go that far to distract me. I've known I was the Plain-Jane sister since I was twelve. You can't live in a house with two raving beauties and not realize you don't measure up. Claire and Judith inherited our Spanish grandmother's looks. I didn't. I look just like my mother and her mother before her. Good enough for daily wear, but no glamour in the mix."

"Is that what you think?" He huffed under his breath. "Your sisters are beautiful, all right. Claire looks like she belongs in a museum, a painting by one of the Old Masters. And Judith could make a fortune posing for pictures instead of painting them." She saw his sharp glance aside. "Audrey, they don't wear well. Claire's cool distance is murderous. She's an ice maiden, not somebody you want to share a sorrow or a joke with. She's unreachable. And Judith can drive you to drink. She's always on the edge, always on the verge of erupting. All that volatility wears me out. You, you're very real. I like the way a little green imp shines out of your eyes. When the sun touches it, your hair has Indian copper in it that makes it sparkle. When you're hurt, pain shows in your face, and when you're happy, you glow with it. You have real beauty, the natural, God-given kind that lasts forever."

Audrey turned to stare at him, trying to see if he was teasing her. His face was solemn enough, though his white teeth gleamed with a bit of a smile behind his beard. "That surprises you, does it? You hadn't thought of yourself that way. I'll bet you've been comparing yourself to your sisters and coming up short all your life." He reached across the seat to cover her hand with his. "I think it's time you used a new standard. Look at yourself for what you are, not what you think your sisters are. You'd be amazed at what a man sees when he looks at you."

Hal found a small Spanish restaurant, near the center of San Antonio, where they shared an excellent dinner and a glass of decent wine. Later they walked along winding streets as old as the city while mariachi music rippled from a hotel ballroom. Audrey pulled her cashmere shawl closer against the chill of falling temperatures.

"Cold?"

"Beginning to be," she confessed.

Hal opened the door at a small art shop. "Let's step in here and let you warm up. Then we'd better get back to the car and start home. Much as I hate to end the evening, I know we both need to be ready for tomorrow, just in case we have new developments."

Neither of them had mentioned the dreary days ahead or the case that seemed to consume them. Audrey pushed the thought of her dad and his trial to the back of her mind. *Not tonight. Tonight isn't part of that world.* The shop was filled with stained glass and silver jewelry. Ornaments for trees and colorful sun catchers sparkled with jewel tones. Bracelets and brooches covered one small ceramic Christmas tree. Earrings in the form of a pair of silver cats, long necked, with sapphire eyes looking down arrogant noses, caught her eye.

"I think Claire would love these. I'm going to get them for her for Christmas." She took them to the elderly lady at the cash register. Hal continued looking around as she chatted with the shopkeeper. When she turned, he was standing at the far end of the store.

"Find something you can't resist?"

"More like something familiar." He held out a key chain with a white marbled glass flower dangling from the chain. "This looks like the magnolias your friend at home has hanging in the windows of the café. I wonder if the same artist made them. The petals have a distinctive tilt and coloring."

"I'll bet it is the same person. Magnolia tries to use local or nearby talent when he can. Judith painted the flamingo mural for him, you know."

Hal fingered the key chain and then abruptly purchased the small item. "Souvenir of a perfect evening," he explained with a slight smile. "I suppose we'd better head home, if you've warmed up enough to face the walk to the car."

They strolled into the night. Traffic had dropped to a slow trickle, making their progress faster. Night wind rose and tugged at her dress and shawl with chilly fingers. Hal took Audrey's hand and tucked it into his pocket. She was grateful for the warmth. As her fingers uncurled in the depths, a smooth ripple of glass crossed her palm. She felt the outline of the stained-glass magnolia.

"It's funny how I keep running into magnolias."

"How's that?"

"Oh, my friend with the café is called Magnolia, and so is his place. Then Dondie mentioned that bar in Arlington to him because of the name, and now this key chain pops up."

Hal stopped and spun to face her. "What bar that the Marshall girl mentioned? She was talking to Magnolia about some place she remembered?"

"I thought Jared told you," Audrey stammered. "I told him, but he didn't think it was useful or important. I supposed he'd passed it on to you, though."

"Tell me now," Hal commanded. As they walked, Audrey filled him in on the incident in Magnolia's café. He nodded now and then when she paused, trying to give him the exact words.

"A bar near the GM plant in Arlington, with Magnolia in the name. And your friend said he'd been there." His steps clipped along faster as Audrey trotted to keep up. "We need to talk to Magnolia and get the exact location." He stopped short and looked down at her. "You said your sister is going to Dallas to wind up her affairs? If we can get the location from Magnolia, we'll send Claire to look at the place and see if they know anything about Dondie Marshall or her family."

"But Jared didn't think this was important," Audrey reminded him. "He checked with information but didn't find a listing. Jared figured it had gone out of business and saw no point in looking further."

"It may prove to be a pointless chase, but it's a clue we can't pass up." His broad hand tipped up her chin and, under the pale glow of a city street lamp, his mouth found hers. The soft brush of his lips on hers wiped out their surroundings. Her fading cognizance registered the brush of his beard on her skin with delighted surprise. "Been waiting a long time to do that, Audrey."

Chapter Seven

"You're sure the girl was talking about a bar in Arlington?" Hal asked Magnolia again. He and Audrey had met with the chef in the small office behind the kitchen as soon as the man could unlock the doors that morning. They'd heard his story, but Hal pried to find any bit Magnolia might have forgotten.

"Had to be Arlington, because she was talking about it being near the GM plant, and that's the only one I know about." Magnolia thumped his elbows down on his desk. "What else can I tell you? It was a one-minute nothing kind of conversation. Soon's I told her I couldn't hire her, the kid shut down like a burned-out bulb and left."

Audrey explained their insistence. "The girl has a memory block of some kind, Magnolia. She can't remember anything before she turned up here. A bar, a young girl, twelve or thirteen—she'd get noticed."

"You got that right, 'specially in that place. It's a hangout where a guy would only take a woman who wasn't his wife. Loud and pretty uncouth. No place I'd take a kid." Magnolia pushed his greying hair under his toque. "If that's all I can tell you, I need to get to the kitchen. Bread ain't gonna bake itself."

Hal stopped him with a gesture. "Just one thing, Magnolia. Arlington information doesn't show a listing for a Magnolia Bar anywhere in the city, not near the plant or anywhere else. It's probably out of business. Could you remember the name of the owner?"

Magnolia grinned. "Now that is something, isn't it?" He laughed a little, his broad white grin crinkling deep trenches in his brown cheeks. "I don't have any idea who owns it. Ever'body just calls it the Magnolia. My cousin took me there, so I don't rightly know the street it's on, but you won't find it listed as the Magnolia Bar. The name is Blue Magnolia. No bar, no grill, no café or anything else added to it. Just Blue Magnolia. It's right there near the plant, across the parking lot and down about half a block along a side street." He paused. "Could be gone by now, but it had a pretty regular trade a few years back. I think it'll still be there."

Audrey had a second thought. "Could you call your cousin and ask?"

"Wish I could, Audrey. Cousin Ebbitt was the last kin I had in this world, but he passed, oh, it's been 'bout two years now, maybe a little more." Magnolia shook a dismal head and tied on his enveloping white apron. "Hope somebody down in Arlington knows about that girl. She's got no cause to go after your dad like this, and she sure as sunrise needs some help getting her head on straight."

Back in Hal's office, Audrey waited while Hal checked telephone information. At last, leaning back in his chair, he grinned with satisfaction.

"I've got it! Blue Magnolia, big as life." He wrote down the address and then consulted a detailed atlas. "Yes, it's right there near the plant. If Claire can take an afternoon while she's in Dallas and drive into

Arlington, we might make some use of this scrap of information."

Audrey felt her spirits lift. At last, something they could actually use. A clue to Dondie's painful history that might unravel the girl's murky reason for her accusations.

Hal held up a cautioning hand. "Don't get too excited over this, Audrey. We're assuming a lot based on one offhand conversation. No one may remember her, or maybe she wasn't even in the place—but for some reason the name stuck in her foggy memory."

"If it was only the name, it would have been the name on the building, Blue Magnolia. Magnolia said the regulars were the ones who called it the Magnolia. Dondie had to have been in there enough to learn what the regular trade called it."

"That sounds logical," he admitted, "but we'll rely on Claire to find out as much as she can."

Audrey waited as he cleared his desk, reminding herself sternly she couldn't afford to get excited over a clue as ephemeral as a wisp of smoke. But she hid a spark of belief deep in her heart and refused to let it die.

"How will Claire go about asking for some trace of Dondie in that bar?" she asked suddenly. "Claire's never even seen the girl."

Hal looked up, consternation filling his face. "I really hadn't thought," he began. "A picture, a photograph? I guess we'll have to send one along. Were there any in the school files from Siding? That would be better than a current one. She may have matured noticeably in the last three years."

"I don't remember Ruth mentioning pictures. Siding may be one of those terribly small, poor schools that doesn't do school pictures." Audrey paced the width of the floor. "Ruth would have some trouble borrowing a picture if there is one. And she could get in a kettle of hot water if she got caught."

Hal agreed. "I hate to ask her, but what else can we do? At least it's Saturday and we don't have to worry about waiting to catch her after school." He dug a phone book out of a pile on his desk, found the Cleburne number, dialed, and was in touch with the schoolteacher. "Ruth, I hate to bother you at home like this, but we may have a thread of information about that girl's background. We need a photograph of her, preferably from three or four years back. Is one in her file? And if it is, could you manage to borrow it somehow?" Hal listened for a bit, shaking his head from time to time. "Then we'll have to do something else, Ruth. Thanks for your help. I hope your mother does well." He dropped the phone into its base and sat heavily.

"She won't do it?"

"She can't." Hal tossed the phone book back on the desk. "Dondie has no picture in the file." He muttered something under his breath that Audrey was reasonably sure she wasn't meant to hear. "School's out for the holidays, Ruth reminded me. Yesterday was the last day of class until January. Ruth's leaving to have Christmas with her mother in Iowa, but she may be back for a couple of weeks after the first of the year, to close up her house. If she's here, she'll do what she can."

Audrey smothered a cry of exasperation. "Too late! Claire has to go right after Christmas. She's given up her apartment so the building management can have it painted as soon as she's out. They won't wait later than the end of the month."

"We may have to make a trip some other time, not depend on Claire." He sounded resigned, but he tugged at his beard in frustration.

"She's the best choice, and this is the best time. She'll be right there, and if contacts can be made, she'll be able to make them. Claire's a whiz at managing things."

"Later on may be better. The holidays are a bad time to try to catch up with people. She could go down and stay a weekend or even several days next month. That might work out for us in the long run."

Audrey tried to quell her impatience. She could feel time running through her hands as if it were a tangible thing.

"Wait. It won't matter when Claire is in Dallas or what Ruth can do at school. We have no photos." Audrey twisted a single curl in agitation.

"So we may as well let this idea simmer for a week or two."

"No! I have an idea. The girl has spent three years in school here. We do make pictures, yearbook pictures, at the beginning of school each year. She'd still be thirteen or so in her first picture here. We could use that. We can get it enlarged. It should be clear enough for Claire to use."

"It's still not available to us," Hal countered. "Annuals and their files are kept at school. We can't go to the publication office and ask for a copy of a back yearbook. First, the school is closed for the holidays, and second, they likely wouldn't give it to us."

Waving his objections aside, Audrey pulled on her jacket and picked up her handbag. "I know. Of course, we can't barge up to the school and ask, even if it weren't closed, but Dad has a full run of yearbooks in his study. He gets one every year. He calls it insurance against letting the years run together. He'll have the one we need, right there in the house."

"Brilliant girl," Hal commended, and followed her out the door.

When Audrey unlocked the door, the house felt empty and shrouded in silence. She and Hal made their way to George's study, where Audrey flipped on the lights and dropped her jacket over a stack of books beside the desk. Every surface in the room loomed with mountains of reference books and hills of folders.

"Your dad has some pretty serious research going on in here."

"I told you he was spending all his time with Jubal Early and company."

"I didn't imagine anything like this." Hal looked around the cluttered, claustrophobic room. "How are we going to find those yearbooks? Is there any system to this mess?"

"Yes, believe it or not, I can usually find things. I've been skirting Dad's hobby horses for years." She pointed to a range of red-and-grey books piled on top of the corner bookcase. "There are the annuals. The problem is finding something to stand on so I can reach them." She stepped over a clutter of books near the cabinet. The stepladder beside the desk had been pressed into service to hold a pile of yellow tablets and multicolored index cards on the steps, but she reached for it.

"Oh, no, you're not risking your pretty neck to climb up there for those books. You're too valuable to lose. Hold on. I think I can squeeze into the corner and hand down a few of them. If George puts the most recent annual on top each year, the one we want shouldn't be more than three down."

Hal used his height and the length of his reach and managed to dislodge the top volumes. They evaded his grasp to slide over his head and thud into the carpet beside him.

"A few inches closer and you'd be going for stitches," Audrey fussed as she gathered up the scattered books.

"No, I applied sound physics to the problem. They landed just where I intended." His smug look didn't fool Audrey.

"You mean you got lucky when no sharp corners made contact with your stubborn head."

"I think this is the one we should start with." Hal waved one volume, deflecting further discussion.

"No room to look at books in here. The family room has light and real chairs." Audrey swept up the remaining volumes, draped her jacket over her shoulder, and fastened the door. "We have to keep this room shut or Richelieu moves in and makes a nest in Dad's papers,"

The cat in question had made his present bed across the back of George's blue chair. He opened one eye, the copper one, to express his annoyance with their presence, and floated to the floor, plumed tail raised with indignation.

"Watch out where you sit. His Eminence has claimed this room for his own, leaving cat hair on everything."

Hal glanced at his khaki pants and sank into the

aging chair. "The least of my worries," he assured her. She took the corner of the sofa, and together they paged through the book. No picture of Dondie Marshall appeared in the class album or in any of the activity shots.

"Maybe she got into school after class pictures were made," Audrey ventured. "I know she enrolled after classes had begun, maybe even late September. Pictures are generally made in August."

Hal pulled out the next book in the sequence. He checked the index and then thumbed through the pages one by one. "She's not in this one, either."

"We must be missing her somehow." Audrey took the last volume and began turning the pages.

The scuff of soft shoes followed the sound of a door opening at the far end of the hallway. Audrey saw her father coming to join them. He was bareheaded, and tufts of his thinning hair stood erect. The jacket he dropped held a fresh, woodsy scent, and the color in his face could only have come from the nip in the December air.

"Hey, good to see you guys working," he teased as he drew close. "What's up? Something promising?"

Between them Audrey and Hal explained their quest and the pile of school yearbooks on the coffee table before them. "So with all the other possibilities running out, we thought we'd make do with a picture from the annual. It might be a little later than we'd like, but perhaps the girl hasn't changed too radically," Hal concluded.

George nodded with a rueful twist to his mouth. "It's a good idea. Magnolia's story could give us a line on the girl. But you're going to have to forget getting a photo of Dondie from the annual, and probably you won't find one anywhere else."

"No pictures?" Hal wore a confused look.

"No pictures. I'd bet on it. Remember, we're dealing with Fred Vanderhill and his concept of Biblical imperatives. 'No graven images' means just that, in his mind. No pictures. None of any kind. No newspaper pictures, no television, no film, and no high school yearbook shots for remembering the golden days of adolescence."

Audrey fell back in dismay. Another promising path cut off by an unexpected wall.

They were still discussing their frustration when Judith and Drake trudged in, bearing piles of quilted pads and packing paper. "This should be enough padding to fill in between the crates to keep anything from shifting. If I can get everything organized this weekend, I'll be able to start loading the day after Christmas," Judith was saying. Audrey waved to her sister. "Looks like a power meeting," Judith observed. "Should we sit in?" Leaving their bundles of packing supplies by the stairwell, Judith and Drake joined the group. "Why the gloomy faces? More trouble?"

Audrey gave a summary of the information Magnolia had provided, then explained the fruitless search for a picture of the Marshall girl. "So we were pouring over the annuals when Dad came in. He says the Vanderhills' religious beliefs prevent Dondie from having her picture made. We're trying to decide if having Claire check out the bar in Arlington is useful, but with no picture, the chance of finding someone who remembers her looks slim."

Judith folded her arms across her black jacket. "If

the only problem is getting a picture of the girl, get me somewhere near her for a little while and you'll have one. I catch a pretty accurate likeness. Dad saw Dondie when she first came here. His memory will help me get her picture back to thirteen or so, only I'll have to get to work on it in the next few days, before I leave for New Orleans. Claire wants to leave the day before I do, so our timing is pretty tight."

"A sketch? Of course, that would work," Hal agreed.

"But the Vanderhills won't let you, or anyone associated with me, near her for any reason, especially to draw her," George insisted.

"Surely I can catch sight of her someplace in public. Along the riverwalk, downtown, somewhere she goes routinely. All I need is a half hour, more or less."

"The Vanderhills keep her pretty close to home," George reminded them.

"Then you just need to let me know where I can find the girl. I'll make sure Claire has a picture to take to Dallas."

"A picture for me to take to Dallas? What's this about?" Claire herself came from the darkening stairs carrying Richelieu over one shoulder, wisps of sleep still showing in her face. The cat's pale fur blended perfectly into her grey knit dress. "I was having a nap when Richelieu announced it was time for a snack. As I woke up I thought I heard voices."

Hal filled in the situation for Claire, adding the suggestion that Judith draw the girl, subtracting a little maturity to be more accurate, for identification purposes.

"Oh, this is good." A bit of color warmed Claire's

ivory cheeks. "Finally something real to do. A piece of the puzzle I can actually work on. I can locate this place in Arlington, and if someone has seen this girl, I'll move towers to find him." Brushing past Drake as if she didn't see him, Claire put the squirming cat on the floor and headed toward the kitchen.

They were still discussing ways and means of getting close to the Marshall girl when Jared dropped by. He was surprised at their enthusiasm over a clue he'd found unpromising. He settled his long frame on the low hassock, the only available seat left in the room, and studied the situation thoughtfully.

"I don't want to throw a wet blanket on your excitement. I still don't think this trip to Arlington offers us much, but since Claire will be nearby, I suppose it's a point to run down. I can't see any harm." Jared crossed his arms over his knees and drew his long legs up against the hassock, never a comfortable seat for a man of his height. "We have two developments you should know about. First, we have a court date for the last of February. Our time frame is pretty tight. The second is that when Dondie heard this morning she would definitely have to testify in open court, she tried to run away. She was at the bus stop asking to hitch a ride. A truck driver was filling the vending machines, and she begged him to take her to San Antonio. Fortunately the minister at the church down the way saw her, knew who she was, and called Fred Vanderhill. The old man will be keeping her even closer from now on." Jared turned to the dark girl across from him. "Judy, you're going to have the devil's own time trying to sketch the girl after this."

****

117

Jared's prediction proved true. In the days leading up to Christmas Eve, the Marshall girl kept to the Vanderhill house or shop. A constant watch bore no results, worrying Audrey as she saw Judith and Drake organizing the crates of paintings for transport. While she helped Claire prepare for the trip to Dallas, and carried on her own business, abruptly, almost as if the week had blown away on the gusty December winds, it was Christmas Eve. Stopping by Hal's office on the way home to invite him to dinner the next day, she found him surrounded by piles of thick volumes.

"You're not supposed to be in the office the day before Christmas," she chided when she saw him bent over a legal tome all but covering the top of his desk.

"Tell me about it. I just finished some research for the textbook and was about to take a minute to write my family. Since we're scattered all over the world, letters are as close as we get to sharing holidays."

"I remember that your dad is with the State Department."

"He and my mother are in London this year. My brothers aren't any closer, so we don't have much time together." Audrey heard a touch of loneliness in his tone.

"I came by because I thought you might like to have dinner with us tomorrow. It won't be very festive, I'm afraid, but the dinner should be good, and having a number of people around will make things brighter for all of us. We can't just grub along worrying over the trial if there are people to feed and entertain."

Hal hesitated, then nodded. "I'll come tomorrow if you'll come with me for a while tonight. A massed chorus made up of all the choirs in town is singing the

Messiah on the steps of the courthouse this evening. I'd like to hear it. Would you join me?" Hal paused, closing his notes and files. "Unless you'd rather not be in such a public place right now."

"I'd love to come. Mom always said she didn't really feel like it was Christmas until she'd heard the *Messiah*." Audrey gathered her things and zipped up her jacket. "It should be a perfect night. Clear, chilly but not cold, and no wind for the first time in days."

"I'll come by for you. You'll have to show me where we can park. One thing Santa Rita doesn't offer is downtown parking."

Audrey laughed. "You're right about that. So leave your car at my house, and we'll walk to the courthouse along the riverwalk. We'll probably get there just as fast, and the walk will be pretty with all the Christmas lights along the river."

****

Audrey's weather prediction proved accurate. Faint stars powdered the evening sky, and the chill in the air was just enough to warrant sweaters and light jackets. The musical program filled the night with uplifting song and the cheer of the season. In wool slacks and a ski sweater, Audrey drew in the crisp night air without becoming cold or uncomfortable. She immersed herself in the music and the moment. For a time she was able to put aside the problems that faced her and escape to another place. Beside her Hal seemed as entranced as she. As one body, the audience stood for the triumphant proclamation of the "Hallelujah Chorus."

"That was just what I needed, Hal. I'm so glad you asked me to come along."

Hal tucked her arm under his and started down the

slope to the riverwalk steps. "I hadn't heard the *Messiah* in years. We have some fine voices in this town."

As groups descended the steps and spread along to the path beside the river, the crowd diminished. Within minutes Audrey and Hal had the softly lit walkway to themselves. Small trees had been covered in crystal lights so their glow lined the sides of the riverbank. Milky white globes above them marked the byways leading to the street level where others returned to parked cars or headed for home.

"See, we're better off not having to search for the car or wait till everyone else has started for home." Audrey pointed to thickened traffic and headlights converging on the street above them.

"Infinitely better off," Hal agreed. Arms linked, they walked in comfortable silence. The river ruffled beside them, white tufts faintly visible beyond the stand of decorated trees. A splash punctuated the night as a fish rose, then fell back into the gleaming water. In the distance the old bridge seemed to be celebrating the season along with the other inhabitants of Santa Rita. The gold lights lining its arched span sparkled against the faint stars of the night sky.

"Time is winding down for this year and the decade," Audrey remarked as the silence became more pronounced. "I hope 1960 is less hassle."

"Time is pressing." Silence, interrupted only by their footsteps along the path, stretched between them. "Your sister hasn't managed to get a good look at the Marshall girl? She still hasn't done her sketches?"

"Not as of this morning. Claire has to leave the morning after Christmas, and Judith leaves the next day. We may not get a picture in time for Claire to take it with her. Maybe we'll get lucky after the first of the year, when both of the girls are back here. I don't see it happening before."

"Damn. Jared may be right and this thing isn't all that important, but we need to check out that bar in Arlington. We have to have the picture. Claire can't just walk in and expect to stir memories without it."

Audrey knew he was right. "We're doing all we can. The Vanderhills are keeping Dondie at home anytime the shop's not open. If the shop is open, the girl is there, helping out. They don't leave her alone for a minute. If the girl hadn't tried to run away, she might have more freedom right now, but as it is…"

"We can't get close enough to do any good," Hal finished. "It's funny that Dondie tried to run off once the court date was set. You'd think having an end to this affair would be a relief to her."

"I think she's scared to death. She's been through a lot, but this has to be awful for her. Even if she's just mixed Dad up with something that happened to her before, she's probably reliving all the emotions."

Hal stopped at the base of steps leading up to the street. "I keep thinking about the incident that brought her here. Perhaps she ran away the last time, too. Maybe she didn't get dumped off here at the church. Maybe she ran away from whatever the situation was, and this was as far as she got."

"What makes you think that, Hal? That she ran away?" Audrey considered the idea.

"Just a wild idea," he answered. "When she found herself in trouble this time, what did she do? Where did she go? The bus stop. She tried to get a bus out of town or hitch a ride to somewhere else. I'm thinking she might have been repeating a pattern—running away from a painful situation."

Audrey stopped and stared down into the ink-dark river. "Running away might be her way of handling fear. No one actually saw somebody drop her in Santa Rita. And the bus stop is across the road from the church where she was found three years ago. If she was scared or hurt before, she might have grabbed the first bus, bought a ticket for as far away as what little money she had would take her, and found herself here. Maybe she intended to hitch a ride from here but didn't have any luck and took shelter in the church. By the time she was found, whatever trauma she suffered had left her so confused and disoriented, she didn't remember what happened." Audrey squeezed Hal's arm with barely controlled excitement. "All along, everyone assumed Dondie had been dropped off here to get her out of the way. Probably abandoned by her family. But she couldn't tell who left her. She might have been running away. She might have brought herself here. And if she did, maybe we can find out what bus she took and where it came from."

Hal stood connecting the ideas. "Is there a bus that comes from somewhere near Arlington?"

"I don't know, but I'll bet there's a way to find out. Oh, Hal, how lucky was it that your path somehow led you here. How lucky for all of us!" She reached up and brushed a kiss of gratitude on his cheek. Her hair fell back from her forehead as he cupped her face between his hands.

"I don't think it was luck, little one. I think it was fate."

"Fate?" she echoed.

"I think so." His lips barely traced a kiss above her eyes. "Back in school, you remember all those long talks we had between the stacks? You don't know how often I thought about seeing you somewhere other than that grim library. I really wanted to, you know. You were interesting and fun and had a practical way of making the place bright and pleasant. I wanted to know you, see who you were outside those silent halls. I didn't pursue the idea. I told myself it wouldn't be right. You were just a freshman and had three undergraduate years ahead, as well as law school, while I was in my last year of law school. I knew I'd be half a continent away and couldn't start a relationship that could only frustrate us both. I told myself it was better to have a brief friendship that we'd both soon forget."

"I never forgot you. You stayed in a special place in my memories. Other things crowded in—school, my mother's death, Dad's terrible grief—all of that filled my time, but I didn't forget you. Then you came here, and we're friends again. Maybe it was fate, as you said."

Audrey watched his expression become grave and still.

"I left that other life with no regrets." He circled her shoulders with one arm, turning her so they both looked down into the river beside the path. "You know why I left?"

"Jared said something happened to a witness in one of your cases."

"Yes, something happened." For a moment he didn't go on. "I got her killed, that's what happened." The bitter tone in his voice emphasized the anger.

"Hal! I don't believe that. You wouldn't."

"No, I wouldn't, not on purpose. I didn't think the man I was defending was guilty, and he played on it. When a witness came forward who could place him at the crime scene, I was convinced she was mistaken. I told my client that I could get him off, that the woman was confused and could be discredited. He asked if we could prove she was lying, and I said she wasn't, that she believed what she said was true, but she was mistaken. I was sure I could discredit her testimony, and my client would be found not guilty. I told him there would always be a question in some minds. I said the woman was sincere, and that after she took the stand some people would believe her, would believe he should have been convicted, though the jury would vote to acquit him."

Audrey could read the rest in Hal's face. "So he saw to it that she never took the stand?"

"Exactly. She suffered a fatal traffic accident two days before she was scheduled to testify. My client walked, but I knew then he was guilty. Guilty not only of the crime he stood trial for but also guilty of arranging for the prosecution's witness to be unable ever to testify against him. I couldn't go on. I could advise others, help them win their cases, but I couldn't do it myself. I'd see the smug, sly look on my client's face repeated in the eyes of anyone I defended.

"So I found myself here, planning a textbook, agreeing to teach, consulting for other lawyers. Now I can live with myself. Besides, I found you again. Suddenly, at that Bar Association dinner, a door I had closed long ago was opened. This time I don't plan to let anything interfere. You're due some serious courting as soon as we can get your dad out of his present trouble, young lady."

It started as a teasing kiss, a promise of things only hinted, but in half a breath Audrey found herself lost in his arms, her last thought obliterated by wave upon wave of sweet possession.

Chapter Eight

The house felt emptier, less alive, Judith realized as she bundled things together before leaving for the gallery. Christmas had been better than she'd expected, what with Audrey bringing Hal over for dinner and Jared popping in during the afternoon. Drake had come by, given Claire a questioning look, and handed a sheaf of prints to George. The two men disappeared into the study to look over the Civil War lithographs Drake had unearthed, though not without catching the brunt of Claire's accusatory glare.

So the Christmas interval was over, Claire had departed to wind up her business in Dallas, and this morning Judith would open the gallery for Drake. Annoyed that she hadn't been able to do the sketch of Dondie Marshall before Claire left, Judith also felt guilty. There hadn't been a moment when the girl wasn't watch-dogged by one or the other of the Vanderhills. *Maybe I could have tried harder, watched closer.*

Judith scooted Richelieu off her black leather jacket and scratched his ears in apology. "Sorry, your royal furriness, but you have a coat and I need this one." The cat rolled on his back and wrapped all four feet around her arm. She rubbed his silvery belly and stroked him under the chin. "I don't know why you decided to sleep in my room when your mama left, but I'd rather you didn't whet your claws on my canvas or play hockey with the paint tubes while I'm gone. Just find a sunny corner and think profound cat thoughts, okay?"

Judith pulled the long straps of her bag over one shoulder and headed for the stairs. Drake was having prints framed this morning, but he'd get to the gallery later. Judith had agreed to go in early. As she reached the landing, the phone began to ring. *Drat! Everyone else is out.* She turned back to the hall extension.

"Judith, I'm glad I caught you before you got away this morning." At the other end of the line Drake sounded uncharacteristically excited.

"I'm on my way out the door. You need for me to do something?"

"Get to the gallery fast. I'll meet you there. Take your sketch pad. I'm at Sue Chow's framing shop, and across the street, at the Vanderhills' shop, Dondie is cleaning a piece of furniture. Looks like she's going to be a while. I'll pick you up with the gallery van. You can stay in the van and sketch while I take the prints in for framing." Drake's instructions seemed unnecessarily complex.

"Why can't I just drive over and park and do some sketches?" Judith protested. "I'd make better time. The girl might finish and go in before we get there."

"Because your jalopy is about as invisible as a Caribbean sunset. No one will think anything about the gallery van parking in front of the shops, but you'd be spotted in about ten seconds in that orange crate of yours."

"You're right. I'll be at the gallery in ten minutes."

Maybe we caught a break at last. Twinges of excitement urging her on, Judith snatched her bag and raced down the stairs.

Mentally trying to hurry the van as Drake drove them to the framing shop, Judith squirmed with impatience. Any minute Dondie Marshall could finish whatever she was doing and leave. As their van was halted by the only traffic light in town, she rechecked her bag of supplies.

"Patience, Judith," Drake counseled. He pointed to the glove box in front of her. "My camera is in there; use it. It has a long-distance lens. If Dondie goes in before you have a chance to finish your drawing, at least you'll have a snapshot."

Judith pulled the camera out and checked the film. "I feel pretty comfortable with this one since we used it to photograph my paintings. I'll snap some pictures of her first, yes. Insurance in case I can't get the sketches."

At last Drake drew the van up to the curb before the framing shop. Across the street a girl in faded jeans and baggy sweater was sanding a small table. She worked with little enthusiasm and less skill, it seemed to Judith.

"She's still there," Drake said with relief in his voice. "Slide back in the corner and go to work. I'll linger in the framing shop as long as I can without being obvious."

Judith shook her head. "It has to be the camera. I can't get a look at her face from this distance. I can't see details."

"Here, try these." Drake took a pair of opera glasses from his pocket. "One reason I wanted to meet you at the gallery was so I could get them."

Judith raised the glasses to her eyes and fingered the focusing knob. "Yes, perfect."

Carrying a stack of prints, Drake left the van, and Judith got down to business, turning to a fresh page in her sketchpad and sorting out some charcoal and colored pencils. She took one more look through the opera glasses and then traded them for the camera. With the window down just a few inches, she focused the heavy lens and framed the picture for two quick shots. Feeling a little conspicuous, she drew back to glance around, wondering if she had been noticed. No one seemed to be paying attention to her or the van. She put the camera aside and, holding the opera glasses with one hand, began to sketch with the other.

Dad didn't give me much of a description to work from. She compared the girl before her with the person George Anderson had described. Brown hair, kind of bushy and thick, he'd said. Her eyes are the main thing, he'd told her. Pale grey eyes, "white eyes" he called them, with the iris almost as light as the whites. "I hope I can get them right. Anybody who met her would remember those eyes." She studied the face that seemed within touching distance.

Judith paused in her drawing but continued to observe the girl across the street through the glasses. She watched how the thin figure moved and how she held her head. *The shape of her head is easy enough and not something that changes radically.* Judith concentrated on the girl again. Dondie's face was more square than oval, she decided, and a heaviness in the brow gave her a furtive look. *With a decent haircut she'd be pretty. That mane of hair isn't just brown, either—it's chestnut and ash brown with hints of gold and honey. The bushiness comes from all that uncontrolled curl.*

Judith flicked her colored pencils over her sketch, catching just a few of the tones. She could fill in the rest later. *If she were my girl, I'd get her to a good stylist and get that hair thinned and her eyebrows shaped. Nice nose, good and straight without being dominant. And that mouth—lots of passion there. Bee-stung, they used to call it. Sensuous—almost pouty. Damn. If that girl had someone to show her how to use what she's got, she could be a knockout. A haircut, a little lipstick, and some foundation to correct the line of her cheeks, and she'd be stunning.*

The girl leaned forward to sand the far edge of the table. As she did, her shapeless sweater pushed against the tabletop, giving a clear outline of a youthful bosom no longer obscured by her baggy garment.

And she's got a figure under there, too. Judith filled in the sketch. *I'll just bet she's begun to look at boys. And somehow, being boys, they'll realize there's something there worth looking back at.*

"Get what you came for?" Drake opened the van door.

"Mostly," Judith told him without looking up, her pencil still dancing across the page. "I'll have to finish up later, fill in color and shading to some extent. I'm not sure I got the eyes just right, and eyes are so important to a portrait, even one dashed off as quickly as this one. Dad was right about hers being unique." She stretched her fingers to ease the kinks.

"Looks good to me." Drake peered over her shoulder. "Were you able to make her look thirteen or so?"

"I don't know, Drake." She turned over a page. "This is what I came up with for the younger version. Do you think it will do?"

He shook his head. "I can't see a lot of difference in the two except she doesn't have the womanly curves beginning to show in the first one."

"She's a hard subject. I tried to capture the girl in what is now a young woman. I'll see what Dad remembers. If you can develop the photographs for me, I'll have more to work with."

"Can do. The darkroom at home is still set up." Drake started the engine and headed the van back toward the gallery. They'd be late opening, but the delay was in a good cause. Turning in the drive at the back of the whitewashed building a few moments later, Drake braked and the van came to a slow stop against the back wall. Judith put the camera in her bag, popped open her door, and wriggled out, pulling the straps of her canvas bag over her shoulder as she slid down from the vehicle.

She followed Drake's dapper form up the back steps, noticing with relief that no cars were parked in the visitor lot. Unlocking the door, Drake held it for her to enter. Judith flipped on lights and adjusted the thermostat to wake up the ancient furnace.

"It's like ice in here," she complained and zipped her jacket closed. "It's colder in here than it is outside."

"This is the end of the old blower. The unit is shot, and I'm getting a new one." Drake lifted one eyebrow and had a sly glint in his dark eyes. "I've called. We'll have a new furnace in by the weekend."

"The clients will probably complain about the inconvenience and racket, but it'll be worth it." Judith handed Drake the camera and tucked her bag into a small locker. "I hope I got that sketch right." Still distracted by her work, she pulled out the drawing case and looked at the sketch under the office lights. "I don't know. I think there's something wrong with the eyes." She put the sketchpad back in the case and closed it. Then she realized Drake had said something out of character. *Disrupt the gallery during a holiday week? One of our busiest times? What's he thinking?* "Drake, we have a lot of people in here between Christmas and New Year's. A new furnace will kill the tours."

"Then we'll close the gallery until New Year's."

"Close the gallery? You can't do that!"

"Why not? I own the damn thing, don't I? And with a work crew coming in for the new furnace, doesn't it make more sense to close?"

"It does when you put it that way." *I guess it will be easier to close while the workmen are here, especially with me gone.* She turned her attention back to the sketch in her hand. "We've got sketches, and the photos, but what do we do with them now? Claire can't do a thing with the pictures here and her in Dallas." Judith thought a minute. "If she still has phone service, I can call her at the apartment and tell her we have them. Maybe we can send a Special Delivery."

Drake turned to face her. His mouth narrowed in a determined line, and his hooded eyes darkened. "Oh, your pictures will get to Claire, and not by mail. I'm going to take them to her myself, just to be sure they get safely into her hands."

"*You're* taking them?" Judith wasn't sure she heard correctly.

"Another reason to close the gallery. I'm taking the

sketches and photos tomorrow morning. I should be at Claire's by late afternoon."

"But Drake, she won't... I mean, Claire isn't likely to welcome a visit from you." She admired Drake's resolution, but Judith doubted it would move her sister. "She won't be thrilled to see you, even if it is in a good cause." Judith bit her tongue to keep from saying more. Why should she interfere if Drake was going to close the gallery anyway? Judith would be gone, out of the line of fire, and Drake could take care of himself. As long as he got the pictures to Claire, was the means he chose any of her business? "Claire will be furious, Drake."

"Judith, it's time your sister and I had a long, uninterrupted talk about some things. She won't do it here, so I'm going to her. This business of the bar in Arlington and the pictures of the girl make as good an excuse as I'm apt to get. I know that I'm running a risk. This may ruin any chance we have of getting back together, but dammit, I'll find out where things went wrong for us before either of us comes back to Santa Rita."

****

By the next afternoon the temperature had dropped abruptly. The first real storm of the winter was blowing in. Audrey shivered. *Central Texas would bring in some actual winter right now.* She'd been caught between an office in Barlow and home with only her cardigan. Shaking in the Canadian wind that invaded the hills of Santa Rita, she rushed to gather the family mail at the curbside box. The envelopes made a double handful that she was glad to tumble onto the hallway table as she drew the warmth of the house around her like a welcome cloak.

"Sounds like Jack Frost has come to stay," George remarked over the file folders filling his desk in the room behind her.

"The wind is bitter, and the mercury dropped twenty-five degrees in two hours." Audrey rubbed her hands to warm them and sorted through the envelopes. A good many, she'd learned in the last few weeks, would contain anonymous, hostile messages. She'd opened one or two in the beginning, unprepared for the ugly, vicious accusations people mailed to George Anderson. The public gossip and whispers were bad enough, but the hate mail made her ill. Since the first few, she'd gathered all unidentifiable mail together and handed it on to Hal. She didn't know if anything in the envelopes proved useful to the case, but Hal shielded her from the psychological blow such mail carried. She saw a number of letters and catalogs for Judith, a few things forwarded to Claire, and a half dozen envelopes for Audrey herself. With both her sisters gone, Audrey put their mail aside and thumbed through her own. Glancing at the return addresses, she concluded some of her clients had paid her end-of-year invoices.

She gathered her dad's mail into one pile to leave in his study. One elegant creamy envelope caught her attention. The return address read "Institute for Civil War Studies, Richmond."

"Dad, you have mail from Richmond. Want it?"

"Oh, you bet. I've been hoping for something from them." He took the envelope she handed him and studied the address. "It comes from the right place."

Puzzled, Audrey watched her father slit the envelope, cutting the flap carefully. He drew out a single sheet of heavy bond and read the short paragraph. A sly smile crinkled the edges of his mouth.

"Yes, indeed it is," he murmured, nodding at the page in his hand.

"What is it, Dad? Did you just win the lottery or something?"

"Just about that good, Audrey. You remember, before all this business with the Marshall girl started, I sent off a proposal to someone about my book on Jubal Early? I contacted this institute in Richmond. They're interested and would like for me to send them the manuscript when I have it completed."

"Oh, Dad, after all these years you've spent working on that book, you deserve to have it published. Maybe the time you invested these last few weeks will have some good result after all."

At her words the light in his eyes dimmed and the smile vanished from his face. "If the trial doesn't go the wrong way."

"Well, I think we should celebrate." Audrey refused to let the dark cloud hanging over them rob her father of this moment of triumph. "I'll pull a steak out of the freezer, make some pasta with garlic, and toss us a salad. We have a whole pecan pie left, and I think I can even find some whipped cream to go with it. We have a good reason to 'festivitate' as Judith used to say. It's not every day we have a famous author added to the family tree."

"Oh, you don't have to go to that much trouble, child, not for just the two of us," George insisted. "And I don't have a book in print yet."

"But you're going to, and we'll all be here to celebrate when you do."

They were able to put the everyday worry out of their minds for a while and enjoy the dinner Audrey prepared. *Good to see Dad laugh again.* Audrey realized it had been weeks since she'd seen him relax and be the man she'd grown up adoring. He tickled her with tales he'd found in his research about the colorful Civil War general and his salty way of expressing himself.

"Lee loved that old coot Jubal Early, heaven knows why. They were as different as white lightning and fine French wine," George concluded.

"Do we have a family connection, Dad? I mean the general's middle name was Anderson, wasn't it? Is he a relative?"

"I've wondered myself, Audrey, but I've never found a family tie." George was about to launch into another tale when the doorbell rang.

Audrey pushed her pie and coffee to one side of the low table in the family room. "I can't imagine who'd be coming at this time of night." She touched the switch and flooded the front porch with light. Through the frosted glass she could see two figures, Hal and Jared, huddling in the inhospitable night.

"What brings the two of you out in this cold? You aren't dressed for the arctic blast out there. Come back to the den, and I'll get you coffee. There's pie left, if you want some."

The two men, wearing only sweaters and casual slacks, followed her lead and stood before the fire. She passed them mugs of coffee and resumed her place on the sofa, waiting for one or the other to explain their unexpected arrival. Jared and Hal exchanged looks. Hal shrugged and took a seat on the sofa next to her.

"We've been at the office kicking things around, trying to figure out what to tell you. We decided we'd better let you know that Jared had a letter today from the school up at Siding. It got held up in the holiday mail, I suppose, because the school sent it before Christmas. It's a reply to our request for information on the Marshall girl. All it says is that the school in Siding received the request to transfer the girl's school records to Santa Rita and has done so. If we have further questions, we should contact the Santa Rita School. End of response."

"But that's *no answer*," Audrey wailed. "It puts us right back where we started. The school here doesn't have anything."

George put his coffee cup aside and leaned back into the worn blue chair. "Well, that seems to be the story of our search, doesn't it? A one-yard gain, fall back two, and punt."

"At least you got some good news today. That offsets this disappointment a little," Audrey reminded him. Her own heart ached with frustration and despair, but she couldn't let her father see how deeply Hal's news had affected her.

"We need to hear some good news." Hal apparently read the suggestive look Audrey gave him. "Tell us what happened."

George hesitated, but Audrey knew he couldn't keep silent about the only bright moment he'd had in weeks. Briefly and with modesty, he described his progress with his manuscript and the interest the institute was showing in it. He took the letter from his pocket so everyone could read it.

"That is worth some celebrating," Jared agreed. "I

just wish we'd been able to bring some equally promising news to you."

Audrey picked up the dessert plates and cups, her agitation making the china and silver rattle. "It makes me so angry to think that the people up there, people who knew that girl almost all her life, won't give us a name or an address. One person could make all the difference to Dad. Someone up there must know what happened to wreck the life of the girl three or four years ago. Siding can't keep the rumor mill quiet any more than Santa Rita can."

Hal caught her hand, stopping her frenzied clatter. "You're right, Audrey. People up there have known this girl for years, and people love to talk. We just need to tap into that well of information."

"The school turned us down, Hal. They don't care to get involved in Santa Rita business. They as much as said so." Audrey left the plates and cups on the bar and drew a long breath. "We'd better hope Claire has some results in Arlington."

Hal leaned against the bar. "I don't think we're ready to give up on Siding, Texas, just yet, not till we've tried tapping that well of information in person. As soon as Judith gets back, and school is in session again, how about you and me making a little field trip? I think Siding is due a visit from some interested parties from Santa Rita. Let's see how much we can learn from the gossip mill up there."

****

Claire heard the wind rising outside her apartment. She shivered at the sound and dismissed the idea of going somewhere for dinner. One bottle of soda remained in the fridge. She didn't feel like eating anyway. That bottle, a few cans of cat food, and two barstools were all that was left of the cozy home she'd made for herself. The rest had gone in the moving truck an hour before. Well, it was finished. She was resigned to the change, she assured herself, and wondered where she would be the next time she saw her pretty red sofa or used her treasured Fiesta ware. A tray of ice melted in the sink, and she'd put a chipped cup in the trash. She retrieved the cup and rinsed it, plunked the scraps of ice in, opened the soda, and poured. The drink foamed and fizzed, bubbling up as she filled the cup. Though meager, it was all the dinner she could manage.

Sheer exhaustion zapped her, leaving Claire no will to resist a blue wave of loss. Her secure life was all over. The work that had taken her interests and talents was gone. The pretty place she'd made into her own nest was nothing but empty cells and silent space. If she let herself go back, let her mind follow her heart, one last piece would shatter her soul—Drake. Their marriage had ended "not with a bang but a whimper," leaving her a heap of bitter regret. Claire pushed memory aside again. She had no energy left to deal with that pain. It still could overwhelm her.

The apartment was packed and cleared. She'd ordered the utilities to be shut off, and her mail was going to Santa Rita until she had a permanent address. If she didn't need to pay some final bills and close her bank account, she'd go back tonight. That had been her plan. She should have been on the road before dark, but the moving van had been delayed by the awful traffic. Now Claire wondered where she'd sleep this bitter, windy night. A hotel, she supposed, but not yet. Not for a while, she decided. Not until she'd had one last luxurious soak in her pretty tub. She had just enough lemon verbena bath salts left in the jar for one final tub. She'd kept a bath sheet and hand towel out of the packing, too. *I'll have a good soak and put on something fit to wear before I try to find a place for the night.* She pulled herself up from the bar, feeling a protest from every tired muscle. A persistent pain burned between her shoulders, and her knees didn't want to straighten out when she stood.

The bathroom mirror confirmed her worst fears. Waist-length brown hair fell in limp strands around a face marked with dust and weariness. The pansy-brown eyes looking back at her were dull and shadowed. She certainly couldn't go to a hotel looking like a waif of the storm. Claire turned on the taps and waited as water billowed and steam began to fill the room. She tossed the last of the fragrant crystals into the water, leaning over to catch the scent floating up to her. Peeling off her grubby white shirt and soiled slacks, she slipped into the foam.

An hour later, wearing a silky sweater and tailored winter white slacks, Claire wound her hair into a damp but serviceable bun at the base of her neck. In fresh clothing and clean hair, she could face the necessity of finding a hotel for the night. She was too tired to drive far, she knew. The wind had grown stronger while she was in her bath. It sounded as if all the lost souls of hell were screaming at her window. The howl made her cringe at the mere idea of going out into that whirlwind. Driving would be worse. Maybe she could just stay— no, what was she thinking! She couldn't stay here through the night. She had no bed, no pillow, not even a sheet or blanket for cover. In an hour or so the utilities would shut down. She would be cut off without heat or light. No, staying here was out of the question. She must push herself out the door, get on the road, and face the elements. She felt relieved she didn't have that picture of Dondie Marshall. Claire didn't know where she would have found the stamina to take the search to Arlington.

Not much left to gather up, Claire assured herself thankfully. She'd packed her suitcase, though she still had a few toiletries in the bathroom. A minute or two took care of that chore. The cat food could ride safely in the trunk. The only hard things to load would be the barstools. They were two of the set of six that had framed the breakfast bar in the Anderson house for as long as she could remember. She'd borrowed them for sentiment as much as for their decorative value. *I have to take them back.* Hauling them down the stairs, across the parking lot, and wedging them into her back seat would be a pain—especially as she'd have to make the trip twice. She'd never be able to navigate the stairs if she tried carrying them together. At least she had only a single flight of stone steps to manage. Claire moved the suitcase near the door and piled the cat food beside it. No, not just the two trips to the car with the barstools, she realized—one trip with the suitcase, another with the bag of cat food, and two final ones with the stools. Too much, her weary body protested, way, way too much. Claire slumped onto a barstool and put her head down. No, she *could not* do it. She couldn't make that trip four times against a raging, icy wind.

Claire wasn't sure how long she sat at the small bar, but it was long enough that the hand under her head became numb. Sitting up at last, she listened to a constant banging somewhere outside. She thought the wind had blown something loose, a door or shutter perhaps, and it was flapping against the building. The howl of the wind, though not as fierce now, made it hard to gauge direction. She listened again. No, the hammering sound came from the building entrance near her apartment. It sounded more like a fist demanding entry for a human visitor than the elements searching for a way into the building. Maybe one of the tenants had gone to the garbage cans or out to a car in the parking area and been locked out. She'd done it herself once. Shivering at the thought of anyone facing the wild elements, Claire stirred herself to make the trek to the outside door.

Frigid currents swept the hall, almost freezing her breath as Claire scurried along the passage and down the steps. As she reached the massive door, another round of banging began.

With all the haste her cold fingers could manage, Claire fought the stubborn, unyielding pushbar. The latch gave way, and she heaved the door open. It took all her strength to overcome the force of the wind. Corridor lights fell on the face of the man standing outside, and she stepped back in confusion and dismay as he crossed the threshold and pulled the door shut behind him.

"Drake Chandler! You can't be here, not here of all places. Not here and not now!" She moved back, trying to put the entrance hall between them.

"Claire Anderson *Chandler*," he echoed with a slight emphasis on the last name. "Why not here? And why not now?" He held out a heavy envelope to her. "I brought you the Marshall girl's pictures. Your Dad needs help, and I could do that much."

"Thanks! Now go away!" She snatched the envelope and ran up the steps toward her own door. Footsteps thudded behind her. She spun to face him. "All right, you've accomplished your mission. Get out."

Adrenaline coursed through her as she wrenched open the door of her apartment. Resentment at his intrusion warred with a crazy urge to throw herself into his arms. Resentment won, and she grabbed the doorknob, intending to slam the door in his face. The lights flickered once, flickered twice—then the apartment plunged into unrelieved darkness.

Chapter Nine

"Do you really think Audrey should make this trip? She has commitments, and George will be alone." Jared addressed his question to Hal, but he watched Audrey.

"I need her there," Hal answered. "She'll be effective in places where I would be obtrusive."

"You're the attorney, you have the expertise," Jared countered.

"But Audrey's the expert in a dress shop." Hal thumbed to a page in the yellow tablet beside him. "The Marshall girl's mother, Donna, worked in one. Audrey knows how to get information in a place like that. The women in the school office will be more forthcoming to another woman. I can manage the county records, verify legal sources, and check out convenience stores and gas stations. But she'll do better in the distaff world. And at least one of her sisters will be back before we're gone."

"Taking time off is hard, though," Audrey admitted. "I'll have to scrunch everybody a little. Tons of updates come at the first of the year." She headed for the hall table. "Let me see what I can juggle."

Though the hall table was still piled with mail, her appointment book was on top.

"Check the thermostat while you're there," George called. "It feels colder."

Audrey tucked the appointment book under her arm, grabbed the loose mail, and checked the wall thermostat. *It is chilly in here.* As she opened the front door to check the outside gauge, a frigid blast took her breath. She plunged back into the house shivering.

"It's below freezing and still dropping." Teeth chattering, she hurried to the warmth of the fireplace.

Jared pulled on his sweater. "I'd better get going. The pipes at the house aren't wrapped yet, and if I wait, I'll be fixing broken pipes till Easter. Audrey, can you give Hal a lift home? We came in my car."

"Sure. He mustn't walk home." She poked at Hal's sweatered shoulder. "You aren't dressed for an arctic blast, either of you."

"Forgot you have winter in this part of the world. Thought you'd outlawed it," Hal quipped.

George grinned. "No, we just canceled it the last four or five years. Looks like this year we get it back."

As her father walked Jared to the door, Audrey passed the mail to Hal. Without comment, she flipped open her appointment book, paging through her notes.

"All of this came today?" He fanned the stack. "Have you opened any of them?"

She looked up in time to catch the grim, set look about his mouth.

"Today's lot was heavier than usual, and no, I don't open them anymore. One batch was enough to turn my stomach. I pass them on for what they're worth."

"And damn little value to the lot." Hal tossed the stack into the briefcase beside him. "I'll check them. Maybe some concerned citizen out there knows something and wants to make contact but can't do it directly."

Audrey glared at the untidy sheaf edging the top of the case. "Don't we ever get one that doesn't malign Dad? Isn't there even *one* that supports him?"

"Sure, we actually get a few positive ones, and if there's a name, I send a note thanking the writer." He paused while she looked down the pages outlining her appointments for the New Year. "How does the schedule look?"

"I'll manage," she said at last. "It's tight because most of the offices are closed between Christmas and New Year's, so I'll be playing catch-up. The second week looks better. I can get the last three days and the weekend open. Will that do?"

"I'd feel better if we could go right away," Hal admitted. "I want to get something nailed down to give your dad some positive action."

"Does it look that bad, Hal?" George stood quietly at the side of the room.

"I'd be lying if I said it was a walk in the park, George. I don't want to mislead you. If we'd been able to get that picture to Claire, take a look at that place in Arlington, I'd feel better."

"But we did," Audrey interrupted him. "Judith made sketches and got a couple of photos yesterday. She spent all evening with Dad, refining her drawing to get a picture of Dondie at thirteen from what he could remember. We think she had pretty good luck."

"But Claire left for Dallas the day before, and Judith left this morning. So now…"

Audrey put her small hand over his. "No, Drake closed the gallery for a day or two, so he's delivering Judith's sketches to Claire."

"I knew I liked that man," Hal exclaimed. "And he might help with that search in Arlington. He'll have an easier time asking questions in a blue-collar bar than your elegant sister."

"You two are going to be a while getting this sortie to the Panhandle planned, probably?" George inquired.

Audrey had taken a book of road maps from the bookcase and added it to the pile of things on the table. Hal's tablet and a fan of pencils filled the rest of the space. "We have quite a bit of planning to do," she agreed. "We have schedules to manage. We aren't just running to San Antonio or even Dallas. We're facing *terra incognito*, and we need to prepare for the unexpected."

"Hal, I hate to see either of you out in this weather later. Why don't you spend the night?" He gestured toward the stairway and the second floor of the house. "We've got two empty rooms upstairs." He paused. "No, we'd better not consider Judith's room. It's a bombsite after all the packing she's done this week. Anyway, there's an empty room for you, Claire's room, if you want it, and I can lend you some pajamas. No need for Audrey to get out tonight, and you two can work out your plans without interruption."

Audrey looked at her father's worn face. "Are you not feeling well, Dad?"

"Child, I'm tired, just plain tired. You and Hal and Jared are handling the legal end of things well, and I'm trying to believe my future doesn't include a jail cell down in Huntsville. I'm going to drive over to the University library tomorrow for some research. Get away for a bit. I have enough people worrying over my business, and I think I need a break." He bent down to pat Audrey's shoulder affectionately. "I've got work to do tomorrow, so I'll say goodnight."

Audrey kissed her father goodnight and watched him mount the stairs. Though he looked weary, he had firmness in his step, and he held his head with pride.

"He's quite a guy, that George Anderson," Hal said in admiration. "I don't know many people who would handle this mess with as much dignity as he has. I'm sure I couldn't do it."

"How could anyone think he'd rape a student? He'd die rather than hurt any one of those kids."

Hal stirred the flames in the fireplace. Gold sparks flew and the fire brightened the russet tones of his hair. "The Anderson girls aren't to be taken lightly either." He put an arm around her to bring her beside him. "Especially this one."

"We have plans to make," she murmured against the nap of his sweater. "It's a long drive and we need…" His lips touching hers stopped both words and thought. The evening held only the warmth of his body and the synchronized beating of their hearts. Time and the problems it carried dissolved around her.

He drew back at last, when the world and its care had lost all meaning, and loosened the clip that held her hair to let the strands cascade through his fingers. "No one else ever sees you like this, Audrey. You keep your hair pulled back, hiding all its shimmer and sheen. And impish thoughts lurk behind those green eyes. How do you keep that side of you, the sparkle and the shine, from spilling out?"

"I don't think I have sparkle and shine, not unless something strange happens to me when you're around."

"Oh, no, it's nothing to do with me, my girl." His

warm breath stirred in her hair. "I think your practical, level-headed, responsible attitude is a cover-up for the romantic dreamer inside. You live a secret life in your head, Audrey Anderson, full of lace and waltzes and starlight. I know that about you."

"No, there's nothing romantic about me," she protested but wished that he were right.

"Oh, no?" A wicked gleam shone in his eye. "I think I can prove it." He stepped back, his look speculative and a little amused. "What do you have on, Audrey?"

Surprised at the turn his words had taken, she looked down. "A ski sweater, a pleated skirt, wool socks and loafers."

"Outside, very sensible." His long fingers brushed across her shoulders. "But I'll bet what's underneath isn't so practical."

Audrey blushed. How could he know that? She did indulge herself in pretty underthings, but she didn't broadcast the fact.

"Bet you don't sleep in fuzzy pajamas or a flannel gown, either." He stopped and the twinkle in his eyes brightened. "I'd say, satin nightgowns, maybe in a shimmering blue, with silky quilted robes in the winter and whispering chiffon in the summer."

The flush in her face must have gone neon. Audrey felt the heat radiating from her cheeks. The man was either psychic or he'd asked Judith.

"Oh, Audrey, don't look at me as if I'd spied on you. It's your nature." He wrapped her in a bear hug that welcomed and felt familiar. "Your face gives you away. I can see sympathy for that Marshall girl in your eyes every time we talk about what might have given her so much pain. You feel her anguish yourself. You hurt for your sister Claire and the muddle her life is in. It's obvious that her shattered romance touches you. Judith doesn't see or appreciate the way Jared feels for her, but you try to bring them together. All that warmth and caring are the other side of you. You're a romantic with dreams and hopes and valentines ready to spill out. You know it, but you haven't recognized the person to show it to."

Hal ruffled her hair and drew her to the sofa to sit. "I said you have some serious courting coming as soon as we clear George." One finger tilted her chin and his lips grazed her lightly. "I think we'd better plan that drive to Siding before I forget that I intend to wait that long."

****

Drake could see the intent in Claire's face. When she grabbed for the door, he knew she meant to slam it in his face. Then she'd retreat into that frosted silence where she took refuge. A half-second behind her, he thrust up a hand to stop the closing arc. As the door slapped against his hand, the lights flickered and the apartment plunged into darkness.

"Turn loose!" Claire tugged to break his grip.

"Not this time." He sidestepped as the door slammed closed.

For a moment Claire's attempt to open it pushed it into his back. Then abruptly he felt her release the knob and pull away. A hint of her scent drifted to him. Drake reached out. His blind grasp met fabric, a clinging knit, and he felt the round warm skin beneath. A hand, slim and pliant, caught his.

"Claire?" His sense of her presence intensified in

the dark. Her hand felt fragile in his, the fine bones almost birdlike in their delicacy. "Are you all right, ladylove?" The old name slipped from his lips unplanned. A tremble shook her. Without thinking, he caught her to him.

"I'm just very tired, Drake." Her attempt to move away was a pathetic token gesture. "Please leave now. I have things to do still. The movers were late, the utilities are off, and the weather…" She didn't go on.

"The movers have been here?" Drake surveyed the darkness around them. Though little light came through the uncurtained windows, he could see no furniture in the room. "Everything's gone?"

She sighed. "I wanted to get it over with."

He heard a note of wistfulness in her words. Coming back to all the memories she'd run from had to be so hard for her. "So what were you going to do? Drive back tonight?"

"I thought so, but the truck was late, and I didn't get everything wound up. I have a little stuff to take with me. I was about to haul the bits and pieces to the car and get a room somewhere for the night."

"No rooms around for miles, Claire. The airport grounded a bunch of flights because of that gale force wind. For fifty miles in any direction everything with a bed in it is booked."

The slim form beside him shook with a shudder of exhaustion. She couldn't go on like this, he thought. She'd pushed herself to the limit.

"Have you had dinner?" He remembered from their life together the first thing Claire did when pressured or weary was to lose her appetite.

"No, I pitched anything that was open and gave the

rest away." A shoulder shrugged under his hand. "I couldn't eat anyway. I was too tired to deal with it." She moved away from him. His eyes were adjusting to the minimal light enough to make out the white of her slacks and sweater. Following her, he found the bar with two high-backed stools beside it. Claire pulled herself into one of them. He dropped the envelope with Judith's pictures on the tile top. Claire's slight silhouette defined a body at the end of endurance. He touched her shoulder gingerly, as he would a wild bird that might injure itself if trapped, and was startled when she let her head rest against his hand.

"Claire, you can't go on like this, love," he began. "Between the worry over George, your firm going under and taking your job with it, moving home, all the mindless rumors circulating in town, you've had more than your share of burdens."

A silent sob shook her. "I know it's selfish of me to act like this, but I've lost everything I've worked for, Drake. I gave everything to the firm. It was my life, my family, my whole world. And this apartment—it's the only place of my own I've ever had. I planned every inch, saved and saved to buy just the right pieces. When I'd come home at night, tired and drained, it lifted me. Just to see my things—each one something special— was a blessing. I could shut the door and be in my own place. The life I worked for vanished overnight. Nothing is left except some boxes."

Drake knew what it was to lose everything that made life meaningful. "You can have it again, darling. This isn't the end of anything. You'll have work you love and a place of your own again."

"We don't know that, Drake. Dad could be

convicted of this awful thing. He could go away, for years and years. At his age, it could be a life sentence. If that happened, I couldn't leave Judith and Audrey to face it alone. I'd have to stay and try to make things easier for them. I couldn't leave Santa Rita again, not if the worst should happen."

Drake turned the swivel seat of the barstool and took her in his arms. She didn't resist. She seemed limp, without strength or will, and he tucked her closer. "It isn't going to happen that way, love. Jared and Hal are doing all they can, and I believe the truth will come out."

He sensed by her silence that she'd passed the point where she could plan the next hour. "Look, you need food and a night's sleep. You can't stay here. With no electricity, this place will be a deep freeze in an hour or so. We've got to get you out of here."

"I suppose," she agreed, but her voice held little interest. "I'll find a phone booth and make calls. I'll find something."

"Nothing closer than Denton will have a room."

She rubbed her eyes. He remembered that gesture. It meant she was about to make a decision and hang the consequences. Trying to drive to Santa Rita—that one frightened him. She couldn't hope to make it, not as tired as she was, and a Canadian blast was howling over the state.

"You could stay with me." He felt her flinch at the suggestion. Good, she was still functioning, he thought. "No, I'm not pushing you for something else, love. I still keep Mother's suite at the Adolphus downtown. They know I'm coming. I have two bedrooms—one of them yours, if you can bear my company in the other one." He brushed a hand over her hair. The silken strands smelled of the same clean citrus scent she'd always used. A mental photo of Claire, her hair falling in inky waves, wearing nothing but an ivory silk slip, flashed in his memory. Ruthlessly he pushed the image away. He didn't need that distraction right now.

"I can't."

"Yes, you can. Just get your coat and tell me where your bag is. We'll leave everything else here and come back for it tomorrow when there's light enough to see what we're doing." He lifted her from the stool and waited.

"My coat and suitcase are in the closet by the door." She led the way through the dim room.

Drake found both and maneuvered the coat over her unresisting shoulders. "Your purse, house keys, anything else you need?"

"My handbag is hanging on the doorknob there." After a moment of groping, Drake found it, and Claire shrugged it over one shoulder. "This is all I need right now. Let's go."

Somewhere above the wind, Drake was sure he heard the angels singing.

****

Jared Pierce climbed out of the steaming shower, felt an icy draft up his naked back, and pulled on the jeans and sweater he'd tossed over the washbasin. Wrapping pipes in a gale was no easy trick. By the time he'd finished up, every bone in his body felt as if ice had replaced the marrow. His skin was leathery from the cold, and he'd cut his hands in a dozen places trying to protect the exposed surfaces. The shower had helped, and so did the generous slug of whiskey he poured into a tumbler.

Hal and Audrey, he mused, were spreading the net to find something to use to an advantage for George. He didn't have much faith in all that chasing around, himself. Most cases were won by digging out the law and looking for other cases that supported the client. In this case, of course, George needed a well-documented miracle. Not that Jared thought George was capable of swatting at a butterfly, much less hurting a child. Still, the law sometimes went astray. Jared had seen it. Look how many times his old man had started a fight in some honky-tonk, then managed to put the blame on the other party. Law didn't seem to fit too well in some instances, and George might find himself on the wrong end. Maybe Hal's creative defense work would be some help, but Jared would prefer to put his faith in black-letter law before making a wild chase to the Panhandle. A wild chase anywhere sounded bad to him, but the Panhandle in winter? Thanks, but he'd pass.

Jared finished his drink and padded around the cabin, putting his tools and supplies away. He liked the look of the place—a little primitive, but comfortable and uncomplicated, without fussies. Fussies, that was Aunt Min's word for things that had to be cleaned but didn't do anything practical to earn their keep. Things like ruffles and ornamental do-dads. He didn't need those, though if he had a woman living here, he guessed she'd expect some of that kind of thing. *A woman living here*. The thought made him smile. Only one woman he ever wanted living here. Judy Anderson and her prickly, flyaway temper. She was the only one he'd have, or he'd do without.

Jared opened the drawer beside the bed to look at

the framed photo he kept there. She'd been something that night, something every fellow at the dance had wanted to take home. The flare of pixie curls framed a delicately boned face. Her eyes really were that black, too, he told himself, with no change in color from the iris to the pupil—just a sheen of obsidian in a background of clear white. Eyelashes, too long to be real, though he knew they were, framed those expressive eyes to make dark fans on her flawless skin. She'd worn red that night, he remembered, the deep red of claret wine. That was before her mother died, before Judy put aside all color to live in one weird black outfit after another. Maybe in some way she was still in mourning.

Sliding the picture back into the drawer, Jared glanced at his watch. Almost midnight. She'd be in her hotel by now. She'd had a full day with the drive to New Orleans and then meeting with that gallery owner and doing whatever else it took to get her paintings up on the wall. The girl sure could paint. Jared didn't have a clue about what made something "Art," but he knew when he looked at one of Judy's paintings he could feel everything going on. He could feel the laughter or the tears or just the wonder that somehow lived right inside the canvas. However she did it, for sure Judy Anderson had magic when she took up a paintbrush.

The phone sat on the shelf by his bed. The round black dial looked like it was grinning at him, just daring him to put in a number and see if a certain voice answered. Oh, what the hell. He grinned back at the phone. She could only hang up, and probably would. One more rejection wouldn't be over his limit. He dialed, and the desk clerk put the call through.

"Hey, Lawyer Pierce, what's up?" Judy's voice sounded bright, even sassy.

"Just called to see if my painter girl got her pictures up."

"Half of them, just half. It takes forever to get the light and space right. Some canvases just can't hang next to each other, and I have to start all over. But the gallery and the owner are perfect."

Jared didn't want to hear her sing the praises of some other man. "I thought you should know we heard from the school in Siding. Guess they were afraid of getting involved in something, so they didn't send along anything useful. Just referred us to the Santa Rita schools."

"Oh, Jared, no! Is Dad upset?"

"No, he took it pretty well. He's heard from that bunch in Richmond, and they want to look at more of his book. I think that took the edge off his disappointment." Jared grinned at the whoop on the other end of the line.

"Dad might get published? Fan-damn-tastic!" She was silent a moment. "But this thing with Siding? We can't get any information about the girl? Guess we'd better hope Claire has better luck."

"Oh, Hal and Audrey have some wild plan to drive up to Siding and do some sleuthing on their own, maybe dig out the untold story. They're going as soon as you or Claire, one or the other, comes back. But Claire has to get that picture if she's going to track down the bar in Arlington."

"Drake shut down the gallery and dashed off for a head-to-head with my iceberg sister. It was the perfect excuse, but I don't know if he can get through to her.

With Drake in Dallas, the two of them can cover more territory and talk to more people. If there's nothing coming out of Siding to help us, we'd better pray Claire and Drake find something."

Jared had serious doubts about either plan bringing up anything useful, but he kept them to himself. He wouldn't blight Judith's hopes, not now, before her big show.

"So when are you getting back, Judy? New Year's will be a bummer without you. I've got some steaks waiting and a bottle of wine we can split." Jared waited for the explosion.

"Find somebody to share it, pal. I'm all booked up."

Jared laughed aloud. Judy was feisty, but she was also predictable. One of the things he loved about her was her flashing response to his teasing. "Well, why don't you come home and tell me what you'd like to do. I'm always open to suggestions."

"Just get my dad out of trouble and give him some peace and quiet," she answered, suddenly serious. "All I want is to have him back where he belongs and see this horrible mess go away."

"Oh, Judy baby, I will if I can. Hal and I are doing all we know to do. If there's anything we haven't tried, it's because we haven't thought of it. You know I love George Anderson as much as if he were family. I keep thinking one day he will be family. I want to pound on doors and shake people to make them listen to me. He's in the back of my mind no matter what else I'm doing."

"What do you mean, one day he will be family, Jared Pierce?" Judith's voice sounded huffy through the lines.

"You know what I mean, Judy. One day he's gonna be my father-in-law. One of these days I'll catch you at the right moment and you'll admit we belong together. You are going to marry me, Judy. Surely you know that."

"Jared Pierce, I don't know any such thing, and neither do you. You've been teasing me about getting married since I was fourteen years old. You've almost made a career out of a teenage crush. But maybe you better watch yourself, and be a little careful about proposing, my friend, 'cause if you get my daddy out of this mess, I just might turn around and say yes!"

Chapter Ten

For Central Texas the day was bitterly cold. The sun floated thin and pale in a buttermilk sky. Audrey plowed through her closet, pulling out the heavy winter things she hadn't worn in years, finally unearthing the down jacket and furry hood she'd bought the only time she'd attempted skiing.

Bundled as well as she could to keep out the seeping chill, Audrey left the house, ducked through the hedge, and scurried across the drive. She should go around; Dad was forever telling her that, but the cold was too intense for her to take more steps than necessary. The damp air made the temperature seem even lower. A rime of frost covered the brown grass, creating treacherous footing. Audrey looked anxiously at the black cowboy boots she'd "borrowed" from Judith. Her sister wasn't fond of sharing. Audrey knew she'd better take care of those prized lizard skins.

Shivering, she reached the car and hurried to start it. Hal needed to get to his office, and she had Jared's work to clear before the trip to Siding. As her little VW warmed, she noticed through a spot clearing in the windshield that her dad's grey Lincoln wasn't in the garage. She spared a hope he would enjoy getting away from Santa Rita for a while, escape into his research at the University library and find a respite from daily stress. Maybe, just maybe, he'd have real luck with his manuscript. A biography on a Civil War character probably wouldn't make the bestseller list, but it might draw some academic acclaim. Heaven knew George Anderson could use some accolades from somewhere.

Hal waved from the porch as she pulled to the curb. "I like your version of Puss-in-Boots, the furry cap and cowboy boots. And for a town that doesn't have winter, this place is putting up a good imitation." He puffed as he took the seat beside her.

"The cap and boots were all I could find to keep out the cold. The arctic blast must be in your honor. We hit record lows last night." Audrey guided her car into the street and made the corner turn at Main Street. "The river iced over for the first time since I can remember."

"So your dad told me." Hal squirmed to find space for his legs in the short compartment.

"You saw Dad? You must have been up with the birds. He probably left as soon as the sun began to rise."

"The cat seemed to think I was in his bed. He kept pushing me off the pillow. Finally I gave up and let him have it."

Audrey laughed. "He's Claire's cat, and you're in her room. I hope you aren't allergic to cats."

"No, fortunately, I like cats, though toenails in my neck aren't my idea of recreation. Why doesn't he come to you? With the other girls gone, I'd think you would be next."

"I shut the door."

"Because I was in the other room? Did it bother you to have me next door, on the other side of a single wall?" His tone teased a little, but she couldn't toss his question away with the same spirit.

She'd been aware of his presence, disturbed by the odd thoughts that drifted through her sleep, but Audrey had no intention of discussing any of that. "No, I close the door because Dad's door is opposite mine, and he sometimes gets up early for his tennis game. The light shines right in my face."

Hal looked dubious. He'd said her face was easy to read. Maybe he saw more than she wanted him to see. They needed a change of topic. "So you think we can go to Siding week after next? You can clear your appointments without too much trouble?"

Hal nodded. "I'm pretty sure I can. How about you? Will Judith have time to get her exhibit under way? Claire will be home in a day or two, I take it."

"If she got her affairs wound up. The weather might delay her. Otherwise I look for her tomorrow or the next day—unless Drake manages to find a crack in her armor. And, brother, I wish he would."

"Your romantic heart would like to see them back together."

"Romantic heart, nothing! Common sense demands it. They've loved each other all their lives, and they're both miserable the way things are now. I want to lock them in a room and tell them they can't come out till they settle things." Audrey gritted her teeth with exasperation.

Hal reached across to run one finger along her clenched jaws. "They'll have to work it out for themselves, Puss. It's not your fight."

She made a determined effort to override her annoyance. "I know, but Claire's so cold and closed up, and Drake's all but bleeding with the hurt he feels."

"I hate to see you focusing on them when you have a life of your own to lead." Hal tapped her cheek. "What do you want for yourself, Audrey? Where will you be this time next year?"

"Here, filing updates, squabbling with Jared, watching Judith pour her heart into her paintings, playing Scrabble with Dad."

"I don't think so."

"Why not? It's a good life."

He made a derisive sound, almost a snort, and ignored her comment as they reached his office. "Looks like you'd better park here. As usual, there's no place closer to the door."

She pulled into the one available space along the street and retrieved her leather case from the back. "I'll run to the post office, then on to get Jared's books caught up. That should give you time to clear up your calendar for our trip."

They hurried along the narrow sidewalk, their breaths leaving puffs of white in the frosty air. Shopkeepers had taken down the Christmas garlands and tinsel to replace them with the glitter of New Year's Eve. A new year coming, a new decade starting, Audrey thought, hoping it would be an easier one.

"We'll be in Siding a couple of days." Hal's words brought her back to the day's needs. "It's a pretty hard drive and we'll see a number of people, I hope."

"It's cold there, too. I'll need warm clothes. Is there a place to stay in that tiny town?" Audrey wondered what amenities their destination offered.

"I'll find accommodations somewhere so we aren't obvious in that isolated place." They reached his door, and Hal caught her hand before she could hurry on.

"When you come back, Puss, I'll have good maps so we don't spend our 'lost weekend' truly lost." He brushed a quick kiss across her lips.

"I thought that was you, Miss Anderson." The voice behind her was dry and cracked with disapproval. "Hoped you were a cut above your wayward sisters, but I guess the apple doesn't roll far from the tree. Carrying on in public, going off with a man—well, we'll keep praying for you all, praying for you to see the light."

Audrey looked beyond Hal's shoulder. Fred Vanderhill stood three paces away, a long wool scarf and a shapeless overcoat masking his identity. She wondered how much he'd overheard.

"Fred Vanderhill's right behind us," she whispered to Hal.

Hal turned to face the man. "Mr. Vanderhill, it's best if you and Miss Anderson don't have any conversation. The court might not understand that you had no questionable motives in speaking to her."

"Man's got to speak out when he sees wrong-doing." Vanderhill stuffed one hand deeper into his pocket and pulled out a handkerchief. His sharp nose reddened in the cold, and he wiped it absently. "You're working to get George Anderson off, aren't you? You're his lawyer?"

"I'm assisting."

"Don't know what kind of man could defend what Anderson's done. Ain't no defense, far as I can see. You planning to claim the girl's lying? That it?"

"Mr. Vanderhill, I can't discuss this case with you. The court will hear all of us. Till then, you should keep away from Mr. Anderson, his family, and his attorneys. We'll be taking depositions in a few days. Any contact before that would be detrimental to both sides."

Vanderhill shook his head. "Girl's not lying, you know. Young girl like that, she don't know enough about evil to lie, wouldn't think to make up that tale. She knows what lying would get her. 'Splained that to her real clear." He pulled the wool scarf closer around his hawklike face. "You're making plans with this woman, sinful plans. I'm telling you both, flat out, to mend your ways. No escaping retribution, not in this life or the next." He pushed between them and stalked away.

"Well, now you've met Fred Vanderhill," Audrey murmured in a low tone.

"Yes, and I feel a lot of sympathy for that girl living under his beady gaze. Her life must be grim in that environment."

"The thing is, Hal, the man's totally sincere. He really does live what he believes. He just can't leave the rest of the world alone. Whatever Dondie's reasons are for her accusations, he's doing what he thinks is right."

Hal put one arm around her shoulders. "I know. I even admire the old coot for taking up for the girl. But he's got to stay away from you and your family." He grinned a little. "Still, however wrong he is about why we're going off together, his version appeals to me."

****

Jared was bent over his desk, giving his complete attention to the plat map spread across it. He didn't look up as Audrey came in with a box under each arm.

"Mail!" she called to break his absorbed study.

"Hi, kid sister," he said as he finally became aware of her presence. "Did I win the door prize?"

"Just grab one of these before I drop it." She tried

to control the sliding package. "You have new binders and pages for your bankruptcy law books."

With little interest, he took one box and shoved it into a corner. "Never mind. Come look at this." He pulled the map higher on the desk.

"What's this? A new boundary dispute you've taken on?" She shucked off her gloves and down jacket. Upside down and covered in minuscule print, the map made little sense to her.

"Nope, it's the plat for Aunt Min's place." One thin finger traced a dotted line. "See, here's the old Winsted place and here's the Lindley ranch. I border both of them. My cabin's here."

Audrey wondered at this sudden preoccupation with real estate, especially Jared's own property, the place he'd bought from his Aunt Min a year or so back. The house was small, but she doubted he was planning to expand already.

"So?" Audrey looked where his finger pointed. "Isn't that where the old barn used to be? I remember picnics when we were kids."

"You got it. The barn stood till an ice storm finally disintegrated it. I was in law school then, and Aunt Min didn't rebuild it." He twisted the map and marked a circle around the point. "The foundation's still there, and it seems sound. Might need a little work, reinforcement, maybe some plumbing, but it's a good, big space with a view to the north over the river."

"What are you planning to build, Jared? You just renovated the cabin." Audrey saw flints of excitement sparking in his eyes. Those honest blue eyes couldn't hide a thing.

"Not for me—for Judy. A studio, a big, beautiful

studio with light and space and room for her to work. Can't you just see her out there?" Jared fell back into his chair, a look of sheer bliss flooding his face.

Jared fantasizing? Indulging in daydreams? "Jared, the question is whether Judith can see herself out there. She has a studio, right in our house. Why would she drive seventeen miles out in the country to paint at your place? What made you even consider such a plan?" Audrey hated to puncture his dream world, but stargazing wasn't like him.

"She won't be driving out to the studio. She'll be living there, with me." He grinned up at her. "You think I've lost my mind, don't you?" He squeezed Audrey's hand, almost painfully. "No, I haven't. I'm just looking ahead. I talked to Judy on the phone last night. I asked her to marry me."

Audrey sat on a corner of the desk. She let a resigned sigh escape. "You've been proposing to Judith since she was eighteen, and she's been saying no for just as long."

"Yeah, but this time, Audrey, she didn't say no." His grin threatened to split his face it was so wide.

"She said yes?" Audrey couldn't mask her disbelief.

"No, but she said maybe. She said if, and she said maybe. It's gonna be yes before long." He opened the desk drawer and pushed a small velvet box into her hands. "I stopped at the bank to get this out of the safety deposit box." Audrey snapped the box open and looked at the exquisite Celtic knots woven into a platinum band. The ring and the hope lighting Jared's eyes made her own eyes mist.

"Oh, Jared, I hope you aren't fooling yourself. I

hope this isn't just Judith being unpredictable." She handed the box back to him. "It's a beautiful ring."

He looked into the box before he closed it. "It is pretty, isn't it? I bought it for her years ago, but I've never had the nerve to show it to her." Pocketing the box, he stood and rolled the map into a narrow cylinder. "I'm not fooling myself, Audrey. She didn't say no this time. The charges against your dad rocked her. With her paintings in that gallery, she feels she's getting recognition. Both things affect her. Judy's changing, coming out of isolation. I hope by summer she'll let me build that studio for her. It feels right somehow."

****

I didn't commit, I really didn't. It was just a quip, a bit of banter. Jared knew I wasn't serious. He had to know I wasn't. Judith walked along Jackson Square, watching other hopeful artists sketch and paint the cathedral inside the square. A small girl tossed bread to a flock of squabbling birds. Judith whipped out her pencil and pad to make a quick sketch. *To be that young and have no fear of tomorrow.* Judith sighed and resumed her place against the aging iron fence.

The color and swirl of the French Quarter filled the air. Breezy, a little cool, but the sun flooded the sky with clear, sharp-edged light. She'd like to come here and paint, capture the colorful scene. Café-au-lait swished in her borrowed hotel cup, now cold, but she drank it anyway. She had to get to the gallery soon. The workmen would be arriving to hang the last of her paintings. Her canvases looked good on the walls highlighted by well-planned lights. And Robey Kearnes was a delightful, elderly man with a true love for her work. She was sorry she'd be leaving him before they had a chance for a deeper friendship.

Home, oh, yes, she wanted to get home. She had to know if Claire made use of the pictures and if Drake managed to get through her sister's defenses. He was in such pain, and Claire, well, Judith could see Claire in a different light. In drawing her sister, Judith had noticed the sadness that lingered below Claire's rigid poise. The ice maiden pose masked a woman with deep, turbulent feeling. Loss and anger were thinly veiled by her cool façade. Drake had his work cut out for him if he hoped to reach her sister.

Never mind Claire. Dad gets all the support and encouragement we have right now. Judith had spent the most time with her father since her mother's illness and death. The lingering threat of Patsy's illness had drawn them closer, as father and daughter fought to keep despair from overwhelming them. They'd tried to be optimistic and positive, even when they had so little hope. They'd supported each other through the last painful months. Audrey had helped—practical, sensible little Audrey, always ready to do whatever came to hand—but George and Judith dealt with Patsy's gradual decline. They took turns sitting at the bedside, worn out but unable to leave, fearing their beloved wraith would waken and find no one near.

Now Dad has his own rough going, and I'll be there for him. But what about Jared? What had come over her the night before? In a sane moment she'd never make the offer she had. Certainly she didn't mean to bargain with Jared over her father's case—and she wasn't marrying anybody. Not anybody—but especially not Jared Pierce!

Judith shook the dust from her black skirt, its

gypsy fringe fluttering in the breeze. She paced the walk along the picturesque scene, seeing nothing, her thoughts lingering in Santa Rita.

Jared's a small town lawyer, and he always will be, with no imagination and no ambition. He'll never dream of Paris or long to visit Rome. He can't see the difference between Van Gogh and Rip Van Winkle. We have nothing in common. And he's homely!

She didn't try for a nicer way to put it. Jared was long and rangy like an old hound dog. He managed his height pretty well—at least he didn't bang into things or get tangled in his own feet—but he was no Nijinsky. His snub nose always had a bit of sunburn from working out in the open. He'd rather string fence wire than sit still for her favorite jazz quartet. And he had freckles, a band of them, right across his sunburned nose and under his eyes. Nice eyes, as blue as the Santa Rita River on a summer day, but nothing romantic to make her heart throb. His hair couldn't decide whether to be brown or blond, but it stood up like summer thatch most of the time. How could she, a painter with an artist's eye for beauty, spend her life with him? She couldn't. That was the end of it.

Judith turned to hurry back to Royal Street and the gallery waiting for her, but Jared, or the thought of him, wouldn't let her alone. Judith thought she'd dismissed him but found herself remembering his strength and quiet support the morning her mother died. She rejected his hold on her but recalled the excitement she'd felt at a dance far back in their past when she'd known the power of being beautiful, at least in one man's eyes. His dogged persistence, his predictable proposals, his stalwart refusal to give up hope, a million pictures clipped from the pages of their lives filled her head.

But I did not say I'd marry him. Judith shook her head in denial. She didn't make that commitment, and he knew she wasn't serious. That being so, why did she contemplate their next meeting with such apprehension?

****

Claire caught herself pacing the length of the sitting room suite. *Stop*, she commanded herself and settled into the red velvet chair near the window. She forced her hands to rest quietly in her lap. Drake looked up from the paper.

"I know you had plans for today, but power lines are down everywhere. Parts of the city are still without electricity." He folded the page in precise fourths and turned to the first section. He'd always done that, she remembered, folded everything into equal parts, tidied away any trace of disarray. She'd once found it endearing. Turning aside, she hoped the painful memory didn't show on her face.

"Drake, I should have taken care of the bank issues first. Then I could go on home and worry with finding this bar later when the power is back on. I hate wasting time sitting here."

"But you *can't* go home, and you *are* stuck with waiting. I'll order breakfast. Room service can be up in a few minutes."

"But I told you I didn't want anything."

"You ate practically nothing last night."

She brushed away his concern. "Too tired to eat." She paced to the window again and looked down into Commerce Street. Its motion hadn't slowed in spite of the windstorm damage. "And I never eat breakfast."

"You used to."

She decided not to hear him. "I'm surprised that you kept this suite after Alice died. You never seemed to care much for the city."

"I didn't care for coming here with Mother. Her endless rounds of shopping and visiting and socials wore me out. I find myself coming often now. My brokers are here, and when I travel I like to use this airport to save transfers and plane changes."

Silence filled the room, as brittle as a cheap water glass. Claire pulled the frayed edges of her poise together. She couldn't stay in the same room with this man much longer. His presence drew her eyes and disordered her thoughts. Her carefully built peace of mind was dangerously close to crumbling.

"I was sorry when Dad told me about Alice's accident." She hoped the subject of his mother's death would send him away.

"The crash—such a terrible end for her. The casket had to be closed. She would have hated having people see her scarred and broken."

"Yes, she was very beautiful."

"I hoped you'd come for the services, Claire, but I know you and she never got on too well."

She turned to him in surprise. "Oh, no, we got on very well, Drake. She told me frequently that she cared a lot for me. She said I was probably the only girl she didn't mind sharing you with."

"I don't believe..." Drake stopped. "I didn't realize you two were that intimate."

Claire continued to look down into the street. A traffic light had frozen, and cars were beginning to clog the intersection. "I know you and your mother were very close, Drake. She adored you. I was glad she could make a little room in her life for me."

Drake came to the window and stood beside her, looking down at the mayhem forming in the street. She turned, surprised to see a deep frown wrinkling his face. Finally he laid a gentle but insistent hand on her shoulder. "Why, Claire, why did you go? What was so bad that we couldn't work it out?" His warm hand pressured her to face him. "I think we should at least talk about it. It's been so long. Can't we clear the air at last?"

"I see no point in going into it, Drake. Not now. It's too late to make any difference. I won't pretend, not any more. No one cares, no one is left to be hurt. Mom's gone, and so is Alice. Dad has misery of his own to live with. Judith and Audrey have their lives and aren't interested in ours." She dared to look up at him, into those dark, hooded eyes, and wondered at the power they still had over her.

He drew a harsh breath and rested both hands on her shoulders. Beneath her silky shirt her skin felt singed by his touch. "Claire, make me understand. I only know that you left, suddenly, with no explanation. I thought you were with your dad while your mother had surgery, and you'd be back. When you came home, you packed your things and moved into the dorm. I'm not pretending, Claire. I do not know, have never known, why you did it."

She couldn't bear any more. She could keep a contained, distant place for herself as long as Drake Chandler didn't become too real. Standing here, in Alice's formal, stately suite, with Drake dredging up the pain and the loss she'd endured that year, the one year of their short marriage, Claire couldn't remain detached and in control. She ripped herself away from his touch.

"I could stand it when you went inside yourself and closed me out. You had a thesis to write and were working hard to finish your internship as well. The demands on you from school were huge. So I could live with having only half of you when you were home."

"It was a pretty tough semester."

Claire gripped the back of the armchair for support. She had to get through this once and for all. This had to be the end of things for them. She'd break if the strain didn't stop.

"I knew it was stressful, and I tried to keep things quiet for you." She bit her lip, struggling to continue. "I knew your background wasn't like mine. You were an only child, wealthy and privileged. Life at your house was quiet, restrained, not like the rowdy place where I'd lived with younger sisters, and cats and dogs, and people banging in and out all day. We were noisy and demonstrative, and that wasn't good for you. Making a quiet home, especially in student housing, was hard, but I wanted you to be comfortable. I tried to be like Alice, dignified and poised, cool and elegant. You weren't happy. I could see it, so I tried to change, to be someone you'd want to come home to. Till you sent for Alice, I thought I was succeeding. Then I saw how far short I fell."

"I sent for Mother?"

Had he forgotten inviting his mother to their seedy apartment? Claire wondered. "I could have dealt with things better if I'd had time to think, but Dad called and told me Mom was in the hospital. She was going in for brain surgery, and her situation was grim. I had to leave. Even Alice saw that. I know she wanted to help us work things out, but maybe it was too late even then."

"Help us work out what, Claire? I can't see what we had to work out. School was a load for both of us, you working and carrying a full schedule, me in grad school. I had that internship, too, but conditions were temporary. They didn't affect our marriage."

He was still denying everything, she saw. Alice had been right. He was a lovely man, as long as he didn't have to deal with unpleasant situations.

"I could have managed everything, Drake. I could have been the cool, poised, gracious woman you wanted. I couldn't do it overnight, I guess. I was young, but I was willing. I'd have won your respect even if I couldn't have your love." She turned away. "I could have done anything, been whatever you wanted me to be, if you'd only—if you'd—" Her voice broke, and the last of her composure dissolved in wracking sobs. "If you'd just wanted our baby or cared a little that I lost it."

Chapter Eleven

Riveted to the floor, Drake watched Claire run from the room. Her white suede pumps blurred into the expanse of cream carpet. He forced his feet to follow her, his head reeling at her words. *A baby? Claire had been pregnant? She miscarried and I didn't know? It couldn't be—no—I would have known.* They'd shared two rooms in student housing and a bed too narrow for either of them to roll over. Two people couldn't live that closely and hide a secret, certainly not a pregnancy. Claire might think they'd talked things out, but Drake wouldn't let her come this far without finishing it. He bent to listen at the door but heard nothing through the aged panel. Even as he turned the knob, he knew the door was locked.

Drake tapped the doorplate, considering his next move. The antique hardware hadn't been changed in the years he'd stayed here. The stately hotel had been updated, but this suite still wore its vintage elegance and brass fittings. Tiptoeing to the bedroom opposite, Drake extracted the ornate brass key from the door lock. One key had always worked on both doors, he recalled. He returned to Claire's door and eased the key into the lock. It turned readily as the tumblers slipped into place. He opened the door.

Across the room, Claire whirled to face him, a

glass of water in her hand. She hurled it full force. It crashed into the doorframe near his head. "I don't want to see your face again!" He ducked another glass, but as he did, she reached for the water pitcher.

"Claire! We have to get this thing straightened out!" He dodged the pitcher, but it smashed against the wall, shattered, and the broken handle caught him on the ear. Ice water splashed his shoulder. Pain sharp as the shards of glass seared his ear from the assault, and drops of blood spattered his shirt. "Damn, woman, when you lose your cool, you go all the way."

Two pillows flew after the pitcher, one smacking him across the face. The knobby trim grazed his eyebrow. When Claire reached for the phone book, Drake knew he had to stop her before she heaved the five-pound weight at him.

"Enough!" He charged across the room and grabbed her wrists, anchoring the phone book between them. She gasped and tried to wrench herself free.

"I told you I didn't want to see you in this room!" Her struggles freed one hand. She raised it to slap him. He blocked her with his arm. She glared and ripped away from him. "Get out!"

"We're getting through this thing. I want to hear it all."

Shoving him away, Claire threw herself across the tester bed, wadding her white skirt and sweater beneath her twisted body, hammering pillows that flew in all directions. Racking sobs tore her. Crossing the room in three steps, Drake knelt on the floor beside the bed. She turned to face the wall.

"This won't do, love." Her wrenching sobs were muffled in the duvet. He'd never seen her lose control before. Hesitating, unsure how she would react, he rolled her over and lifted her to sit against the bolster. "You can throw all the bric-a-brac at me if you need to, but you can't throw accusations in my face and then run away, my darling. Tell me what I did, all of it. Then if you want to heave the phone book at me, at least I'll know why."

She tried to pull away. "Liar! You know!"

He pulled her to him. "No, Claire, no." She twisted in his grasp. "You're going to tell me, tell me everything that went wrong. But first there are three things you've got to know. One, I love you, have always loved you, and nothing changes that. Two, I did not know you were pregnant or that you'd miscarried. I would never let you go through that alone. And third, if after we talk, you want me to go, I will."

Claire's sobs subsided, but she'd lost the remote, hidden look. Drake took heart from that. "When were you pregnant, love? In the spring? Those last weeks?"

She leaned back into the pillows, resignation dulling her eyes. "The baby wasn't the beginning. I guess it was the end."

"All right, start earlier." He thought a moment. "You said I'd asked Mother to come. Let's straighten that out. I was as surprised as you were when she turned up. She hated being near the University. Students offended her."

"But she told me you'd asked her."

"Ladylove, listen. She came to present an internship to one of the art students. About that time, I got an offer from a small art gallery in New York. It meant a fellowship, too, and postgraduate work with some of the authorities in American folk art. I asked for time to decide, because your mom's treatments weren't going well. George expected surgery ahead. You'd be across the country if anything happened. Regardless, I knew you'd insist that I accept. So I waited, hoping for better news from home."

"That was the opportunity you dreamed about. You wouldn't keep it to yourself." Her tone was sullen, disbelieving.

He had longed to tell her but had held back. "I had to, for your sake, but I couldn't keep from thinking about it. I was torn."

"You went all silent and broody those weeks before spring break. You were worrying about what to tell me? How I'd feel?"

"I was, but news leaks in the art gallery and museum world. Mother heard about it from one of her dealers. She came to see us, hoping to keep me from accepting. If I did, she wouldn't have me to run the gallery for her when I finished grad school." Drake knew Claire's question before she asked it.

"So why did Alice say you'd sent for her? She didn't mention an internship or a New York gallery."

"When I met her at the hotel, she asked me about it, and I told her I hadn't even discussed it with you. For your mom's sake, she agreed to keep quiet."

"If she wanted you back in Santa Rita so badly, why didn't she enlist my help in keeping you there? With Mom's situation so precarious, certainly I would have agreed." Claire was sitting upright now, her mind engaged in their talk. Her emotional overload had eased. Drake decided she could face another truth, an ugly one.

"She could accomplish two goals, Claire. She

wanted to split us up and to get me back home as well." Claire's eyebrows rose in disbelief as he continued. "Alice didn't love you, my darling. Love wasn't necessary to Alice. I was a nice accessory, well-mannered and trained to her standards, and she never expected the situation to change. Our marriage was a blow to her. She did everything she could to stop it. When she couldn't, she made trouble and cast doubts at every opportunity."

"You really didn't ask her to come to me? To tell me what you couldn't, that we'd made a mistake and you'd decided I wasn't the girl you should have married?" Embers lit the dark shadows in Claire's eyes. He felt her anger.

"Is that how she did it?" He took her hands in his and kissed the place where she'd once worn his ring. "I should have known. She was much too consoling and supportive to be genuine." A question stopped his thoughts. "But why didn't you come to me? Why take her word for how I felt?"

"I brooded all day, telling myself she was wrong, she'd misunderstood." Claire buried her face in her hands. "I skipped my late class and took the bus over to her hotel to talk to her again, to make sure I was clear about what she was telling me, that you really wanted someone else. I saw you come out of the hotel with a girl, a beautiful girl. She kissed you. Alice had said you had someone else, and I saw her. I didn't need for Alice to say it again. I saw the two of you together."

Drake wrapped her close, his body rocking hers in his embrace. "Damn you, Alice, if I could get my hands on you this minute, I'd wring your conniving neck." He brushed a hand over the coil of hair at the back of

Claire's head. A pin had worked loose. He began freeing the rest of them. "Claire, you saw the young woman who received the internship at the gallery. Alice asked her to dinner at the hotel and insisted I be there when she made the offer. Then she implied that I'd arranged it, making sure the girl felt grateful to me. Did Alice know you were coming by?"

Claire nodded. "I called her during the morning and told her I just couldn't believe you'd hidden your true feelings from me. I asked her advice. She said she was intervening on your behalf, that you were hopeless at dealing with unpleasantness. She said you were having dinner with her because of my late class and suggested I come by in time for after-dinner coffee. Maybe we could all talk." Claire's full lips thinned and she pushed her loosened hair back. "You think she planned it—the girl, my seeing you, all of it?" Claire looked doubtful. "No, it's too chancy. I don't believe it. You're making it up."

"No, Claire, I'm not. Alice knew we'd converge at the hotel at some point. You'd walk in and find me at dinner with another woman or see us together somehow. She couldn't know that the girl would kiss me, but she'd set the stage for a show of gratitude. She suggested you come, didn't she?" At Claire's reluctant nod, he went on. "Mother set it up and let the pieces fall where they might. She took a risk, Claire, but not much of one. And I'd bet she had other plans cooked up if it failed."

Claire looked down, hiding her expression. "The next day, she came by the apartment and asked why I missed dinner, if I'd talked to you. I told her what I'd seen. Drake, I told her I might be pregnant and didn't know what to do." Claire pushed her flowing hair back over her shoulders to raise her eyes to his. "She insisted I make an appointment at the clinic to be sure. She even went with me to the doctor. The tests were positive, of course, and I knew if I told you it would be the end of us. You were interested in someone else and thought our marriage was a mistake. Alice said a baby was no excuse for staying together, not in your mind, anyway. I was frantic trying to think things out. Then Dad called to tell me about Mom's surgery. Alice insisted I go on home. She said she'd tell you and try to help us work things out. I threw a few things in a bag, called a couple of professors to explain, and headed for Santa Rita."

Drake moved higher on the bed. He wanted to take her in his arms but knew the time hadn't yet come for him to get that close. "You have to believe that she never told me, Claire. She just said Patsy was in the hospital so you'd gone home. I expected you to call, but you never did. Then you came back, packed your things, and moved out. I got the notice you'd filed for divorce the day before Easter. I was so lost and angry, too, I didn't know which way was up."

"I miscarried the day after Mom's operation, I'd been at the hospital most of the night and drove home early in the morning to catch some sleep. I started spotting right after I got home, but I didn't realize it. Then I waited till office hours to drive myself over. I couldn't tell anyone. Dad was too worried over Mom, Audrey was too young, and Judith was in New York. It was too late to save the pregnancy anyway, so I just said I had a touch of the flu. Mom couldn't have visitors. Dad didn't pay attention to anything but Mom, and Audrey never realized what was wrong. It wasn't hard to keep things to myself. I went to see a lawyer as soon as I could get away from the house. It seemed best to bring things to an end."

"So you went through all that alone." Drake shut his eyes to hold back the well of black misery he felt at her pain. "It shouldn't have happened that way. I would have been there if I'd known, Claire."

"I was sure you did know. I called Alice." Claire's voice became dull and weary. "She said you were furious and thought I'd tried to hold on to you with a baby. She said hearing I'd lost the baby was the best news you could imagine."

"No wonder you hated me." He took her in his arms, as if to shelter her from her memories, to blot away the things that had gone awry. They couldn't go back, he knew, but could they find a way to have a future together? Could they put their lives back together? Would Claire even consider trying?

****

Audrey looked up from her filing as Hal came through the door. "Just made coffee." She waved at the percolator on the credenza. "I'll be through here in a minute."

"You look pretty good behind my desk, Puss." He shed his coat and fetched two cups from the rack above the fireplace. "Want a permanent job there?"

"I don't think you can afford me, and my other clients would raise Cain. While I was waiting for you, I called the bus company and checked out some routes and schedules." She tore two pages of notes from a steno pad. "A bus leaves from Arlington twice a day, and either one could have dropped Dondie Marshall in Santa Rita. They leave Arlington at 11:30 at night and

3:00 in the morning, go to Fort Worth to make a connection to Dallas, and then San Antonio, and they pass through here about 5:30 and 10:00 in the morning. She could have been on the early one, Hal. She could have come that far, maybe trying to get to San Antonio or make connections there, and not had enough money. The bus stop is on a state highway, and she might hitch a ride from here."

He took the pages and the map she handed him. He scanned the area at the tip of her finger. "You're right. She might have done that. And when she didn't flag a ride, she went to the church across the street just to find a place to rest."

"She was disoriented and suffering from some sort of memory loss," Audrey reminded him. "Could she have formed any kind of plan in that state of mind? Planned to hitch a ride or had a definite destination? What I'm wondering is if she had family in San Antonio and was trying to get there. She might be only a hundred miles from people who are searching for her, but they'd never find her here."

Hal poured coffee and handed a cup to her. "You and your valentine heart. You always want to make things better, don't you?" He looked at the map again. "Let's try tracking her from the Arlington bus and see if anybody remembers her. She should be a pretty memorable figure, a young girl, late night bus, probably not many riders. She gets off here before daylight with no one to meet her. Yes, the driver or the ticket agent might remember. It's worth a try. Sounds like another errand for Claire and Drake. Have you heard from the Dallas branch of the enterprise?"

"No, but the storm up there made ours look like a

spring breeze. Power lines are down and the city's blacked out in a lot of places. I tried to call, but I couldn't connect. Maybe I can get Claire this evening. She won't leave without letting us know if she found out anything at that bar, I'm sure."

"You're positive Drake got the sketches to her?"

Audrey nodded, and Hal reached across the desk to tilt up her chin. "I guess he'd have called us if he had a problem. I hope…" Hal paused and she saw the twinkle spark in his hazel eyes. "Okay, let's just say I'm on Cupid's side." He drew a chair closer and opened his desk diary. "Can't you free up some time this week? I'm anxious to make that trip to Siding. We've got to look into that end of things as soon as possible. The minute one of the other girls is back, in fact. I don't think we can wait for both of them."

Audrey saw the furrow between his brows. He raked his fingers through his mane of russet hair in an unusual display of nerves. "I could do the courthouse library the first of next week, I suppose," she said slowly. "And Jared will understand if he has to wait a day or two for that tax service. I might leave the day after Judith gets back. That should be, um, Tuesday? Will that do it?"

"Tomorrow's New Year's Eve, Friday is the first, and Judith is supposed to be here on Monday." Hal nodded. "I think we'd better plan on it."

****

Audrey answered the phone late in the evening and was relieved to hear her older sister at the other end of the connection. Claire sounded distracted, as if she had only part of her mind focused on the conversation. "Are you sure you're okay, Claire? I know the storm was awful up that way."

"Just a little tired, Audrey. You know what moving is like."

Audrey didn't know. She'd never moved in her life beyond taking a couple of boxes to and from her dorm room at school. It looked sort of exciting to her. "Did Drake get Judith's sketches to you? Can you get to Arlington all right?"

"Sketches are here, but I'll probably stay over a day or two so I can get to that bar. I can't see any point in trying to talk to people in a bar over New Year's. The place will be packed with revelers. I'll go Monday if they're open, otherwise Tuesday."

"That makes sense." Audrey told her sister about the possibility of the Marshall girl catching a bus from Arlington and finding herself stranded in Santa Rita. "So if you can, take the pictures around to the bus station while you're there. Maybe the agent will remember her."

"Mmm," Claire murmured, "it sounds like a long shot, but we don't have any other kind, do we?"

"Not at this point. Hal and I are going to Siding next week to see if we can get a line on the girl's family. Judith will be home Tuesday, so Dad won't be here alone."

The sisters ended the call with Audrey still mildly concerned about Claire. She'd never been close to Claire, she reminded herself. She'd been only twelve when Claire, very much the sophisticated older sister, had left for the University. And Claire had never really lived at home after that. She'd been home for holidays, but she'd stayed at school to take summer classes in the long break between semesters. Just as the two girls might have become closer, Claire had ended her marriage and fled to Dallas. Her visits home since were measured in hours.

"I was hoping she'd stay here," Audrey told her father over dinner. "I thought maybe she and Drake would patch things up. He's a terrific guy."

"You can't arrange people's lives, child. You can't make your hopes theirs."

"I know, but he loves her. Surely she can see that."

"And Jared cares for Judith," he added. "But we can't make choices for her either."

"Jared thinks Judith is on the edge of saying yes." She giggled at his astonishment. "He really does. He's got a ring and all kinds of plans." She told George of the conversation she'd had with Jared about his hopes.

"Jared is a good man, and Judith could do a lot worse."

****

"New Year's Eve! And my own show!" Judith laughed with uninhibited glee at the girl in the mirror opposite. The strapless black dress was barely on the right side of decent, she knew, but it was so gorgeous she couldn't resist. Black silk clung closer than a second skin from bosom to mid-calf, where it bloomed into a froth of ruffles. She'd make her mark tonight. She would. She could feel it. The paintings were beautifully placed, lit with artistry to show them to the best advantage. A number of important people were coming, including Kearnes' friend who wrote freelance art criticism for major publications.

Champagne and trays of tempting little sandwiches and decadent sweets would entice the guests. A jazz combo would add background. Mainly people were coming to see her work—people who knew something about paintings and collected them, and could make her name. Not New York, not San Francisco, not any of the major cities yet, but New Orleans might be a beginning for her.

Judith ran a comb though her short curls and dabbed a touch of blue shading above her black eyes. Best she could do with herself, she decided, and that wasn't bad. Her artist's eye recognized the girl in the mirror had beauty. It wasn't conventional beauty, not like Claire's classic features, but rather a piquant look, memorable and a little off-beat. Not a bad look at all, she decided and tossed a black-and-gold paisley shawl over her shoulders. Knuckles tapped at the door.

Kearnes, perhaps? She shook her head. Robey Kearnes was nearly eighty and left the apartment above his gallery on Royal Street only for dinner on Sunday. Who else would be—oh! A face flashed as her mind gave birth to the thought. *He wouldn't have. He couldn't have. Jared can't be on the other side of that door. He doesn't belong in this part of my life. He has sense enough to stay away.*

She wrenched the door open and confirmed her worst fears. Jared leaned his tall frame against the doorframe.

"You look like cold beer on a hot summer night, Judy. Where have you been hiding all that?" His look traveled the length of her daring gown.

She had to laugh. She must have got it right, because Jared didn't know how to fake a compliment. "Jared, what are you doing here? Why aren't you in Santa Rita where you belong?"

"Just came to wish you luck, and to bring you

these." He passed a white box tied with ribbons to her.

Reluctant to think what he might have in the box, she opened it cautiously. Nested in pale straw sat a cluster of tiny white orchids. Translucent loops of silver ribbon cupped the blossoms. "Oh, Jared, how perfectly beautiful. They're just the right thing. How sweet of you."

"Wanted to do something special for you tonight." Taking the box from her, he lifted the flowers. He raised an eyebrow at her strapless gown. "But there's no damn place to pin them."

Judith took the corsage and pinned it into the curls above her ear. "How about there?"

He stroked her cheek with an awkward hand. "Perfect, Judy. I thought they looked like you."

She hadn't had a corsage since the white roses he'd sent her for the Harvest Festival dance. She'd never thought what flower she might look like. White orchids? Why not?

"I need to leave," she reminded him.

"I know. I just came to wish you luck."

"All the way from Santa Rita? And you aren't coming to the gallery?" She was surprised and vaguely disappointed.

He grinned wider. "If you want me, sure, I'll come. But I'll stay out of the way. I know you've got to spend time with the people who can help you."

He understood more than she'd known, and the realization touched her. "I'll be glad to have someone from home to give me a boost." She left an appreciative kiss on his cheek. He slipped an arm around her waist and hugged her to him.

"Good girl! You'll rock them on their heels

tonight. Nobody can miss the talent in your work."

"Why, Jared, I didn't know you could see anything in what I paint."

"See anything, Judy? I'm not sure how you do what you do, but you make me feel everything on the canvas and all the hints hidden just off the edge. I don't know what to call it, unless it's what they mean when they talk about genius." His honest blue eyes were bright with sincerity.

"Oh, if just one other person feels that way about my stuff, I'm a success." Judith looked into his eyes, level with her own. "That does make everything perfect."

"Well, almost, I guess, except the one thing that would make things truly perfect."

What could be better than having her own showing, feeling beautiful, and floating on a cloud of optimism? Well, getting Dad out of that mess of trouble, of course, but that wasn't part of tonight. She started to ask him the question.

"It's just lacking the one element, Judy, just one thing." He had both of her hands in his, and the passionate, hopeful look on his face made him almost handsome. "You stopped saying no, and you moved on to maybe. This would be a perfect time for you to say yes. Will you marry me, Judy?"

She didn't mean to say it. She couldn't stop the word. It flew out with no thought from her. "Yes!" she answered and instantly slapped both hands over her impulsive, irresponsible mouth.

Chapter Twelve

New Year's Eve. She looked down into the street at the revelers on their way to parties at the hotels and clubs. It wasn't the worst New Year's Eve of her life, Claire reminded herself. It wasn't as bad as the first one after her divorce. Certainly it wasn't as bad as the first one after Mom died. No, this wasn't the worst one, but it was up there in the top five, for sure. She watched the traffic, the streams of lights that lined the avenues in all directions. The city had recovered from the storm for the most part, enough so that the celebrations would go on. Celebrations everywhere but in one corner of this gracious old hotel.

The lights below drew her eyes hypnotically. Did she believe Drake? Could she accept what he'd told her? She didn't know. One minute it seemed as if he'd answered all her doubts, the next his words seemed too theatrical to believe. Alice Ainsley Chandler had been beautiful, elegant, and aloof, never really part of the small town where she lived. Her life centered on buying trips to both East and West Coast cities. She'd lived in this hotel suite almost as much as she had the museum-like home she'd shared with her husband and son. The quiet joke around Santa Rita was that Alice had opened the art gallery just to have a place to keep her paintings and other art works after she filled the house. Drake's father, as Claire remembered him, was a quiet little man with an office in the corner room on the second floor where he spent his days on the phone happily turning money into more money. He'd died of a sudden, massive heart attack when Drake was ten.

As a boy, Drake had been something of an outsider, but he'd been one of Patsy Anderson's students. He'd walked home with Patsy from school one day, and perhaps sensing his loneliness, the teacher invited him in to meet her girls. Though he was four years older, he'd become Claire's special friend. *We grew up together, loved each other, but we let it all slip away. We were such good friends, such caring lovers.* Could Claire doubt Drake's sincerity now? But then, could anyone be as coldly calculating as he'd painted Alice? Claire didn't know, didn't see a way to be sure. She didn't dare risk her heart a second time. She couldn't survive having her life torn apart again.

Claire heard the door of the suite open and saw Drake's familiar form outlined by the hall lights. He snapped on the table lamp beside the door as he came in.

"Oh, I didn't realize you were in here, Claire. Did you get everything finished up?" He shed his coat and came to stand beside her. The traffic below drew his glance as it had hers.

"Yes, I dropped the utility bills at the night depository after I cleared the last of my things out of the apartment. Thanks for driving me over." She didn't trust herself to look up at him. She continued to watch the traffic.

"Glad I could help." He was silent for the space of two changes in the traffic light down the street. "I wasn't sure you'd come back here."

"I wasn't either," she admitted, "but I had to stay somewhere in the city. I can't go to Arlington before Tuesday. Hal and Jared want me to check the bus station in Arlington as well as the bar, and it isn't open on Monday. They think the girl might have come to Santa Rita by bus."

Drake drew up the hassock to sit beside her. "Would anyone remember after all this time? One girl, one trip, three years ago?"

"Any possible avenue needs looking at, and I'm already here. Might as well try."

"I'll go with you. Bus stations aren't very savory places."

"You don't have to do that," she began.

"Don't have to, but I will. I don't like the idea of you questioning people in bars or bus stations alone. We'll cover more territory together."

A day in his company, the two of them alone in a car, would be awkward, but it would also be more efficient.

The silence held to a disturbing length. Drake broke it at last. "I ran into an old friend, a retired Episcopal priest, while I was having lunch. He and his wife were on some charity boards with Alice. He invited me to dinner tonight, just to welcome the New Year with a few friends. Would you like to go? I think you'd like them."

Claire shook her head. "I'm wretched company tonight."

"We can order dinner in up here and bring in the New Year together."

Claire closed her eyes against the carnival scene

below. "I wish you'd go anyway, Drake. You needn't stay here with me. I'll have a bite and go to bed early. I'd like to be alone for a while." The day had been hard, and Claire couldn't face sitting opposite Drake for another evening—not this particular evening.

Drake took one of her hands in both of his. "It's no good for us, is it, Claire? You can't bring yourself to believe me. You can't take the chance and trust me again."

She pulled away, withdrawing to the other side of the room. "I don't know what to believe, Drake. Alice was gracious to me, sympathetic if not warm. You were the fellow all the other guys admired and all the girls wanted to take home. The one parents held up as an example to their own kids. But you changed after we married. You were different. You say it was the decision about New York, and maybe that was part of it. But you shut me out so I couldn't tell you I suspected I was pregnant. You were so unreachable—and I saw that girl."

The resignation shading Drake's eyes hurt more than any words he could have said. He expelled a long breath. "You're right, Claire, things did change between us. I've told you what was happening, the stress I was feeling. I can't prove that girl was part of a set-up. Only Alice could tell you the truth, and she wouldn't admit anything even if she were here."

Drake turned away, a portrait of defeat as he crossed the room and picked up his coat. "I guess I'll accept Father Will's invitation, but I'll be back early." He buttoned the cashmere and looked back at her. "You know, Claire, I can't prove anything. I can't convince you that Alice was trying to destroy us. But you could remember I've never lied to you in all the time we've known each other. You could look back over the years and just decide to believe me, take the chance. It's no harder than cherishing your anger and hiding from life again."

Claire had no answer. She watched him leave. It wasn't anger she was holding on to. It was peace of mind. She wasn't hiding from life. She'd worked to make a life. Not as warm, as fulfilling as the life she'd wanted, but she'd survived. A reproachful voice inside reminded her that she'd survived with a cat to love and a job in place of a family. Did that constitute hiding from life? No matter. She couldn't go back. She and Drake were different people, led different lives now. They'd gone down other paths and become strangers. And he hadn't said he wanted her back. *He said he loved me. Is that the same thing? No!* It was not, and besides, she'd passed the place where man-woman, love-marriage was possible. A snide voice inside chided her. *So a cat and a job and an apartment in a big, soulless city are every bit as good as a loving man in the house and kids on the stairs?* Who was she kidding? Not that nagging little voice in her head. She couldn't fool it.

Claire paced the thick carpet soundlessly, gnawing a fingertip and brooding. Surely she could find some way to discover if Drake was telling the truth. Not about Alice's part in all this, Claire supposed. Alice didn't leave a note saying, "I want Claire Anderson out of my son's life." But there should be something that showed Drake had been offered that fellowship. She could probably find out at the University. It would be a kind of proof, at least a token of his good faith. How to get at it? Someone kept records of that sort of thing, people she could call and ask. Somebody knew about fellowships and places that offered them. Maybe if she saw a list, something would sound familiar. Drake must have dropped a clue about it sometime to somebody. *You can find out, but not tonight. Not on New Year's Eve,* her little voice countered.

Claire paced the room in restless circles. She could find the information, but not tonight, not this minute, when she felt strong enough to deal with it. Could she wait, or would she lose her nerve before she found a knowledgeable source? The question in her head was abruptly halted by the peal of the phone in the suite.

"Mrs. Chandler? Dr. Chandler said you might want to order dinner this evening. The kitchen will close in an hour, so perhaps you'd like to do it now?"

Not sure what she answered, Claire put the phone aside and sat heavily on the bed. *Dr. Chandler? Drake?* Did the operator mean Drake? She did, of course. And Claire realized she should have known, should have added it up long before. Drake was in grad school when they married. He'd stayed at the University a couple of years afterward. She'd pushed him out of her mind, refused to hear any word of what he did, and isolated herself from Santa Rita news. No wonder she hadn't known. Though she'd ignored his activities, it looked as if in the fallout from their divorce Drake had acquired postgraduate degrees and the academic titles that went with them. Dr. Drake Chandler. It sounded, well, it sounded like Drake hadn't let their divorce shatter all his dreams.

You poured your life into your work, that insistent internal voice reminded her. *Why wouldn't he do the same?* The sound of someone tapping at the door halted her ruminations. Claire hurried to the sitting room to admit the young waiter with a rolling cart.

"Your dinner." He gestured to the tray. "Where do you want it? There by the window?"

Thinking of the merrymakers below, Claire suggested the quieter table near the bookshelf. The waiter whipped off covers and placed linen and dishes. Tucking a bill into his hand, Claire shooed him on his way as soon as she could.

Pretty dinner plates, the sheen of silver, and the savory scent of pot roast and potatoes drew Claire to the small table. She should eat, she reminded herself. Perhaps if she had a book, something to hold her attention, she could manage to eat a little something. The offerings in the bookcase were sparse. Claire dropped to her knees beside the shelves and skimmed the titles. Art books, every volume related in some way to art. Then a sedate, deep blue cover caught her eye. The work stood out in its somber hues against the brighter covers around it. She pulled it from the shelf.

"*American Folk Art and Its Influence* by Dr. Drake A. Chandler." It was a fairly small work, just over a hundred pages, but filled with copious illustrations and color prints. Claire carried it back to the big armchair and sank into the cushions, her dinner forgotten as she skimmed the slim volume. She flipped to the back page and the short biography of the author. "Though offered the prestigious Kleinschmidt Fellowship, Dr. Chandler chose to continue his graduate studies at the University of Texas, where he concluded his doctoral program with the publication 'Catalog of the Ballard Folk Art Collection with Annotations.' His frequent monographs

197

on Texas folk art offer the serious scholar fresh areas for exploration. In addition, Dr. Chandler showcases promising new artists at the Chandler Gallery in Santa Rita, Texas. His highly acclaimed new work examines American folk art with an original perspective."

He had a fellowship, he really did, and passed it up. He didn't come home to run the gallery for Alice. If he gave up the fellowship and didn't come back to Santa Rita immediately, does that mean—could I believe—everything else he said was true? Was Alice behind it all, using us as pawns she moved around to suit her whims?

Claire shut the book. She put her untouched dinner in the hallway, closed the drapes, and turned off the lights. With a sleepwalker's steps she returned to her own room. Pulling pins from her hair, she let its dark waves cascade over her shoulders. In the bathroom she filled the tub with steaming water and closed the door. She had serious thinking ahead, and Claire wanted no distractions. Her life might hang on the conclusions she reached.

****

"Happy New Year!"

Audrey accepted the glass Hal passed her. "It's not champagne, not even wine," he apologized as he handed a glass to George. "Santa Rita doesn't offer late night shoppers much choice. So I brought sparkling cider. The intent is the same."

"And a good choice," George agreed.

"I didn't expect you to come by." Audrey wondered what had brought the man to their door moments before midnight.

"I had a question or two for George. I just took a

198

chance you might have stayed up to see the Old Year out."

George led them to the family room and offered Hal a seat. The attorney had to step around the chessboard to reach the sofa. He looked it over. "You're playing against your dad, Audrey?"

"Very badly. I'm no competition. He needs Drake for a proper opponent."

George didn't deny Audrey wasn't much of a player. He set his glass aside. "What did you want to ask, Hal?"

"I went over my notes, the ones we made that first evening, and I need to clear up one or two things before we leave for Siding." The yellow tablet was beginning to look frayed, and most of its pages were lined and circled till no space remained on the sheet. He flipped to a dog-eared portion and took two pencils from his pocket. "Tell me again about the Marshall girl. You said you didn't know her very well. She hadn't come in for counseling? No discipline problems?"

George was silent for a moment. "No, I don't think I'd ever had a conversation with the child before that day I took over classes for Ruth Cleburne. I knew her by sight, of course. Nothing more."

"Did any of her teachers ever mention her, say she was difficult or disruptive?" Hal was still, attentive. Audrey thought he watched her father with unusual care.

George shook his head. "No, not disruptive. I remember her math teacher said she didn't have the background to handle geometry, no foundations."

Hal made a note on his page and turned to the next one. "You said her previous grades were pretty good, the ones transferred here?"

George nodded vigorously. "They were good, very good. Math and science had been her best subjects. But here, well, she can't count on taking senior courses next year based on what she's done here so far."

Hal made another note. "Can you explain that, George? The nosedive in subjects she'd enjoyed at the other school?"

George shut his eyes. "A number of things could account for it. Whatever trauma turned her life upside down and made her close off all memory could be part of the reason. Some kind of physical injury, maybe. Or Siding being the tiny place it is, the school may be inadequate, or they inflated the grades up there. It happens."

"But you tried to make a difference," Hal suggested. "You tried to help her improve her work, even to the point of tutoring her yourself."

"I thought I could help."

"Outside of her schoolwork?" Hal circled a portion of the page. "Could you help her there? With the emotional trauma?"

"I told her we could make a search for her family, get in touch with the school at Siding, try to find someone who belonged to her." George sighed. "I guess it was too much for her, or too soon. She wouldn't hear of it."

"Scared her, did it?"

George leaned forward, his arms on his knees, nodding. "I thought she was going to run out of the office. Said she didn't want to know what had happened to her, that the people who dumped her couldn't have cared about her. I hoped she'd accept my help when she felt more secure."

"Okay, that raises some questions." Hal folded up his tablet and put the pencils away. "I've done some research on memory loss. Usually when people lose a piece of their lives, even an hour or a day, they pick at that loss like a knot. Happens with head injuries and severe shock. The victim can't stand not recovering those moments. You ever see somebody who lost a memory and didn't want to know, George?"

George twisted his head to look up at Hal. "No, can't say I have, but then I've never had a child with such a massive fear eating at her, either. That suggest a new way to go?"

Hal picked up his notes. "Just gives me something to chew on, something to think about."

Audrey walked Hal to the door. "You have something on your mind?" She handed him his jacket. "You look like you're thinking way deep inside."

"I'm trying to get a feel for the girl. See, something keeps nagging at me."

"What?" Audrey couldn't see any new information in the talk she'd just witnessed.

"I'm trying to figure out those boxer shorts."

That didn't convey anything to Audrey, either. "We know they're Dad's. And the towel, too, I'm sure."

"They are. But you don't believe she came by them the way she said, that she took them after a sexual encounter with George, to use as a threat of exposure, do you?"

"No, of course not!"

"Neither do I. That means she acquired them in some surreptitious manner. She took them, and she had a reason. I want to know how she got them and why."

"She could have, I don't know, found them? Dad dropped them from his gym bag, or they fell out when he put the bag in the car? A number of things might have put them in her path."

"Audrey." Hal pulled on his coat. "Those shorts are the only tangible, physical evidence the prosecution has. We need to know how they got into the girl's book bag. She knew the boxers were your dad's. She also knew the Vanderhill woman would find them. Premeditation? Thinking ahead of a way to implicate George? Preparation? It sounds like a pretty sophisticated program for this girl. So I asked George about her mental processes—how she thinks and reacts. She's lost her memory, does poorly in school, and is withdrawn. In other words, she's a not a creative or industrious student. Could she have planned this campaign against him from the start? Is she clever enough to come up with a plan like that?"

"Deliberately planned it, you mean? In advance?" Audrey reeled at the thought. "From what we know about her, she doesn't sound like someone who could concoct a devious plan. And why would she? To what purpose?"

"I want to find out if she is capable of forming intent, and did she do so? And what would it gain her? I hope we'll get some hint in Siding. But I promise you one thing, Audrey. If they put that girl on the stand, and they just about have to, if the prosecution is to make its case, Jared and I will take her apart and put her back together till we find out how and when she stole those shorts from your dad. We will get the truth out of her."

Audrey, stunned by the ruthless look in Hal's face,

tried to protest. "But Hal, she's just a kid. You can't do that to her."

His hands dropped heavily on her shoulders. "I can, Audrey, and I will. Get this into your head. Jared is a pretty fair lawyer, and I'm a son of a bitch in court. Between us, we can get your dad off, get the case dismissed on lack of evidence or legal technicalities. But we can't prove what the Marshall girl claims actually didn't happen. George may walk out of a court of law a free man, but he'll forever be condemned in the court of public opinion. Either that girl spits out the truth, or George Anderson gets branded a rapist. We can't afford to let her off easy just because she's a troubled kid."

In the hard light of the porch, Hal's shadow filled the doorway. For a moment Audrey imagined she could see his Norse forebears, fierce and implacable, looming in the night sky beyond. A chill touched the base of her spine. Viking they called him and Viking he was.

"It's barbaric," she objected. "It's barbaric to ruin a young girl who may have just tangled memories and old troubles together. Dad wouldn't want you to do it that way."

"If she stole his shorts? If she planned their discovery? If she plotted to ruin him?" Hal buttoned his coat. "Your dad may have room in his heart to forgive her, but you'd better be glad I don't. When I take on a case, I see it all the way through. If that girl planned this charade, don't you want her stopped?"

"She can't be that conniving," Audrey insisted.

"We don't know what she may be, Puss. And until we find out, I'm not in favor of bestowing sainthood on her." He put his arm around her shoulder. "Did you get things cleared up enough to leave when your sister gets back?"

Audrey nodded. "I did, but I've got to go into Jared's office for a while tomorrow. I don't want him to get back and find the place in a mess. I went over and put in some time on his loose-leaf services this afternoon, but I couldn't finish. It's a disaster over there."

"Jared's gone somewhere?"

"To New Orleans, to see Judith's show. He couldn't sit still. He left early this morning."

"Well, I wish him luck. He's hell-bent to win the girl's hand. Maybe he's got a chance."

****

Jared was at that moment standing in a long, crowded room surrounded by the wave of people flowing around the paintings highlighted on the walls.

"You're a hit, Judy." He rested a hand on her bare shoulder and felt her shiver.

"I think so," she whispered without turning to look at him. "Three of the canvases sold outright, with hold tags on two more. Robey's pleased. He says it's all he hoped it would be."

Jared lowered his voice. "Who was that fellow, the one who looked like a walking turquoise mine?"

A note of excitement raised her voice. "He's from Santa Fe. He's on the board of the Art Institute."

Jared gave the man across the room a second look. "He's a phony, baby. Watch out for him."

Judith bristled at his words of caution. "Robey wouldn't invite anybody he doesn't know. And what do you know about artists, anyway?"

Jared knew he was on treacherous ground but

couldn't keep from warning this impetuous girl. "I know a New York accent from a Western one."

"Just because you never left Santa Rita, you think everybody stays in the town where they were born. Not these days." She turned away and took the glass of champagne a passing waiter offered.

"That one certainly didn't." Jared mentally tallied the tasteless amount of turquoise and silver the man sported. "I wonder if he bought stock in an Indian trading post. He could hold an auction all by himself."

Judith glared at him. "For your information, Jared Pierce, he's asked me to do a master class at the Institute next summer. I think I'll do it. It's an advantageous career move."

"Good luck, Judy. I hope it works out. But I'd keep him on formal terms, if I were you. He looks like a tomcat on the make." Jared glanced at the man again. "The way that jewelry weighs him down, he clanks when he walks."

She turned, irritation flushing her cheeks. "Jared, about what we were talking about earlier. You know, getting ma-, ma-, mar—"

"Getting married, is that what you can't quite get out?" He sighed. "What about it? You want to reconsider?"

"I'm moving it back to maybe."

He put his glass on the table, familiar resignation making his shoulders tighten. "You do whatever you need to, baby."

"Jared, I never meant to say yes. It just sort of flew out on its own. But I'll let the 'maybe' stand."

With one finger he touched the curve of her cheek. "Maybe leaning to no, or maybe tilting toward yes?"

"No degrees of qualification right now. Just maybe." She moved away from the table and into another knot of chattering strangers.

Jared watched the girl he loved walk away once more. She'd done it to him again. "One of these days, Judy Anderson, I'm gonna ask and you're gonna say yes, and I'll hold you to it." He put his plate down on the table. The tiny sandwiches and soggy salad looked no more appetizing than they had when he picked them up. The sweet champagne left a taste in his mouth he couldn't abide. He edged through the crowd and finally managed to get a spot beside Judith.

"It's going really well for you, baby. You don't need me here, and there's a lot to do in Santa Rita before Hal and Audrey leave. I can walk to the hotel from here to get my truck, so I'm heading on back. You have a real good time. I'll see you when you get in. Happy New Year, Judy."

****

Drake stopped beneath a light in the hallway and searched his pockets for his key. He glanced at his watch. Only a little past 12:30, he saw. Not late, but he was sure Claire had gone to bed. She hadn't wanted his company earlier, and he didn't suppose she'd changed her mind. He let himself into the suite and put his coat in the closet. A dim light from the lamp in the corner surprised him. Claire must have left it on. He glanced toward her bedroom. Closed door and no light showing underneath, he noted. She'd gone on to bed. He reached for the lamp switch. Something rustled across the room. A movement drew his eyes.

"Was it the Kleinschmidt Fellowship, Drake? Was that the one you turned down?"

Out of the shaded corner where the high-backed chair faced the window, a figure emerged. Claire stepped toward the light. The lamp cast a glow over her pearl pink satin robe but kept her hair in midnight shadows.

Drake swallowed hard to answer the question. "It was, but how did you know, Claire?" He took a step toward her. "I'm sure I never mentioned it."

She brushed his question aside. "It doesn't matter." She came out of the blackness and into the pool of light. Her ink-dark hair fell to her waist in heavy waves, making a frame for her delicate face above the pale shimmer of satin.

"I'm surprised you're still up," he said, forcing words around the tightness in his throat.

"I thought I'd see the New Year in with you after all." She slipped the cord loose and let her robe fall, swirling from her shoulders to the floor. The pink gown underneath did nothing to mask the gifts nature had given her. "Happy New Year, Dr. Chandler," she murmured, moving to his arms. This time Drake knew the angels were singing.

Chapter Thirteen

"I hope it isn't true that how you spend New Year's Day predicts the way you spend the rest of the year," Audrey told Hal as she bundled up the discarded pages that littered the floor of Jared's office.

"This wouldn't be my first choice either."

"Was there something we needed to discuss?" She continued to straighten the office. "I didn't expect to see you out today. I thought you were in your office getting ready for the great drive to Siding."

"A piece of information I picked up from a friendly source interrupted my plans." Hal shifted some loose-leaf binders from a chair and sat down. "The Vanderhills took the Marshall girl in to see the doctor last week."

"Please don't say the girl is pregnant!"

Hal held up a hand. "No, she's not, but she's not an untouched blossom, either. No way to know when she became sexually active, but she's been intimate with a man at some time."

Audrey digested the information. "Doesn't that add weight to their case?"

Hal shrugged. "It cuts both ways. Equally incriminating George or suggesting the girl had some fellow on the sly. Maybe she thought George knew it and threw suspicion on him to confuse the issue."

"If Dondie escaped the Vanderhills' watchful eyes, she's pretty clever."

"We don't know what her life was before. She may have developed a sly streak to survive."

Audrey pitched the last of the discarded pages into a trash bag and closed it. "You're thinking rape? I can imagine a girl forced into relations at that age could shut off her memory just to be able to cope with it."

Lost in thought, Hal paced the small office. "Maybe, but I'd expect the girl to close off memory of the event, not her entire life."

"Do you think whatever happened was in Siding?"

Hal scooted a stack of mail to one side and leaned an elbow on the corner of the desk. "The time frame indicates it. Her school records show she completed the school year there. By the next September, she was here, and unless Claire finds she was actually in Arlington, her crisis was in Siding." He added an afterthought. "Do you think Vanderhill could be the man in her life? Could she be covering for him?"

"Vanderhill? Not a chance." Audrey waved the idea away. "Fred Vanderhill's narrow-minded and unforgiving, but moral as they come. He couldn't live with himself if he'd done something to Dondie. No, she has to have a boyfriend, hard as it is to believe."

"Still, Vanderhill is someone we have to consider, even if it's only to discount him as a possibility." A wry grin twisted Hal's mouth. "It's interesting that you reject the idea of Vanderhill molesting a girl in his care, but he doesn't hesitate to accuse George of the same act."

"His righteous attitude is so aggravating you'd love to see him slip. He won't. He'd never violate his beliefs." Audrey tossed down a new stack of paper-wrapped pages. "If Dondie has a boyfriend she's protecting, can we find him?"

"I don't know, Puss, but I'll ask Jared to see what he can learn while we're in Siding. He's local. He'll have a better chance to draw out anyone who might have seen the girl with someone." Hal rose as if to leave.

"Here's Jared now. His truck just pulled up in front of the office, and he's coming this way."

A moment later, the young attorney sagged against the doorframe. Jared's red-rimmed eyes had the look of a man in need of sleep. His rumpled pants and dress shirt suggested he'd driven back to Santa Rita straight from the gallery opening. A sandy stubble glazed his cheeks and a gaunt greyness shadowed his face.

"Did we schedule a meeting and I missed it?" he asked as he lifted his feet heavily over the threshold.

"You look like the back end of a long night," Audrey told him. "Hal came into some information, and we were discussing the best thing to do with it."

Jared swiped his eyes with the back of his hand. "I drove straight from New Orleans. Was heading for my place, but I thought I'd check in first. What's up?"

Hal filled the other attorney in on the information from the Marshall girl's medical exam and the talk he and George Anderson had had the night before.

"I can't see Vanderhill, that puritanical old goat, being part of this. He's too damned busy exposing other people's sins to have time to commit his own." Jared pushed a carton to the floor and straddled the chair that had held it. "If there's a kid out there—or a man with a yen for young girls—somebody knows it. I've talked to the guys at the convenience store and the ticket girl at the Palace Theater. None of them remember seeing Dondie with a guy. In fact, the girl at the Palace said Dondie sometimes stopped to read the movie posters, but she never bought a ticket. Near as I can tell, the girl hasn't been in any of the teen hangouts at all. Not at Luke's Drug Store or even the picnic tables over by the riverwalk."

"An older man, a college boy, or somebody with a job that lets him get out? Delivery guy or repair man?" Hal suggested.

"I'll look for one." Jared scrubbed his eyes as if rubbing the tiredness away. "Wish I had one of Judy's sketches or a photograph. It might help."

Audrey frowned. "We were in such a hurry for Drake to get them to Claire that I just didn't think to have Judith make extras."

Hal nodded. "We should have thought of that. George said the likeness was good. Still, Judith said the eyes didn't come off as well as she'd hoped."

Jared pushed up from his chair. "I know what Judy's problem was. I saw Dondie the night they brought George in. I've seen the look she has in her eyes before. It's that wounded look that you sometimes see in a kid who's way too experienced for somebody twelve or fourteen or even sixteen. It goes with keeping the defenses high and the world out. Judy's never seen that look before. She didn't know how to interpret it."

Audrey thumped Jared on the shoulder. "Speaking of my sister, how'd you two do last night? Still thinking you're going to win her over?"

Jared rubbed his stubbled cheeks. "Pretty good, I guess. We were engaged for almost three hours."

Audrey laughed at the pained expression on his face. "Something of a record for short engagements, isn't it? Did she get cold feet or did you quarrel again?"

Tugging at his ear, Jared gave her a rueful grin. "Some Long Island lounge lizard wearing enough turquoise to pave the Sandia Mountains talked to her about teaching a class in Santa Fe. I said he was a fake, she flew off the handle, and the next thing I knew we'd gone from 'I do' to 'I don't think so.' She's doing really well at the gallery, and she didn't need me, so I headed home."

"You're out on your feet, brother," Hal counseled. "Go on home and put in some serious sack time. There's nothing pressing here today. Get some sleep."

"No quarrel with that plan." Jared looked around the office. "You got that service ready for me already? Thanks, Audrey. If I could afford you, I'd put you to work full time."

"And leave me to update my own books?" Hal rejected the idea, holding up a hand to stop Jared's suggestion. "I'd be dodging malpractice suits. You have to share her."

"Nice to be appreciated, guys, but I'm leaving now. Ruth came home this morning. Dad and I are expecting her for dinner, so you go along home and leave me a free evening for once." She shooed the two men out, watched Jared shamble toward his pickup, and wondered if he'd ever stop chasing her elusive sister. His quest looked hopeless from where she stood.

Looking forward to a quiet dinner at home, Audrey pulled her VW bug in behind her dad's Town Car. Ruth was a pleasant person who shared George's historical interests. She'd looked to him as a mentor when she first came to Santa Rita. Her love of history and teaching equaled his, and they'd had many lively discussions over bits of his Jubal Early research. Her help with the Marshall girl's records had been useful, but Audrey hoped the trial and all references to it would be tabled for the night. The heady scent of her father's beef stew greeted her at the door.

"Hey, you must have put Jubal to bed early to get this going in time for dinner."

George answered in a mock-stern voice. "Have a little respect for the subject of my definitive biography, young lady."

"Yes, Papa." She laughed and dropped a kiss on his cheek. "How is the great work coming?"

"I've wrapped it up. I want Ruth to skim the last few pages. I re-wrote them about sixteen times, and I've re-read them till I don't know which version is the good one anymore."

Audrey took salad greens from the fridge and tossed them into the sink for washing. "Ruth will be delighted to read your manuscript. She's been encouraging you for as long as she's been here." Audrey glanced at the clock. "When is she supposed to arrive?"

George chewed his lip. It galled him, Audrey knew, for Ruth to feel she must wait until dark and walk up the back footpath to come to the Anderson house. How awful that she couldn't openly visit a friend.

"In about half an hour." George turned away to stir the stew simmering on the stove.

"Good. That gives me time to make a pan of cornbread. We'll have a real Texas dinner tonight. I brought a pecan pie we can cut for dessert."

As she worked, Audrey wondered if she should tell her father about the impromptu meeting in Jared's office earlier. The medical information would worry him, she decided, and she'd leave Jared to deal with the news if, or when, he found a man in Dondie's life.

"Jared came by the office this afternoon. He'd just driven in from Judith's opening."

"How did it go? Was it a promising start for her?" George left the stew to listen to his daughter's news.

"He said the showing looked successful. He also said he and Judith were engaged for about three hours, till Judith got an offer from some art dealer from Santa Fe. Then, Jared said, they went from 'I do' to 'I don't' in a minute flat."

George laughed ruefully. "Our Judith scares herself half to death every time she lets somebody get inside her shell. She can deal with the way other people feel when she catches them on canvas, but she doesn't know what to do when her own feelings get involved. I think she's afraid she'll have to face losing someone again. She got tangled up when Claire went off to college. They were so close growing up. Claire didn't ever really come home again, and that hurt Judith. Losing your mother and giving up the art school in New York, I guess those two things were too much for her. She shut down everything except her work."

"I didn't remember Claire and Judith being all that close."

George nodded. "I guess it seems to you that those two have always been scratching at each other." He drew up a barstool and settled on it. "They were best friends as well as sisters, as young kids. They had differences, of course, but they didn't really drift apart until Claire left for college. That started a rift that grew more strained when Claire got married. Claire and Drake splitting up finished the falling-out. Judith felt like Claire was being unfair and sided with Drake. Your mother and I had a hard time with the divorce, too, especially with Patsy sick. It seemed wrong and impulsive, but since they haven't been able to work things out, it may have been for the best."

A soft tap at the deck door interrupted their reminiscing and sent George to answer the knock. He held the door back to greet Ruth and took the coat she shed as she entered.

"We have a hint of ice or snow in the air tonight," their visitor announced. "Some real winter weather may hit us this year." Ruth followed George to the breakfast bar and accepted the glass of red wine he offered her. "Just the thing to thaw out the chill in my bones." She sipped gratefully and sniffed the aroma around her. "And what's that heavenly perfume? Beef stew? Perfect."

"Dad's specialty," Audrey told her. "And he's got a surprise for you. Dad, why don't you get your masterpiece while I finish things in here? You'll have time to look it over before the bread is done."

George rubbed his hands. "Oh, yes, a new captive audience. I'll be right back."

"He's really finished the biography, Ruth, and someone is interested in publishing it. He's been writing night and day since they asked for the manuscript. I know he's dying for you to read it."

Ruth put her glass aside. "How wonderful that he's been able to concentrate on his work. Hanging about the house with no purpose and fretting would be so unhealthy for him."

Audrey started to tell Ruth that it would be a favor to George to forget the trial, at least for the evening, but her dad returned with a thick stack of white pages.

"Here, I want you to see some of the sources I found. I located letters and a diary that opened up new lines of study. Come over to the sofa, where the light's better."

The manuscript and its research made up the major conversation topics throughout dinner and into the evening. Dondie Marshall wasn't mentioned until Ruth gathered her things and prepared to leave.

"By the way, I had an interesting conversation this afternoon," she told George as she buttoned her coat. "At the school."

"Who could you find on the campus this afternoon?" he asked. "Surely you had more interesting places to be on New Year's Day."

"Oh, I guess it was nostalgia. Knowing that I won't be back, I wanted to walk along the paths once more before I left. I thought I'd do it today when no one was around. I won't get to see this year's class graduate, and that hurts. I know every class is wonderful in its own way, but this class is unique. It's my first homeroom class to graduate. Saying goodbye is unbearable, and I wanted to take some mental snapshots when no one could see me get weepy."

Before the teacher could tear up, Audrey touched her shoulder. "Someone did see you, I suppose. You said you had a conversation with someone while you were there."

"Oh, yes. Our groundskeeper. I don't think he ever

takes a day off." Ruth squared her shoulders and regained the composure that had begun to slip. "Keefe Dublin was hauling fallen limbs and bundling them for the refuse collectors. He saw me and waved. I couldn't act like I didn't see him, so I stopped, and we talked a minute. He asked about you, George. He's one of your biggest fans."

George smiled with a little hesitancy. "He had his grandson living with him a while back. Boy got in with a bad crowd, an older bunch. I did what I could to get the boy back on track. Keefe keeps on telling me how much he appreciates it."

"Well, he asked about this mess we've got and how you're doing. He told me an odd little thing. Maybe it doesn't mean much." Ruth put her hand on George's arm. "I wouldn't mention it, except I know your lawyers want to look at anything out of the ordinary."

"What did Keefe tell you, Ruth?" Audrey leaned forward anxiously.

"He was working over in the flowerbeds near the parking lot a day or two before Thanksgiving. He's not sure exactly which day it was, but he knew which week because the kids weren't in school. He saw your car in the lot, George, and he said he figured you were at the tennis courts hitting balls like you did most days. He didn't pay much attention, but later he saw you put your gym bag in the car and go around to the front of the building. Probably picking up faculty mail or making a call. Nothing he'd normally notice, but then he saw one of the kids hanging around the parking lot. He says he always worries about vandals during holidays, and seeing your car was the only one out there, he kept a half an eye on it. He says the kid may have put something into your car. He's not sure, but he thinks the kid was just shutting the back door when Keefe spotted him." Ruth looked first at George, then at Audrey. "I didn't want to spoil our evening, and this may not even be worth worrying about, but if someone put something in your car, George, you should know about it."

As Ruth left, Audrey waited to close the door until their guest was well down the path where other lights could help her along the way. Puzzled by Ruth's information, she turned to her father. "Dad, if someone put something in your car while you were on the tennis court, wouldn't you have found it?"

George looked out into the night, his brow wrinkled with a frown. "I would, because I washed the car the day after Thanksgiving and vacuumed it inside. I even took up the mats and moved the seats to be sure I got everything. No one put anything in the car."

Audrey followed him back into the family room. "No, Dad, but what if this unknown person actually was taking something out? Taking something from your gym bag, like a towel and a distinctive pair of boxers? It might look the same to an observer, but it's a matter of interpretation. I think one of your legal eagles will want to talk to Mr. Dublin."

****

Jared hopped on one foot, then the other, to pull thick socks over his ice-cold feet. He should have turned down the bed and crawled under the quilts before he fell asleep. Too drugged with exhaustion to do more, he'd slipped off his boots and outer clothes and crashed into oblivion for several hours. When he finally came back to reality, his feet were bricks of ice, cold had sunk deep into his bones, and he was stiff from sleeping in a half-curled knot. He doubted his back would ever straighten out.

This floor could be used for ice skating. He swore at himself for his laxity as he lit the fire in the fireplace. Lighting the oven and all four of the burners on the kitchen stove helped. The cabin would warm soon, but the delay didn't appeal to him. He filled the percolator with water and tossed coffee into the basket. *Five or six minutes to get the pot going. Coffee should help.*

While the coffee burbled in the pot, Jared pared away the stubble that shaded his face. As soon as the temperature in the house began to rise, he poured coffee, added a little of Aunt Min's peach brandy, and carried it to the bathroom. By the time he'd finished a shower and pulled on jeans and his favorite sweatshirt, so faded and worn the color was debatable, the cabin was warm and his back no longer protested at standing up.

Awake and functioning in a reasonable way, Jared realized he'd missed more than one meal. The last thing he could remember eating was a dime-sized sandwich and a dollop of green stuff at Judith's gallery. He foraged through the leftovers in the fridge and stacked together a decent sandwich.

Wool socks toward the fireplace, Jared sat back in his armchair and breathed in the fragrance of pecan logs, peach brandy, and coffee. *Practically perfect. Now if instead of that stand of wild grass and brush outside the window I had a good-sized studio under that pale winter moon, and if a certain obstreperous, black-eyed wench lived out here with me and used that studio, that would qualify as perfect.* But it looked as though those last two things might have to be kept as hopes rather than reality. *Blast and bless Judy, she's a trial and a challenge, but she's mine whether she admits it or not.*

Jared set the coffee mug on the table beside the armchair and leaned back, listening to the winter wind curling around the roof and the fire snapping and crackling before him. He thought he'd only closed his eyes for a moment, but he must have dozed off. The sound of someone banging at the door went through the little cabin like a rifle shot. He shook himself awake.

"Coming, coming." He stumbled across the dark room to the door.

"Could I borrow a cup of coffee on a cold winter night?"

Jared rubbed his eyes to be sure he wasn't still dozing. "Judy? I didn't... I mean... You're here? Aren't you supposed to be at some big do in New Orleans?"

Judith pushed past him and his garbled inquiry. Her black leather jacket wasn't zipped, and she had nothing over her short spiky hair. Her face was icy when he touched her cheek.

"I told Robey that I couldn't endure another cocktail party or the conversation that went with it." Judith hustled to the fireplace and rubbed her hands briskly.

"You're half frozen," Jared scolded, and poured the last of the coffee for her. She started to take it. "Wait, I have half a bottle of Min's homemade liquid peaches in here." He dribbled a little into her cup. "That'll warm you up a little quicker."

She inhaled the scent of the coffee and swallowed a gulp. "Thanks, you're a lifesaver. The heater went out on the van about eighty miles back. I thought I'd never get here."

"I'm glad to see you, but what the hell are you doing here? It's fifteen miles farther than going straight home."

Judith took another swallow. "Yes, but if I'd gone on home, I'd probably lose my nerve. I came on over here first because I owe you an apology. If I wait till tomorrow I'll talk myself out of making it."

"Judy Anderson apologizes? To me? Can't happen, Judy baby. I've known you, child and woman, all your life. You don't apologize. You just barrel on."

Jared was amazed to see Judith's face flush scarlet. "You've got every reason to think so, after the way I barreled on last night at the gallery. You came all the way from Santa Rita to see my show. I got all caught up in how important I was. It went to my head." She cast him a shamefaced smile. "It meant a lot for you to come. So I'm sorry I was a big-headed brat on an ego trip."

"Judy, you were the center of attention and deserved the applause. I didn't expect you to cling to me all night, not unless things went wrong and you needed a little hometown support. You had a bunch of people telling you how good you are, so you didn't need me."

"You didn't go off mad at me because I, well, I unsaid yes? I thought this time I'd really hurt your feelings." Judith held out her cup. "Any more of Aunt Min's favorite drink?"

"I'll make another pot." Jared took her cup and went back to the galley kitchen to start the coffee. Was Judy actually considering someone else's feelings?

Where was this sudden sensitivity coming from? Judy never acknowledged that she offended or hurt someone's feelings. She was oblivious to the possibility. He trickled fresh coffee into her cup, slipped the pot back into place, and added a gurgle of brandy to fill her mug. She still stood by the fireplace, rubbing the chill out, when he returned.

Jared handed her the cup and put his hands on her shoulders. "Come over here and sit, painter girl, and tell papa what's going on with you." He drew her to the armchair and patted the arm as an invitation.

With a show of reluctance, Judith sat on the worn, brown leather. "I don't know, Jared. It's just a little of everything. Dad, Claire, all the turmoil, I guess it just got to me. And then that creep—the one who was supposed to be from the Santa Fe Art Institute—turned out to be a free-loading octopus. He was all hands and vague promises, and Robey Kearnes didn't even know him. He was a gatecrasher! Suddenly all I wanted was to get away from him, the crowd, the show—everything—and come home. I ran out on Robey and the show."

"You're pooped, kid, and you've been riding on nerves for weeks, ever since Thanksgiving." He pulled her into his lap, where she curled up like a weary kitten.

"You want to go home, Judy? I'll drive, if you do." He ruffled her hair lightly, the silky spikes falling at his touch.

"No, I don't want to go home, Jared." Her head drooped against his shoulder. "I'm not sure what I want."

"You want to stay with me tonight? The bed's small, but you know that. We've managed it before."

Black brows knitted in a frown and her dark eyes held a sheen suspiciously suggesting tears. "I think I'd like that. And maybe I didn't really mean maybe, after all." Her voice fell to a barely audible tone. "Maybe I did mean yes."

Chapter Fourteen

Claire's classic suede pumps made distinct clipping sounds on the hard floor. She stretched to keep her paces even with Drake's longer stride. At the turn of the hallway he hesitated a moment.

"Are you sure you want it this way, Claire?" An anxious note deepened his voice.

The way she wanted it? Claire looked up at his face half hidden by the winter light of the hall. That handsome profile hadn't changed, but the hooded eyes no longer suggested a tragic poet. She saw something sensuous, heated in their expression.

The way she wanted things? She couldn't have put her wants into words. Mom had always had a superstition that what one did on New Year's Day was how the year would be spent. Claire hoped that was so. Nothing had ever been as right as waking the morning before with Drake sleeping beside her.

"You are sure?" he asked again.

"It's exactly the way things should be, Drake." She put her gloved hand on the cashmere sleeve of his coat. "You aren't having second thoughts, are you?"

"And third and fourth, ladylove, but not about the rightness of this. I'm having qualms about doing it without calling your family."

"They'll have a fit." She chuckled, then gave him a

sober, thoughtful answer. "But we can't do it at home, not as things are with Dad right now. And I'm not waiting till we get through with the courts. So it's here and now, isn't it?"

Drake tucked her arm through his. "Then, here and now, we go see the clerk."

The office they sought was at the end of the hallway. A pleasant lady with streaked grey hair and a twinkle in her eye met them at the low counter. "How could I help you folks today?"

Drake slipped his arm around Claire. "A marriage license, please."

"Right you are, sir." The clerk opened the cabinet beside her and removed a long, gold-trimmed document. "Now, have either of you been married before?"

Claire and Drake exchanged looks. "Yes," Drake admitted, "we were married before."

"And were either of you divorced within the last thirty days?"

"Oh, no," Claire answered. "It was years ago."

"You have Texas driver's licenses?"

Both reached for their cards, Claire fumbling in her bag and Drake smoothly sliding his from a convenient card case. The clerk took each one and filled in the blanks on the sheet with the pertinent information.

"Both of you sign in the places I've marked. It's valid in seventy-two hours, folks." She cast Claire a teasing expression. "He looks like a keeper, my dear. I wouldn't let him out of my sight between now and Thursday. Some Dallas hussy might carry him off if you turn your back."

Claire laughed at the quip but agreed with the

bureau clerk. Thursday seemed like a very long time away. Drake paid the fee and took the official envelope. He put it away in his inner pocket and waited as Claire put her driver's license back in her bag, fastened her coat, and pulled on her gloves.

"What do we do until Thursday?" She laughed at the suggestive look he gave her. "Besides that, I mean."

"We have that errand to do for Jared and Hal, but we can't talk to the people at the bar till tomorrow, you said. No point in making that trip twice."

"I hate to sound like a complaining woman, but when I left Santa Rita, I planned to be here a couple of days. If I'm going to be here all week, I need some clothes. And I'd like something a little special for when we use that piece of paper in your pocket."

"Haven't got a thing to wear, huh?" Drake grinned. "Does that mean you need to spend the day shopping?"

Claire sighed. "It does. Is that a terrible drag for you?"

They reached the car, and he held the door as she climbed into the low-slung black Thunderbird. "No problem at all, love. I have a little shopping to do myself." He took her left hand, removed her glove, and kissed the third finger. "This hand is indecently naked. I think it needs a ring." His gaze met hers and rocked her with its intensity. "I never gave you an engagement ring, but I'd like to get you one now. A diamond? Would you like that?"

"I don't need a ring, Drake. A band, a simple gold one, will be fine."

"No. I've waited a long time to put a ring on your hand again. Isn't there something you've secretly wanted?" He didn't release her hand, and his look demanded an answer.

"Yes, but probably not what you imagine." Claire exhaled and let her thoughts find words. "I've always wanted a ruby, a deep, dark red one, in an antique setting, ornate and looking like it was handed down, bride to bride, for two hundred years."

"Now, I wouldn't have thought of it, but it's absolutely right for you. I know a couple of places over in the Park Cities area that deal in antique jewelry. Surely one of them will have something or know a dealer who does." He started the car and waited as the heater began to take the chill from the interior. "And what about shops for you? Lord and Taylor? Neiman-Marcus? A designer's shop?"

Claire made a rejecting gesture. "Way too expensive for me. I'd better find something in my range."

Drake pulled out his wallet and took a thick stack of currency from it. "I don't think I ever bought you a dress, ladylove." He pressed the money into her hand.

"Oh, I don't need—"

He placed a finger over her lips. "You remember how it was, those few months we were married? We lived in that tiny apartment we shared with the occasional cockroach and the ant colony. We survived on the trickle of money from Grandpa's trust, what you made working in the registrar's office, and the minuscule stipend the art museum paid me. We lived as well as any of our friends, but there were no luxuries, nothing extra."

"It wasn't too bad. Everybody lived just like we did."

"Sure, we were students. We didn't expect more.

But I wanted to give you things, and I intended, once I came into the estate my dad left, to do more for you. Alice controlled things by making sure I never had money for non-essentials. It galled me to think we were scrimping to have an occasional meal that wasn't pasta when we had no necessity for it. I have money now, and I want to give you things."

Claire was uncomfortable with the idea. "I've never spent a cent I didn't earn, not since I finished high school," she insisted. "If I hadn't won that scholarship, I would have had to go to school on student loans like everyone else. I didn't intend to let Dad pay my way, not with Judith and Audrey still to send to school. I don't think I can change now. It's my pride, I guess."

Drake ran a finger over her lips and teased the line of her chin. "Then I appeal to the love we've rediscovered. Sacrifice your pride for mine this one time, Claire. Let me do something for you. I've got money, a disgusting amount of the stuff, and it makes me happy to spend it on you now that I can. Go to the best shops, the most interesting stores, and do something extravagant."

She opened her palm and looked at the wad of cash. "Well, a girl needs a wedding dress," she conceded. "Last time, I wore Mom's. It wasn't very becoming. I could do better this time."

"Do exactly what you want. The most perfect dress you can find. And hang the cost. Don't even ask the price."

"No long, white, misty veil. None of that."

"Not if you don't want one." He cocked his head to one side in consideration. "But maybe something classic in white? After all, ladylove, you are still my bride."

****

The room felt cold and bleak when Judith woke up. For a moment she couldn't remember where she was. The dim light and the shadowy furniture loomed in unfamiliar ways. A patch of bright quilt rumpled the other side of the bed. *Oh, Jared's cabin.* The evening came back to her, how cold she'd been and how distraught she'd felt. *That art dealer from Santa Fe—though he wasn't from Santa Fe, and I'd bet all he knows about art was how to spell it.* His persistent, unpolished attempt to lure her to his hotel room had almost ruined the gallery show for her. When he reappeared on Sunday at Robey's cocktail party, she packed her things and left. The van heater went out when she was two-thirds of the way home, the old vehicle letting in every icy draft. When she reached Santa Rita County, all Judith could think of was her shivering misery and how right Jared had been.

A sound outside the one-room cabin caught her attention. The door opened slowly, as if to eliminate the slight creak of its hinges. Jared slipped in and dropped his rancher's coat over the back of the brown leather armchair.

"Judy? Are you awake?" He came with careful steps to the side of the bed. "Oh, finally came back to life, did you?"

She stirred languorously under the quilts, reaching above her head to stretch every muscle. "I must have slept like a boulder. I didn't notice when you got up."

He sat on the opposite side of the bed. "And I suppose you've forgotten the status of our no-maybe-yes discussion?"

"I believe we settled that pretty definitely about two this morning, if I'm not mistaken." Judith wriggled under the covers. "Or did we change the question?"

Jared scooted so he sat with his back against the tall, thin bedpost. "Not this time, Judy Anderson. You said yes—in fact you said it twice—so as far as I'm concerned, you've committed yourself. Not trying to get back to no, are you, baby?"

"If I wanted to take it back?" Judith closed her eyes, waiting to hear him tell her that if she needed to reconsider, he'd let her.

The bed bounced under him as he leaned over, trapping her under the quilts. "Not this time, Judy. I'm holding you to it. I love you, and you love me, too. At least you put on a mighty fine imitation of it last night. Are you saying you didn't mean it?"

Judith managed to free one arm and used it to pull his head down to hers. She rubbed her forehead against his, her fingers tangled in the thatch of his hair. "Nope, not this time. I just wanted to be sure you know how to handle a yes as well as you've always handled no."

"Anybody told you you're a brat? Told you today, I mean?"

"Just you." She squirmed loose from the confining covers. "Do I make coffee or do you?"

"Made it an hour ago while you were sleeping the sleep of innocent children."

Judith pushed the covers back, shivered when the cool air touched her nakedness, and unselfconsciously reached for the awning-striped bathrobe he'd left on the other bedpost. She wrapped her slim length in it and ran her fingers through her short locks.

By the time she'd washed her face and put on heavy socks, Jared had coffee and toast waiting on the table. "It's colder," she commented, brushing at the frost on the lower edge of the windowpane.

"With more coming from Canada, accompanied by raging wind. I had to run those spindly cows of mine into some shelter. It could get seriously bad tomorrow." He poured a second cup of coffee and sat beside her.

"Too bad your Aunt Min's old barn went down in that ice storm. You could have herded them in there for the duration."

He smiled, and she saw something sly in the way he looked. "Oh, I don't think that would have worked out. I think the painter lady who's going to put her studio out there would have objected to cattle for roommates. I hear she's a little persnickety that way."

"A studio? A studio for me out there where the barn was, with that grand view of the river and everything? Jared!"

A slow flush filled the man's face. "Well, Judy, it makes sense, now, doesn't it? It's tight enough, two of us in this one-room cabin. No way could you fit your painting stuff in here, too. You'd hate having me around when you're working. So I just figured I'd give you some space of your own. Probably you'll want to draw the plans yourself, but I thought I'd get a contractor out here to see how long it's gonna take. I don't suppose you'll consider making this thing legal till you've got a place to put your paints and pots."

"You're coming suspiciously close to bribery, Counselor." She swallowed her coffee and hurried to get her coat. "Come on, Jared. I want to go out there and look at my place. I want to check the light and the way the shadows fall. Come on!"

"Put on something warmer than my bathrobe under your coat, painter girl. I don't want to be responsible for you taking pneumonia. I suspect you're a rotten patient."

She scrambled around the room and tumbled herself into an acceptable number of garments to go outside. Not pausing to fasten everything, Judith wrapped a scarf around her head and dashed outside into the cold morning.

"I want windows, great big ones, so I can look across the river, and I'll need some plumbing, a half bath at least, for washing brushes and hanging rags and so forth." Judith kicked aside the brush that had grown up around the old foundation. She paced off the space and felt in her pockets for a scrap of paper and a pencil.

"I can see it, Jared. My mind can see every detail." She waved toward the river below the bluff. "I'll have a great view and fabulous light. A woodstove for heat and an attic fan for the summer. Maybe a loft, for all my books on technique and style and Old Masters. Redwood would be nice—it's practical, too. Doesn't need painting." She stood in the center of the dirty concrete, turning slowly, looking up at the building taking shape in her mind.

"Let's see what the contractor thinks he can do with what I can afford, baby, before you get too carried away," Jared cautioned.

"Oh, but I'll pay for a lot of it myself. I sold a raft of paintings, and at some pretty decent prices, too." Judith put her hands on her hips and glared at him. "If this isn't a fifty-fifty partnership, it isn't a partnership at all."

Jared threw up his hands. "You're as independent as Aunt Min. Good thing I like that in my women. Let's meet with the contractor, put our finances together, and see what we can afford. Okay?"

"Very much okay." She crossed the dusty span with little prancing steps till she stood before him. "I seem to be in love with you, Jared Pierce. I hope you realize that I'm just plain hell to live with."

"That is such a surprise." His dry tone said it all. She would be hell to live with, and for some reason that suited him very well. "Let's get back to the house, Judy, before we freeze to the spot out here. We should talk about the more ceremonial aspects of this thing. Like where and when can we get married?"

She lifted her shoulders with a shrug of indifference. "We'll elope."

"No, we will not. Aunt Min would skin me alive. I'd like your family there, the girls and your dad." His blue eyes took on a sly twinkle. "Just think, it's your chance to get back at Claire for that bilious green dress she made you wear at her wedding. You can pick something she'll never live down. Puce, maybe, whatever color that is? Fluorescent orange?"

"Pomegranate? Dry snuff brown?" They were still giggling over the possibilities as they slipped out of coats and gloves inside the warm cabin. "If we have to make a show out of it," Judith suggested, "can't we just do it here? Throw a party, have mariachi music, cook enchiladas, drink beer, dance on the floor of the future studio. You wear your best jeans and boots."

"And you'll wear some black gypsy outfit with fringe and shawls? That should get folks talking."

Judith looked down at the black denim skirt and

blouse she'd put on that morning. The hem of the heavy skirt just brushed the tops of her favorite lizard boots. "I guess I can give up black, at least for one day."

"White dress, Judy? Something simple, but something that will let everybody know you're the bride?"

She was about to offer another solution when the phone rang. Jared picked up the handset. "Hal? What's that? A possible witness at the school? Al Hayes is going? Okay, I'll meet him there. Oh, Judy's back. She's here with me. The heater is out on her van, and she thought I could get it going for her. I'll drive her into town as I come. Tell George she's fine, will you?" He put the handset down.

"Trouble?" Judith asked.

"Don't know yet, baby. Ruth Cleburne found someone who saw a kid possibly tampering with things in your dad's car just before Thanksgiving. Sheriff Hayes is going over to interview him. He asked me to meet him there. I can't do much, just listen to what's said, but it might be a break for George." Jared picked up his coat and tossed it over his shoulders. "Your dad's been trying to get you at the hotel. He's relieved you're with me. I said I'd drop you off as I came in. You want to tell your family when you get there, or wait till I can come over later?"

"I don't want to tell them at all. I think I'm going to look like an awful fool after slamming the door in your face for ages." Judith walked into his waiting arms. "I guess we'll tell them when you come over, so we can face the taunts and laughs together." Between kisses they moved toward the door. "Could this witness actually help Dad out? Did he really see anything?"

He kissed her, and lingered to kiss her again. "I intend to find out. This could be a real break, Judy. Hold a good thought. Maybe we'll have lots to celebrate tonight."

****

O'Keefe Dublin lived in a dog-run cabin not far from the highway. Jared noticed the trimmed pyracantha hedges as he parked his truck. A few of the orange berries still clung to the dried branches. Red trim brightened the small grey house, and the wide front porch held metal outdoor chairs. Sheriff Al Hayes, bundled in a sheepskin coat, was sitting in one of the yellow chairs, rocking peacefully in the pale morning sun.

"Mornin', Jared," the sheriff called as Jared started up the walk.

"Sheriff." Jared nodded at the man. "What have we got here?"

"Not sure yet. Lindstrom called me this morning with a tale about Keefe seeing something at the school, some kid messing with George's car. May be nothing to it, but he thought you should be along when I talk to Dublin. You can't say anything. Understand? It might be taken as coaching the witness. Ever'body knows how Keefe feels about George. Not much he wouldn't do to help George out. So sit to one side, where he can't be reading things off your ugly face, and we'll hear what he's got to say."

Jared looked around. "Is he waiting inside?"

"No, gone down to the other side of his pecan orchard. He's got a ewe about to lamb out of season, and he wanted to see about her."

Through the trees Jared could see a small, wizened

man in work clothes coming toward them. His short grey hair glistened like polished silver in the early sun.

"Sorry to keep you boys waiting," the old man said as he approached. "Have to keep an eye on Daisy. It's her first, and she's just a mite nervous. You fellas come in out of the cold. Got coffee on the stove."

The small house was as plain and well-scrubbed as the man who lived there. Four straight-backed chairs surrounded the bleached table, and soon hefty red mugs steamed before the three men sitting around it.

"Now tell me what this is all about," Keefe Dublin suggested.

Jared sat as far to the side as he could. He could see just the back of Dublin's head and the glint of light on his thinning hair.

Al Hayes plopped his Stetson on the table. "I understand you saw someone put something into George Anderson's car a day or so before Thanksgiving. Anything you can tell us might have bearing on the case. Just what did you see? As detailed as you can remember, Keefe."

Keefe Dublin tilted his chair back and looked up at the ceiling. "Well, now, I was working the flower beds there along the parking lot. I can't be exact about the date, you know, because I didn't really think too much about it at the time. I know school was out for the Thanksgiving holiday, 'cause all the students were gone. It was early, before lunchtime, but not first light. George's car was in the lot over near the tennis courts. Figgered he was swatting balls around and thought I'd catch him when he finished, wish him a happy holiday." Dublin gave the sheriff a hard look. "He's a good man, never mind what some folks say. They'd talk different if they'd had the trouble with their kids some of us have."

"You were working on the grounds and saw something," Hayes prodded.

"So I was, and I saw George coming back with his tennis racket and bag. He stopped at the car and put his things in the back seat. I was going over to say hello, but he went up the walk to the administration office. He was walking away from me, not seeing me, so I thought to catch him coming out. Five, maybe ten minutes later, I saw some kid messing around the car. George's car, you know. Kid shut the back door kinda quiet-like, then walked away, fast. Not running, you understand, but moving with some hustle. I meant to tell George when I saw him, but I took a load of trimmings out back. Guess George left while I was away. His car was gone when I came 'round the building. That's what I saw, fellas. All I saw."

"Mr. Dublin, did you see what the kid put in the car, if anything? Large or small? Soft bundle or a box? Maybe leaving a holiday gift or something like that?" The sheriff had a notebook on the table beside his coffee. He snapped his pen open and waited.

"Don't have a notion, Al. Didn't actually see the kid put anything in the car. Just the way it looked to me at the time." Dublin pushed his cup to the middle of the table. "And I won't say I saw somethin' I didn't. Understand that."

"We don't want you to do that," Hayes assured him. Jared held his breath, hoping he knew the next question. "Is it possible the kid took something out of the car rather than put something inside it?"

Dublin sat silently for a moment. "I didn't think of

237

it, no, sir, I didn't, but it sure could have been that way, just as easy one way as the other. Kid's hands were empty, but sure as the world, those ski jackets have deep side pockets."

Hayes nodded. "Ski jacket, was it? And the kid's hands were empty." He made notes on his pad. "Now could you describe the kid you saw? Height, build, hair color, that kind of thing?"

Dublin mused over the question for a moment. "Well, I'll tell you, the kid looked just like a dozen others. Not tall, no, sir, not much over five feet. Could have been a youngster, twelve or so, that hadn't got that teen growing spurt yet. As to build, I can't say much there either. Jeans and sneakers, like they all wear, and that bulky jacket. Can't tell if a kid wearing that garb is fat or thin. It's like a uniform with them these days."

"Anything you can tell us might help," Hayes coaxed.

"The hair now, I couldn't see the hair at first. Coat had a hood to it and the kid had it pulled up. But it slipped a little and I caught a glimpse of brown hair. Long brown hair, it was."

Hayes leaned forward. "You think the kid at the Anderson car might have been a girl?"

"Can't swear to it, Al, but there is some difference in the way men and women function. And I ain't too old to notice. When the kid walked away, moving on at a pretty good clip, I watched a minute. I've gotta say, that kid had the rolling motion of a girl trying not to swing her hips as she got up speed. 'Course, it's just my impression, and like I said, I couldn't rightly swear to it."

Chapter Fifteen

"Hal, I think it's starting to snow." Audrey pointed to the fine white veiling that misted the sky.

Hal nodded at the direction she pointed. "I know, little one. The weather report predicted the possibility this morning. I thought we needed to get on the road and get ahead of it, but it's coming in even earlier than expected."

Audrey pressed her nose to the glass to see the individual flakes. Snow was such a rare occurrence in her life she didn't want to miss anything.

"It could get nasty up where we're going, Audrey, with high winds and maybe drifts as much as thirty-six inches. Hazardous road conditions tonight." Hal flipped on the windshield wipers to clear the flakes turning to droplets as they hit. "It's not cold enough for snow to stay on the ground now, but the temperature will drop as we go north."

"I've never been in really deep snow. We get a dusting of it about once in five or six years, but nothing more. Heavy snow is pretty dangerous, isn't it?"

"Don't be too concerned. I've been driving in the stuff most of my life. I had the snow tires mounted on the car yesterday when I first heard the reports."

"Snow tires? I've never even seen snow tires."

"Probably just being overly cautious, but I thought

I might as well use them one last time. I really used them in Chicago, but chances are we won't need them here. Are you warm enough?"

"Beautifully warm and toasty." Audrey watched the thickening white cloud outside. The thin mist deepened to discernible flakes as the road rolled out before them. Still the flakes only touched and melted, leaving a damp blue sheen on the highway. "Do you think Keefe Dublin will do us any good in court? Even if Dondie took those things from Dad's car, we can't prove it with Keefe's testimony. He can't identify her."

"It raises the possibility, casts a shadow on the girl's story." Hal eased into the outside lane and turned onto a narrower road. "I'm convinced Dublin did see her. She took those shorts and the towel from the car. The only time they would have been accessible was when George's gym bag was in the car and the car was in an isolated place. The time frame fits. It's a crack in the solidity of her accusation."

"Were you able to get us places to stay in Siding? I know you were trying to find a hotel or inn in the town."

"Nothing in Siding itself. I found a small hotel in Bailey, the county seat, about sixteen miles from Siding. Siding doesn't even have a motel inside the city limits."

Audrey considered the situation. "Probably Bailey is better, Hal. In Siding, small as it is, everybody in town would know who we are and what we're doing by the time we got our coats off. If we're in Bailey, we're less likely to create discussion."

Hal agreed. "I thought so too. Living in Santa Rita and, in particular, dealing with your dad's case, has given me a very strong appreciation for the dynamics of small-town life. There simply isn't any way to keep secrets. I'm always surprised at how fast private things become general knowledge."

"Speaking of surprises, were you stunned at Jared and Judith's news last night? Coming in, cool as ice water, saying they're getting married? You looked pretty astounded."

Hal turned the wipers up to a faster tempo. "I was knocked flat. After the way Jared looked in his office yesterday, I thought the whole thing had gone down in flames. I couldn't imagine a turnaround anytime soon. Is the condition permanent?"

Audrey smothered a chuckle. "I think Judith is happy at last. She was waltzing Richelieu around the kitchen this morning and singing about wonderful guys." She couldn't hold back—her laughter burst forth. "As for what made the change, I think Judith came back from New Orleans and was at Jared's place long before you called yesterday. And in between the time she got there and the time she and Jared drove into town, something pretty wonderful must have happened. Something during the night—while she was there."

"You think she spent the night? Why?"

"I'm inferring, but she was babbling about a studio Jared wants to build her. And about how small the cabin is for two people. And a bunch of details adding up to Judith being there a lot longer than a couple of hours yesterday morning."

"Your romantic heart approves." Hal raised an eyebrow over one hazel eye.

"Not my business, romantic or otherwise," she insisted. "I'm just delighted to see Judith so happy. And

Dad, too. He's going off in private to chuckle anytime he thinks no one is paying attention to him."

The snow had become heavier, wet feathers sliding down on a whispering wind. The landscape slowly took on a coat of white, and details began to disappear under the cover. The car purred along, though Audrey felt the wind was growing stronger with every mile. Trees began to dance to an orchestra only the bare limbs could hear.

"I see a roadside café ahead." Hal interrupted the fantasy Audrey had created in her mind. "I think we should stop, eat, and get a weather update if we can."

"Do you think we can get to Bailey?" She watched a tumbleweed roll along the road till it collided with a highway sign. In moments it lost identity as snow stuck to the dry twigs.

"I'll find out," he answered. "I don't take reckless chances, Audrey." He pulled into a parking lot with gusts blowing across it, halfway hiding the small café beyond the white billows. *Will he push on in this weather? Does being driven to find answers count as a reckless chance?* She glanced up at Hal with a query in her thoughts.

"No, I wouldn't take chances, Audrey, not with the woman I love in the car."

Too stunned to answer, Audrey watched him leave the car and dash to the door of the café, his mane of hair a plume in the swirling grey. He tugged at the red door, fighting the wind to get it open, and stepped inside. Minutes later he was back to the Mercedes, helping her climb out and catching her arm when a blast of wind flattened her against the side of the car. Shielding her from the elements, Hal led her to the door of the café, where icy drafts and a shower of white burst into the entry with them.

"They're open, but only for the next hour or so. I'd stop here, but there's no hotel," he told her. "We'll make a run for the next town and spend the night if we have to." Hal took her hand, and together they followed the trim, dark waitress to a corner booth.

"We're all out of most things on the menu," she told them. "But I got good hot coffee, fried chicken, and red beans—food's good, and it'll stick to your ribs."

"Sounds like just the thing," Hal answered with a good-natured smile. If it wasn't exactly what they wanted, it didn't matter. The young woman was doing what she could to help out unexpected guests, travelers driven to her door by the storm.

The coffee came quickly, and Audrey clasped the thick cup in both hands. She watched Hal stir in a packet of sugar and take his first sip.

"What?" he asked when he noticed her intent look.

"What you said in the car. Taking chances with—" She stopped, too self-conscious to go on.

"With the woman I love?" He tilted her head so her eyes could only look into his. "Surely you know, Audrey. If it wasn't love at first sight exactly, it was love at the first real opportunity. I'd closed the door on my feelings for you long ago because I couldn't, in conscience, pursue them. When I came back to Texas, there you were, filling my mind, messing up my sleep, and making yourself indispensable in my life."

"I didn't know."

"But you don't feel the same thing for me?" Hal pressed his hand over hers. "Can you say you aren't in love with me at all?"

She looked down at her cup. "I was infatuated with you when we were in school. When Dad's trouble looked impossible, and Jared couldn't handle the case alone, all I could think was that you'd know how to deal with it. You're amazing, making things as easy for me as anyone could with this mess, but I don't know… I mean, you've kissed me and it's sweet. We've been out together and had a pleasant time. If we'd been more than casual friends when we were in school, I'd have walked on clouds for weeks. Maybe I'm too wrapped up in Dad's problems to feel anything right now. You think I have a romantic heart, but you're wrong this time. I don't, not for myself, anyway." She ended her miserable speech by closing her eyes and looking away.

"Damn, woman," he said softly, "if you're not every bit as mule-headed as your sisters!"

****

Drake slowed the car to exit the highway. Arlington was a city in its own right, but urban enclaves had sprung up and surrounded it. What demographers had begun to call the Metroplex had covered the area from Dallas to Fort Worth with continuous subdivisions and incorporated sites chained together by bands of interlocking roads.

"It looks like we might get a spatter of snow, love." A light film of dampness formed on the car windows.

"Oh, how perfect! A winter wonderland, and all for us." Claire sighed ecstatically. "I think snow is gorgeous. How did you arrange it?"

Drake reached over the console to take her hand. "You're giving me far too much credit."

Under the questing touch of his fingers, she felt the

ring on her third finger turn a little. It was too big, and they'd discussed taking it to a jeweler to have it sized. Claire wasn't sure she could let it out of her sight. She held her hand up to the window so the pallid January light fell across it.

"The little bauble was acceptable, I take it?" Drake looked away from the wheel a second, and she inclined her head his direction.

"I think it most satisfactory," she said in an arch tone and then laughed delightedly. "It's the most perfect ring in the whole world." A faint ray of light pierced the dim afternoon for a moment, touching her hand and releasing the deep fires hidden in the wine-red stones. A Victorian half-hoop ring of filigree, rubies, and rose-cut diamonds, the band glowed when the least bit of light touched it. It was even better than the image she'd kept in her dreams for so long.

"I spoke to my friend, the retired priest," Drake began. Claire stopped admiring her ring and gave him her full attention. A disturbingly serious tone deepened his voice.

"The priest, Alice's friend?" She bit back a rejection of what she feared he was going to say.

"*My* friend," he insisted. "He and his wife knew Alice. I don't think they considered her a friend." He caught her hand again and held it as if urging her to hear him out. "We need someone to officiate, love, and I guess we could find a JP or somebody, but I'd like for it to be someone who at least cares about us. Father Will is a good man, someone I've known for a long time."

"He wouldn't want to..." Claire looked for words. "I mean, would we have to tell him how everything happened with us before?"

"We would, I think. Will takes marrying people pretty seriously, and I think he'd need to know how things went wrong with us. He's a priest, after all. I think he'll see this is the right thing, and he'll be pleased we've been able to overcome past misunderstandings. He did know Alice, but he knew the real Alice, not the façade. I don't think he'll be surprised at her part in our break-up." He stroked the finger with the ring. "Can you deal with it?"

"You think he'll understand?" She wondered how any outsider possibly could appreciate the depths of Alice's scheming. Claire herself was still trying to cope with the revelations Drake had made about the woman she'd thought she knew.

"I really do, love." The affirmation in his tone was reassuring.

Claire shut her eyes and nodded. "Then let's talk to him about it. If he says no, he'd rather not, we can still hunt up a JP."

Silence enveloped the car as both contemplated the questions they might face with the priest. Gradually the snow seemed to thicken and cling to the ground in low spots. Claire watched a wisp grow into a pile as they neared a crossover and turned.

"Do you detest cats?"

"Ailurophobia could be a deal breaker, couldn't it?" Drake smiled at the serious tone of her question. "You're speaking of a certain spoiled ball of fur that thinks he owns you."

"Richelieu is part of my life. He was a tiny thing when I got him, right after I lost the baby. He filled a huge empty hole in my world." She felt urgency rising inside. Drake had to understand how important her purring bundle had become to her.

"I always wanted a cat, especially a Persian cat, when I was a boy," he said at last. "I read about Persians and went to cat shows and talked to breeders, but Mother always said no. She wouldn't risk her precious furnishings. Cats had claws and left hair on things, so I never got a cat."

"So you won't mind Richelieu? I can't leave him behind." Drake had such a kind heart. She didn't think he'd really wanted a cat when he was a child. She didn't remember him ever saying anything about it.

"As long as he isn't too resentful of my presence in your life, we should get along fine."

"I won't have him declawed," she went on. "He's very well behaved, though he can't help shedding quarts of hair."

"Why would you even think of it?"

"Well, there are all those antiques and precious rugs and miles of carved woodwork in your house."

Drake's glance held an element of surprise. "Do you want to live there?"

She shook her head. "No, but you live there, and I want to live with you."

"I thought we'd build a house, something suitable for a family—a family with a cat."

"A house? For us?" Claire hugged herself. "Us and Richelieu and maybe, before long, babies?"

He nodded. "I thought it was a good idea. Of course, we'll have to live somewhere while the thing's being built. We always talked about living in the coach house when we were dreaming dreams. It's still there, just empty space doing nothing. It needs paint and furniture, but it's four solid rooms with a bath and a closet-sized kitchen."

Claire laughed with glee. "I have furniture! I just sent it to storage, remember? Not four rooms of it, but a collection of things I hold dear. A red kidney-shaped sofa, a zebra-wood table with four chairs, linens, dinnerware, basic things but special to me. I wondered where I'd be the next time I saw my treasures. And I'm a demon with a paintbrush. You should recall all the times I painted my room at home."

"So we'll make a nest in the coach house while we plan a forever home," Drake agreed. "But, darling wife, what are we going to do with Alice's monstrosity? Nobody could afford to buy the thing, and who'd want to live in it anyway?"

Claire was still, but a churning silence filled the car with the whir of unseen wheels. "You said I should tell you about the things I want," she said at last.

"Anything this side of the moon, love. Just tell me."

"I've always thought I'd like to run an inn. Wouldn't your house be fabulous as a very exclusive inn? People would spend a lot of money to sleep in those massive beds or sit in that prissy parlor. The house is full of fascinating knickknacks and collectibles. We'd need a couple to help with the housekeeping, I guess, but I'm used to managing arrangements for groups of people. I could do the business end. It's no harder than managing offices for a partnership."

Drake's sudden laughter filled the car. "I think you're brilliant, ladylove. It's just the thing for you. You'll enjoy it, but it won't tie you up every minute.

And I think there's an element of revenge in there somewhere. Alice will spin in her grave if you are arranging for strangers to sleep in her precious house."

Claire laughed with him. She hadn't thought of how satisfying it would be to make Alice's mansion a monument to her treachery.

"Look there, Claire." Drake gestured toward a small side street on their right. "I think we've found the place. Isn't that neon light supposed to be a magnolia blossom? This must be the bar Hal meant. And it looks as if it's just now opening for business."

****

The snow blinded any traveler foolish enough to go out in it. Audrey gripped the edge of her seat in sheer terror as Hal inched the car along a path they hoped was part of the road. They'd left the diner as soon as they had eaten, but the storm had rapidly overtaken them. She looked at the tense expression on Hal's face and remained silent. She didn't dare distract him or interfere with his concentration. The windshield wipers fanned at the thickening accumulation on the glass, each swipe making less headway against it.

"We can't go on in this, Puss. The snow's thick, and I can't tell where the pavement is unless I stay right in the center. We'd better look for shelter till this blows itself out."

Audrey knew he was right. The strain of keeping the car out of ditches and drifts was taking a toll on Hal, and they hadn't seen a house or a store since they took the smaller road to Bailey.

"I think there's a drive over there." Hal pointed to what might be a level path going off into the distance. "It should lead to a house or some kind of building." He eased the car into a turn. Audrey felt the back end slide and forced herself not to cringe. The slide was brief as the snow tires bit into the surface, and they cautiously coasted along what might be a drive.

Against the snow and wind, a small shape emerged. Not a house, Audrey decided, peering into the gloom, but something solid, intermittently obscured by whipping sheets of white. She couldn't tell exactly what it was.

"I think it's an abandoned service station," Hal announced. "See how one side extends out toward us? It could be a service bay. It's not elegant, but it'll give us shelter on three sides and keep us out of the wind. If there's nothing under the snow, we can drive right in."

Audrey nodded and kept her fears to herself. Even if they could get the car inside the bay, it would be unbearably cold unless the car was running. She pulled her down jacket closed and zipped it.

Hal turned the car and backed into the space under the awning. "If there's a service pit, I hope it's square with the opening," he muttered as he eased the wheels further back. The hood drew even with the edge of the supports, and the shriek of the wind dropped to a low rumble inside the car. Hal cut the engine. "At least we're off the road." He leaned back into his seat as if exhausted by the effort of coming this far. "We're only about sixty miles out of Bailey. As soon as the wind drops and the snow lets up, we'll drive on in. We'll be there by nightfall."

Hours to spend, and the car is already cooling. We'll be icicles by the time the storm passes. Hal must have sensed Audrey's concern. He opened his door. "We'll be all right, Audrey. Hold on a minute." A blast of frigid air caught her breath, chilling her down into her lungs, as Hal slipped out of the car.

Through the back window she saw him hauling a box from the trunk. "Here, this will help." He slid in beside her, then peeled back sealing tape and pulled a bag from the box. "I thought I'd be giving this away." He tore open the bag, unrolled a quilted expanse of white, puffed fabric, and spread it over them. "A down comforter. I needed it in Chicago but thought I'd never use it here. Down has been keeping Europeans warm in unheated houses for centuries." He tucked it tightly around both of them. "It will keep out the frost in Texas for the duration of this storm, I think. Sit close to me, and we'll be fine." A delicious sense of well-being filled her as Hal held her close and the down cocooned her in heavenly warmth.

****

"Are you sure you want to do the bar alone?" Drake asked anxiously as Claire buttoned her coat and climbed out of the warmth of the car. The pale curtain of snow falling from a grey-and-white sky thickened to clumping flakes.

"I can handle this end of the quest." The snow spiraling in the street still didn't look too treacherous. "It's faster for me to check the bar while you to go on to the bus station than for two of us to trek around to both places. The weather is going downhill fast. The quicker we get back to Dallas, the better, I think."

Drake wiped away a spray of snowflakes blowing across his face and agreed. "I'll be back here in an hour, at the most," he promised. "You do what you can between now and then. If you don't get any information here, don't go somewhere else asking questions. Just

251

wait. It looks like a pretty safe neighborhood, but I wouldn't want you walking around in bad weather."

"Just do your part of this investigation and I'll do mine, so we can get through with it." She opened the folder and selected Judith's interpretation of a younger Dondie. "Here, you take the other one, and the photos, and see if anybody remembers her at the bus station." She gave him the folder and pushed him gently toward the car. "Go on now. The quicker you go, the sooner you'll be back."

Claire held her sketch to her coat, protecting it from the wind and drifting snow, and hurried across the street to the Blue Magnolia.

A bald man in a Hawaiian shirt and white apron looked up as Claire scooted through the door. "Come in out of the storm, lady. I don't expect a crowd here in this fine weather." He polished a spot on the bar and put down a cocktail napkin and a bowl of nuts. "What'll it be?"

"A glass of red wine?"

He shrugged and reached for a bottle on the back shelf. "You got it." Claire put the sketch on the bar and took the glass he offered. His look drifted over the picture, but she couldn't see a sign of recognition.

"I'm hoping you can give me some help," she began. "This girl, a teenager, had a painful thing happen to her. She doesn't know what it was, but it was bad. My family and I are trying to help her connect with her relatives. She has no memory of anything more than three years back, when she was found abandoned in a church. She has a hazy idea she was in or near Arlington, in a place called the Magnolia. Does this picture look familiar to you at all?" Claire held up the sketch so the dim light fell on it. The barkeep took it and studied it a minute.

"Don't think so, miss. This isn't a family kind of place. Not where people would bring kids, anyway. And I don't let teenagers hang around. They're trouble. Trouble I don't need, not the juvenile delinquent kind." He handed her the page, shaking his head.

"You would have been here then, three years or so ago? You'd remember if a young girl created some kind of disturbance?" Claire felt she had to prod his memory just in case some incident might come to light.

"Oh, yeah, I was here then. I'm always here. It's my place, and I work any time the joint is open. Found out long ago nobody watches your money as close as you do yourself. So if the sign says open, I'm here."

Claire sipped her wine, shuddering at the too-sweet taste. "And there's never been any kind of trouble?"

He laughed shortly. "Trouble, lady? Hell, 'trouble' is just another name for a bar. There's ever' kind of trouble you can mix up." He leaned one elbow on the polished surface and nodded off toward the tables along the wall. "You want to talk about trouble, you shoulda been here the night one of our local 'ladies' decided her competition was cutting prices. We had a hair-pulling in the middle of the floor that left two grown men nursing black eyes when they tried to break it up. Yes, sir, bar equals trouble, all right."

"But was a young girl, this girl, ever part of something?" She prompted him with the sketch.

His mind seemed still to be on her first question. "Tell you, one night some dame came in here, popped open the register while I was at the other end of the bar. Had a birthday party going on, lots of noise and moving around. In all the excitement, the gal thought she could tap the till and I wouldn't see her do it. I saw her all right, but she still got out the door with about sixty bucks. Never did catch her." The bartender took a mug from a rack below the bar and dried it, slowly polishing the surface. "And one time, oh, two-three years back, the cops found a stolen car out in the parking lot. Been there a couple of days. They thought it was used in a hit-and-run. Me, I never noticed it. They made quite a show of fingerprinting, making pictures, and what all. They dragged it off after tying up my parking lot half a day." He put the mug up on a glass shelf. "You wanta see ever' garden variety of trouble they make, just open yourself a bar. It'll all come to you."

Claire picked up the sketch again and turned it toward him. "But you're sure you've never seen this girl in here or around the neighborhood?"

He dismissed it with a shake of his head. "No, I can't say I have." He started to hand it back to her and hesitated. "Something about her, those funny eyes, rings a bell. Too young to be hanging around here, though. An older sister? Mother? I don't know. But a kid like this, no, not in here, lady. Not in here." He gave her the sketch with some finality in the gesture. "Another glass of wine for you?"

****

"Are you asleep, Audrey?" Hal's voice tugged at her mind, and Audrey tried to brush it away. A cold wind washed across her face. She stirred and halfway sat up.

"I was dozing a little," she mumbled. The icy blast forced her to open her eyes.

"I think we need some fresh air in here." She

realized the car was running, and Hal was pressing the button to raise the windows. The glass behind him was sliding back into place. She rubbed her eyes and sat up.

"What time is it?" She peered at the face of her watch in the near blackness of the car's interior.

"Coming up on 4:30. Dark as midnight, but the snow is thinning."

Audrey stretched and shifted her position under the enveloping comforter. They would have frozen without it, she was sure. "We should be able to leave soon?"

"I don't know, Puss, but I hope so. The wind is still fierce out there."

She listened and became aware of the constant groan and creak of the walls holding back the force of the blast. Its keening sound suggested despair.

Our wind at home isn't like this wind. She was accustomed to wind raging or blasting for a time, then blowing itself out. This wind threatened, did not relent, and sang in a mournful, minor key. She shivered at the sound.

"It sounds like a living thing, howling and shrieking all around us."

The silence between them inside the car could scarcely be called silent. The wind rattled a loose board and spun tree limbs across the open space outside their sanctuary.

"You mustn't worry too much about what we're going to find in Siding." Hal was perhaps trying to direct her mind to something beyond the moment. "Even if we don't find anything, Jared and I will get George out of this situation. The school groundskeeper is a start. What he saw is valuable to our defense."

Audrey nodded, though she knew he couldn't see

the motion in the faded light. "I know," she added aloud. "Dad is such a good man. Kids got an education or vocational training because he saw to it, when nobody else cared or would try. You can't imagine how many people owe him for the success they're enjoying. Not one of them has stepped forward to help him through this awful thing. Not a single one has called or written to say 'I'm with you. I'll come to court and tell everybody what you did for me.' Not one has stepped up and asked to be heard."

"We've had some letters, supportive letters, from people who cared and wanted to say they didn't believe the rumors," Hal reminded her.

"I've seen them. Most don't sign their names, and none offer to go public and take a stand. It kills me to see people turn their heads and look away if they run into Dad. Without my sisters and you and Drake and Jared, oh, and Ruth and Keefe, we'd be isolated. No one will take the chance to support Dad, because they'd be criticized just like we are. Look how Ruth has to slip in and out like a ghost when she comes to see us."

"I think the sheriff is on your side, though he can't be public about it. He broke speed records getting out there to talk to the school groundskeeper."

"Oh, he's impartial and trying to do his job." An undertone of defeat strained her voice. She felt the pressure of unshed tears behind her eyes. "Keefe didn't even see any importance in his own story. The sheriff checked it out, but he didn't put much weight to it, I suppose."

"You're working yourself up to a huge depression, Puss." She felt Hal's large hand close over hers. "Between the weather now and the drag and pull on you these past weeks, you're overwhelmed."

"Every new idea keeps fizzling out, Hal, but the threat hanging over Dad never goes away." She stopped as the wind hit a higher, wailing note. "Hear that? In the wind? As if someone was crying with no one out there to hear. That's the way I feel, as if I were crying against the wind, and no one can even hear me."

Chapter Sixteen

Drake joined Claire at the table beside the window. The suite was comfortably warm, its tall windows looking down at the snow in the street. Traffic moved, though slowly, and pedestrians took care to walk in cleared paths along the sidewalk. The city seemed to be taking its second storm in a week in stride.

"Most of them haven't seen this kind of thing in years, but they just get up and go on about their business," Claire observed over her morning toast.

"None of us knows how to drive in it. We don't get enough practice. I expect fender benders are crashing all over town." Drake drew back from the window and poured coffee into the waiting cups. "Did our jaunt to Arlington gain us anything? Or was it a total loss?"

Claire turned from the window. "All I got from the bartender was a listing of the trials of running a bar. He was interesting but not informative. He thought he might have seen someone who looked like Dondie, but he may have just said it to get rid of me. I pushed him pretty hard."

"The ticket agent at the bus station was sure he'd seen the girl, didn't know when, or where she'd been going." Drake cut his toast in precise quarters and buttered one. "I think he'd identify a raccoon for the fifty dollars I gave him. I don't see we have anything to report to Jared. Maybe Hal and Audrey will do better."

Claire agreed. "If they could make the trip."

"So we have today and tomorrow to ourselves, love. How about planning our special event? Shall I call Father Will and see if he can meet with us? We need to decide on the place. Here in the suite wouldn't be bad. We could order flowers and have a small buffet set up. The string quartet in the lobby might agree to play."

Claire looked around the suite, noting the lovely appointments and artful décor. She shook her head. "If we were having people in, family and friends, yes, but it's silly for the two of us." She felt a little sad at the thought of getting married without her father and Judith and Audrey, no one at all to witness her happiness.

"We'll talk to Will and see if he can take care of the formalities. Then we can decide on a place." Drake reached for the phone. "I'll call him and see what he has to say."

Apprehension gnawed at Claire. What could Drake say to the retired priest? How could Drake explain their situation without raking up the old pain?

"Want to get on the extension in the bedroom?" Drake must have read her thoughts.

She hesitated. "I have to deal with this some time, don't I?" She put her coffee aside and went to the room that until two nights before had been hers.

****

"You seem to be in better spirits this morning, Audrey." Hal was waiting at her door as she started out.

She hadn't expected him so early. *He must be made of stronger stuff than I am.* "I'm fine." It cost her to put an energetic expression with the answer.

They'd finally crept out of the abandoned service

259

station sometime in the night. The wind had dropped to an unceasing murmur but didn't buffet the car like a ping-pong ball, though the biting cold had not abated. Through a world of eerie white shapes, they'd progressed at a crawling pace over the last miles to Bailey. In spite of the hour, Hal insisted on dinner when they arrived. Audrey barely tasted hers before putting down her fork and heading for her room. Her boots weighed more than her whole body, and she'd thought she'd never get her feet up the last steps.

"So we're ready to take on the wilds of Siding?" Hal looked her over carefully. She straightened her shoulders and stood as tall as her five feet four inches permitted.

She hooked her bag over one shoulder and gave him a mock salute. "Onward for king and country, sire."

The drive to Siding told the travelers much about the place. Small farms lined the road, the farmhouses showing no one had money for paint or new roofs. As the car passed the city limits sign announcing a population of 862, a few businesses began to appear along the road. In the distance stood a brown, square building with a nearly empty parking lot.

"The local industry, I suppose," Hal remarked. A moment later a sign marked a plant entrance: *Winkley Electronics, Siding, Texas*. "Oh, the landing gear people."

"Landing gear?"

"Winkley makes aircraft landing gears. I'd guess this plant takes unfinished parts from vendors and puts them together." Hal gazed at the empty parking spaces. "Looks like they're not doing too well. Two hours into the first shift with hardly anyone at work."

"Maybe Dondie's mother left because the town's drying up for lack of work."

Hal nodded and followed the arrow pointing toward the business district. "The girl's mother worked in a shop, Miss Bobbie's Dress Shop. Let's see if Miss Bobbie will talk to you. Meanwhile I'll take the car to the service station and fill up, maybe make a contact or two." They drove the length of Main Street, five blocks of mostly boarded-up shops, then made a U-turn and started back. Miss Bobbie's was the glass-fronted white shop on the corner. Hal pulled over to let Audrey out.

Snow still stood in crisp white ripples along the street. No one had cleared the sidewalk. Audrey had to watch to keep from plunging into snow over her boot tops. She reached the door only to find a closed sign hanging at an angle in the glass pane.

"Oh, fine. Where am I supposed to go until they open?"

"It won't be opening any time soon unless I can find a buyer," a cheerful voice called. A small woman, middle-aged, all but buried in a quantity of sweaters and scarves, came puffing along the walk toward her.

"Are you Miss Bobbie?" Audrey hoped the answer was yes. This bright-eyed, cheerful soul looked like she'd happily talk all morning.

"No, no, she's my aunt, Roberta Spires. I'm Jessie Hamlin. Aunt Bobbie was taken bad right after Christmas. She's eighty-seven, you know, and not as spry as she was a year or so ago. Looks like she'll have to give up the shop. I came over from Bailey to help her out, but land sakes, I can't stay and run the place for her. I've got a husband who wants his dinner, and two lazy boys who think Mama's going to look after them till they retire. Can't stay more'n a day or two." Jessie managed to sort a large key from the dozen on her ring and opened the door. "Come on in here, young lady, and get warm. My heavens, we had us a storm last night. Hope you weren't out in it. Like to have blowed the house over, I swear."

Audrey followed the plump form into the shop. Jessie pulled cords to raise the blinds, and the sparkle of snow reflected in the wide windows. "Now, you needed to see Aunt Bobbie, Miss…" She waited.

"Anderson, Audrey Anderson," she obliged.

"Audrey. What a pretty name, and one you don't hear so very often. Aunt Bobbie's not up to visitors yet, Audrey, but I can tell her you came by for a visit, if you want. What was it you said you needed to see her about?"

Probably this well-meaning woman couldn't help, Audrey decided. She didn't live in the small community and wouldn't have any reason to know a teenage girl who'd been gone three years or more.

"I needed to ask about a former employee." She eased her bag over her shoulder. "I guess I'll have to see if I can find someone else who knew her."

"Oh, too bad, hon. Hate to see you make the trip around over town. The cold out there'll eat you alive. Not many shops left here since the plant's closing down. Guess I'm gonna have myself a time finding anybody to buy this place. Folks are moving out ever' day, and this bad winter ain't making things any easier." She waved a hand at the silent store. "It was a good little business in its day." Audrey looked around at the mannequins in the window and the racks of garments along the walls. It probably had been a nice little shop not too long ago. "Real good business. Bobbie had her own alteration lady and ever'thing, just like a big city store."

"Alteration lady? Donna Marshall worked here as an alteration seamstress. Did you know her, by any chance?" Audrey felt her hopes rise.

"Donna? You're asking about her?" She slapped her palm against the countertop. "Now, that beats all." She laughed. "I surely did know Donna. Sweetest girl Aunt Bobbie ever had working for her. Her and her little girl used to come to our place for ice cream on a Saturday afternoon in the summers after Aunt Bobbie closed the shop for the day. Pretty as dolls, both of them. Different types, but pretty. How do you know Donna?"

Audrey hated to tell Jessie the true reason she was in Siding, but she felt a falsehood would come back to haunt her.

"I don't know Donna. I only know Dondie, her daughter. The girl has had some kind of terrible accident or injury. She can't remember her family and doesn't know where they are. She's a very troubled child. I want to find her mother and bring the family back together, if I can." It was the truth as far as it went, and Audrey couldn't contemplate explaining more.

Jessie pushed a stray wave behind her ear. "I hate to hear bad news about those girls. They'd had enough trouble. Donna's young husband dying when they both were still just kids. Coming back here with a baby to live in her mama's house and scrabbling to make half a living. Break your heart to see the look in Donna's eyes sometimes. When they left here, seemed like things were finally going good for them."

"They left here? When did they leave, and where did they go?" Audrey reached into her bag for a notepad.

"Just about the same time me and my husband sold the ice cream shop to move to Bailey. Or maybe we left a little before the girls did. Guess it was, 'cause I couldn't go to Donna's wedding. We'd just opened the dry cleaners and didn't have anybody to keep the store." She took a moment to think back. "Been three, no, four years, come summer."

"Donna got married and they moved away?"

"Oh, didn't she just. Audrey, you should have seen her. She was as happy as ever a bride hopes to be. And pretty! Aunt Bobbie gave her a dress from the shop for her wedding present. I saw it. A little yellow tulip of a dress. 'Course Donna was tiny, like a doll, and her red hair just flamed when she let it loose. Too bad the baby didn't take after Donna, but she was a cute little thing. Blonde, she was. Wonder if it stayed yella, like the down on a baby duck. Mostly that kind gets darker."

"It's brown now, a light brown with red and gold highlights," Audrey told her. "But she's not very tall, so I guess she got height from her mother." Audrey made some notes in her book. "You said Donna got married. Who did she marry? Where did they move?"

Jessie thought a minute. "I don't recall his name now. He'd been in the military—navy, I'm thinking—and come here afterward to work in the plant. He was a manager or some such. Then he got some offer from somewhere, and they moved. I know Aunt Bobbie told me all about it at the time, but it's water over the dam now."

"Would your aunt remember?"

"Aunt Bobbie? Land sakes, hon, she can't remember my name or even her own, most times. She's had a bad spell. All the medicine, I suspect, has just muddled her head all around. Half the time she don't know daylight from dark."

Audrey poked for other bits of information, but it was soon clear, though Jessie enjoyed visiting and would talk at length with anyone who came by, she knew nothing more about Donna Marshall, her child, or the man she married.

****

Claire shredded a paper tissue in her lap. She'd worn one of the extravagant purchases Drake had encouraged and felt especially bright and beautiful when she left the hotel. The wine-red knit dress matched the color of her ring and gave a glow to her ivory skin. She'd been waiting in this busy restaurant for Drake and the retired priest for half an hour, and her anxiety was rising from apprehensive to outright misery. Drake had assured her all would be well, but the moment he left, Claire's doubts began to take over. *At last*, she sighed, as two men came out of the elevator and into the room. Drake led a squareish, greyish man to the table. He wore no priestly collar, and she was glad. She didn't need formality to increase her tension.

"Will, this is Claire." She could hear pride and a note of passion in Drake's words.

"I'm so pleased you could come, Father Will." The men seated themselves and disposed of ordering lunch as rapidly as possible.

"So you're the mystery girl I've been hearing about all these years," the priest commented. "I'm happy you and Drake have found each other again. I always felt Alice's deeds would find her out. She made a life of meddling."

Claire put her fork aside. "You knew what she did to us?"

"Not exactly, my dear, but I suspected something of the sort. She told me there had been a separation, and she was sure, given time, you'd have the marriage terminated. I didn't know all the specifics, but she was very pleased with herself. Drake gave me some of the details." Will's genial square face held a look of regret. "Alice had a fine mind and an excellent understanding of art. What she lacked, I fear, was empathy and any ability to distinguish her wants from what others might need."

Drake uttered a short, unamused laugh. "You're being very charitable, Will. Alice was completely self-centered and consumed with the need to control everyone around her. It's nothing short of miraculous that Claire and I found our way back to each other."

Father Will nodded in agreement. "True, but don't forget, the miraculous is my stock in trade." He put one hand over Claire's left hand and a second over Drake's right. "Now it's all come right, hasn't it? Tell me what you want to do about getting married. Do you think we can get it right for you this time?" The quiet twinkle in his eyes warmed Claire.

"We're going to be together for as long as there is time."

"At least a hundred years," Drake added.

****

"Well, we're a little forward," Hal decided as Audrey filled him in on her chat at the dress shop. "I was told Donna had married, too, though I didn't get a name. Best any of them could come up with was it sounded like an Indian name, Longbow or something similar. The man hadn't been here long, as I get it. If you aren't born here, it takes about forty years to stop being a newcomer."

"True of most small towns," Audrey agreed. "So where do we go from here? You talked to the guys at the service station and the convenience store. We could try the plant. The man Donna married is supposed to have worked there."

Hal didn't look happy about her suggestion. "We can, if there isn't any other way, but if we go there, we're talking about personnel files and employee records, touchy stuff. I'd rather leave it till we don't have any other place to go. We can check the courthouse tomorrow for a record of the marriage. Likely they got the license here in the county, though there's no certainty. Today, I'd like for you to see if you can pry anything out of the women who work in the school office."

"But they already sent us a letter with no information. Why would they be more forthcoming now?" Wouldn't it be wasting time to check with the school when there were more fertile areas to work?

Hal held up a hand and marked off his points finger by finger. "The girl was in school here all her life until a few years ago. Then, in one year—less actually—the girl's mother marries and the family leaves. According to the letter we got, her records went to Santa Rita. But the family didn't move to Santa Rita. So those records should have gone somewhere else. They shouldn't have still been here. I want to know why they were. Wasn't there a request to send them on, wherever the family really did move?"

"You're right, Hal. Jessie said Donna married in the summer and they left. Those records should have gone on."

"So the next stop on your list is the school office, right?"

"I don't know if I can get confidential information out of them," she admitted.

"You can, Audrey. Just be sweetly persistent. I know you can do it."

The school was like the one in Santa Rita where her father had spent so many years. Audrey immediately knew the smell of chalk and books and misplaced coats. The grey filing cabinets of the administration office loomed against one wall. Faculty mail slots banked the other side. A low counter divided the entry door from three desks cramped together behind it. One woman, thin, dressed in a heavy cardigan, her white hair scraped into a small knot at the back of her head, was tapping on a typewriter. The desk before her almost disappeared under the piles of papers stacked on it. She looked up at Audrey's entrance.

"The school is still closed for the holidays," she said pleasantly. "We'll be back in session next Monday. Do you have a child you want to enroll?" The last question sounded wistfully hopeful to Audrey.

"No, I needed to ask about a former student." Caught by the memories the room brought her, she suddenly felt at home. "My dad's a teacher. Or I should say he was. He's been serving as student counselor for the last few years. This office feels just like his does."

The woman stood up. "I suppose all classrooms

and school offices eventually absorb the same influences. Gym socks and chalk, brown bag lunches and cough drops, they stick around a long time." She came to the counter. "I'm Mildred Ross, the principal here. You came about a former student?"

"She's a student at my dad's school. She's in a bad place right now. A court case. It would help if we had some way to find her family. Some kind of injury, physical or mental, left her with no memory of anything before she was abandoned at a church in our town. She knows her name and how old she is, and nothing more."

"Oh, poor child." The principal's empathy vibrated in her words. "But how did you trace her here? Through her name?"

"The county social worker traced her here. Unfortunately, the information was thin. The family left here after her school year, and then some tragedy separated them."

"I see," Mildred Ross said. "You need to find the family. You said a court case is involved?"

"The girl may have confused some vague memory with a current happening and not be able to tell truthfully what she knows." Audrey knew she was skimming the edges of veracity but was reluctant to reveal her father's plight.

"A head injury could have that effect. Who did you say the child is? I'll look and see if we have records for her."

"Marshall was the family name. The girl's name is Dondie, or Donna Denise."

"Dondie? Dondie Marshall?" Miss Ross paled.

"You know her?" Audrey reached to steady the older woman. She seemed quite shaken.

"Of course. I know every student in this school, and their parents before them, most of the time. Dondie! I can't bear to think of something tragic happening to her. She's such a loving, gifted little girl."

Audrey waited as the principal composed herself. "What can you tell me about the family?"

"Not a great deal. The mother was a pretty thing and worked hard to make ends meet. She was widowed when the little girl was just a baby. Came here because her parents, maybe his parents, I'm not sure now, left them a little house. Took in sewing to help stretch her income. Dondie wore the cutest little outfits Donna made for her. We were all so glad when Dondie told us her mom was getting married. It was a good thing for both of them. The man had a son and no wife. Donna had a little girl with no daddy. We hated to see them leave, you know, but Dondie was bright, and we couldn't give her everything she needed in this small place. We don't even have a decent library. It was better for her to move."

"And who did Donna marry?"

Miss Ross looked downcast. "I just don't remember. I didn't know the man. He'd only been here a couple of years, not a local boy."

"But he had a son of his own. Wasn't he a student here, too?"

The principal gave her a sad smile. "Our town is dying. We've been fortunate to keep the school open this long. We can only manage by sending our high school students to the consolidated school in Bailey. Our classes here stop at the eighth grade. From here, our children are bussed to the county high school."

"And the boy was a high school student?"

"Graduated from there before Donna and his father married. I never knew the youngster."

Audrey's hopes deflated, but she couldn't give up yet. "If Dondie left here because her family wanted to give her a stronger academic background, surely her records were sent on."

"To your dad's school, apparently."

"But the family didn't move to Santa Rita. The girl came sometime in September. Why were her records still here?"

Awareness began to fill the older woman's face. "A very good question, my dear. I'd like an answer myself." She opened the small gate at the side of the counter. "Come with me, and we'll see if we can find out."

Audrey followed as Mildred Ross led the way to the bank of filing cabinets. "You keep copies of the records transferred?"

"Oh, no, we don't have the space for that, I'm afraid. We mail the records when a request comes from a new school. All we keep here is a file jacket with the request letter and any correspondence we have with the new school. Usually it's just the transmittal letter."

A file drawer marked Closed—A-M stuck a bit. Mildred Ross expertly maneuvered the drawer in its compartment. "It's as old as I am, and the cold makes both of us cranky," she apologized as she finally opened the drawer. She flipped through worn tabs and pulled a brown file jacket free.

"Here we are." She carried the file to the counter and spread it flat.

"I see the letter from Santa Rita there."

"Actually there are two from Santa Rita, one from

the school and one from a lawyer asking about Dondie's family." She looked up. "We didn't give you much help, did we?"

"No, Miss Ross, though I'm sure no one meant to be callous about the girl's welfare." Audrey hoped she'd said the right thing.

"I didn't see the request myself." Her voice suggested such an omission was not to her liking. "I would have at least made a phone call to see what it was about. Our office help is mostly volunteer, you see, and the ladies sometimes take on more than they should handle. I should have seen this attorney's letter."

"Is that all? Nothing from another school?"

Mildred Ross shook her head. "No other records." She raised the letters bradded into the file. "Oh, no, wait, something else is here. It's still folded, just fastened into the jacket and left. What on earth were those girls thinking?" She unclasped the fastener and slid the top pages free. The folded letter came last. She slipped it over the prongs and opened it.

"What have you found?"

The principal bit her lip in frustration. "Another request came to transfer the girl's records. Apparently we never honored it. It's dated the first of July, so it predates the request from Santa Rita by more than two months."

"Why weren't the records sent?" Audrey asked. Then another question occurred to her. "When the new school didn't get the records, why didn't they make a second request? Wouldn't that be the normal thing to do?"

"Usually a school will send a follow-up in about sixty days if they don't hear something. We do, at any rate." She smoothed the letter and neatly clipped it back in the file. "I don't know why they didn't ask." She returned the file to the drawer. "I'll bet it was the Perrit girl. She did some harebrained things while she was in the office." Mildred Ross shut the drawer with force. "When a young girl is in love—or heat—she's all but useless. Around the beginning of July she flitted off to be with her boyfriend. Probably the letter came in and her head was somewhere else. She just tossed it in the file and forgot it. When we sent things to Santa Rita, we didn't even notice it, or took it for a doctor's note or permission slip. We wouldn't have transmitted either of those with the grade and attendance records."

She was more concerned with the foul-up in her own office than Audrey's quest. Audrey started to ask the question burning in her mind, but the principal was still focused on the clerk's blunder.

"That Perrit girl was in her own world. She volunteered here to get away from home. When her young man graduated, they broke up. She was wailing and sniffling around the house till somebody told her to get something to do and stop whining. I let her work here. She wasn't much good at office work, but I hoped I could help her. She wasn't stupid, just obsessed about that boy. Then one day she flitted in, said he'd sent for her, and she was going. Didn't even finish her day out. I guess she'd been brooding over the decision all day and finally made it. She was on the evening bus out of town the same day. And left us a lot of little messes like this one to clean up."

Audrey sympathized but was running short on patience and time. She had only one question left to ask here. "Miss Ross, I didn't actually see the request for

Dondie's records. Where was it from? I need to see if I can connect it to Dondie's family. Could I take a look at it, please?"

"Of course you need to know what school was asking for the files. But I can tell you without hauling a cranky drawer out again. It was Travis High School, a good school, though bigger than I'd want for a child from a small-town school. Travis High, down in Arlington."

Chapter Seventeen

For the most part, small drifts of snow sparkled pristine and white around Bailey, Texas, but in places dark frozen puddles edged black treacherous mud. Audrey left the hotel and looked for the coffee shop Hal had said was only a step away. Audrey caught sight of the brown cup sign, Hava Java, far down the street. *Closer to two blocks.*

Audrey's attempt to contact Jared had been futile. The office phone had rung endlessly. She had no response at Drake's gallery or at home. *So much for trying to report progress.* Audrey zipped up her coat. Breakfast seemed like a better idea anyway.

Wrinkling her nose at the sludge and goo waiting between the door of the hotel and the coffee shop, Audrey took a hesitant step. Clear frigid air encircled her as she left the relative warmth of the hotel entrance. Her earlobes numbed almost as she stepped into the street. She should have worn her furry cap, she realized, and dug gloves out of her pocket. Her bag slipped as she pulled the stiffened leather over fingers clumsy with the cold. Two blocks to the coffee shop began to feel like miles.

Audrey reviewed the puzzle as she picked a path along the slippery walk. The blank areas were taking shape now with a better picture of Dondie Marshall's background. The mother married and the child apparently was happy about it. The boy, the son of the man Donna married, had he been the root of the trouble? Audrey considered him, sidestepping as a car splashed a stream of mud and ice her way. Teenage boys were sometimes bullies, or just plain self-centered. Maybe the boy wasn't pleased about the marriage and took his resentment out on Dondie.

Audrey dodged puddles but slid into snowy mush, leaving her boots caked with grime. She grabbed a street sign, knocked the toes of her boots against the base to loosen some of the goo, and went on.

The man Donna married might not have been the person she thought he was. Audrey picked up her review of possibilities. He had no daughters, and sudden exposure to the hormonal angst and drama of a thirteen-year-old girl accustomed to all her mother's attention might have been more than the new husband bargained for. Maybe he'd been insensitive or overwhelmed and treated the girl harshly. Audrey conceded she didn't have enough of the story to explain why Donna Marshall, respected and admired in Siding, became a woman who abandoned or endangered her child. The story left too much unexplained. One thing was clear in Audrey's mind. Every piece of the puzzle invariably led back to Arlington. She hoped Claire hadn't started for home yet. Arlington appeared to have answers, if they could find the right questions.

The sound of crackling ice pulled Audrey out of her thoughts. Her footing gave way, and she found the thin skim of mud under foot covered a patch of unmelted ice. One foot slid left and the other right. She clutched wildly for a handhold. The swing of her weighted bag dragged her further off balance. Hair loose and flying across her eyes, half blinded by sun glinting off bits of ice, Audrey flailed at thin air, desperately grabbing for a support. A parking meter saved her from falling ignominiously on her face into the mud. Clinging with both hands until she regained balance, she looked down to see what damage the impromptu skate down the sidewalk had done. Grey gunk coated her boots, and her green slacks were spattered to the knees with greasy brown residue. *Next time we have separate errands,* she promised the absent Hal, *I'll take the car and you can hit the streets.*

****

Claire let her slippers slide off her feet. She curled up on the loveseat, wrapping the pink satin robe tightly around her. From the bathroom beyond the bedroom she could hear water cascading over tiles. Drake's voice rose above the splash and gurgle with the Spanish love song he was crooning. It was a very nice voice, she decided, untrained but pleasant as a backdrop for the morning's first efforts. *We're going to wear well together. Probably better than before, because we were kids then. We didn't know we could lose the most valuable thing life would offer us. We did lose it for a time, but we got it back again. We'll take better care of our love, protect it and each other, this time.*

Time, she mused as Drake changed songs in mid-chorus, time ran so fast and at the same time so slowly. *I thought waiting seventy-two hours would be like waiting for Christmas when it's only July. Now the waiting period is almost up and we still don't have a place to get married. Well, we do. This suite will be fine. We can have it here. Father Will doesn't have a parish anymore, and we don't have a church here.* In her heart, locked in a place where she was sure Drake couldn't see, was a lingering regret—she'd have no aisle, no candlelight, no stately organ. Her dad wouldn't escort her to her groom, and no sister would stand with her. She wouldn't have well-wishers to witness her happiest moment.

Father Will had seen her regret, she thought, but he'd also seen the problems. George, because of the pending trial, couldn't come clear across the state. A wedding in the midst of the other family burdens at home would seem insensitive, and waiting till the trial was over wasn't an option they were willing to consider. So their choice came down to a quiet ceremony, no fanfare, no guests or other flourishes. She was happy to have a second chance at the love she'd believed to be only ashes and regrets. Claire told herself if her dad could be cleared of those awful charges, she wouldn't ask for more than what she had at this moment.

The shower stopped and Drake appeared in the doorway. He'd draped one of the hotel's generous towels around himself like a toga. He padded across the carpet and sat at the end of her loveseat, the towel slipping a little as he sat.

"You're far off in dreamland, ladylove." He reached under her robe, fully aware, she was sure, she had nothing under it. One slow finger drew a line along the sole of her bare foot. She shivered as his tender touch stirred her.

"I was thinking about where we could get married," she admitted. "I guess the easiest place is right here in the suite. It's a lovely room, and the place is just a detail anyway. You're the only important, essential element."

Drake's fingers closed around her ankle. She stretched her legs against the brocade, letting the textures and his touch fill her senses. "If this room is acceptable," he said leaning forward to the further detriment of his toga, "we can spend today exploring some other uses for the place. I have some very creative ideas."

His long clever fingers sought the knot securing her robe. The pink satin loosened under his questing touch. The spicy scent of his soap and aftershave enveloped her, and her robe was falling free. His towel slipped away. His arms were around her, his lips touching hers—and across the room the phone cut the moment with a shrill peal.

"Ignore it," Claire suggested, her finger smoothing the line between his eyes. The phone rang again.

With a groan of frustration, Drake sat up. "It could be Hal or Jared trying to reach you. Judith has my number here." Reluctantly he drew back. "I'll be just a second." As the strident ring filled the room again, he dashed for the phone, his towel only a crumpled streak blending into the carpet.

It could be something about Dad, Claire reminded herself to overcome her annoyance at the untimely interruption. She caught a fragment of conversation, "...looking forward to seeing you," and a silence following.

"Who was it?" she called, re-tying her robe and reaching for her slippers. One was beside the loveseat, and she stepped into it while looking about for the other.

When she turned, Drake, holding briefs and a T-shirt, stood in the bedroom doorway. "It was Bird." He pulled the shirt over his head. Claire had to smile at the leopard print briefs. His dark gold hair emerged from the neck of the shirt.

"Bird?"

He tugged the shirt down over his shoulders. "Bird is Father Will's wife. She's downstairs and on her way up. Will must have told her about us, because she wants to talk to us about the wedding. She'll be here in about two minutes."

"The minister's wife is coming? I'm not even decent!" Claire found her other shoe and put it on. "Strangers popping into our love nest before breakfast? Sedate art historian in a scanty costume? Is this what life is going to be like with you?" She picked up the towel and tossed it to him. "Here, put that away and try to be dressed by the time she's at the door. She's going to think we're Bohemian enough, sharing this suite without benefit of clergy. We don't want to embarrass her more." Stifling a laugh, she dashed for the bedroom to dress. What a scene for the minister's wife to walk into. And what if she hadn't called first?

****

"Next time *you* walk and *I'll* take the car." Audrey held out her booted foot for Hal to see the sludge covering it.

"Unfortunate." Hal barely glanced at the mess. "I can recommend the pancakes and sausage."

She plopped into the chair beside him and turned up the cup before her. A waitress filled the cup and passed her a menu.

"Your dainty footwear aside, did you get the

information to Jared?"

She skimmed the menu as she told him of her various attempts and failures. "We've got to reach Claire before she starts home. She needs to hang out in Dallas for a day or two more. At least till we can get a name for her to check out." Audrey looked up at the waitress poised with pad and pen. "Oh, just bring me whatever he's having." She waved the girl away.

"The courthouse doesn't open till nine." Hal checked the clock above the counter. "Half an hour." He poured sugar into his cup and stirred. "No reason for both of us to go. We have the woman's name and an approximate date for the marriage. It should be a fairly straightforward question. Either they got the license here or they didn't."

The waitress slid a huge plate of pancakes, sausage, and eggs in front of Audrey. "Right." Audrey shook her head at the serving. "This place must cater to ranch hands, not regular appetites." She took a bite, savored the tang of the sausage, and began buttering her pancakes. "It wouldn't make sense, Hal, for Donna and her fellow to get the license somewhere else. They were married in Siding, and no one indicated she had out-of-town family."

Hal pushed his plate aside and took a pencil from his pocket. Without being asked, Audrey freed a tablet from the jumble in her bag and passed it to him. He grinned, not commenting on how well she read his mind, but Audrey knew he thought it. "I think that makes the most sense, too. Let's see, the school principal put the marriage about four years ago come summer, didn't she?" Audrey confirmed it. "And summer, that's June or July, isn't it?"

"No, I'd make it May or June," Audrey contradicted. "The letter from the school in Arlington was dated July. The wedding would have been earlier."

Hal made a note and circled it, adding a question mark to the side. "I'll start in May and go forward. July is probably the latest possible time." He closed the pad. "What are you going to do while I'm plowing through musty records at the courthouse, little one? Visit the local centers of culture or shop in the vast array of emporiums?"

She laughed at the suggestion. "Charming as your program sounds," she answered facetiously, "I have a quest of my own. The town has a newspaper—the *Bailey Banner*—published twice a week. I gleaned that bit of information from the helpful soul minding the desk at our hotel. I'm going to look at back issues. Small town papers print everything, who made the honor roll, who's having a birthday, and especially who's getting married. I'm bound to find something about the Marshall wedding, maybe names of the guests. One of them might have a current address for the family. We can check for contacts here while Claire looks at the other end, in Arlington."

"I knew I fell in love with you for something besides your pretty green eyes, Puss." Hal grinned his approval. "You have a lawyer's mind behind your sweet face."

****

"You're every bit as lovely as Will said, Claire." The woman standing in the entrance of the suite was smaller than Claire's five feet six inches, but she wasn't the tiny creature one expected from her name. Her silver hair waved softly about her face, and her eyes matched her immaculate blue suit.

"Won't you come in," Claire invited. "We were about to order breakfast. What can I get for you?"

"Not a thing," the older woman began, then reconsidered. "No, actually I would love some tea. I feel the cold more than I used to."

Once settled in the sitting room, Claire wasn't sure what to say to their unexpected guest.

"Bird, you served a wonderful dinner to Will's New Year's Eve guests." Drake managed to break the awkwardness.

"It was a nice evening. Will was delighted you were able to come." She looked from Drake to Claire and back again. "Isn't this silly? We're sitting here making chit-chat when you two have things to do. Will told me about your situation, you see." She put a hand over Claire's. "He thinks you're not quite happy about the wedding arrangements, dear. It does seem less than joyful to have Will come up here and read the wedding service over you."

Claire swallowed a desire to agree. "It's fine, Bird. Drake and I will be married—we must remember what's important."

"I had a thought—it's not exactly traditional, and it won't be like having a large family wedding in your own church—but it's festive, and a few dear people would share your happiness and offer their congratulations."

Claire glanced at Drake. Had he secretly seen into her heart and known the regret she'd hidden? Had he said something to Father Will to lead the priest's wife to come with a suggestion?

"No point in going for elaborate planning, and we

don't have anyone who could come on such short notice."

"I know, Claire, but it would be so very little trouble. The people I'm thinking of would feel blessed to share your joy." Bird leaned forward, emphasizing her sincerity. "I volunteer at a senior citizens center three days a week. It's a place where perfectly healthy, active older people come to do some community work, make craft items for various fundraisers, and socialize. I play the piano and lead an hour of singing. We have a little non-denominational chapel at the center, where some of the retired clergy take turns holding Sunday services. Last year two of our members were married in the chapel. Will did the service. When we were talking last night about how disappointed you must be, Claire, the image of that chapel just popped into my head. Would you let my senior citizens host your wedding? It would be a privilege and a joy for them to do it."

Claire looked at Drake in something like panic. Let total strangers, frail and elderly ones, take on planning her wedding—and in only two days? She could see disaster looming. "I don't think…"

"Now before you scare yourself, Claire," Bird interrupted, "let me assure you these dear people are used to putting events together. They do two bazaars every year, with games and refreshments and events. Last year we had a storytelling day and people came from all over Tarrant County. We even did a reception for the mayor and his wife. And we do a community dance for retired folks about once a month. We're used to doing things, and a wedding is just adding a reception on to a church service. What do you think? We can provide it all, anything you want. You just need a groom and a dress. You have a dress?"

Claire could only nod. She did have a dress, a wonderful, incredibly expensive dress.

Bird looked at Drake. "Well, young man, what do you say? Shall we give the girl a pretty little wedding in a proper chapel? Don't you want to see her coming down the aisle, the way you've imagined it, and know you two aren't giving up dreams for the sake of expediency?"

Drake moved to the loveseat and sat beside Claire. "Up to you, ladylove. We'll do it any way you want, but I suspect you'd like to do this in a church this time. Your parents' backyard under the old oak tree was fine when we were kids, but this is different. This is for always. If your family can't be here, at least people with loving hearts could be."

Claire looked up at his concerned, loving face and knew, whatever her fears might be, this was the answer to her unspoken prayer. She could have the wedding her heart longed for. "Yes," she murmured, tears stinging her eyes. "Oh, yes, Drake."

****

The *Bailey Banner* was housed in an aged brick building on a side street off the main drag. Its weathered front and sagging door didn't suggest a bustling hive of activity inside. Behind the lone desk, a young man sat reading the sports page from a metropolitan daily. His feet, large and covered only by his striped socks, were propped on one corner, while a cup of cold coffee sat on the other. He didn't stir till Audrey tapped her knuckles beside his ankles on the desktop.

He dropped the top of the paper an inch or two.

"Whad'ja need?"

"I need to look at some back issues of the paper," she told him, her voice crisp with impatience.

He gestured toward a cabinet behind him where stacks of volumes were stored. "Have at it."

She could see the dates on the books. They started ten years back and receded into fading decades. "No, issues from May and June four years ago, not ancient history."

"Yeah, right." He turned the newspaper to a new page. "The loose issues. No reason to have those bound." He waved a negligent hand at the untidy piles of newsprint bundled into a run of shelves in the darker recesses of the room. "Help yourself."

"Just tell me where I can find the year I need. I can handle the rest." She was finding it difficult to keep her temper.

"The date, more or less, is on a sheet of paper tacked behind the stacks. 'Course they get mixed up, put back in the wrong pile sometimes."

"This is for a court case, and time is a factor. Can you give me a hint about where to start?"

"Your case, your funeral." He shrugged. "Might start up there." He motioned to two boxes, dusty and threatening to topple from the uneven heap. "Those are about the right time, I guess."

Audrey slipped off her coat and put it over the back of a straight chair. The law school library had been better controlled but not much tidier. She hadn't forgotten how to organize a search.

Standing on the chair, Audrey sorted through the jumbled piles of disorderly, dusty papers. One box slipped from her reach and fell to the floor, leaving a chaotic wave of yellowing newspapers across the floor. The man at the desk barely looked up from his football scores as she climbed down from the chair and retrieved the box. A glance at the label assured her these were from the time period she sought.

Audrey stacked the tumbled pages on a side table, handling them as carefully as she could. The brittle paper threatened to crumble with any touch, and the dust and ink on her fingers smudged the print where she touched a page. She began turning through issues, moving back through the events making up the daily lives of the communities nearby.

A column headed "Sightings at Siding" appeared in the first issue of each week. Thinking she might find her answers in the daily gossip, she slowed her search, checking dates at frequent intervals. May issues at last came to light.

Myrtle Mae was home after her recent surgery and was looking forward to getting back to her garden, one item told her. Audrey wondered briefly who Myrtle Mae was and how she felt about the county reading her saga of the gallstones. Endless reports of travel, whether short hops or extended tours, filled pages. Every account of a party or celebration listed the attendees and the refreshments served. Audrey noted the same names came up in every issue. Were they popular, or did the limited population make repetition a necessity? Though the snippets from life were intriguing, it was the wedding announcements she read with avid interest. The descriptions went on for lengthy paragraphs and included not just the bridal finery. Every garment, flower, favor, and food received microscopic attention. Surely Donna Marshall's nuptials had not been overlooked.

May passed in a stream of grey-toned images that blurred before her eyes. Audrey pulled out the June issues. The first publication date rewarded her search. "Marshall-Rainwater Plans Announced." The headline stopped her eyes. There it was. The announcement that Donna Marshall and Noah Rainwater would be married the next weekend in the garden of Mr. and Mrs. Norman Hale. A small, informal ceremony was planned, and afterward the couple would be spending the weekend in Palo Dura Canyon. Short, no details, but Audrey was within sight of the end of her search.

"Can I buy this issue of the paper? And maybe a couple more?" she asked the indifferent office keeper.

He put his feet down and laid the paper aside. Stuffing his long arms into a jacket, too short in the sleeves and too tight around his paunch, he nodded. "Okay by me. Fifty cents for the issue, leave the money on the desk. I'll be 'cross the street getting a doughnut and a sody water."

"You're just leaving the office to run itself?"

"Sure. You ain't gonna steal that pile of kindling you're reading, are you?" He sounded almost hopeful. He shoved his feet into shoes, leaving them untied, and sauntered to the door. "Later," he said, and headed into the daylight. An icy blast from the opened door sent cold needles up her back. Audrey retrieved her coat and returned to her page. She wasn't sure whether she should be amused or annoyed with her laconic host.

"Rainwater," she murmured as she turned to the next stack. "I guess it was an Indian name at some time. Just like Longbow was."

Discarding issues outside of her dates of interest,

Audrey scanned for the actual wedding announcement. When she located the first paper of the next week, the announcement was prominently placed. "Marshall-Rainwater Vows Read."

"Right!" she cheered and skimmed through the paragraphs. The account fairly gushed with sentiment. Audrey saw Noah Rainwater's son Drew had served as best man and Dondie had been her mother's attendant. A long description of the bride's yellow dress and each flower in her colonial nosegay followed. Audrey read on, skipping the effusive details and looking only for names. Miss Roberta Spires was mentioned as an honored guest, but others were lumped into the "host of well-wishers" who waved the newlyweds off to their weekend honeymoon. At the very end something useful caught Audrey's attention. "The happy couple will soon be leaving our city. Noah Rainwater and long-time friend Tad Houseman will be opening an appliance dealership in Arlington, where Donna and Noah will make their home. Miss Dondie Marshall is looking forward to her new school, though she says she will miss her many friends here. Drew Rainwater will be leaving for military service in the fall. Are there wedding bells in the near future for you as well, Drew? We hear Rhonda would like to know."

Home town gossip and small town happenings, Audrey chuckled. *Even a high school romance gets covered.* She had what she was looking for. Not as many names as she'd hoped, but a bit of information she hadn't expected to find. She had the name of Noah Rainwater's partner and the type of business they were opening. The name gave Claire more leads to follow, even if Audrey and Hal hit a blank. Audrey found a crumpled dollar bill in her bag. She dropped the money on the desk and set the coffee cup on it to keep it from blowing when the door opened.

Before sliding the folded pages into the side of her bag, Audrey looked over the wedding article once more. Family moved to Arlington, Dondie happy about school, the boy planning a tour of military duty. It looked so promising, a new start. What happened? Where did it fall apart? What made Dondie become an isolated, confused child? Surely someone could tell her. Audrey ran a finger down the page. The boy had a sweetheart, a fairly serious one, it seemed. Maybe the girl knew some of the answers. Audrey put her pages away and picked up her coat. She didn't have very many names to check on. Many people had moved from the dying town, everyone said, so the Hale family might no longer be here. People lost touch after moving. They might not know the story even if she found them. But the girl Rhonda probably did, not that it mattered. The hope of finding her was less than the hope of locating the wedding hosts. At least Audrey had last names for them. She had no real chance with the girl, not with a fairly common name like Rhonda, the passing of time, and no last name at all.

Audrey shouldered her bag and zipped up her coat. Not until she stepped into the street and felt the icy sludge seeping into her boots did she remember Hal had once more taken the car and left her to walk.

Chapter Eighteen

Judith watched the two men pacing the length and width of the concrete plot. They'd been talking back and forth in mumbles for an hour. Judith leaned her back against the cottonwood tree, cocked one boot against the trunk, pulled her jacket closer, and waited. Sooner or later they'd remember she had a say in things. They strolled to the other side of her tree, the contractor pointing toward the panorama before them.

"Nah, Jared, it was me doin' it, I'd turn the thing forty-five degrees west. Forget all that glass and such. Too hot. How you gonna clean winders so high up? Now, me, I'd put a couple of partitions, make myself a big front room, a little bedroom, a bath, and put a galley kitchen here along the wall. Show you what I mean." The contractor picked up a twig and drew lines in the dirt. "See, you turn it this way, put yourself a sliding door right here, a patio outside, you got all the light anybody needs, and save yourself a heap of work to boot. And you got somethin' you can sell one of these days and make a little profit on."

Judith waited for Jared to ask her opinion. He seemed to be studying the lines on the ground with interest. She pulled away from the tree, dusted the back of her saddle pants for leaves, and sauntered to stand between the two men.

"When you boys get tired of playing in the dirt and are ready to hear what I plan to have in this studio, come over to the house. I have some sketches and a floor plan. If you can follow simple instructions, I might let you look at them." Judith stalked between them, heading for the house.

"Girl's mighty sharp-tongued," she heard the contractor complain.

"You don't know the half of it. And if she doesn't get what she wants, you'll see how fast she can turn into a wildcat. She wants windows on the north two stories high, so you do what the lady wants." Jared's words faded as Judith reached the house. A smile tugged at her lips, but she kept walking. She heard the phone ringing inside and hurried in.

Dumping her sketch bag, she grabbed the receiver. "Hello."

"Judith, I finally caught up with you." Audrey's voice sounded as if she'd been running.

"Sis, what's up? You find the missing family?"

"We found a lot of interesting stuff, but I need to talk to Claire. Has she started home yet?"

"Still in Dallas, last we heard. The bar in Arlington didn't have anything new, but she had a nibble at the bus station. Claire wasn't sure it was on the level. Maybe some guy just saying what he thought she wanted to hear. She said the weather was rotten in Dallas, so she's staying till the snow's gone."

She heard Audrey mumble something to another party, probably Hal, and then she spoke into the phone again. "We need to reach her. Where is she staying?"

Judith fumbled for a notepad. "I didn't ask her, but Drake's at the Adolphus. He'll know." She read the number off the pad to her sister. "Try him there."

"Hal needs to talk to Jared. Is he there?" Audrey sounded hurried, as if she had too many things on her mind.

"Sure, Sis, he's here, reading the riot act to a contractor about my studio. Hold on. I'll get him." She walked out the front door and waved to get Jared's attention. He was still propounding the facts of life to the contractor. Finally he looked up. Judith mimed answering a telephone, and he came at a run.

"Hal has information and needs to talk." He headed back into the house and snatched the dangling phone.

"Rainwater? That's the name?" he was saying as Judith returned. "Okay, married in Siding but moved to Arlington. Arlington? I'll be damned. What else? Appliance store, partner named Houseman." Jared listened. "Oh, George? He left early this morning. Good lord, the man's a prisoner in his own house. He's not getting on a plane for Rio. He drove to San Antonio, had some lunch, mailed his manuscript, and is on his way back. I'll tell him the news when he gets in. We'll keep trying to get Claire from this end. You heading back?" Jared listened again. "Right, see you then."

The information Hal and Audrey had dug up cheered Judith more than she wanted to admit. A name to locate, a connection to find, at last some solid facts to work on, if Claire could locate the Rainwater family or their store. "Hal and Audrey will arrive tonight?"

"No, Audrey found the names of some friends of the Rainwaters. She and Hal are trying to locate them before coming back. Hal questioned your dad leaving town, but I think he sees the need."

"So we're moving along, getting answers?" Judith

saw a degree of hope.

"We are, Judy baby, we are. I didn't think much of your sister's Arlington connection, but it may be a hot lead." He put an arm over her shoulders. "Let's continue educating the contractor, and then we'll call Drake. He'll know where to find your sister. Claire probably stayed with a friend, but I'll bet Drake can pinpoint her every move."

****

Claire sat in the shadows of the little chapel, where she found the atmosphere healing. One look at this tiny sanctuary had convinced her Bird's suggestion was good. A short, central aisle with six pews to each side would seat sixty guests. She'd have nowhere near so many, but she'd have a proper aisle to come down. Stained glass windows filled the room with rose-and-gold light. Bird sat at the small piano beside the altar. On the other side, three women, all over seventy, compared notes.

"What do you think, Claire?" Bird looked up but continued to spill light, shimmering notes through the air. "Will this do it for you?"

"Bird, the chapel is perfect."

"I'll play for the service, of course. You'll want a processional, even if there aren't any attendants. What would you like?"

Claire almost said she would let Bird decide. Then she caught herself. Drake would tell her to speak her heart. "Would it offend anyone if it wasn't church music?"

"You didn't want 'Mack the Knife' or 'In the Mood,' did you?" Bird riffed through a few rollicking bars of the swing tune.

Claire laughed in delight. Bird was proving to be a rainbow of surprises. "Perhaps a little too informal." She mulled a more serious selection. "When Drake and I were starving students, our entertainment was limited to free movies and concerts on campus. One piece became sort of our theme."

"'Shake, Rattle and Roll'?" Bird suggested.

Claire gave up and dissolved in peals of giggles as Bird romped through a chorus.

"Not that one," she insisted when both had regained their composure. "It was from an old movie— *Cover Girl.* It's called 'Long Ago and Far Away,' and Drake and I thought if it as our song."

"I think Jerome Kern and Ira Gershwin would be honored." Bird fingered a chord. "Will and I enjoyed *Cover Girl,* too." She struck the first haunting notes of the melody, and Claire once more felt a shiver move up her spine. This was the piece she wanted. Drake would remember it, too.

Claire heard the last note fade. "Would it be all right? It's very special to us."

"I think it's perfect." Bird played through the short piece again, holding Claire almost spellbound.

She rested both hands on the piano. "You play with such feeling."

"Oh, in my green and innocent years, I thought I would be a concert pianist, but I met Will and plans changed. I've played instruments with half the keys missing, and I've played some truly splendid grand pianos, but all of them served to lift someone's spirits or ease someone's pain. There's no better feeling." She turned to face Claire. "Now, what about a recessional? Something light and lilting?"

"Surprise us. Anything you choose will be exactly right."

The three older women beside the altar came to join them at the piano. Bird made introductions. "This is Mattie, who makes the best Italian cream cake in the world." She turned to the other two women. "And Joyce and Olla help out in the kitchen. They have the reception well in hand. Right, girls?"

"Reception?" Claire felt panic rising.

"Honey, you didn't think we were gonna let you walk down the aisle and right on out the door, did you? 'Tain't decent." The woman Bird called Mattie whipped open a loose-leaf notebook and turned to a page. "Gonna do the cream cake, put some rose petals and doodads around, make it wedding 'stead of retirement or birthday, two tiers. What time you thinkin' for this affair, Claire honey? Evening?"

Claire shook her head in confusion. She hadn't thought about time. "What's best for you?"

"Well, we get the day crowd out of here by five so they can get home early. Then we could clean and get the tables set. We'll need a bite to eat and time to dress up a mite. Say you plan the wedding for seven, and we'll have reception things ready around eight. Leaves time for you to get your pictures made after."

Pictures? Claire hadn't thought about pictures either. Had Drake?

"So if we're receiving between eight and half past, our crowd's had dinner only two hours earlier. Not gonna need much of a buffet. Say we'll do cucumber sandwiches, toast points with crab salad, those little tiny quiche things, a cheese-and-fruit tray, and the cake. Coffee and claret wine punch?" Mattie had her lists made before Claire could say yes or no. She didn't have a better scheme, so she nodded in agreement.

"Good, everything's settled. Now, you got a color scheme planned?" Mattie had turned to a new page.

"Well, uh, no, I really hadn't thought—"

"Then we oughta get our flower lady to help you out. You called her, Bird?"

Claire felt like the ball in a ping-pong tournament. The women seemed to know how to get things done, leaving her the pleasure of agreeing to major choices while they took care of details without her.

"Mary-Suellen said roses work best in here. She's sure she can get them. She's done flowers for the chapel a lot this year. What color, Claire? I'll call and tell her."

For a moment Claire couldn't think, then a glint of light touched her ring. "This color, the color of the center stone in my ring." She held it out for them to see.

"My, my, did you ever see anything so pretty?" Mattie held Claire's hand up to the light and admired the rose-cut diamonds and the deep, glowing rubies. "A handsome color. I just bet we can get flowers to match. Bird, you tell Mary-Suellen, and I'll get going on dressing up the hall out there. We gonna have ourselves a humdinger of a show here, ladies, come tomorrow night."

Claire and Bird watched the three bustle off, chattering among themselves and laughing over the plans they'd made. "It can't be so easy," Claire exclaimed.

"Well, generally not, but in this case there's no time to fuss over the little stuff." Bird closed the piano. "Let's go over to the office so I can call Mary-Suellen.

She'll want to know what style you want her to create."

"Candles, lots of candles, ivory ones with globes around them. And poufs of ivory tulle with velvet bows. Romantic and…" She stopped. "Am I getting too carried away?"

"If I'm reading you right, you want Victorian elegance and frills, right?"

"Oh, Bird, exactly right. And I have to find a photographer, too. We need pictures. Especially since Dad and my sisters won't be here to see it."

Bird agreed. "All taken care of, Claire. When I told our group they were invited to a wedding tomorrow, one of our gentlemen reminded me he does a bit of photography. Of course, it's for his birdwatching society, but he knows how to use a camera. He's excited. In fact he'd like to attempt a portrait before the ceremony."

"It's all going to be perfect, Bird. I just know it." She looked at the meeting room where the reception would be held. Its cream-and-gold walls would look splendid with her ruby-red roses. She was sure Mattie could make even peanut butter sandwiches look like a feast. "I hope Drake knows this is costing him a fortune," Claire said, a worry-note in her voice.

"What was the last thing he said to you as we left the hotel? *Don't even ask the price, just do what makes you happy.* Aren't those his very own words?" Bird's voice was stern. "This is one time, probably the only time, I'd suggest giving in to the man."

****

Drake closed his book and listened. He heard the door to the suite open. "Claire?" he called. "Are you back at last?" He swung his feet off the bed and hurried to the sitting room. Claire, her arms full of packages, looked windblown and rosy. He kissed her over the top of the pile and took the stack from her.

"Find some pretty things, love?"

"A bride has to have a few things—underthings."

"I knew Bird was a good influence on you. Did you get the wedding put together the way you wanted?"

"It's going to be grand." She slipped out of her topcoat and turned to hang it up. Drake enjoyed the sight of her in her simple taupe suit, one he suspected had cost him serious money. She was beautiful, without a single flaw in face or form. She wore her beauty the way she wore her elegant suit, without fanfare or show, just being who she was.

"I was thinking of taking you to dinner later. Is there something you'd prefer?"

"Mmm, anything will be fine." She unbuttoned her jacket and stepped out of her shoes. "I keep thinking I should have heard from the family. Has anyone been trying to get me?"

Drake went to the phone and learned the desk had messages for him. "They've been trying to get in touch." He covered the phone. "Shall I tell them I can have you call? Or do you want me to tell them you're here?"

"No, no, not yet."

Drake had the desk place the call to Santa Rita. "I can find her, Jared." He grinned as he glanced at the girl across the room. "What's up?" He made writing motions in the air. Claire nodded and a moment later put a hotel pen and a pad beside him. Drake scribbled notes as he listened.

"What is it? What did he tell you? Is there news?"

Claire's tone was taut with curiosity.

"Hal and Audrey made a find in that little town in the Panhandle. The Marshall girl's mother married and left the town, moving—guess where?"

"I don't know. Here?"

"More or less. The new husband intended to open an appliance shop in Arlington. Name's Rainwater, Noah Rainwater. Hal didn't know if he opened the shop or if the family moved there, but they intended to. Your job, or rather ours, is to find the family if they're still here. The girl was supposed to attend Travis High School in Arlington, but her records were never sent. The supposition is whatever happened to the girl prevented her from enrolling there. Time frame's between the first of July and probably mid to late August, because Hal and Audrey have accounted for her until she left Siding."

"If we have the name and the kind of shop, I guess we see if it's listed in the phone book." She got the thick volumes and spread them over the bed. "Are Hal and Audrey on their way home?"

"No, they have other names they want to check on. They'll be back in Santa Rita tomorrow afternoon." Drake watched her page through the books and scan the columns. "Find them?"

"No, not a listing for Rainwater, not in Arlington."

"It's been almost four years. People move, especially inside the metro area. Let's check some of the other suburbs."

In the following hour they located three families with the last name of Rainwater. None of them were either Noah or Donna, nor did they know another Rainwater family. Finally Drake resorted to calling information.

"Yes, a Noah Rainwater in Arlington," he confirmed. "Or a Donna Rainwater."

"The number is unpublished at the customer's request," the disinterested voice told him.

"Well, we know such a person lives in Arlington. We just can't get the number or the address."

"What about the shop? Can we get a number or a location for it?" She flipped the classified pages open and found the listing for appliance stores. "Dozens of them," she moaned.

"Okay, we don't know what name the business has, and we don't know a street address, but we know the owner's name. Rainwater has a partner, a fellow called Houseman. Look for a shop using one or the other of those names or some combination, maybe initials—H and R or something."

Claire ran her finger down the columns. "No, I don't see..." She stopped in the center of the page. "RainHouse Appliances? What do you think?"

Drake took the book from her. "It's Arlington, and the name is possible. Let's try." The number was local, so he could dial it directly. "It's ringing." Drake held the receiver away from his ear but close enough to hear if the phone was answered. "By the way, you have two weddings in your family. Jared worked some kind of black magic on your sister, and she finally said yes. Looks like miracles at the Anderson household."

"Jared and Judith?" Claire jumped up from her chair ready to demand details.

Drake waved her away as the ringing went on without interruption. "Closed, I guess." He looked at his watch. Just five minutes past six. "We missed them,

301

love." He sat on the sofa and pulled her down beside him. "I see no way to reach them tonight." He could see the disappointment in her eyes. "Come on, I'll buy you dinner, your last one as a single woman."

Over dinner in the hotel restaurant, Drake and Claire discussed the information gathered and the conclusions the two lawyers had made.

"Is Dad excited or apprehensive?" she asked.

"Jared said George was cautiously optimistic." He sat back in his chair. "Of course, he's delighted about Jared and Judith. I think he's hoped for them to get together almost as long as Jared has."

"I can't believe Judith finally said yes. What on earth changed her mind? Judith's always been her most obnoxious to him."

"Must be that old black magic called love. I can't imagine anything else influencing your brilliant sister. Hope her painting doesn't suffer for it."

"Drake! What a thing to say. I'm sure Judith will be even better with Jared in her life." She stirred restlessly in her chair, glancing at her watch and pushing dessert away.

"What's bothering you, love? You're not eating your mousse."

She frowned and looked out the window to the traffic passing. "Drake, don't shops post emergency numbers, a number where the owner can be reached in case of fire or flood? I've seen signs like that on doors, right below where they give the hours."

"You want to drive to Arlington, Claire? See if it's the right shop? Maybe find a number for the Rainwaters or the partner? Is that what you're thinking?" Drake sighed. He read her intention in her face.

"I know it's probably pointless, but if we could find something to help Dad, I'd feel better. I've been here longer than I planned and not discovered anything useful. Everyone else has done something. Judith's pictures, Audrey's trip, but I'm just indulging myself."

Drake took her hand across the table. "You talked to the bartender. It didn't turn out to be anything, but you did what you could."

"I know, Drake, but everything comes back to Arlington. Maybe if I'd known something else to ask..." She looked across at him with determination in her eyes. "Tomorrow we'll have a lot of other things on our minds. I want to do something tonight. You don't have to go. I don't mind driving out there by myself."

"Oh, no, love, if you want to go, I'll take you. I don't think I could sit in our hotel suite and know you're out on the road somewhere." He picked up the restaurant check and signed it. "Let's get your coat if we're going into the wilderness. It's miserably cold out there."

Drake made the drive out of town in silence. He kept his eyes open for the vagaries of other drivers, and traffic was heavy. Most of the snow was gone, only darkened drifts showing up in niches along the road. The trip might be pointless, but he understood Claire's urgent need to do something. He, too, hoped they'd find some kind of information at the shop, for Claire's sake. He looked again at the address printed on the hotel pad.

"Don't be too let down if we can't get anything tonight, will you, Claire?" He sought her hand and held it against his knee. "We might get lucky, but try not to be crushed if we're not."

Their road led them along a commercial avenue

filled with small shops offering floor covering, discount furniture, and plumbing fixtures. *Perhaps Rainwater located his shop with an eye toward giving customers a range of similar services. A good business move.*

"Look, Drake, RainHouse, right in the middle of that strip center." Claire directed his attention to the group of four shops housed in a line of attractive brick units. "I think the lights are on."

"Probably just a trick of the street lights," he began, but then he saw overhead lights in the shop and people moving about. "Stay in the car, Claire. It could be a robbery in progress."

"You can't go up there and interrupt if it's a robbery. You'll get shot."

Drake pulled the car closer. "Looks like a meeting of some kind. They're all sitting in a group talking, and they have brown bags and Cokes. It's no robbery." He slipped out of the car and went to the glass-paned door. He stood a moment, then came back and opened her door. "Looks like the staff is doing inventory," he said helping her out. "We may be in luck after all."

Drake and Claire stood outside the shop and watched the group inside for a moment. "Do we have Judith's sketch or one of the photos in the car?"

"We do. I meant to take the file into the hotel yesterday, but I forgot it. Do you think we can get somebody here to look at a picture? If Rainwater isn't here, I mean."

Drake gave her hand a squeeze. "It's worth a try." He returned to the car, came back carrying the file folder, and knocked sharply on the door. A young man looked up, then turned away. Drake knocked again, harder and with more authority. A pretty blonde girl in rolled-up jeans and a St. Anne's High School sweatshirt came to the door.

"We're closed for inventory, sir. If you'd come back in the morning?" Her ponytail danced and her indigo eyes sparkled even in the dim light.

"We need to see Mr. Rainwater, miss. It's a matter of some urgency, a legal matter." Drake's tone held an element of authority.

"Oh! " The girl's pretty face lit up. "Is it about the accident?"

"It's about an accident, yes."

The girl stepped back and let them enter. "Noah, some people here to see you. It sounds important. Maybe you should give them a minute." Her voice had the crystal clarity of a born cheerleader.

A solid-looking man in his late forties removed himself from the group. His hair held its dark natural color and his eyes were warm with a humorous gleam. Drake stepped forward.

"Mr. Rainwater, I'm Drake Chandler. I'm sorry to interrupt you like this, but it's a matter of some urgency." He passed the folder to the man and opened it. "Mr. Rainwater, do you know this girl?"

Noah Rainwater looked up, the good humor gone, his eyes as dark and expressionless as slate.

"You know where she is?"

"Yes," Drake told him. "We know."

"Do you know what she's done?"

"We know about the last three years."

Rainwater stepped back and motioned toward a small room in the back. "Come and tell me. We've been searching for her, but in the last year we've just about given up. I'd like to hear what you've got to say."

They started toward the corner room. Rainwater turned to the blonde girl. "It's pretty important for me to talk to these folks. It may be what we've been hoping for. We'll be a while. Get us some coffee, will you?"

"Sure, Noah, I'll make a fresh pot."

"And bring us some of those cookies your mother sent, will you, Dondie?"

Chapter Nineteen

Audrey came out of Miss Bobbie's Dress Shop carrying a box and a small shopping bag just as Hal pulled up to the curb.

"Taxi, lady?" He opened the door and tossed the parcels into the back seat. "Any luck? With the search, I mean, not the shopping."

"Jessie told me the Hales moved to Florida about two years ago. Her aunt probably knew where, but Bobbie's memory being what it is, she's not likely to be able to tell us. Jessie didn't have any idea who Rhonda is. I called Miss Ross at the school, but no one answered. The woman who wrote the local column for the paper isn't here anymore, either." Audrey sighed and fell back into the plush car seat. "I took so much of Jessie's time, I felt I should buy something. So I have a new dress but no new information."

Hal laughed at her saga. "I've heard some wild excuses for buying a new dress, but I think that one's original."

"Well, laugh if you want to, but I'm out of ideas. I can't find a soul to ask another question, even if I could think of one to ask. Do you have any thoughts?"

"I believe I do." He pulled away from the curb and drove down Main Street to the place where it met the highway. "I learned about a place just over the state line, maybe half an hour from here, that serves rare steak and cold beer. They serve wine, too, but it comes in brown jugs, so beer is safer. Could I interest you in my agenda?"

"I'm starved. Lead me to this oasis in the wasteland."

Boots and Spurs, according to the red neon sign, served the biggest steaks and the coldest mugs of beer in the country. When Audrey was served her plate, she believed the claim. "It's half a dinosaur." She sampled the first bite. "But it's good."

"I don't think the restaurant-rating people have found this one yet. It might not make their list anyway. A quarter head of lettuce drowned in a cup of bottled French dressing probably isn't their definition of a salad."

"Real ranch hands don't eat green stuff."

They concentrated on the plate-sized steaks and fluffy baked potatoes in silence. Gradually Audrey became aware of the slow, sweet waltz drifting into the dining room from the room beyond.

"I hear a real country fiddle." She closed her eyes to listen.

"I haven't heard 'Faded Love' in about a century."

She looked at him in surprise. "You know country music? I'm amazed."

He took her hand and pulled her to her feet. "I've been around a place like this once or twice in my life. Come on, let's see if the dance floor's big enough to turn around on."

It was a good-sized floor, and they went around it more than once. The boy with the fiddle had two sidemen backing him up, and the group poured out some country favorites like fine old wine.

Audrey liked the way Hal danced. She'd noticed, when they danced at the Bar Association dinner, he moved with ease and power for such a big man. His lead was easy to follow. "You've danced to this music before."

"A time or three," he admitted, "but never with such an interesting partner."

Something was happening that Audrey didn't want to examine too closely. She'd decided her feelings for Hal were just the same infatuation she'd felt in school. If she looked closely at the effect he had on her, she might find it was turning to something deep and disturbing. *The middle of a family crisis is not the time to fall in love.* The last weeks had taken a heavy toll on her emotions. Her worry for her dad, the rumors and gossip, trying to hold her head up in the face of public scrutiny—all of it had drained her. Hal was reliable, ready to fight the battle her family faced, but she mustn't let admiration and friendship color her judgment.

"It won't do, Audrey." Hal's voice was a murmur in her ear.

"What won't?"

"Your face is as readable as a child's picture book." He spun her lightly over the floor and stopped at their table. "You can't run from it. It's there, right under the surface, anytime we're together. It's attraction, it's rapport, it's even—lust. And sooner or later you're going to admit it."

"Hal, with the way things are right now, Dad and this damnable mess... I don't know... I can't deal with any more. Don't you see? I've got to keep my head.

Judith's finally let Jared into her life. Claire's got to sort out her feelings for Drake. They're both emotionally tangled up in their own lives. They have distractions affecting the way they see things. I'm left to be Dad's sounding board, to make a safe haven for him in the middle of all this strife. I can't fall off the edge too."

"Can't or won't?" He waited for her answer.

"Both, I guess. If I lost my head, let infatuation take over, I wouldn't be any use to Dad, or to you either. My judgment would be questionable."

"You're not in love with me? You're going to keep telling us both that story?"

Audrey looked up at him with every intention of saying just that. Something in the hazel gold of his eyes held her. Something in the half grin behind his beard wouldn't let her say the words.

"Can you say it and mean it, Audrey? Say you don't love me the way I love you?"

"I… I don't…" She couldn't make the words take shape. The man mesmerized her somehow. He seemed to fill her field of vision, to wrap her in the warmth of his personality, till she couldn't distinguish anything. She felt she was drowning, and he was the only secure point she could reach. Audrey found herself in his arms, arms that stopped all her answers, and the heat of his kiss melted what reserve she had left. She could only cling to him blindly. "I don't know where this is leading," she finally managed to say.

"It leads us to each other, to the place where there isn't anything else."

Audrey knew little of the ride back to the hotel. She was hot, she was cold, Hal loved her, but Hal was the Viking, as intractable and implacable as his seagoing ancestors. Could she love him? All sides of him? A jumble of questions passed through her mind as the wheels spun over the highway. Through the windshield, a quarter moon glimmered like a silver scythe in the sky. The ink-black night had only a thin veil of clouds thrown over the stars. The night didn't lend itself to clear thinking, not when her heart was pounding in her ears and her skin tingled with the need for his touch.

Hal parked beside the hotel, held the door for her, took her hand to help her from the seat. The packages in the back seat caught a bit of light from the streetlamp as Hal bundled them from the car. A dim glow from a wall sconce met them as they entered the small hotel lobby and climbed the stairs.

At the door of Audrey's room, Hal held his hand out for her key. "I can stay or I can go, Audrey." His low voice was as intimate as the brush of his hand against her cheek. "I'd rather stay and see where this all leads. But if it bothers you, if you aren't ready to let me stay, I'll go."

"I don't think you'd better stay, Hal. I need to think." She saw the thin lines near the corners of his eyes tighten. She could feel him draw away from her, though he didn't actually move.

He nodded. "The time will come, Audrey, when you won't run away. You'll want me as much as I want you. I'm looking forward to the moment." He put her key and her packages into her hand and brushed his lips across her forehead. "Goodnight, Puss. I hope you sleep better than I'm going to."

Audrey closed her door and leaned her back

against it, too shaken to move a step, letting her parcels fall to the floor unnoticed. Her breathing was shallow, as if she'd been running, and the pulses in her temples were drumming. She forced herself to take long breaths and exhale slowly.

That never happened before. Just losing herself in the moment—no, she didn't drop her defenses. *Audrey Anderson is coolly professional, practical, and always thinks ahead of her actions.* She needed the reminder. *This is no schoolgirl crush, and you aren't going to fling yourself at him, not when your judgment is questionable.* She continued to lecture herself as she took her hair down from its slightly frayed ponytail. Scolding herself for a lack of foresight, for not seeing this ambush in the road, she brushed her teeth and showered. A cool washcloth over her face didn't remove the heat behind her eyes, but she assured herself it helped.

When this is all over and I can look at Halvard Lindstrom in a clearer light, I'll know if this silly feeling is just gratitude and passion or something substantial.

Agreeing with the girl in the mirror, Audrey patted on a bit of her favorite lavender cologne. It was good to feel clearheaded about the situation. She opened her travel bag and took out the pale blue nightgown. It was such a comforting garment. The satin slipped over her skin like a cascade of spring water. The blue slippers, so soft, let her move like a silent sprite across the floor. Her quilted robe was hanging in the closet. How nice it matched the gown so well. She brushed her hair until it rolled over her shoulders, a silky cloud of gold and brown and copper.

Yes, it's good to be in control of things. The evening had been highly charged, and she could have made a foolish mistake. Hal's confidence and charisma could easily undermine her defenses. Not now, not with her mind clear and working. Audrey slipped into the robe and buttoned it from hem to neck. It swished with a pretty sigh as it brushed the floor. Her gown moved softly over her hips and thighs. She took a look at the girl in the long mirror on the door. No question, she looked cool and collected.

Audrey opened her door and walked soundlessly to the door opposite. She knocked, quite firmly she thought, and waited. The door came slowly open. Hal stood a moment looking down at her.

"I've had time to think. Could a girl reconsider the offer?"

****

Claire rolled to a sitting position and tucked a pillow behind her head. Drake was already at the phone, nibbling a breakfast roll while the front desk put through a call. "Who are you calling first?"

"Jared. I think we have to start with him." Drake held the phone in silence. "Judith, let me talk to that man of yours, will you?"

Claire smothered a laugh. Judith was at Jared's house at six in the morning? Good for her!

"It's Drake, Jared. Listen, we found the Rainwater family last night. It's an interesting story, and I think you and Hal should hear it. George, too, if we can get him here." He listened a minute. "No, it's too long and involved to get into it on the phone. The questions you lawyers will ask won't even occur to Claire or me. The plane out of San Antonio will get you here by mid-afternoon. Can you and Judith make it? I'll have tickets waiting for you." He listened again. "Yes, of course, bring her. Bring clothes, too. I'm taking everybody to dinner tonight. I'll talk to Al Hayes and see if we can get George down here. He should meet Dondie Marshall's family and know what kind of people they are."

Once Drake put the phone down, Claire rolled closer and put her head against his bare shoulder. "Is he going to do it? Will he bring Judith?"

"I think we roused his curiosity enough to bring him down here, and Judith isn't about to let him out of her sight." He slipped an arm around her and teased her ear with a strand of her hair. "The hard part will be getting your dad here. I'll tackle Hal first."

His call to Hal followed the same general line, but he suggested Hal and Audrey drive from their Panhandle hotel to Dallas instead of heading for Santa Rita. He promised to have hotel rooms arranged for them and mentioned a family dinner.

"Okay, Miss Fix-it, your turn. Let's see what it takes to convince Al Hayes to spring your dad." He passed her the receiver and waited while the desk made the call.

"I'm guessing Al's at the office this morning. If not—oh, hello." Her voice became crisp and authoritative. "This is Claire Anderson. I need to speak with Sheriff Hayes, please."

"Is he there?" Drake whispered.

She nodded and held the phone away from her ear so he could hear. "Hello, Sheriff, how are things?"

"Busy, Miss Claire, right busy. What can I do for you?"

She winked at Drake and dropped her voice a level. "Al, do you remember who took the motorcycle engine apart in Mr. Sims' office his senior year in high school? And Dad let him off with cleaning up the mess and a warning about not doing it again?"

"Claire, I haven't forgot your dad did my nephew a favor by never letting that go public. Your dad's done a lot for the kids in this town over the years, when he thought it was justified."

"Do you think reminding Judge Lindley of his small transgression might make him feel like giving Dad a little of the same leniency…"

"I get the idea, Claire. Sam owes your dad a favor and you're calling it in. What do you want?" He seemed in a hurry to get to the heart of the call.

"I've found Dondie Marshall's family." Claire gripped the phone tighter. So much depended on getting the sheriff to cooperate. "They have quite a story, and I think it will clear Dad's name. I want you to bring him up here to Dallas. You need to hear the story, and Dad deserves to."

"Good lord, Claire, I can't do that. I'll come, and if it's really useful, I can take a deposition. Get it to Sam, let him decide if you've got something, but I can't take George to Dallas. Can't do it, girl, just can't." Al Hayes sounded very definite.

"Sure you can, Just think about it. You get on a plane in San Antonio this afternoon, bringing Dad, of course, have dinner with us, spend the night in a good hotel, go listen to these people and hear their story, and tomorrow you're back in Santa Rita, a hero for clearing up this case."

"Claire, we can do it just as well without your dad.

Why get his hopes up if this turns out to be a goose chase?" The sheriff sounded firm and unimpressed. Claire decided to push for the last argument.

"Because Drake and I are getting married tonight, and I want my daddy there." A hint of tears lingered in her voice. "We're getting married, and Dad's going to be sick at heart if he doesn't get to be here. We haven't told a soul—just you—and Sheriff, I'm depending on you to make this happen for me. You just can't let me down."

"And there really is evidence I need to hear?" Hayes asked. "This isn't some shenanigan just to get your dad there for the shindig?"

"Honest to God, there's evidence, Sheriff." Claire waited, almost sure she'd reached beyond the sheriff's crusty exterior.

"Okay, for all the old debts, I'll do what I can. Give me a flight number and time. Maybe I can convince Sam to put George in my custody for twenty-four hours. I know he isn't happy about what this case is doing to George or the town. He might be willing to listen."

"It's going to work." Drake grinned over the pile of pillows after she relayed details to Hayes and ended the conversation. "You're going to have your family here for the wedding. And wait till the sheriff hears Rainwater's story. Everything's going to be fine, love."

"Oh, yes, yes, it is." Claire sank into the froth of pillows and nuzzled his cheek. "Wonderful man." She touched the thin planes of his face and traced the line of his mouth. He nibbled her finger. " Stop! Richelieu nips like that, too, when it's time to feed the kitty. Oh, no!" She sat bolt upright in the bed. "If everyone is coming here, who's going to take care of Richelieu? He doesn't do boarding or cat sitters."

"Claire, I thought it was something serious." Drake pulled her back to the place beside him. "It's no problem. We'll just get him a plane ticket, too. He'll love coming to the wedding."

****

Hal looked at the bundled covers on the bed. Over the back of a chair a sheen of pale blue glimmered in the half light. Two smaller bits of blue spotted the dark floor. He caught a scent of lavender lingering in the air. Hal put the phone down and came back to the bed. The ringing bell hadn't disturbed her. A few strands of hair spilled from under the quilted cover, silky and fine as a child's curls.

"Audrey." He bent close to the pillow. He felt her stir a little, then roll over so the faint light washed her face with a pale glow.

"Hal?" Her eyes fluttered open, dark in the shadows of morning. "Did I hear the phone?"

"You did, little one." He brushed the tumbled waves from her face. "It was Drake."

"Drake?" She sat up, pulling the cover higher, and looked for her scattered garments. "Has something happened? Is Claire all right?"

"He said they found the Rainwater family. He wouldn't give details, but he insists we drive to Dallas instead of Santa Rita. He says Jared and Judith are coming, and with luck the judge will let your dad be there. It sounds like they've really got an answer, but Drake didn't want to tell me on the phone. Oh, yes, he says he's giving a dinner for the family tonight. Do you have something to wear?"

"I bought a little thing at Miss Bobbie's. It will do for most anything." She brushed his question aside. "But are we going? If Jared and Judith are there, we might be more use in Santa Rita. We might need to file motions or contact the judge."

"Wouldn't you rather see what Claire's found out?" Hal picked up her robe and handed it to her. "Is this what you're looking for?" he asked in a different, more intimate voice. She flushed deeply enough for him to notice even in the half-light of daybreak.

Audrey took the robe and slipped into it, her back turned modestly. "I'm trying to think what the best use of our time would be."

Hal sank down onto the bed and caught her hands, hands having a devilishly hard time with slippery covered buttons. "You're going practical on me, Puss. You want to be there when the package is opened, and so do I. We're going to Dallas." He loosened one button, the only one she'd managed to fasten. "And since we aren't going to be on the road as long, we don't need to leave as early. I can think of a thing or two we haven't done, or we could do again." The lavender scent of her hair spilled over him as he buried his face in it. Her lips met his in silent agreement. They'd leave for Dallas in an hour—or maybe two.

****

Jared watched Judith run to the far end of the airport lobby to greet the last arrivals. George, a small bag in one hand, hurried along the concourse. He was followed by the lanky sheriff. Jared looked down at the wire cage beside his feet. A baleful look met his. "Don't blame me, buster," he told the irate ball of fur inside. "I didn't make you get in that cage or leave your warm place in the window. Tell your mama about it when you see her." The cat turned his head, dismissing the insignificant human who'd bounced him down stairs and abducted him, transporting a high-born Persian to this unseemly place.

****

The family converged in the stately lobby of the old hotel. Drake thought he'd braced himself for the clamor of questions, but he'd not remembered the level of noise surrounding the Anderson family *en mass*. Judith and Audrey were demanding information, new points occurring to them every moment, and even if he'd intended to answer, he couldn't. Hal and Jared had legal concerns. Poor George just looked stunned and resigned to the chaos. Hayes stood by in silence.

Drake waved his hands for quiet. "Folks!" He waved harder to get their attention. "Folks, all this is going to get a full airing in the morning. Right now, Claire is waiting for us. We have a limo outside to take everyone to dinner. Let's have an evening when this wretched case isn't the center of our lives for a change. We'll enjoy the evening more if we put the case aside for the moment." Drake directed the group out the door to where a driver was waiting to help them into the limo. He was glad to see Judith in something besides black. *Jared's really turned things around for that girl.* She was glowing, and the royal blue dress clinging to her long, svelte figure did great things for her. Audrey looked as if she were lit up like a candle, too. Her gold wool jersey dress showed off what the kid usually kept hidden, that she was a lovely girl with a figure to make a man look twice. *Wonder what they'll say when they find out what's really happening tonight.* Drake smiled

319

and felt like strutting a little. He'd convinced Claire, he and Will and Bird. And Claire, who wouldn't give up, had her victory, too.

****

Claire walked through the meeting room of the center one more time. Bird, the florist, Mattie and her crew, and a host of people Claire had never met had made a magnificent effort. Baskets of ruby roses filled the corners and showered each table. Fat ivory candles lent a warm glow through their hurricane globes. Miles of tulle and ruby velvet ribbon covered the plain white chairs with froth. Claire turned to the corner where Mattie was placing the cake. Rose petals drifted over ivory basket-weave icing, and a pair of crystal swans graced the tiny top tier. Beside the cake stood a cut-glass punch bowl waiting for the wine punch. Mattie turned to her.

"Looks like a fairyland, now, doesn't it, Claire honey? Told you we could do miracles."

"I believe you could turn the proverbial sow's ear into silk. It's just everything I could ask for."

"You seen the chapel?" Mattie went on as she dusted the tabletop with a handful of ruby-colored petals.

"No, I haven't looked at it yet. I wanted to see the cake and all the flowers."

"Bird's in there now. You oughta go take a peek before you dress. Good chance you won't remember to look when you come down the aisle."

Bird met her at the door of the chapel. "It's almost time for Windy to come do your pictures. I'll help you dress when you've looked around."

Claire opened the arched door cautiously.

Everything looked so perfect for the reception. She could only hope the chapel had fared as well. Bird held the door, and Claire's eyes adjusted to the light. There were candles, a shimmer of them, spiraling down a confection of lacy white iron trees, standing higher than her head and leading to the altar. Each tall spire had roses woven into the frame until the candles and the roses seemed to float above the floor. A cloud of tulle and candles framed the altar with only a scattering of buds to accent the arrangement.

"This is incredible!"

"It's not too much?" Bird asked anxiously. "I told Mary-Suellen you said romantic Victorian, and this is how she saw it."

"It's too, too much, and I love it. I feel like a princess, a doll in a dollhouse. I never dreamed anyone could match my most secret fantasy, but this does."

Bird looked at her watch, prompting Claire to hurry. Claire caught the gesture and nodded. Yes, she was ready now. She had seen what she wanted to see. It was time for her to dress.

****

"Okay, pretend you're a bird and there's a...no, not a good idea." The spry, white-haired man sighed. "Just think of something wonderful." He held the camera up.

"Think of your family arriving at the doors and the surprise waiting for them," Bird suggested.

Bird's image did spill joy and elation over Claire. She felt her smile warm to the picture Bird suggested.

"Now, that's the look of a ladybird waiting for her mate." Windy chuckled and snapped the picture. "I'm finished here, pretty. I'll see you in the chapel, but you won't see me. Your eyes will be on your young man."

He gathered his bags and bundles and scurried out.

"He's a sweetheart," Bird told her as the door closed. "But he tends to relate everything to critters with feathers." She picked up the cascade of shaded pink and crimson roses and passed it to Claire. "You do look like an angel, my dear, and I'm so proud to have been here to help this happen."

"I couldn't have done it without you." Claire wasn't mouthing a gracious platitude. This wedding truly could not be taking place if Bird hadn't come to the rescue. A knock tapped softly at the door.

Bird shook her head. "Somebody's telling me to get out there." The person on the other side of the door had another mission, however. A soft exchange took place and Bird closed the door smiling. "A gift from the groom." She passed Claire a small, flat, white velvet box. Claire lifted the lid and gazed at the daisy chain of rubies and rose-cut diamonds gleaming in a nest of satin. A card caught the edge of one stone. She lifted it and read the words written in Drake's neat square printing: "They match the ring. I thought you wouldn't want to break up the set. I like to keep things that belong to each other together. Like us. Drake."

"Don't you dare cry, Claire Anderson." Bird's tone was sharp, almost stern. "I won't have you sniffling down the aisle."

Claire, braced by the snap in Bird's command, bit her lip and smiled. "I'm not crying." She dabbed at her eyes with a tissue and passed one to Bird. "But you are."

"Oh, nonsense." Bird wiped at the corner of one eye. She opened her hand and pressed something into Claire's palm. "You're supposed to have this, too. He said he still had yours."

Claire held up the circle of gold and tilted it so she could see inside the ring. "It's his ring, the one I gave him when we got married in the back yard. When we were college kids," Claire said in wonder. "He's kept it and mine all this time."

"He said he'd like to have them back where they belong."

"And he will," Claire assured her, "forever and forever again."

Bird looked her up and down, checking to see nothing had become disarranged during the photographic session. "Perfect, Claire, just perfect. I've got to get to my piano before everyone is seated. Are you sure you're all right here by yourself? You can get to the chapel okay? I could get one of your sisters."

Claire brushed the idea aside. In truth she was looking forward to a few minutes alone. "No, I'm just fine right here." She lifted the necklace free from its swirl of satin and clasped it around her neck. The gold and stones felt cold against her skin for a moment, then warmed to her touch. Bird kissed her cheek and turned to go. "I wish your mama could see you right now. She'd be so proud."

"Somehow I think she knows, Bird. I'm sure she does."

Bird left quietly as Claire stood once more before the mirror. The necklace was a wonderful surprise and the perfect touch. Her silk velvet gown glowed with the warm crystal fire the gems gave it. She'd felt the low, dipping neckline needed something, but she'd not found the right thing to go with the dress. Its long sleeves and close skirt clung to her like a sweep of fine snow, and the pleats pressed into the short chapel train flowed behind her in an elegant curve. The ivory dress was simple but with the understated perfection only a master of design could manage. A spray of creamy feathers in a wreath of illusion replaced a bridal veil. It was her style, her look, and it made the perfect final touch. A tap came at the door.

"Bird said ever'thing's ready, honey. You need help gettin' over there to the chapel?" Mattie waited outside.

"If you could just hold the door for me," Claire answered, and gathered up her bouquet.

Mattie got the door and then took her elbow. "Gather up your skirt, honey. Don't want you tripping on it, now." She held on until they stood outside the closed doors of the chapel. Claire dropped the hem of her skirt and Mattie smoothed it for her. "Be just a minute now, and then I'll open the doors so you can start down. Ready?"

"Ready," Claire answered, more than ready to begin anew with Drake and the future. Through the doors she heard the first few bars of the song she and Drake had loved. Mattie began to open one door and one of the women from the kitchen hurried to take the other one.

The arched opening spread before her. At the end of the row of candles Claire saw Drake waiting with Father Will at the altar. She glanced toward the front. George and her sisters, and Hal and Jared were looking back to see her.

Whether it was a trick of the light or somehow past and present linked for a moment, Claire saw another face, a beloved and long-absent face, in the dark beyond the candlelight. Claire drew her breath, heard the rising chords, and took the first step into the chapel.

Her last glance assured her Patsy indeed smiled on her daughter's wedding day.

Chapter Twenty

The Rainwater home was a modest Arts and Crafts cottage dating from the early years of the twentieth century. As a connoisseur of American art, Drake appreciated the well-preserved details and the simple furnishings. Of the eight people descending on the house at the bottom of the cul-de-sac, he suspected he was the only one with attention to give to their surroundings. The others were almost rigid with anticipation or anxiety.

Noah Rainwater waited in the doorway, a granite rock of a man, his Indian-black hair slicked away from his face and a grim calm in his eyes.

"Folks, come on in and find a seat. We're going to be a tad cramped for space, but it's better you came to us rather than us trying to get to you." He held the door and nodded as each one entered. Once they were inside, Drake made introductions. He was anxious to see how the Rainwaters' story would affect the family and the sheriff. Drake had heard it before—he and Claire—so he could watch the faces around him as the tale came to light.

The group squeezed into the room, though Drake sat on an unpadded deacon's bench beside the front windows and Judith took a place on the hearth near the low-burning fire.

Glancing at his audience, Noah Rainwater began. "I'm a pretty fair hand at talking among friends, but I don't take to holding center stage." He paced across the small room to one beyond and came back with a ladderback chair. "Now, we're just friends having a gab session," he said, straddling the rush-bottomed chair.

"You know how we came to be here, Noah," Drake prompted. "I told you about George and the trouble he's facing."

"You did, Drake." He looked back at George. "Sorry for your trouble, sir, and I hope we can help put it to rest." He was silent a minute, collecting his thoughts. "I better start back a ways. I put twenty years in the navy, married a girl I met on leave. It didn't work out like I expected. The girl didn't like being a navy wife. After the war, she took off with a man who lived a nine-to-five, weekends-off kind of life. Early on, we'd had the boy, Drew, and he got to be a handful for her. I left the navy and took a land job so he could live with me. Wound up running the plant up in the Panhandle. Met Donna and her daughter the summer before Drew started his last year of school."

"Then you moved here?" Jared asked.

"Hold on. You need to understand how it happened."

Drake smiled a little. He'd learned Noah Rainwater wouldn't be moved off his own path.

"Drew got in with the wrong crowd. Not the sort you want to see your son hanging around. Nothing serious—smoking, driving around late, kid trouble— but the kind you can see leading to something bigger."

He looked away to the windows as a sedan pulled into the drive. "Donna's here." Tenderness roughened his voice. He excused himself and left the room. The sound of an opening door was followed by the swish of something moving over the polished floor. In a moment a lovely red-haired woman entered the room in a wheelchair.

"My wife, Donna," Rainwater said by way of introduction.

"I wanted to be here when you came," she said, "but I had an early therapy session I couldn't miss."

"Donna," Drake said, "it's a pleasure to meet you." He made the introductions again.

"I was just telling them about Drew," Noah explained. "And how he was when we met."

"Drew wasn't a bad boy," Donna interjected. "He just didn't have any purpose in life. After Noah and I started seeing each other, he sort of came around. Started talking about going into the military when he finished school until he could decide how to spend his life."

"He had a girlfriend," Audrey mentioned.

"Oh, yes, he had a girl," Noah agreed. "She was part of the problem. Fool girl latched on to him like a tick on a newborn pup. Wanted him with her all hours of the day and night. I was half expecting the girl to up and swear she was pregnant."

"Your son joined the military after graduation?" Hal queried. "The wedding announcement in the paper mentioned it."

"Silly woman's nonsense in the paper stirred a hornet's nest, I'll tell you." Noah looked across at his wife. "Probably put Donna in her wheelchair, you get down to it."

The group exchanged confused looks. While they

saw the family's pain, Drake could read their doubtful faces. They hadn't heard about Dondie.

"I had a navy buddy who had a notion to open an appliance store here where he grew up," Noah continued. "He had a little money, I'd saved quite a bit, and Donna had some from selling her folks' house. We put it together and set up our business. Dondie needed better schools, and I wanted Drew away from that girl, so we'd decided to leave Siding."

"Such a terrible summer," Donna added. "It tore all our lives apart."

Noah patted her shoulder. "I'll tell them, sweetheart. Don't fret about it. It's all coming to an end." He looked over at Hal and Jared. "The insurance company has been real good to us. It looks like one more operation and Donna will walk again."

Claire's dark eyes filled. "Oh, I hope so, Donna."

"Come summer—we'd barely got settled here—the girl showed up again, right on our doorstep. She wanted to see Drew. He didn't want to see her, but she kept hanging around, stopping Drew on the street, even following Dondie over to the park or around the neighborhood. We couldn't get rid of her. One day she came to the house while Donna was here alone. Donna's got red hair and, sweet as she is, she's got the temper to go with it. She let the little vixen have it. Told her to stay away, leave us and the boy alone, and then told her if she had any pride she wouldn't be chasing after somebody who didn't want her. Three days later Donna was run down, right out there in the street."

"You don't mean the girl…" Audrey couldn't finish the thought.

Donna nodded. "I saw her as I fell. Her face is in

my head every waking minute. She stole a car and sat out there waiting. I'll see that car bearing down for as long as nightmares can haunt a person."

"And your injury, all the suffering it cost you, made Dondie run away?" George asked.

"Dondie?" Donna looked surprised. "Oh, Dondie never ran away. She's a wonderful girl, doing well at school, and she's a tremendous help to us both. Why did you think Dondie ran away?"

Drake held out the folder with Judith's sketches in it. "Because this girl, calling herself Dondie Marshall, accused George of rape."

Donna took the folder. "But this isn't Dondie. This is the girl who ran me down, the one who kept pursuing Drew. We've been searching for her ever since. She's Rhonda Perrit, and if she's a high school student, I'm Whistler's mother. This girl is twenty-one years old, every day of it."

Drake and Claire had known the story, but they had shared none of it with the others. Better, they decided, to let the people who'd lived the story tell it.

"Perrit?" Audrey sounded stunned. "A girl named Perrit worked in the office of the school in Siding. Her sloppy filing kept the records from being transferred…"

Hal interrupted. "But Dondie's records never came to Arlington. We learned they were still in Siding until someone requested them for the Santa Rita school. How could Dondie be in school here?"

Donna pushed her chair forward. "She's in Saint Anne's, a private school, on a scholarship. She took the entrance exams and we had her medical records. Saint Anne's didn't need anything else once they saw her scores, but when we moved, I wasn't sure what it would take to get her into Saint Anne's. I filled out enrollment and requested a transfer for her at the high school, just in case. I suppose Rhonda found out where we lived from the transfer request."

Audrey nodded in agreement. "The principal said Rhonda took a bus to meet her boyfriend about the time the transfer letter came to Siding."

"But why come to Santa Rita?" George asked. "What brought her there?"

"We think after she attacked Donna, she got out of Arlington fast, maybe took the first bus she could," Drake answered, "and probably with the money she had, Santa Rita was as far as she could go. Made up the story about not remembering anything to cover things up."

Claire put in another note. "The bartender at the Magnolia said a stolen car had been left on his lot, a car involved in a hit-and-run. The police identified it as the car that hit Donna."

Drake added, "Fingerprints should establish the case against her here."

Al Hayes interrupted the chatter. "Folks, I'm going to need statements, and Mr. Rainwater, I think Santa Rita would take it kindly if you came down in the next few days to identify the girl. We should have her in custody by then. I sorta think we'll be able to match up those fingerprints." Hayes looked around at the people in the room. "This clears up things here, but we still have to deal with charges against George. Lots of interesting facts coming out here, but nothing that proves he didn't mess with a girl he knew as a student."

The clamor rising up to him was deafening. Drake saw Claire's face fall and felt the wave of anguish sweeping her sisters from exultation to despair. He could see the sheriff's point. The girl might be guilty of attempted vehicular homicide, but her false identity had nothing to do with George or the rape charge against him. The ordeal still wasn't over.

****

"We can end the case on a technicality," Jared said three days later as the family grouped around the dining table for a strategy session. "The girl isn't a minor. She was in school fraudulently. We know George didn't rape her, and the prosecution can't prove he did. The shorts lose any value to the case with Keefe's testimony. The girl's previous history blackens her credibility, and we'll get the case thrown out."

"But he's not exonerated," Claire told him in protest. "We want Dad's name cleared."

"I don't see it happening," he said with a note of defeat. "We have nothing else to use. No means of proving she lied, no witness who saw her with someone else. What else can we do?"

A wave of bittersweet satisfaction filled George Anderson as he looked from face to face. "I'm getting out of this thing without a conviction. A terrible wrong's made right, now, with Claire and Drake back together. Judith and Jared are on their way to making a good life. Audrey seems to blossom every day and looks more and more like her mother. I have a new friend in Hal, who plays chess almost as well as Drake does. The Jubal Early book is going to be published. I guess I can't grouse about one small fly in the ointment. A reputation is a small price to pay for all I have."

Claire pulled away from Drake to sit on the hassock in front of her father. "But it's not fair," she protested. "You didn't do anything wrong. You shouldn't be branded for something you didn't do."

Audrey interrupted her sister. "I blame myself for not realizing while we were in Siding that the girl who lived there wasn't the same girl we knew as Dondie. Everyone talked about how bright she was, how she loved school. And no one mentioned her haunting eyes. Here everyone said she was a terrible student, but they always remembered her eyes. Obviously two different girls. If I'd been really listening, I would have known."

George stopped her. "If anyone should have seen through the girl, it should have been me. I'm the professional educator. I should have realized she was no sixteen-year-old kid." He turned back to Claire. "And on the subject of fairness, do you have any idea how often in history people have had to live with worse said about them? With far harsher consequences than a smudge on the record?" George waved aside her complaint. "At least I live in a place where I can't be convicted without evidence. Girls, you have to have some perspective about things, take a long-range look."

"I can't," Audrey said sharply. "I don't intend to let some little felon who tried to run over an innocent woman ruin your good name."

"Neither do I," Judith agreed.

The doorbell cut through the debate, though George heard the discussion wind a note higher as he left the room to answer the bell. Sheriff Hayes stood on the porch. Apprehension and a flash of anger clutched George.

"Don't look at me like I'm the enemy, George," Al Hayes said, waving a placating hand. "I haven't come to bring the house down. Can I come in? Are you having a family meeting?"

"Something along those lines. Come join us. Better the girls fuss at you than at me." The two men entered the dining room, where expressions from outright hostility to guarded acceptance swept the room.

"Folks, don't get down on me for doing my job. I work for you just like I do the rest of this county." Uninvited he took a chair. "I've been over at the school board meeting, George. Had to speak to the board about vandalism and what to do about it." He stretched his long legs out.

"I forget there are such meetings these days," George answered.

"Yeah, but you've been to a passel of them over the years, haven't you?" Hayes raised an eyebrow. His face had a slight look of satisfaction. "I know you have, 'cause while I was waiting to talk, I thumbed through some files of old minutes. I'd swear your name appeared at every meeting, taking up for kids in trouble or trying to find new programs to keep kids in school."

Hearing the rustle of impatience around him, George interrupted the sheriff. "You going somewhere with this, Al?"

"Maybe," he answered. "George, do you recall a dinner meeting held at one board member's house, oh, last fall sometime? November, maybe?"

George thought a minute. "November? Seems like a lifetime ago, but, sure, we did meet one Saturday night last fall to talk about some standardized tests we were asked to evaluate. Louise Tannerly had some experience with the tests, and she was getting us up to date on how they worked. Meeting ran pretty late, and I gave Louise a ride to and from the meeting. She doesn't drive after dark anymore."

"It was the night of the Bar Association dinner dance, Jared. You remember? Dad had gone to pick Mrs. Tannerly up just before you came to get me." Audrey looked at the sheriff. "Is it important?"

"Kinda might be," he said. "I was looking at the report of some meetings, and one date rang a bell. I went back to the office and checked the times the Perrit girl said you and she were together. Most were the hour right after school was out. Nothing to say those were anything but counseling sessions, and being right there in the school with lots of people around, I don't see how anybody could think different. Still, one, a Saturday night, was significant. It was about eight-thirty or nine the girl said you were together, and it was the night where she claims the rape happened. Problem is, it's the same night as that special meeting of the school board. The minutes say you attended, and the meeting didn't break up till right around ten. Got to believe nobody fiddled with the board minutes."

"Dad couldn't have been with Rhonda Perrit," Audrey exclaimed. "He picked up Mrs. Tannerly, they went to the meeting, he took her home, and he was here watching the news when Jared and I came in."

Judith spoke up as well. "I was home when Dad came in. We listened to the news and heard about Claire's firm closing. No way the Perrit woman can claim anything happened that night. Dad had somebody with him every minute of the evening, and they would say so."

Hayes nodded. "I figure the girl was watching the house, waiting for a night everybody was out. She saw all y'all leave home. Couldn't know there would be a record of where George was and witnesses to swear to it. Might have been any Saturday night, with no one remembering just where they were after the fact. Her story was a risk, but minimal. Most folks can't tell you what they did any particular night—especially a couple of weeks after the fact. I can make a case to the DA that if the girl lied about one night, a night she had such explicit details about, she was lying—period. Especially given her record as we now know it." Hayes tilted his chair back and let out the wide grin he'd been holding in. "It's over, folks. I think we can safely say it. This mess will be cleared up. I plan to ask our local newspaper man, Ned Garrett, to come sit in on the hearing when I go over everything. We've no cause to protect Rhonda Perrit from public opinion. It's gonna make a hell of a splash in the paper next week. Just thought you'd like to know."

Shock filled the house on Stafford Street. George felt the room reel with relief. Everyone talked, babbled, even cried a little. For weeks to come, the people who'd been through it would be taking the facts and turning them all directions to be sure, but his name was clear.

****

The girl's hair no longer covered her eyes. The thick bush had been cut and styled till it wreathed her face with tapered curls. A line of mascara on the lashes made her strangely light eyes dramatic. Lipstick made the pouty mouth sensual and alluring. A black sweater, clinging to well-developed breasts, topped lime-green capris outlining a shapely bottom. She wasn't a child in trouble for copying a paper on a school assignment. She was a woman in trouble with the law. George looked at the young face across the table from him and saw nothing childlike or innocent.

"You wanted to see me?" he began, not sure why he was here.

"Yeah, I just wanted to say it wasn't personal." The childlike timbre of her voice was gone, as well. "What I said about you, it wasn't personal."

"Why did you do it, Rhonda? What did I ever do to make you target me?" George sincerely wanted to know.

"It wasn't you," she said again. "It was what you said about getting in touch with people in Siding, finding out about my family. I couldn't let you start looking there. Somebody in Siding could have put me together with Drew Rainwater, which would take them right to Arlington. I was sure I'd killed the woman Noah married, just knew I did, and the law was looking for me. I figured I'd throw up enough dust to keep you focused right here. You'd be too busy fighting off the wolves to bother about looking into my past."

"Your story could have cost me my family, my work, and my freedom, Rhonda. Did you think of the consequences of your charge?"

She shrugged and reached for a cigarette. "Your lookout, George. We all gotta watch out for the sharks." She lit up and drew in a lungful of smoke.

She'd never weigh the aftermath of her actions or feel for the people she jeopardized, George realized. "So what happens to you now?"

"They're taking me to Arlington this afternoon. I guess somebody will get me a lawyer. If he's any good, he'll get me off. If not, who knows?" She seemed to be through with the interview, but something still bothered George.

"Why pose as a high school girl, Rhonda? Why pretend to be sixteen?"

She blew a puff of smoke. "Why not? Kids in school, they have it pretty good. Somebody pays the bills, gives them food, clothes, a good place to sleep. School's not bad, even if you've been through the grind before. I didn't do so well when I got in with the Vanderhills. All the church going and praying and stuff. Not that they got in my way—they'd never believe sweet little Dondie could lead them down the garden path. And it wasn't a bad gig, just so damn boring, and a drag listening to the old man go on and on about what was wrong with the world. I was about ready to chuck it, just waiting for warm weather and a few minutes alone with the cash register before I hit the road. Then you poked into my life. Too bad, George. You should have ignored poor little confused Dondie and saved yourself a bucket of trouble." She blew another puff of smoke. "Might have saved me some, too."

No remorse showed in her face or her voice. She didn't feel a thing about the people she'd hurt.

"So why did you take on Dondie's name and history? What did her identity offer you?"

Rhonda laughed with a sharp note. "Why not? The little twit had everything going for her. Looks, brains, a great-looking guy—my guy—who was just all caught up in having a family, especially a little sister. Noah took on over her like she was his own kid. He never had a good word to say to me. I thought I'd see how it was to be her for a while. And if I left a few black spots on her clean white record, too bad. She could live with it. After all, I only borrowed her background for a while. She didn't lose much."

"Her mother could have died and may never walk again. Her school record is hopelessly mixed up. And she's been exposed to a side of life she should never have seen. She didn't lose anything?" George shook his head at Rhonda's blank look. She didn't care, would never care, about hurting the people who got in her way. He took another look at her, saw she'd already dismissed him from her mind, and picked up his coat. George walked slowly from the room. Hayes sat at a desk, writing, as George passed.

"I hope you got all that, Al." The vile taste in his mouth choked him. "I can't seem to find any sympathy for her, but I hate to think what all this is doing to Fred Vanderhill. He was her victim as much as anyone."

"Hit him hard, but he and his church are all praying for her." Hayes flipped the closely written pages before him. "Took her story down word for word. She's nailed for your case by her own admission. Think she'll be behind bars for a long time. By the way, your girls are waiting outside to take you to lunch. Give them my best, and thank them for their persistence. It made the difference."

****

"We just had a call from the sheriff's office," Hal announced. "Rhonda Perrit is on her way to Arlington to face enough charges to keep her attention for a good while. Seems there may be a few other incidents in her life to sort out."

Audrey let a sigh of relief escape. "And good riddance."

"So, Dad, I guess the school will have to let you have your job back now," Judith suggested.

"Judy, they'll let me come back, and I suppose

they'd let me sit in the counselor's office again. But that would be pretty uncomfortable for them and for me. I think it's time to do something else with my life—go out and explore new worlds." He glanced around the room, and Audrey caught a hint of glee in his tone. The room exploded with protests.

"Dad!"

"You're a teacher! The school, the kids, those have been your life!"

The objections and exclamations filled the room till George held up both hands for silence.

"What did you have in mind?" Hal asked. His quiet note of curiosity lowered the decibel level a little.

George's smile had more than a hint of satisfaction. "A week or so ago the Institute in Richmond asked me to be a guest lecturer next fall. They'd also like for me to help develop a curriculum for high schools to use in teaching about the Civil War. I'd sort of considered it, but with this affair hanging over my head, I couldn't accept. Now, it's possible. I'll have access to some primary sources I haven't been able to reach before, and I'm excited about the offer. I'll be here for your wedding, Judy, but then I think I'll take a slow drive through the South and be in Richmond by September."

Audrey felt her heart drop. She'd planned to be here with her dad after Judith's July wedding. She'd thought he'd be alone and need her to keep him company. Hal was watching her, and she remembered how easily he read her face. She tried to hide her sense of displacement. Claire and Judith had new lives and loves, new dreams to fulfill. What did she have? Claire and Judith voiced a chorus of questions. Jared and Drake expressed concerns as well, and as George explained his plans, the group drew together around him.

With a hollow, lost feeling, Audrey picked up her discarded jacket and slipped out the french door. She stared out into the evening light. She was home, the danger had subsided, but nothing would ever be the same. The cold snap had passed, leaving a sharp chill in the air, and she pulled her jacket closer. No, nothing would ever be the same, and somehow the old oak tree, toppled by the winter storm, was tangible evidence of the changes in their lives. The hardy tree had stood for a hundred years looking over the Santa Rita River. It had been in the background of their lives for as long as she could remember. Claire and Drake were married under its massive boughs. Judith had used it as the focal point of the first serious painting she'd created. And Audrey had helped her mother to the now-shattered bench the last time Patsy had left the house to sit in the afternoon sun. Audrey remembered how the leaves had cast a dappled pattern over her mother's pallor. Now the tree was gone, taking with it so many precious memories.

Looking at the fallen oak made a sharp pain twist within her. *Things end, everything comes to an end. Even mighty oaks reach a point where they can't stand up to the forces around them.*

She walked down the slope of the lawn to the mass of branches and limbs splayed across the path. The stone bench had caught the brunt of the fall and crumbled from the force. She stooped to pick up a shard and held it, tracing the edges with one finger.

"It was a very old tree, Puss." Hal's words were soft in the fading light.

Tears stung her eyes, and she couldn't look at him.

She knew she'd never hold back the pain if she did. "It was part of our lives, part of so much of what we did. Family picnics, and telling secrets, and wishing on stars. Somehow having it fall, just now, just as everything is different, feels like the end of an era. As if we'd turned a corner and could never go back."

Hal's hands rested on her shoulders in a comforting way. "I suppose your family has turned a corner, Audrey. In a good way, it seems to me. Claire stepped out of her snow-maiden exile and seems to be on her way to rebuilding her life with Drake. Judith is dealing with all her loss and anger in a healthy way. Looks like she and Jared will never lead a quiet, humdrum life, but they seem to be happy with it. And your dad has a chance to follow a private dream and build a new career. So, yes, things have changed. Sometimes you have to let go of something before you can move on. If nothing had changed, Claire would still be walling herself off from life, Judith would still be an angry woman growing in bitterness every day, and your dad...well, he might be imprisoned by a false charge or by a time gone by. Neither one would be fair to him. You wouldn't want that for the family, would you, Audrey?"

The sting of her unshed tears burned her eyes. Not trusting her voice, Audrey shook her head. Of course she was glad for Claire and Judith. She was relieved her dad wouldn't be branded by Rhonda Perrit's awful lies. Even the new work George was taking on seemed like a blessing for him. "I'm being sentimental about an old tree, and it's silly of me. Just a bit of emotional overload, I guess." She straightened and stood taller. "The tree service people will be here tomorrow to cut it up and haul it away. I'll be all right by then."

Hal turned her to face him. "Everyone has a new beginning, everyone but you. That's what you're thinking, isn't it? Feeling a bit lost because the lives closest to you have taken a turn? But what about Audrey? Where is she in all this change?"

She tried to turn away. "I'll think about me once things settle down. I mean, I have my business to run, and you lawyers depend on me. I like my work, and now the crisis is over, I can get back to my routine."

"And what about me, Audrey? What will I do for excitement? No green-eyed girl coming into my office with a problem to solve. No treks off into the frozen flatlands to find missing families. No invitations to a family conference laced with impromptu weddings and missing teenagers." Hal's tawny eyes, somehow both teasing and tender, crinkled at the corners. "I don't think I'm ready for total tranquility, Puss. And I'm afraid I'd miss the colorful Andersons if I let you get too far out of my sight."

Audrey settled back against the rough trunk of the fallen tree. "I don't think I'll be very far away, Hal. I still have your books to look after. And you'll need my services for some time yet, if you're ever going to finish that textbook you keep talking about."

"It's not just my books that need you, Audrey. It's my heart. I don't think I can even imagine life unless you're with me. At least, I don't want to try. I know the women in this family are mule-stubborn and have a bad habit of keeping a man waiting for years before they say yes." He reached into his pocket and took out a small velvet box. "Can we forego the waiting period? Will you marry me, Audrey? You know I've loved you since my law school days. And after our night in Bailey, I think you might care for me a little, too."

"I…care for you, Hal, but how can I know, how can I be sure it's not just the old infatuation mixed with a lot of gratitude? Maybe… A little time… A year—"

"Damn, woman, you are every bit as obstinate and perverse as your sisters." His kiss wasn't tentative or gentle this time. It demanded response, and the response filled Audrey with a fiery need to answer in kind.

When she thought the world would never stop spinning, he released her. She drew a long, shaky breath.

"Hal? Oh, Hal, I do love you, and I will marry you. I will, and we won't wait ages, either, but…"

"But what, Puss?" He drew her close, so she had to look up to see the grin behind his gold-tipped beard.

"Hal, I don't want to wait either, but do you think it's good for Dad to marry off all three daughters in one year? I mean, Claire and Drake in January, Judith and Jared in July, and us…well, when? Sometime later this year? Won't it be hard on him?"

Hal chuckled. "George Anderson is more resilient than you think." He lifted the lid of the small box and loosened the glittering solitaire from its satin nest. The platinum band slid over her finger, and he brushed the back of her hand with a kiss. "But since you're so worried, Puss, let's go in and ask the man himself how he feels about another wedding in the family." He laughed aloud. "Later this year?" He tucked Audrey into the curve of his arm, and they started toward the house. "Christmas? A Christmas wedding? Sounds perfect to me."

Audrey let the warmth of his arms shut out the winter chill. The nap of his jacket rubbed against the curve of her cheek. "I don't think there's any point in trying to argue with a Viking raider bent on having his own way. Christmas will be perfect."

A word about the author...

A fifth-generation Texan, Fleeta Cunningham has lived in a number of small Texas towns. Drawing on all of them, she created Santa Rita and its inhabitants.

After a career as a law librarian for a major Texas law firm, writing a monthly column for a professional newsletter and other legal publications, she returned to her home in Central Texas to write full time. Fleeta has been writing in one form or another since the age of eight.

When she isn't writing, she teaches creative writing classes, serves as the wedding coordinator for her church, and keeps house for her feline roommates.

Her other musings can be found at:

www.authorsbymoonlight.com

or her website

www.fleetacunningham.com.

She loves to hear from readers.

~*~

The Santa Rita Series includes:

DON'T CALL ME DARLIN'
BLACK RAIN RISING
ELOPEMENT FOR ONE
HALF PAST MOURNING

www.ingramcontent.com/pod-product-compliance
Lightning Source LLC
Chambersburg PA
CBHW071516260626
47170CB00002B/393